PRECIPICE

A Novel

BOB MADDUX

BOB MADDUX
For information, contact:
Ezekiel 12 Publications
San Deigo, California
bob.maddux@gmail.com

Printed Worldwide
First Printing 2025
First Edition 2025

10 9 8 7 6 5 4 3 2 1

Interior Book Design by Walt's Book Design
www.waltsbookdesign.com

PRECIPICE

CHAPTER ONE

BIG SUR

AUGUST · 1970

The morning chill cut into Andrew as he waited at the Highway 1 turnout. Behind him, the cliff dropped away to the invisible sea below, waves breaking against rocks in muted crashes, while predawn darkness pressed in from all sides. A thin fog drifted up from the ocean, veiling the landscape in gauze. He stood with his back to the Pacific, facing east across the highway where a dirt road wound up into the hills. Through the mist, he could make out the road's beginning and the slope rising away from the coast, but the darkness swallowed everything beyond the first bend.

Blaire should have been here by now.

Images of her invaded his thoughts like the waves below, her dark hair catching light, the asymmetry of her smile, three freckles beneath her left collarbone he'd traced in stolen moments. He could almost feel the curve of her waist, her body both fragile and unyielding. Blaire moved like a dancer, drawing eyes wherever she went, especially Ash's possessive gaze. Ash, or whatever his real name was, had always been secretive about his past, and his jealous intensity over Blaire made Andrew's betrayal even more dangerous. These memories weren't just desire; they were fuel for the fire he'd ignited.

His black Triumph Bonneville motorcycle stood ready, its paint still pristine after five years of hard riding. The classic bike gleamed even in the dim light; chrome pipes catching what little illumination existed, the parallel-twin engine silent but promising. His leather bag was secured to the seat, emptied of most of his belongings to make room for the cash, with just enough space left for Blaire to press against his back. He imagined her arms around his waist; her body molded to his spine as they rode. Inside that leather bag, fifty thousand dollars in bundled bills waited. Stolen money. Enough to disappear completely. Enough to get them both killed if Ash discovered what they'd taken before they could put miles between themselves and the commune.

Andrew checked his watch. Blaire was late.

Someone was coming up the road.

He squinted into the murk, trying to pierce the veil of mist, expecting Blaire to emerge any minute. The highway stretched empty in both directions, the silence so complete he could hear the blood pounding in his ears between the distant crashes of waves below. The darkness pressed in from all sides, thick and suffocating. Then, across the road, he spotted the faintest outline moving toward him. Footsteps hit the asphalt, moving at a run.

"Is that you, Blaire?" he called out.

A frantic reply came back, expelled between deep breaths. "Yes, it's me."

Andrew kicked his bike to life and moved toward her. "Is everything cool?"

Her chest was heaving when she met him in the middle of the road and slid onto the bike behind him. "No, I think Ash is on to us."

"Did he follow you?"

"I was sure he was asleep when I slipped away, but then, when I was halfway down the hill, I could hear him calling after me." Her voice trembled. "He was shouting that he's got a gun. He threatened to kill us both. Let's go!"

Just then, Andrew heard the roar of an engine off to the east on the road above them. Moments later, he could see the beam of headlights jostling up and down as a truck clamored down the hill toward them.

"That's him," cried Blaire as she wrapped her arms around Andrew's waist. "You can't let him catch us."

"Don't worry, babe. Just hold on."

He gunned the throttle and headed south, the Triumph's engine screaming against the salt-heavy fog that clung to the cliffs like a living thing.

"How will we get away from him?" Blaire shouted over the roar of the engine, her voice thin in the wind, her hair whipping like prayer flags against his leather jacket.

"Don't worry, I've got a plan. Just stay steady and lean into the curves with me." The words came out ragged, torn apart by the Pacific wind. They both bent low against the rushing air as the bike sprinted along the road to the first turn, the pavement slick with predawn mist, the drop-off to their right a yawning mouth of darkness and churning waves. The headlights of Ash's truck swerved onto the highway behind them as they went into the first bend, cutting through the fog like yellow eyes of some prehistoric beast. His engine growled into full throttle as he shifted into second gear, the sound bouncing off the canyon walls. Once in third, he'd be closing the gap between them.

The one advantage in their favor was that heading south, this route had some of the tightest curves on any road in America—curves that had claimed more than their share of dreamers and drifters. In a flat-out race, Ash would overtake them in no time. But if Andrew could stay ahead until they got through several sets of turns, they could pull into one of the side roads and hide as Ash passed, disappear into the redwood shadows like they'd never existed at all.

Andrew lost sight of the truck as they passed through a series of softer curves, the road rising and falling like ocean swells. But as they headed into the next bend above Redwood Gulch, where the trees pressed close and the air smelled of decay and rebirth, Ash's headlights came back into view. Andrew only had seconds to make it to the next turn, or they wouldn't have a chance to hide. The headlights emerged once again, and he could see Ash closing in through his mirror, the truck's grille like bared teeth. Andrew shifted down.

Pop pop pop! The exhaust backfired, sharp as gunshots in the canyon acoustics, but Andrew's heart was racing like they'd just been shot at. He had to slow to take the next turn, the bike's tires screaming against wet asphalt. Coming out on the other side, he twisted back on the throttle. The engine howled as they flew toward the next curve, the speedometer climbing past sane numbers.

Blaire hugged him tighter, her body pressing against his back, her heartbeat hammering through the thin cotton of her peasant blouse, reminding him again why he'd caught himself in this wild escape. He'd do anything to keep her in his life, even if it meant facing the anger of her jilted lover. He'd done it with complete abandon, stolen her away like some outlaw from a dime novel, and he'd do it again just to have her. It was worth it all, he told himself, worth the danger, worth the madness of this midnight flight.

Again, they eluded Ash, hidden by another hill crowned with wind-twisted cypress. But within moments, they were back in his sights, caught in those relentless beams. They roared up the slender highway for several minutes until they came to another curve near the Soda Springs Trail, where the fog grew thicker, turning the world into a tunnel of gray. Coming out of the bend, Andrew looked back to see that their pursuer had fallen slightly behind. He twisted the throttle to full, and the bike raced through another series of curves until they veered into a tight bend at Salmon Creek, the bridge beneath them groaning like old bones.

Just as they came out of the bend, Andrew spotted a path leading off the highway to the left and up into a stand of trees—barely visible, more deer trail than road. He pulled onto the path and shut off his engine, killing the headlight as they glided up the trail, momentum carrying them forward, coming to a stop behind some towering brush that smelled of wild sage and fear.

Several long heartbeats later, Ash's truck rounded the bend, its engine rumbling like distant thunder. For a moment, Andrew was confident Ash could see them. He was heading right toward them, the headlights sweeping across their hiding spot like searchlights in a prison break, but at the last minute, he shifted up, turned out of the curve, and roared up the road around the next bend, taillights disappearing into the fog.

No sooner was Ash gone from sight than Andrew kicked the motor to life and headed back onto the highway, this time bearing north, back toward the safety of their commune, back toward morning. "Okay, Blaire," he shouted over the snarl of the engine. "We've got to go all out now. It won't be long before he realizes we've switched back. Hold on tight."

Blaire heeded his warning, hugging him in a desperate grip, her fingernails digging through his coat. Andrew dashed up the road, hoping Ash hadn't noticed their last maneuver, praying to whatever cosmic forces might be listening. In moments, they were heading away with all the thrust he could crank out of his bike, the engine screaming its mechanical fury into the night. Once they neared the next curve, where the road came to a point jutting out over the void, Andrew could see across the gorge. There in the twilight was Ash's truck, a dark shape against the purple sky. They were totally exposed. If he was watching, he could see them as well, two figures on a motorcycle silhouetted against the predawn darkness.

Ash braked, his taillights bursting red like sudden wounds in the darkness. He turned and headed back their way, the truck fishtailing on the narrow road.

"He's seen us!" cried Blaire, her voice cracking with something between terror and exhilaration.

CHAPTER TWO

MOONLIGHT BEACH

JUNE • 2000

Thirty years later, and the sound of the ocean still stirred something primal in Andrew Foster: equal parts wonder and warning. Some mornings, the crash of the waves dragged him back to that night on the cliffs, when headlights cut through the fog and the taste of betrayal hung thick in the air. He told himself he'd outrun the past. But the ocean remembered. It always did.

This morning, it wasn't just a memory. The black SUV had reappeared again: same tinted windows, same appearance down the street from his apartment, like a predator stalking a wounded animal. He hadn't told Jade. Not yet.

Now, crouched beside a sandy-haired boy as they shaped uneven towers into a sandcastle wall, Andrew tried to bury the gnawing tension beneath the rhythm of salt and wind. Jade, who nannied for the boy's family part-time, sat beneath a striped umbrella a few yards away, engrossed in a paperback, unaware of the shadow that had followed them to Moonlight Beach.

Chandler barked an order like a tiny general, demanding a moat around the east side. Andrew nodded, carving with a plastic shovel, trying to match the boy's intensity. The tide was out, the sun was warm, and for the moment, just the moment, the fear stayed buried in the sand.

The ocean put Andrew at rest like nothing else could. He'd read about negative ions and wave rhythms syncing with human heartbeats. Still, for him, it felt more personal, like Moonlight Beach had been explicitly designed to calm the frequency of his anxiety. The late-afternoon sun fractured across the water into millions of diamond-like shards, hypnotic and bright. Salt crusted on his lips, mingling with the aftertaste of lukewarm coffee, while waves rolled in with a rhythm steadier than his own pulse: a metronome that had steadied him through every crisis since childhood.

He needed that steadying influence now more than ever.

His eyes drifted to the parking lot crowning the bluff. The black Range Rover sat in the far corner, its matte surface swallowing light instead of reflecting it: a void in the otherwise sunlit tableau. Even from this distance, Andrew could make out its aggressive stance: custom rims that suggested wealth mixed with recklessness, a blacked-out grille that gave the SUV the face of a predator.

The windows were tinted well beyond the legal limit, transforming the glass into obsidian mirrors that revealed nothing of what lurked behind them. Andrew's pulse quickened despite the ocean's calming influence. Whoever watched him now did so with perfect anonymity while he sat exposed, vulnerable as a specimen under glass.

He ran his fingers through the sand beside him, letting the coarse grains slide between his knuckles as he tried to ground himself in the tactile sensation. The heat from the day had penetrated several inches deep, warming his hand as he dug in further. He focused on this small physical comfort while his mind cataloged the pattern that had emerged with disturbing clarity over the past eleven days.

The first sighting had been here at Moonlight Beach, a place where he came to escape rather than be found. He'd dismissed it initially; luxury SUVs were familiar enough in this affluent coastal community. But then the Range Rover had appeared outside his office building in Solana Beach, parked with strategic precision just beyond where the security cameras would capture a clear view of the license plate. It always maintained that same calculated distance: close enough to establish presence but far enough to evade identification.

The sun dipped lower now, casting Andrew's shadow across the sand in an elongated distortion of his seated form. He watched as it stretched away from him, reaching for escape but finding none. A cold bead of sweat traced the line of his spine despite the warmth of the late afternoon.

He glanced back up at the parking lot, hoping irrationally that the Range Rover might have vanished during his moment of distraction. It hadn't. In fact, it seemed to have inched closer to the edge of the bluff, its front tires now aligned with the painted line of the parking space as if straining forward, eager to close the distance between predator and prey.

He created a dummy contact in his saved numbers under the name "Strange SUV," typing the license plate number where the phone number would typically be entered.

Andrew turned his back on the car and the boy by his side for just a moment, trying to center himself. Out over the water, a squadron of pelicans glided on the currents of air, effortlessly making their way north. They appeared so unconcerned, so peaceful. Andrew envied their freedom, their ability to lift off and disappear into the sky if threatened. He chose to be like them as he let the blue sea under their wings work its magic on his worries. And suddenly, he felt a sense of calm returning, a feeling that was short-lived with the next thought: Chandler. What if the car was here about Chandler and not about him at all?

He'd been coming out here on Fridays for the last month to meet with the boy, ever since Jade, his sister and Chandler's nanny, suggested the boy could use some quality time with a father figure. The nanny gig was new for her, something she'd fallen back on after the tech company she'd worked for gutted half its staff in the latest round of layoffs. She'd done childcare years ago, and when this opportunity came up through an agency, she took it. The pay was surprisingly good: wealthy clients willing to shell out serious money for quality care. Right now, she was taking a much-needed break, lounging in her beach chair a stone's throw away. The other half of that deal was unspoken, of course: that even though Andrew had never managed to father a child, at least he'd get some time to experience what it might have been like.

From the start, she mentioned that since Chandler was the child of one of her high-end clients, she wasn't really at liberty to tell him a lot about the boy. Some of the rich types around here were worried about kidnapping, so they'd told her to keep the family's identity quiet. Andrew didn't give that a second thought at the time, but now... now he was wondering if that had anything to do with his mysterious stalker. He wanted to grab for this explanation like a lifeline. Maybe it wasn't about him after all. But the hard truth was the personal failures of his past hadn't left him without enemies.

Either way, there was danger here, and he was starting to worry.

His six-year-old little buddy pulled him from his thoughts as the child scurried by, back and forth from the sea, bringing buckets of water to mix with the dry sand for their castle. Andrew decided to put the car out of his mind for the moment. He resolved not to allow it to spoil the joy of his time with Chandler. They were on their second sandcastle of the day. Encroaching waves had already swallowed their first attempt. They'd gradually retreated to the edge of the dry sand, confident that the water wouldn't reach this spot till they were gone.

Soon, Andrew was lost in Chandler's excitement and simple joy over their endeavor. It would have been great to marry, but it just never worked out. It wasn't that he didn't have that option. He'd loved a few women over the years, and plenty of them had loved him, but they never made it to the altar.

He thought of Carolyn, one of Jade's friends. She would have been his first choice. She'd come into his life when he was on the rebound from Blaire, and they'd had an on-again, off-again relationship that lasted for years. He'd thought they might eventually tie the knot. But then, fifteen years ago, Blaire had come back into his life. That tumultuous and short-lived affair that followed ended with Carolyn gone for good.

It was clear to him now why his relationships never lasted: either he was overly critical or just impatient. His eye wandered too. There were so many beautiful women here in San Diego that it was easy to get distracted, primarily when you're motivated by shallow pleasure. Simply put, he was selfish. Even now, he was embarrassed by how easily he'd thrown away what he had with Carolyn for another round with Blaire. One thing is for sure: if he ever got another opportunity at a relationship, he'd approach it much differently. He was hoping for another chance.

Finding someone who'd be interested in him was still not a problem. Finding something deeper, well, that took more than physical attraction. Andrew thought he could confidently say he wasn't a bad-looking guy; he had a full head of hair and still showed no signs of salt and pepper. At fifty, he was only a few pounds over the weight category for his 5'11" frame. He worked out three times a week, and there was no sagging at his jawline. But other things sagged. For one, his soul sagged. When it's all about you, well, you end up weak inside and unable to bring anything of lasting value to others. That's why he was really working on that part of his life. That's why he was taking time to be with his sister and her charge. He wanted to invest in someone and take nothing in return but the simple joy of seeing them fulfilled.

Chandler's voice suddenly broke through his thoughts. "Oh man." He pointed to one side of their sand structure that had caved in. "Hey, Andrew, you've built a lot of buildings. Why is this one falling over?"

Andrew reached down, mixed some sand and water, and started to patch up the break. "You see, you must get the mixture right. We need to add more water. It's all about the water. Not enough, and the sand dries and crumbles."

"Awesome," Chandler said, studying how Andrew's hands shaped the mixture. "You know what? When I look at sandcastles, I imagine them as real buildings. I draw buildings sometimes, like really tall ones with lots of windows." His small hands sketched shapes in the air. "Maybe I could show you my sketches sometime? Mom says they're pretty good."

"I'd like that," Andrew said, smoothing another section of the castle wall. "I used to draw buildings, too. Still do sometimes."

For a six-year-old, Chandler was remarkably articulate, perhaps a sign of the genius Jade always insisted lay beneath that tousled hair.

"Really?" The boy's eyes widened. "Like, for your job?"

"Sort of." Andrew had earned an architectural degree in college, but contract work initially paid better. After a few years, he'd moved into development, so he didn't build buildings in the literal sense any longer. His ventures had mostly been smaller projects here and there among the shrinking real estate opportunities in this overpriced coastal region. He'd dreamed big but never made the giant killing he'd hoped for. If you visited his office, you could see some of those visions posted on the wall: a twenty-unit condominium development and a small, yet fashionable, shopping center.

But the one that haunted him most was Precipice: his father's dream project, passed down like a torch he couldn't quite carry. The renderings were now yellowing at the edges, but the vision remained sharp: a development that would change everything. His dad was in his eighties now, frail but still asking about it whenever Andrew visited, those expectant eyes making the weight of the unfulfilled dream feel heavier with each passing year.

But he hadn't given up yet. He still had visions, and he was confident that his development dreams would become a reality someday. But that someday better come soon, or there wouldn't be one. He was on his last dime.

Chandler's busy movement stilled, and Andrew looked down to see him staring out at the water. He could see the wonder in the boy's eyes as his young mind took in the distant horizon. He looked up at Andrew, his eyes filled with questions.

"Andrew, why does the water always have to wreck our castles, but never go past the volleyball courts?" He pointed toward a set of posts and net, thirty feet away, where a pair of well-tanned couples were battling it out in an intense game, churning up sand and shouting into the sea breeze.

"That's a great question," Andrew said. The boy's face was focused on him now, his hands stirring the sand, his hair tossed by the salty gusts.

Andrew tried to come up with a good answer, searching his mind for a simple way to help Chandler understand the mystery of the ocean that even he didn't fully comprehend. "It's called the tide. You see, it's the influence of the moon. It pulls the huge ocean back and forth. It's similar to the way your hand can move the water in your sink at home. It's just that you can't see the hand that moves the tide; it's an invisible force."

"Kind of like the one in Star Wars?" Chandler asked.

"Yeah, kind of like that. But it's not good or evil, it's just there moving things around," Andrew replied.

Chandler thought deeply about that for a moment, staring out at the water again and then back at their building project. "Well, I think it's kind of evil: it always knocks down our castles."

At the word evil, Andrew's eyes strayed back to the parking lot. Yeah, it was still there, the car looming above them like a black cloud. It reminded him of the other things that had been stalking him in his dreams and waking him well before dawn. These tormenting thoughts seemed to perch at the edge of his consciousness, waiting for the right moment to bring forth their accusations. They were the deeds of his younger self he'd tried to put out of his mind, the lies he'd told and people he'd betrayed.

Andrew managed a distracted grunt in return to Chandler's words. "I guess you're right," he added.

Now confident in their agreement, they both went back to shoring up the side of their gritty construction project. They knew it was futile once the watery assault of the ocean reached this spot. But Andrew rallied them with an encouraging word, "But it's nice we're always left with fresh sand to build another one once the sea's done with it."

"Yeah, but I wish just once we'd come back here and find one we'd built last week still standing."

"That would be great. Who knows? Maybe someday that might happen." Andrew decided that next time they'd build one farther from the ocean in hopes that it would be beyond the tide's reach. But he knew it wouldn't last. Within a day, the wind or mischievous children would wreak havoc with anything left unattended.

"Remember the one we built last week? It was the best one ever. I really liked it..." Chandler looked closely at their current project, a crease in his brow. "It was better than this one."

"We'll do better next time. Do you want to start over now?"

"No. I think Nanny Jade wants to go soon. We won't have time."

They both looked over to where Jade was collecting her things. He was right; it was time to say goodbye for the week. Andrew felt a little twinge inside. He'd grown to care for this boy, and he'd miss him.

Chandler paused suddenly, and Andrew could tell there was something on the boy's mind, something he'd like to say to him but couldn't. Andrew knew this because it had happened repeatedly over the last few weeks, and each time Chandler had ended up telling him he had a secret he'd like to share but couldn't. Andrew didn't push him to speak. He wasn't about to go probing. He was sure it would come out with time. He figured it must be about problems at home or maybe something bad the boy had done, such as telling a lie or using a naughty word.

"It's time to go, Chandler," Jade said, pointing up the hill toward the parking lot, where her white late-model Toyota Camry sat. Andrew's eyes followed her motion, and he saw the mysterious SUV. It was just across a few rows down from hers, its tinted windows glaring at him.

Andrew really hoped this was about an overprotective parent. If he'd put Jade and Chandler in danger, he'd never forgive himself. But could anything harm them here on this beach among hundreds of people at the edge of this safe neighborhood? Why should the appearance of an unknown car put him in such a state of anxiety? The first time he saw it, he hardly noticed. The next time, he thought, Hmm, a strange coincidence. But somewhere between the second and third time, it got him thinking. It always came when Jade arrived and left shortly after her.

Andrew brought his thoughts back to the task at hand. "Better finish packing up, Chandler."

Chandler agreed by picking up the green plastic sand bucket as Andrew gathered the two yellow shovels they'd set aside earlier. He took the moment to catch up with Jade. "So, you're still dating that Jeff guy?"

"Of course," said Jade, her brows narrowing.

"Can't say I like him much." Andrew was recalling the lunch the three of them had two weeks ago. The guy was a financial planner, super successful with all the ego that went with it. "He seems really into himself."

"I guess you'd know that from experience."

"Ouch," Andrew's brows now tightened. "Yes, you're right, it takes one to know one." He gave his comment a few beats to sink in before he spoke again. "But you've got to admit I've made some strides in that area."

Jade's brows relaxed, and she gave him the slightest smile. "True, you're not the same guy you were ten years ago."

Andrew finally had to face what a jerk he'd been to Carolyn. Thank goodness Jade sat him down one night and, over a few beers, set him right on this relationship thing. That was painful, but he was sure not as painful as his treatment of Carolyn. After that session with Jade, he called Carolyn. She didn't answer, but he left a message of apology on her voicemail. He sent an email too, but never got a reply. He saw her last summer with her new friend. He could tell she was happy, and that was a good thing. It wasn't the place for apologies, but he could tell by her warmth she'd forgiven him.

"I'm a work in progress, thanks to you."

"I know! You might actually be ready for a healthy relationship."

"Speaking of healthy relationships, that's why I'm concerned about Jeff, but like you said the other day, you're a big girl."

"Yes, so let me work it out."

"Okay, I will but just hear my note of caution."

"I do. Sorry for being a bit defensive. I'm glad you care, big brother," she said through a laugh.

Chandler, all packed up, took Jade's hand and turned to Andrew. "Oh... can you have lunch with us today, Andrew? Maybe we can go for burgers?"

"That would be great, but I've got to meet a potential client at my office at one. Maybe next time, buddy."

"Okay," he said with an eager smile. Andrew tossed the small beach bag over his shoulder and headed toward the parking lot.

"Looks like you two have had another great time together," said Jade as she led the way to her car. "So, Chandler, how did the building go on the second castle?"

"Not as good as last week," he said with a slight frown. "But Andrew says we'll do better next time."

Jade brushed aside a few strands of hair caught against her dark eyebrows. "I'm sure it will be better next time," she said with a wink. "Right, Andrew?"

"For sure."

A minute later, they were at Jade's car. "So, you'll have lunch with us next week?" said Chandler as Jade opened the door and made sure he was buckled into his booster seat. "Let's go to In-N-Out."

"I love their burgers," Jade said, "haven't had one in months."

"Me neither." Andrew patted his firm stomach and reminded himself why he hadn't had one in a while.

"Thanks for hanging with us again," said Jade as she gave him a peck on each cheek. "It's always a joy."

"Next Friday, same time?" asked Jade as she slid into her seat.

"I'll be here."

"Oh, I almost forgot. Will you be able to meet us on Saturdays once school's back in session?"

"Shouldn't be a problem."

"Good. I know it's a way off, but I just wanted to give you a heads up so you could plan."

The door closed. Jade started the car and pulled away, rolling down the window to wave goodbye. "Bye," Andrew called out as he bent down to wave to Chandler. When he looked up, the black Range Rover was backing out of its space with deliberate precision, its tinted windows revealing nothing. It moved down the line of cars like a predator tracking prey, then eased into position behind Jade's Camry, maintaining a careful distance as both vehicles disappeared into traffic.

CHAPTER THREE

LA JOLLA

JUNE · 2000

Glass and steel inspired him. Landon Strand loved to see form, function, and art working in harmony to create something beautiful. It was a habitat for humility because if you let it, it could humble you. Whether standing at a building's base, like he was now, or perched on its pinnacle where you could look across the landscape and out toward the Pacific, you found yourself caught up in the spectacle of it all. It made you realize how tiny you were against its massive frame. Humbling. Still, that wasn't enough to distract him from the mysterious assignment he carried in his briefcase.

For others, it could be a habitat for hubris. These spires rising around him would soon form a place where wealth creators labored, and with a man's labor often came an overblown confidence, an attitude, an assurance that he could do anything. His boss, Donovan Lasseter, watched as the massive crane moved things into place above them. Their obligatory white safety helmets weren't quite the proper match for their Cucinelli sports coats, crisp open-collared Ricci shirts, Zanotti leather belts, and Ferragamo shoes. Donovan had always had great taste, and Landon had been more than happy to emulate it.

Donovan might be full of hubris, especially today, but Landon shouldn't call it that. It was just an extreme sense of self-assurance born of accomplishments. He'd come to believe he could achieve anything. Many had accused him of overweening pride. But Landon couldn't bring himself to agree. He admired the man too much. Donovan had given him the sort of opportunities that few men his age enjoyed. After five years as his assistant, Landon had seen what Donovan had done to get where he was today.

And it was more than that. Like Donovan, Landon came from an impoverished family, so he knew what it took to achieve great success. Pure hard work had gotten them here. Landon put in his share of long hours, but he had to admit no one worked harder than Donovan Lasseter.

Donovan stood beside him, looking up at his latest handiwork. The steel girders of this creation pierced the blue above them like a bold but lanky skeleton waiting for the "masters of construction" to lay a skin of crystal glass upon them.

Donovan beamed like a proud father. Landon had seen that stance before—hands on hips, chest puffed out, that big unrestrained grin. He was proud, and he didn't care who knew it. A moment later, they headed toward the modular trailer on site to meet with the construction manager and his staff. They walked up the switchback entry into a room lined with paneled walls made to look like wood. The worn, rented furniture was a perfect match for the torn screens on the windows.

Donovan was there to get answers from John Farina, the construction manager. Landon wanted answers too—answers to the questions raised by his latest assignment. He was preoccupied with the contents of his briefcase. Landon's curiosity burned beneath the surface, but he forced himself to stay composed. As they approached the trailer, he kept pace without betraying the urgency that tugged at him with every step.

Farina was a burly man whose arms were layered with the type of tattoos one gets in the Navy. He didn't fit the mold that had become increasingly common in the industry: guys with college degrees and an air of sophistication. Farina had obviously honed his skill from years on the job. He was much older than Landon's boss and clearly had things in hand, but he was respectfully attentive to Donovan's questions.

"So, John, how soon will they start on the framing?" Donovan asked.

"The subs are ahead of schedule, so we should start in a week. Plus, the lead time for our glazing is exactly on schedule," said Farina.

"Excellent. It looks like it will turn out even better than our last project. I'm glad I brought you on again."

"It's good to be here, sir. I'll bring it in as I promised."

"If it turns out like our last job up north, I'll be a happy man."

"I'm confident it will. We've had a few more challenges and some overtime that wasn't expected."

"No worries, you'll always have that in this business. Just keep an eye on it."

"You can be sure of that."

"Let's hope you do. We can't have our quality slipping, can we, John?" Donovan gave him a pat on the back that looked friendly enough, but the words didn't sit right with Landon. The Donovan he knew was an encourager, not prone to passive-aggressive threats like the one he'd just heard. Maybe he'd misunderstood.

But from the look on Farina's face, Landon thought he'd understood all too well. Farina only nodded and flashed an uncomfortable smile. What was that about?

"I'm watching them like a hawk. I'm just glad it hasn't slowed us up," added Farina.

This tower was just one of Donovan's masterpieces. He'd built two in San Francisco and another massive business center for one of the Silicon Valley giants that decided to move its headquarters into the city by the bay.

"Okay, Landon and I will be back next week. Before we go, we'd like to see the view from the top."

"The construction elevator is available. Do you want me to go with you, sir?"

"No, we can manage. We'll check in before we leave."

Landon grabbed the briefcase he'd set down beside Farina's desk and followed Donovan to the lift. They rode to the top floor and walked over the unfinished steel floor.

Reaching the edge, they looked out toward the Pacific. Donovan drank in the view and exclaimed, "I'm so glad we moved our operations here, Lanny."

Don was the only one who called him that. To everyone else, it was either Mr. Strand or Landon. Even his wife, Britney, called him Landon. It was more urbane, she'd said on the day they first started dating. He had introduced himself by saying, "My name's Landon, but you can call me Lanny."

"I like Landon," she had said, and so it had been Landon ever since, except when the boss talked to him.

"It's been great here, Don," he said, still distracted by the uncomfortable exchange with Farina. The use of Donovan's nickname was second nature to him by now, though he was always careful never to use it in front of the other employees. He smiled to show he agreed with his assessment of this lovely coastal city. "Britney loves San Diego, and she threatened to leave me if I ever try to move away."

Should he say something about Donovan's response to Farina? Ask what was going on? Maybe he was having an off day, Landon convinced himself there was no need to get into this now.

"I'm so glad Jacqueline didn't let up on me until I gave in and moved us down here," said Donovan. His wife, Jacqueline, was a tall, slender former model who had finally had enough of the damp summers in San Francisco and decided to move south. Additionally, she was a Southern California girl, raised in Newport Beach. When her father died, her mom cashed in his considerable life insurance policy, sold the house, and moved Jacqueline and her sister into a waterfront mansion on Coronado. She's been a driving force in Donovan's life, not only wanting him to succeed but also wanting kids right away. They had Payton in the first few years of their marriage, but none since then, but not because they haven't been trying.

Donovan leaned against the safety rail, his expression softening. "My son loves it here, too. He was struggling for a while—probably because I've been working too much, always traveling, never around when he needed me." He paused, the admission clearly weighing on him. "I was so caught up in everything else that I didn't see how much he was falling behind. Thankfully, my brother stepped in and recommended Santa Loma Academy. The tutoring program there has been a godsend. Since he started, his grades have improved dramatically, and he appears to be happier as well. I was really worried about him for a while there, but now..." He trailed off, watching the water below. "Sometimes it takes an outsider to see what you're missing when you're too busy to notice."

Landon was relieved to see the conversation turning to more familiar territory; this was more like the Donovan he knew. "I'm glad to hear that. I guess the recommendation was a good one."

Donovan shook his head with a rueful smile. "It wasn't the first time I've had to lean on my brother. Between work and everything else, I'm constantly calling him for advice about parenting stuff. The tutoring program there has been a godsend, though. Since Payton started, his grades have improved dramatically, and he appears to be happier as well. I was really worried about him for a while there, but Ryan always knows what to do when I'm in over my head. Jacqueline was at her wits' end, too. Now that Payton's doing better, it's given Jacqueline time to develop her design business. With him being older as well, she wants to occupy her days with something productive."

"Payton is a great kid and really bright."

"Yes, he is."

Donovan stood still for a moment, as if he were gearing up for something. "I really appreciate the way you've listened to me this past year. All my worries about Payton, the guilt about not being around enough. It's embarrassing, and I wasn't sure who I could confide in about all that parenting stuff."

"I'm glad you feel comfortable talking to me about it. I know it's personal, but you can trust me. Sometimes you need someone to bounce things off of, you know?"

"Exactly. And you never make me feel like I'm failing as a dad, even when I probably am." Donovan managed a small smile. "It helps just having someone listen who doesn't judge."

"Well, I will always be here for you."

Landon sincerely admired Donovan and was honored that he'd grown to trust him. In seven years, Donovan had built an empire that amazed his peers, humbled his competition, and put him on the cover of four or five financial periodicals. He was making his mark early. Even by his first year out of Stanford with a business degree, he was off and running. He entered the real estate industry and became an instant success. He always had an uncanny sense of knowing where the market was headed. He was a lot like some of the brilliant individuals who made it in Tech; he just applied his skills to real estate.

From there, he quickly focused on development, and that's when his rise became meteoric. Landon knew that was an overused term, but he swore that sometimes, just being near Donovan, you could sense some cosmic heat filling the room. It was as if he were being propelled through the business atmosphere, burning with an intensity that seemed to make him glow. Only, he wasn't burning out. Somehow, his star just got brighter.

First, it was those small but strategically placed posh shopping centers, and then he took on a few key buildings in the business parks that were springing up to house the growth of the tech industry. Then the towers became his financial constellations, gleaming against the cityscape at sunset or twinkling like bejeweled pillars as they took their places among the pantheon of the city's glass majesties.

When Donovan invited Landon aboard straight out of Stanford grad school, Landon discovered that he'd hitched himself to a star. Now he was Donovan's second in command, and what a ride it had been. Donovan had led the way, or should he say lit the way, from the beginning, and Landon had grown in his wake. It had been a stellar journey for sure. Though he never understood why Donovan had favored him, maybe it was because he was from his alma mater, whatever the case, he was grateful.

All of which made Donovan's more recent behavior turn more disquieting. It was restrained, just below the surface. But Landon could tell he was on a mission, and it was an angry one. He kept telling himself it was temporary, that if he waited it out, they'd go on like they always had. Still, he wondered if Donovan would realize that he was allowing his work to become more critical than his relationships with his family, friends, and himself. He could only hope so. Landon didn't like to rock the boat, especially given all that Donovan had done for him.

Two years ago, Donovan had made him vice president of Lasseter Enterprises, in charge of acquisitions. Landon had minored in real estate management, so it was a natural fit. From there, Donovan soon added other portfolios for him to handle. Then he also put him in charge of special projects. This could be as simple as making a potential investor feel important by wining and dining them at a five-star restaurant, or as stressful as putting out one of the frequent fires that arose when Donovan had cut an unproductive employee or trimmed the fat from a lagging department. But more than any of those, it had been his job to be a confidant and sidekick.

But he was genuinely fascinated by this latest assignment, and it appeared that now was the appropriate time to bring up the issue that had been burning a hole in his briefcase. Donovan had given him a list of three people to locate. So, he hired a private investigative firm, Cassidy PI, here in San Diego, to find them. Now that he'd gotten a report back from the PI firm, this was a perfect time to bring it to his attention.

"So, Don, I've got the info from the Cassidy firm on those guys you had me run checks on."

"Great. What did they find?"

"Well, the folks they've investigated are an eclectic bunch. It's interesting the different kinds of people that go into development."

"That's funny. Are you including us in that group?" Donovan said with a twinkle in his eye.

"No," Landon said after a chuckle.

"I didn't think so. Go ahead."

He removed three sheets of paper from his briefcase and referred to them as he talked. "The first one's Jared Olsen. He's a former professional surfer who invested in small developments with the money he earned from his endorsements. He made a small chunk of change on his last project, but he's had hit-and-miss results on the others. He works out of his home and truck. No office, just an answering service."

"Sounds like a lot of athletes that blow through their money and connections."

"The next one's Manny Rodriguez, a failed mortgage broker who buys and flips homes. He's done okay, but nothing spectacular. He's got a small office just off the PCH. It's in one of those houses that was zoned for offices, and five or six folks are crammed in there. He does okay for himself, but from what I can tell, he'll never make it big."

"Listen, you never know. All it would take with one of these guys is the right break, and they could take off."

"Maybe so, but not this last guy. He's a bit of a has-been. His name is Andrew Foster, and he works out of one of those office complexes where the businesses get a tiny office with access to a conference room and a cute coed to answer the phones and make you look like you're successful. Like the others, the PI firm ran a check on his career, and it didn't turn up much. A few corner mini-malls and one larger one. Its sale was probably the only thing keeping him afloat. He does have initial permits for something called Precipice, on the coast. It's a state-of-the-art, premier research enclave with lavish amenities designed to attract the best medical and scientific minds. But he has no funding. Other than that, nothing of substance."

"Well, maybe his luck's about to change."

Landon extended the three pages to Donovan. "Here are all the details from personal to business dealings. They're a motley group."

Donovan took them and scanned the list, running his finger down each page, his lips tight and his brows knit. After a few minutes, he tapped Foster's page. "This one. Foster." "Foster?" Landon glanced at his own notes. "The guy with the coastal property?" "That's the one. Been around North County for years but never hit it big." Donovan's eyes stayed on the report. "Interesting background though—Big Sur, Joshua Tree. Not your typical developer path." "The PI firm was thorough," Landon said. "Even tracked down his college transfers." Donovan looked up with a slight smile. "Good. I like to know who I'm dealing with."

Landon was always amazed at the way these PI firms came up with such innovative ideas. A brief stay in Big Sur... he could only guess they must have found some friend or acquaintance from thirty years ago and either cajoled or paid to get this sort of history from them.

He looked at the paper in Donovan's hand, then up at his face, noticing the slight bit of gray encroaching on the hair at his temples. His sophisticated appearance was part of the reason he was successful, his was the sort of handsome face that didn't leave you feeling jealous; it inspired trust somehow.

"Good work. So, here's what I want you to do," Donovan said, looking over the report from Cassidy. "It says here that Foster has a piece of land on the coast that's permit-ready, and the final map has been recorded. He's calling the development Precipice. His architectural working drawings are complete, and he needs to record his final map to start grading. The big holdup has been the lack of funding. He just hasn't been able to get a bank to come on board due to his financial statement. That will all change once we're involved."

"So, we're going to bring him that funding?"

"We are," Donovan said matter-of-factly.

"The Precipice project actually aligns perfectly with the bold vision we've been pursuing." Landon was still shocked that they were considering any of these guys. They were all losers in his book. "But Don, I saw those plans. This is truly ambitious—a cutting-edge medical research facility with world-class amenities. Foster has never executed anything remotely on this scale. He's completely out of his league."

"I know, but I sense there's something unique here. I want to make him an offer to partner on it."

"The scale is exactly what we're used to, but Foster..." Landon shook his head. "Are you sure he can handle it?"

"Yes, and this time I'd like to keep the Lasseter name out of it completely."

"The property is extraordinary," Landon pressed. "A premier research facility that could revolutionize the medical field. It's just... Foster has never shown he can deliver something this significant."

Donovan's eyes flickered with something unreadable before he answered. "What you might not know is that Precipice has been a dream of Foster's father, Joseph, who was a top architect in his day. I read about him when I was in graduate school. This is now his son's project. When I was starting, I took risks. I stepped out and took a bold action, and it was successful. Maybe this is Foster's chance to fulfill his father's dream. Sometimes the motivation to honor a legacy can drive people to achieve things they never thought possible."

They'd worked through shells before, but this seemed odd. "So, are we going to let him know who we are?"

"No, and you're going to have to trust me on this, Lanny. I know I'm keeping you in the dark, but I've got my reasons."

Landon looked him in the eyes, trying to read him. This felt like a red flag, but Donovan's eyes weren't giving anything away. He couldn't think of anything to say or any apparent reason not to trust him on this. "Okay, Don."

"I've already had legal do all the background on this sort of project. They've cleared it completely. They've created a totally new entity."

Landon raised an eyebrow. "What kind of entity?"

"You'll be CEO. I'm calling it Teknon 2 Partners."

"Wait—me? CEO?"

"I'm going to fund it from one of our offshore accounts. Shirley, in management, has already leased a suite of offices in La Jolla and hired a temp. They should have it furnished and ready for operations in a few days."

"And what exactly am I walking into here?"

"All you'll need to do is show up. I've had a lawyer set up an LLC for this, and we'll bring Foster on as the managing member. Tell him to make a big draw the first week to get him motivated, and then from there we'll fund monthly."

"So Foster's going to run this thing?"

"As far as your usual responsibilities, I'll have some of our current team set up in the new offices—that way you can oversee their regular work while they also help with this new corp."

Landon frowned. "Is this thing even on the map?"

"Shirley's even set up the website and the entire background story. She's also found a group that created a total history for you and the company—it comes up legit on the background checks."

"Wow. Okay." Landon was a bit surprised that Donovan was so far ahead of him on this, but it wasn't the first time.

"You'll work out of that office when you're on this project and have a PA take care of the day-to-day operations. You'll only need to be involved with it one day a week at first, and then not much after that—mainly monitoring developments for me."

Just then, something strange seemed to rush across Donovan's face, and then a glimmer in his eyes. It wasn't a pleasant glow but something weird, troubling, almost hostile. It burned there for a moment and then vanished behind one of his generous smiles.

Landon had to admit, though, he was seriously intrigued, and a little troubled, by the whole thing. He did his best to hide it with a return smile and nod of affirmation. "I trust you, Don. That's never been a problem. You have my full support." Even though it seemed full steam ahead, he felt compelled to ask again.

"Are you sure you want to do this? I'm not sure Foster has any drive left. This Precipice project would challenge even our most seasoned development team. He's probably sucking on the vapors of those last small deals he did a few years ago."

"Yes, I'm sure." Donovan's eyes burned with the sort of intensity Landon had only seen when they were in full battle mode with a competing corporate entity or when a frustrated tenant brought a lawsuit against them. "Sometimes people need a chance to prove themselves. This project is exactly the kind of bold, visionary development we specialize in. Foster may surprise us all."

Landon nodded reluctantly. He didn't fully understand Donovan's confidence in Foster, but he'd back his boss's play. If Donovan believed Foster could rise to the challenge of building a state-of-the-art research facility, who was he to argue? He knew where Donovan's intensity came from. It was an almost animal territorialism, the part of him that had made him so successful and ruthless when necessary to get what he wanted. And when he got that look, nothing and no one would stop him.

"Okay, Don. I don't get it, but it goes without saying that once you know what you want, you get it, and it always seems to work out." He'd seen that with the Standish project in San Jose. They had used a shell then, and it worked like a charm. In fact, when Stone Enterprises found out what they'd done and how they won, they took them to dinner and treated them with a bottle of Macallan Scotch even though they'd beaten them out on the deal. "I remember the Standish deal. Sam Stone was in awe. I haven't forgotten that Scotch either."

They both had a big laugh as Donovan handed the file from Cassidy back to him.

"Thanks, Lanny," he said, smiling.

They took the elevator back to the bottom and stopped at the construction trailer. Donovan took the time to talk with an assistant superintendent, asking about his children and his ailing mother living in Mexico. He also chatted with a couple of the supervisors. He was a natural with them, making sure they felt like valued members of the team. Landon wondered for the first time if this was genuine or a ploy, but he reminded himself that Donovan had never once made anyone working for him feel unimportant.

They left their white construction helmets at the trailer and soon found themselves in the parking lot. Donovan opened the door to his Ferrari and called out to Landon, "I won't be back in the office till tomorrow. Jacqueline and I are going to a meeting and then to an early dinner with the Tanners."

Landon stopped at his Mercedes and replied, "I get it. We're booked up too. We've got a soccer game for Eva, and then the Greenbergs have

invited us to their son's bar mitzvah. It should be an interesting evening."
Britney and he were lifelong Episcopalians, but that wouldn't stop them
from gracing one of the highlights of their neighbors' lives with their
appearance. It all came with the package of living in the high-rise apartment
complex in downtown San Diego.

Donovan's Ferrari pulled out ahead of him into the traffic, but the
look was still there. Landon could see it in his eyes as he waved goodbye.
Where had he seen that before, and why did it make the hair on his neck
stand up?

It had only been a week ago. Maybe that's why it was still echoing in
his subconscious—or perhaps it was something more profound. A sense of
betrayal. A promise broken. That was the real reason he was going to make
someone pay. The man had lied—some high-powered corporate head
who'd made assurances and then walked them back when it mattered most.
And then Landon remembered. Donovan's words from that day came
drifting back to him: "I won't let him get away with it. I'm going to make
him pay." Landon had overheard the statement during a heated phone call.
What unsettled him more than the words themselves was not knowing who
had been on the other end. When Donovan hung up, he'd had that same
look in his eyes—the same one he had now. It had chilled Landon then,
and it still did.

Landon could sum it all up in one word, one word that really shouldn't
be there in the world of a man who had so much. One word that shouldn't
be part of a life graced with wealth, a beautiful spouse, a handsome son, and
a fantastic career.

Revenge.

CHAPTER FOUR

BIG SUR

JULY • 1970

Andrew loved the way the fog drifted in from the Pacific, California's version of an ancient Avalon. The mist did something with the trees that made them magical. Their branches swayed in what seemed to be an astral wind, even though it was just the gentle breeze coming in off the sea. Still, it left an earthy moisture that dripped from their leaves like an organic elixir. There was a sense of transcendence that made one believe the entrance to Middle-earth might be hiding somewhere nearby. This was Big Sur's particular magic, where the Santa Lucia Mountains plunged into the Pacific, creating a landscape that existed somewhere between dream and reality.

He and Amber, his steady girlfriend, were planning to return to San Francisco State in the fall, at least, that was the loose idea they tossed around between swims in the stream in the upper meadow and long talks by the fire. But lately, he wasn't so sure. Part of him felt like something here, in this place, still needed to play out. There was an undercurrent to the summer he couldn't quite name, something unfinished, almost fated. Yet even in the languid rhythm of Big Sur's Redwood-shadowed mornings and coastal haze, Andrew felt the hum of his deeper ambition. Architecture, development, those weren't just career choices to him. They were the language through which he made sense of the world. Where others saw empty lots or decaying beams, he saw potential, design, destiny.

Amber noticed it too. She'd said as much one night, curled beside him in the tent, her fingers tracing the lines of his wrist like she was sketching blueprints. She said his passion grounded her, pulled her toward something real in a world that often felt unmoored. It was that intensity, his vision, his discipline, that had first drawn her in. Even here, while they let the summer carry them on its strange tide, that drive never left him. It burned quietly beneath the surface, just waiting for the right moment, the right project, to reignite. And perhaps that was the tension he couldn't shake, the feeling that Big Sur hadn't finished with them yet, but also that he wasn't meant to linger too long. There were cities to shape, skylines to carve. And he couldn't ignore the sense that his path, whatever it was—would demand sacrifice.

Just a few hours before, he had hiked under those magnificent redwood arbors, now returning from a grocery run from the general store just up the coast. He'd parked his Triumph Bonneville by a small house in the woods; the same model Steve McQueen had ridden in *The Great Escape*. Andrew had been thirteen when he'd first seen that film, watching McQueen tear across the German countryside, and he'd known instantly what he wanted. Every dollar from his after-school job, every birthday gift, every lawn mowed had gone into a jar until he could afford his own Triumph. That first bike had been his freedom. This one, years later, still gave him the same thrill.

It was perfect for taking the curving Highway 1 that hugged the high cliffs like a lover's embrace. He'd been good on a bike for years, but this place demanded respect, one moment of inattention and the Pacific waited eight hundred feet below. The danger was part of the meditation.

He'd firmly chained his bike to a thick tree near the end of the gravel road, next to a dented Ford pickup, a rusted '58 Plymouth Belvedere, and a stripped-down VW Beetle that looked like a refugee from Haight-Ashbury. No one would likely steal it, but around here, some hippies still believed that everyone owned everyone else's stuff. Satisfied it was secure, he made his way along a fern-filled pathway leading up towards the crest of the hill. The trail wound through groves where the fog collected in hollows, creating ghost gardens of mist and shadow. Overhead, the redwoods formed cathedral arches, their ancient presence making human concerns seem temporary. The path led him through a narrow arroyo carved by a chattering creek, water that had been falling toward the sea for millennia, until he finally arrived at the huge stone house perched high on a ridge just above the fog line, where the everyday world fell away and only Big Sur's timeless mystery remained.

Nestled beside the house was a washbasin fed with water from a nearby spring. An outdoor rock barbecue and stone oven crouched beside the building like two granite offspring. This rugged place was home to one of the few remaining communes from the late sixties. Its location in idyllic Big Sur and its reputation for altruism had continued to make it a destination for a new generation of seekers.

A broad gathering area had been created in front of the dwelling, where Andrew now sat in a drum circle, ripping out a lead on a borrowed guitar. His Gibson J45 was stolen the first day of summer, and he'd had to use others since then. Another guitarist and a flute player backed him up, accompanied by a variety of congas and bongos. They were jamming their way through a twelve-bar blues song, high on some great Acapulco Gold. The sun seemed to simmer just above the western horizon as if it were about to be plunged into an icy haze. The fog spread toward them like a broad, lacy prairie leading to some mystic kingdom.

Andrew had sojourned here for most of the summer with his girlfriend, Amber Reed, living off the meager funds left over from his last student loan. They'd both taken the summer off from college classes to explore this communal life in Big Sur. Amber was in the kitchen at the moment with the cooking team, preparing the commune's next meal—she loved to cook, and he loved her cooking, especially the way she could transform their bulk supplies of rice, beans, and vegetables into something that actually tasted good. Her blonde hair would be tied back, flour probably dusting her cheek as she kneaded bread alongside the others.

College had started well enough. Studying architecture sparked his imagination and gave him a sense of purpose. But a strange wind was blowing through his generation. With the war abroad, protests at home, and the rise of the counterculture, it was a time of searching, and of chasing sensation. Drugs flowed freely, promising freedom but often leading to confusion. Somewhere along the way, his focus drifted. His heart wasn't in it anymore. He'd only made it through his first year.

That summer, like many of his peers, he chose the visceral over the cerebral. School could wait. The cultural upheaval had left many in a fog, idealism fading into pot smoke, free love, and the haunting headlines of Charlie Manson. They were still searching, but not as hopefully as a decade before.

Andrew looked around the musical circle at their eclectic group. Sam Costas was a remarkable individual whose most notable gift was a keen sense of rhythm. He was beating out a drug-fueled cadence on a conga drum, setting the tempo for the blues riffs Andrew was playing on the battered Martin. Dave Hester, who was playing rhythm on a cheap gut-stringed generic that someone had left there months ago, accompanied him. There was an assortment of other guys on bongos, random wooden sticks beating on logs, and Ash Murik, whose gift with the flute showed that he was by far the best musician in the group.

Andrew drifted back to a road trip he took with Ash last year to Mount Shasta. The memory surfaced with cinematic clarity—the three of them against the backdrop of that mystical mountain that seemed to generate its own legends like a power plant creates electricity.

Blaire had been with Ash even then. She was the gorgeous, leggy girl he'd been shacking up with, her presence in their circle still new enough that Andrew found himself stunned by her beauty at unexpected moments. Her face had the kind of symmetry that photographers chase throughout their entire careers; her movements were fluid and deliberate in a way that drew all eyes to her.

The three of them were sitting around sharing a joint and a grilled trout they'd caught in the nearby lake. The cannabis had loosened something in Ash, transforming his usual controlled demeanor into something almost approachable. They were laughing and joking like the best of friends, the mountain air crisp in their lungs, the night stretching before them with possibilities.

But when Ash got up to take a leak, disappearing into the darkness beyond their small circle of lamplight, Blaire's demeanor changed instantly. The languid smile fell from her face like a mask removed, and she leaned across the space Ash had vacated, pinning Andrew with her intense stare.

"You know Ash is into sorcery?" she'd said, her voice so low he almost thought he'd misheard.

Andrew wasn't sure what to say to that, so he laughed it off, assuming the weed had sent her mind in strange directions.

"Not the Disney fantasy type," she continued, unsmiling. "It's the real deal, sacrifice and stuff like that. And Andrew... Ash isn't even his real name. He told me once when he was really high. Said he had to leave his old life behind when he found 'the path.'"

The laughter died in his throat as he registered the seriousness in her expression. The floating, pleasant feeling from the joint curdled into something uneasy.

"Why? What for?" he asked, unsure how to respond to something so unexpected, so discordant with the carefree evening they'd been sharing.

"There are powers in this mountain," she'd said, her eyes darting toward the place where Ash had disappeared. "Ancient ones. He knows how to reach them, how to bargain with them." She swallowed visibly. "He makes offerings. Sometimes small things, blood from his palm, objects of personal significance. Sometimes...larger things."

Andrew wasn't sure what unsettled him more, Blaire's warning about Ash, or the intensity in her eyes as she shared it. Her words were sharp-edged, but her closeness softened them. Her breath carried the faint sweetness of clove, and when she leaned in, a strand of hair brushed his arm. He hated that he noticed.

A part of him wanted to dismiss it all as weed-induced paranoia. Ash might be theatrical, even dangerous, but blood rituals? Offerings? It sounded like the stuff of underground comics.

Ash had developed a following in the Haight, almost cultish. His charisma and supposed spiritual powers drew people to him like moths to a flame. There were several in the commune that had followed him here from wherever he'd been before, devoted disciples who hung on his every word and treated his rambling philosophies like gospel. They called him their "guide" and spoke of him in hushed, reverent tones when he wasn't around.

Yet Blaire wasn't joking, and worse, she wasn't just scared, she was reaching for him. And that's what disturbed him most. Something in Blaire had already turned.

He knew the look she was giving him. He'd seen it before, in girls who were searching for escape. And despite himself, a part of him wanted to be the one she escaped to.

That want made him furious with himself.

Her words spilled out in an urgent stream, as if she'd been holding them back for too long and now couldn't contain them. With each new detail about midnight rituals and strange artifacts hidden beneath floorboards, Andrew found himself wondering if the weed had been laced with something more substantial, something that distorted perception more profoundly.

He doubted it was true, of course. Ash was manipulative, volatile, even dangerous in the conventional sense—but a dark wizard? It seemed more likely that Ash had spun these tales to impress Blaire, knowing her fascination with all things mystical. She was clearly into cosmic stuff, always talking about the I Ching, chakra readings, and other metaphysical pursuits, but this stuff with Ash was clearly on the verge of being demonic.

But something in the way she'd looked at him that night, with fear threading through her conviction, had planted a seed of unease that had never fully died.

She was quiet when Andrew didn't seem to encourage her. Then, as if she read his mind, she was lighthearted again. "Well, at least he's good in the sack." She flashed him a mischievous grin.

Some women were like that. The more edgy a guy was, the more it turned them on.

Andrew hadn't seen the two of them for months after that until they arrived here this summer.

The memory faded as Sam's conga drum hit a particularly loud flourish, pulling Andrew back to the present. He blinked, readjusting to the fading daylight and the circle of musicians around him. His fingers continued to play the blues progression on autopilot, while his mind wandered, muscle memory carrying the melody.

Near their drum circle, spread out in loose clusters like birds drawn to music, were a collection of eager young girls who'd joined their little commune. Some were dressed in flowing robes, while others were wearing very little, warming themselves with the last rays of the setting sun. It had been a lovely day of feasting on the fresh food Andrew purchased up the coast, fresh water from a nearby well, and the powerful pot that Ash seemed to have an endless supply of.

Ash and Blaire were just one part of their little community on the side of this mountain. The hippies believed these mountains held the same power the Esselen and Ohlone tribes had held sacred for thousands of years, holy ground where the veil between worlds grew thin. Young seekers fled here after Haight-Ashbury turned dark, after Altamont's violence and the Manson Family's nightmares poisoned the dream of peace and love. Big Sur became their refuge, the last pure place.

They'd become a group made up of hippies, would-be rockers, bikers, druggies, hangers-on, college students on break, and even a few rednecks from towns like Hollister, who had found out about the free sex and wild nights here in Big Sur.

Their jam session ended as if on cue as the final traces of the sun vanished beneath the distant fogbank. Andrew returned the borrowed guitar to Eric Bishop, the unofficial leader of their commune. He had promised to build a fire on the hearth of the stone house. So, they all agreed to continue the performance up there once they'd finished with the dinner.

Bishop was about ten years older than Andrew, and he'd been into the bohemian thing since his beatnik days. He was shacked up with a woman named Janice who'd anointed herself the camp nurse and had a little medicine kit filled with everything from antibiotics to herbs. She fancied herself the den mother for their group, and Eric acted as a kind of father to this little flock of seekers. Besides, he'd known Angelica, the owner of the land, for years, and she'd permitted him to do some social experiment with the place for the summer. Andrew thought she had long-term goals to develop it into a bed and breakfast, but for now, her altruistic bent had overcome her commercial interests. So, she'd given Eric free rein of the place for a while.

The aroma of cooking food from the stone house wafted over their group, and they packed up their instruments and headed for supper. Ash and Blaire were ahead of Andrew as they walked toward the house. He couldn't help but admire the couple's good looks. Especially Blaire. No doubt Ash's charisma had attracted her. Many of them had. However, there were also rumors about Ash, some of which were troubling.

Stories that he'd been the NorCal link for the Sons of Molku out of Laguna Beach. One especially grievous report was that he was involved in a murder, and that the money he got to launch his business was from that killing. The large knife hanging from his belt in a sheath did little to dispel those impressions.

Andrew had chosen to ignore those rumors and focus on the good things he saw in Ash, such as his musical talent. Looking at him now, though, he had to admit there was a haunting aura about him sometimes. Andrew got a contact high just playing with him musically, but at times, there was something else there. It was a wildness that rose like a burst of flames. He did his best to steer clear of any conflict with him.

But maybe Andrew had been wrong to ignore the warning signs and Blaire's claims. If he was being honest with himself, it was sometimes freaky. Ash said all the right things about brotherhood and love, but Andrew sensed that if he ever crossed him, he'd be in for some serious karma.

A chill ran through him as they approached the stone house, and it wasn't from the evening air. In the gathering darkness, the shadows seemed to shift and lengthen across Ash's face, transforming him momentarily into something almost inhuman. Andrew shook his head, trying to dispel the image. It was just the drugs, he told himself. Just the Acapulco Gold playing tricks on his mind.

But even as the warmth of the house enveloped him and the sounds of laughter reached his ears, Andrew couldn't shake the feeling that he was walking into something darker than he could imagine. Something that had been set in motion long before this summer and would continue long after the commune disbanded, and they all went their separate ways.

Something he might never escape.

CHAPTER FIVE

CARLSBAD

JUNE · 2000

The sun blazed against the Pacific as Andrew drove north along PCH toward Carlsbad Village. These Monday visits to his father always left him feeling hollowed out.

The Sterling Grove sat near the center of town, a modest Spanish colonial building that looked more like a luxury inn than a senior care facility. Andrew parked his ten-year-old Subaru and grabbed the paper bag containing dinner ingredients.

"Good afternoon, Mr. Foster," the receptionist greeted him. "Your father is expecting you."

"How's he been this week?"

A flicker of hesitation crossed her face. "He's had some good days."

Andrew understood. His father was slipping further away, one brain cell at a time.

He found Joseph Foster in apartment 209, sitting in his leather armchair by the window, reading an architectural journal. Once a commanding presence, at eighty-two, he seemed diminished, though his eyes remained sharp and critical.

"You're late," Joseph said without looking up.

"Only by ten minutes. Traffic was brutal."

"Traffic is always brutal. Plan accordingly." Joseph finally looked at his son. "What's in the bag?"

"Sea bass. Fresh from the market."

Andrew began preparing dinner in the spotless kitchen while his father returned to his journal.

"I saw Jade last weekend," Andrew said. "She called yesterday, said she's landed another startup gig. She'll keep her nanny side hustle going, though. You know how much she loves kids.

"So, she'll still do administrative work? She's too bright to be answering phones."

"It's a foot in the door, Dad."

"And you? Any new projects?"

Andrew sliced the lemon with more force than necessary. "Nothing solid."

Joseph set his journal aside. "What about Precipice?"

Andrew froze. The premier medical research facility had been Joseph's masterpiece design, state-of-the-art labs perched on coastal bluffs. The plans are still gathering dust.

"Still looking for investors."

"You've been 'looking' for two years now."

"These things take time. Finding someone with vision and capital is proving difficult."

"It's my finest work," Joseph said softly. "All those years designing corporate towers... they were practice for Precipice."

The vulnerability in his father's voice made Andrew's chest tighten. "I haven't given up."

"That land option won't be available forever."

Andrew's stomach tightened. The option had been steadily draining his savings.

"I know, Dad."

As Joseph spoke about the project, his hands moved expressively, sketching invisible buildings in the air. In these moments, he transformed back into the vibrant architect who had once captivated clients with his vision.

"I know you're doing your best," Joseph said finally. "If there's one thing Fosters don't do, it's quit."

The simple vote of confidence warmed Andrew more than he expected.

"How's Carolyn?" Joseph asked suddenly. "Will she be joining you for dinner?"

Andrew's hands stilled. "Dad, I broke up with her fifteen years ago. You're thinking of Marilynn. And we haven't been an item since December."

Joseph frowned, confusion flickering across his face before his expression hardened. "Of course. I was just testing you."

But Andrew could see the lapse had unsettled him. For a moment, neither spoke. Joseph turned back to the window, watching the traffic pass below. Andrew busied himself with setting the table, a familiar ritual that offered them both a graceful exit from the uncomfortable moment. They ate in comfortable silence by the window.

Joseph took a bite of the sea bass and nodded approvingly.

"You always had a talent for cooking. Your mother would be proud."

"I miss her," Andrew said simply.

Joseph's hand trembled slightly as he reached for his wine. "Every day. Every single day."

After dinner, Andrew prepared to leave. He placed a hand on his father's shoulder. "I'm going to make Precipice happen, Dad. Somehow."

Joseph covered Andrew's hand with his own. "I know you're trying, son. That means more to me than whether it actually happens."

The unexpected absolution caught Andrew by surprise. For once, his father wasn't measuring him by his achievements, but by his effort.

"I love you, Dad."

"I love you too. Now go home before it gets too late."

Driving home under a canopy of stars, Andrew pulled over at a viewpoint. Below him, the Pacific stretched endlessly, silver waves catching moonlight. Somewhere along this coast was the land that held their shared dream.

He thought of the dwindling time to secure the property, find investors, and make Joseph's vision a reality. A sense of urgency washed over him, along with renewed determination.

Tomorrow would bring new possibilities. Tonight, the memory of his father's words, "I love you too", was enough to carry him through the darkness.

CHAPTER SIX

ENCINITAS

JUNE · 2000

Andrew sat in his apartment on the last day of June, the afternoon light slanting through the blinds, casting prison-bar shadows across the worn carpet. The Fourth was just three days away. Usually, he'd be planning which beach party to hit, whose barbecue would have the best food, which rooftop would have the perfect view of the fireworks over the bay. But those thoughts now felt like they belonged to someone else's life.

His fingers tapped nervously on his phone. What he needed wasn't someone far away. What he needed was someone close, someone who could get answers about the dark SUV he believed was stalking him or those he cared about. The vehicle had appeared too many times to be a coincidence—outside his apartment, trailing him from meetings, parked across from places he'd only decided to visit at the last minute.

The holiday weekend loomed ahead, but instead of anticipation, all he felt was dread. Three days until the city exploded in celebration, and all he could think about was who was behind those tinted windows.

The name Jimmy Ramirez flashed in his mind. He was a PI and an old friend, someone who might help. Andrew had been tempted to call him sooner about his potential stalker but had held off, dismissing his fears as paranoia. After seeing the car at the beach repeatedly over the last month, however, he was finally ready to act. He couldn't risk putting Jade and Chandler in danger.

Andrew scrolled to Jimmy's contact and pressed the call button.

Jimmy Ramirez had been a former classmate from SDSU, on a basketball scholarship during his first year when they'd met. Andrew had been a sophomore then, a year older and a late starter, having wasted twelve months drifting through hippie communes in Marin, Big Sur, and Joshua Tree. Unlike many students struggling with tuition, Andrew had more than enough money to pay his way through school. The source of those funds remained his secret, never shared even with Jimmy. Instead, he'd concocted a story about a wealthy East Coast uncle who had left him a trust fund that could only be accessed if he attended college. Jimmy had believed it. Everyone had.

That lie wasn't the worst of Andrew's faults, not by a long shot. He tried to push back the sting of his conscience as he punched in Jimmy's number. The phone rang twice before someone picked up.

"This is Ramirez Security and Investigations. How may I help you?" The voice belonged to a charming young Latina whom Andrew had gotten to know over the years. She was always gracious when he called.

"Buenas tardes," Andrew offered in his very limited Spanish. "I'd like to speak to Mr. Ramirez. Tell him it's Andrew Foster calling."

"Of course, Mr. Foster. I'll get him right away." Her tone made it obvious she knew Jimmy and Andrew were friends and that Jimmy would be glad to hear from him.

As Andrew waited, an Enrique Iglesias song played quietly in the background. Then the music cut off, and Jimmy's voice came through.

"Hi, Andrew. How are you, hermano?"

"Good, thanks for asking."

"How's business?"

"About the same. I'm still working on that deal in Carlsbad and hoping it will go through. But nothing yet."

"Well, I'm sure something will come through for you." Jimmy had been saying this on and off for years. He had always been there to rejoice with Andrew when he succeeded in a significant development and to commiserate when he was depressed about his failures, always offering encouragement. And it wasn't just about business. Jimmy had been there for Andrew through a bad breakup, too, nursing him through his pain with margaritas and shots of tequila until the bar closed.

"Yeah, I'm sure it will. How's your family?"

"Tina's great. She's been with Raquel all week in Phoenix. You know she just had her second child, it's another girl."

The mention of Raquel reminded Andrew of her quinceañera. He realized how long ago that must have been, she was married now and had made Jimmy a grandfather for the second time.

"Armando's great too," Jimmy continued, "he's expecting his first, a boy."

Andrew was happy for his friend, but the mention of grandkids revived a deep ache somewhere inside him. What had he done wrong? The answer was complicated, and he knew it. He pushed the thought away rather than dwell on his failure to marry and build a family.

"That's great news, Jimmy," Andrew said in a cheerful voice. "I can't wait to see the latest addition to your growing tribe. Soon you'll have your own barrio."

Jimmy gave a courtesy laugh at Andrew's failed attempt at humor, and Andrew joined him.

"So, give mis saludos a tus niños."

Jimmy laughed again, this time at Andrew's poor pronunciation. Andrew was at the end of his Spanish, and they both knew it.

"Okay, enough of your jokes and your miserable attempts at Spanish, my friend," Jimmy said over his laughter. "Just be glad you haven't tried to get hired by the border patrol or make a living doing stand-up comedy."

"Amen to that," Andrew agreed.

"So, what can I do for you, Andrew?"

Now that the moment had arrived, Andrew struggled to voice his concerns. But he knew he'd be angry with himself if he chickened out, so he took the plunge.

"Well, you know that I've been helping Jade watch one of her charges, the boy, Chandler. I help babysit him on Fridays at Moonlight Beach."

"Yes, I remember you told me."

"For about a month now, each time Jade arrives with Chandler, this strange car shows up. It's one of those cool-looking Range Rovers, the kind all those rich dudes in North County drive."

"Yeah, I've seen them. The new rich down here in 'Chulajuana' drive them too. They're even becoming a hit in TJ. So, what about it?"

"It's just so strange. Each week, it pulls into the parking lot just after Jade drives in, and then they wait, just far enough away where I can't make out who's driving or how many people are in the vehicle. Additionally, it's black and features tinted windows, even on the driver's side. Aren't those illegal?"

"Yeah, they are, but a lot of people ignore the law and take the risk of a ticket."

"Then it started showing up at my office now and then. Last week, when I got home, there it was, parked down the street from my condo..." Andrew paused, frustrated and a little anxious as he relived the whole scenario. "At first, I thought I was just being paranoid, but it's obvious now that someone is stalking me. It's really getting weird."

There was silence on the other end for several heartbeats, almost like Jimmy was analyzing the dilemma before answering. "Well, that is a little odd. And you haven't seen who's in the vehicle?"

"No."

"Have you gotten any strange phone calls, like the caller hangs up?"

"Not one."

"What about threats?"

"No threats either."

"Well, those are both good signs."

"What do you make of it, Jimmy?" Andrew heard the pleading in his own voice. He must have been more distressed than he thought. The phone call to his friend had brought everything into focus, and suddenly he realized just how concerned he really was.

"Well, I wouldn't be that alarmed. If it were really a threat, they'd have acted by now. It seems that most of the interest centers on the boy. I think the occurrences around your office and home are just coincidences. Are you sure it was the same car?"

"I'm pretty sure." But Andrew wasn't really.

"As long as I've known you, you've always been a straight shooter. I'm sorry, but I need to ask. Have you been involved in any illegal activities? Or had any recent bad business deals?"

"No."

"Have you made any enemies?"

"No, nothing like that."

"Well... I could put one of my agents on it, but it's going to cost something."

"Jimmy, that would be great, but things are a little tight right now." Andrew hated to admit that his bank account was nearly empty.

"Yeah, I get it. Maybe I could do it gratis for a few days."

Andrew wasn't going to put his friend in that position. "No, let's hold off for now. I'm not ready to get overly serious about this thing." Inside, though, he realized that he was serious. He was worried, but he didn't want to admit it to Jimmy. He didn't want to admit it to himself.

"I tell you what I can do. Did you get the license?"

"Yes, I got it."

"Well, I can run a check on it for you, find out who the owner is. We can start there."

Relief flooded over Andrew with Jimmy's suggestion. That was it, a check on the owner. Once he knew who it was, he'd have a better understanding of who he was dealing with and what he might be facing. "Great idea. I'll get that number to you."

"Okay, I'll get right on it and get back to you in a day or two. At the same time, I don't want you to worry too much. And that offer's still open.

I can put one of my staff on it if something really worrisome comes of this whole matter."

"That would be great, thanks." Andrew was sure Jimmy could sense the relief in his voice. Andrew sensed it too. "You're a great friend, hermano." There it was again, his poor Spanish slipping out. But it was from the heart, and Jimmy knew it.

"You are too, hermano," Jimmy said with absolute conviction. "It's almost time for one of our taco meetings at Lucia's."

"Yes, I'm looking forward to it. Hopefully this whole thing will be resolved, and we can have a big laugh about it over some cervezas."

"I'm sure we will. Well, my secretary just came in and says I've got an important client on the line."

"Okay."

"Talk to you soon."

"Yes, soon." The line went dead, and Andrew hung up.

He stood up to stretch and walked over to the window. His office was on the second floor, offering him a view of the street below. He glanced down at the line of cars parked at the curb, and his legs went weak. There it was, the black Range Rover sitting just up the street under a tree. He couldn't quite make out the license plate, but he was sure it was the same car he'd seen before. The front seat was dark, and the shadows cast by the tree only enhanced its obscurity.

Who was after him? He hadn't done anything illegal. There had been no shady business deals. It was true he wasn't as successful in business as he wanted to be, but he hadn't made any enemies recently. He was honest about that.

But that hadn't always been true. He had made an enemy once, years ago. The man was formidable; someone Andrew was all too eager to put behind him. And he thought he had. Could it be? Was this him, rising from Andrew's past, where he thought. Could it be? Was this him rising from the past where I thought I'd buried him all those years ago? Hopefully, it was only an empty fear.

Days later, Andrew stepped into his office in Solana Beach, feeling the familiar weight of depression settle over him. The space wasn't messy or dirty, but he constantly worked to keep it clutter-free. Appearances mattered, a potential investor might appear, or one of his pending proposals might finally come through. There were at least half a dozen such scenarios that could happen at any time. Except that not one had occurred in the last six months, and gloom settled in like the fog clinging to the coast for the third day this week.

Glancing around, Andrew saw remnants of his past endeavors gathering dust. Plans of failed projects sat in two heavy cardboard drums behind his desk like giant paper cigars, yellowing with age. Two severely abused whiteboards hung on the wall across from him. One tilted slightly to the left, he kept forgetting to straighten it. Those boards had been erased countless times, and now they were so scarred with color markers that the tint wouldn't come off. Faint green, red, and blue-hued bullet points and outlines, some made years ago in a flurry of energy with a magic marker, now haunted the surface. They were gone but not really, just pale images of a faded dream, a washed-out idea, a discolored plan.

Sometimes they mocked him. Everything from a twenty-unit condo project on the coast in Leucadia to a retirement project in Oceanside had been plotted out there. The list went on and on. A faded acrostic near the left corner of the board still carried the ghostly images of the step-by-step game plan for one of them. But Andrew wasn't one to give in to depression. He'd encouraged himself a hundred times, and now the caffeine in his tall dark was kicking in. He'd soon push away these apparitions of past ideas and move on. After all, he was in the land of dreams: California. Hopeful folks from the Gold Rush pioneers to the families who pushed west during the Great Depression had made it here. It worked for them, and it would work for him.

There, amongst them in the corner, gathering dust, was the model his dad had put together and the companion plans for The Precipice, his father's dream project of a state-of-the-art medical research center, with all the amenities that would draw the best of the best to its premier site on the San Diego coast. He could still remember the pride in his father's eyes when he'd unveiled the model at the dining room table all those years ago, explaining every detail with the passion of a man who believed in something with his whole heart. "This will be my legacy, Andrew," he'd said, resting a hand on Andrew's shoulder. "Something that will actually help people." The irony wasn't lost on Andrew that it was the same project he'd taken on himself years later, only to watch it fade like a dream at dawn, the way most dreams did in his life. The plans for The Precipice remained tucked away, quietly gathering dust like forgotten promises, a tangible reminder of not just his own failures, but a legacy of dreams deferred across generations.

Andrew ran his fingers along the tube that contained the blueprints, leaving trails in the fine layer of dust that coated it. He hadn't looked at them in years, couldn't bring himself to unroll them and see the meticulous drawings that represented so much hope, so much ambition, first his father's, then his own. Maybe someday he would find the courage to try again, to breathe life back into The Precipice and make it more than just another ghost project haunting the corners of his office. But not today. Today, he would focus on the here and now, on the small victories that might someday lead to something more. After all, even the most magnificent redwoods start as tiny seeds.

Andrew started in on his mail. It contained the usual bills, junk mail, and postal flyers advertising everything from pizza to reverse mortgage offers. But there was something different among them today. It was a pristine white envelope addressed to him with the embossed logo of some group called Teknon 2 Partners in the upper left corner. The font and color spoke of class and wealth most subtly. Instantly, his curiosity was aroused. He'd never heard of them. An inner voice chastised him: 'You'd *better check them out before you go any further, you fool.'*

He started to tear into the envelope with his index finger, but something told him this one deserved the edge of his long-lost letter opener. He pulled open the center drawer of the desk, banging his gut, and searched around amid old cell phone cables, paper clips, and used pens. There it was. He couldn't remember the last time he'd used it, smooth bamboo with some Tahitian maiden engraved on the handle, a souvenir from a trip to the South Seas years ago. He slid the blade into place and savored the way it cut through the textured paper envelope. The crisp white stock of the letter felt rich in his fingers. He saw the company's logo at the top. Below was the date, followed by his name and address. He started to read:

"Dear Mr. Foster," the letter began.

"Allow me to introduce myself. My name is Hayden Quinn. I am the CEO of Teknon 2 Partners. I'm inquiring about a specific development project that you submitted to the Coastal Commission last year. It's called The Precipice. This project is currently on hold due to a lack of funding. Although we're new to the San Diego Market, we've had great success in bringing projects of your type to fruition. We are interested in partnering with you on this endeavor, with the goal of making it a reality. If you are equally interested in partnering with us, given our influence and financial backing, please reply at your earliest convenience.

I've included our website address, along with my private email and cell phone, as a sign that we are serious about moving forward on this endeavor. I will look forward to your timely reply.

Sincerely, Hayden Quinn, CEO, Teknon 2 Partners"

The rest of the letter contained the website address, a somewhat luxurious or prestigious sign in an era when digital presence was still a rarity. Then there was Quinn's personal email address and cell phone number. Andrew stared at the letter and then reread it, feeling the quality of the paper between his fingers as he tried to absorb what was being offered. Could it be some scam letter? He'd gotten those before. Not the Nigerian type, where someone wanted to share a fortune if you just put a few thousand in their bank account, but ones from groups offering great financing or partnership with strings attached, or should he say tentacles. Once they'd drawn you in, the other shoe would drop as they found some excuse to take over your project and push you out. Thankfully, Andrew had never been taken in by one of those.

This offer seemed legit, though. Whatever the case, it was worth looking into. First things first, he told himself as he laid the letter aside and fired up his desk computer. As he waited for it to boot up, he contemplated how he might respond. If this were a valid offer, it could be the sort of thing Andrew had dreamed would come along. Every developer hoped for one of these. He'd heard the stories over the years of how some tiny little firm partners with one of the big guys, and overnight they're made into millionaires.

Geoff Peters of Rancho Properties was like that. He was once a foreman on one of the prominent citrus and avocado farms in East County during its early development. One day, the owner came to him and said he wanted to develop the land. He made Geoff a partner and put him in charge of the project. The next thing you knew, not only did he make a fortune as lots sold off in the high six figures, but later he started his own development firm. He began with a small shopping center in a growing area and then expanded to a larger one. Now he had projects in other states and a couple of maquiladoras in Mexico generating revenue.

The computer was now on, and the browser had popped up. Andrew typed in "Teknon 2 Partners," and shortly a sophisticated and tasteful site appeared. He went to the "About Us" tab, and a pull-down menu appeared. He scrolled through the list of personnel. There he was: Hayden Quinn, CEO. His smiling, handsome young face looked out at Andrew. He had perfectly styled blond hair and a close-cropped beard with the appropriate level of stubble that many younger hip executives wear today. Andrew looked over at the paragraph beside his picture. It listed his portfolio and bio. Achievements such as graduating cum laude from Stanford University. It listed the various positions he'd held in the company and how long he'd been in each one. It seemed he'd been with Teknon 2 Partners his entire career. That seemed unusual, but then some of the good companies developed loyal team players that stuck with the group for years. Andrew saw that as a good sign.

He was starting to think he was dealing with the real deal here as he looked through the rest of the site, exploring their properties and developments. He scrolled through the personnel page again. Hayden Quinn was looking youthful and confident. His warm expression made Andrew want to trust him and filled him with hope. He was impressed, deeply impressed. He closed his eyes, took a deep breath, and looked up again to stare at the screen. Was this really happening?

Andrew wasn't sure how he felt. He'd had such hopes for years, and most of them had never been realized. They'd incubate in his soul, nurtured by his mind and heart. Fed by his labors, they seemed to thrive for a while, and then somewhere along the way, they'd either die or get lost in a sea of regulations and paperwork. All this had left some real scars inside, the kind that still ached.

But now, maybe this was the one project he'd been hoping for, the one development that would kick-start his business again and get him back on the map. With something like this, he could have a good run for the next ten years and then be set for the rest of his life. He could buy an oceanfront condo, get a new car, and gain the confidence he needed to re-enter the dating scene. More importantly, this offer could finally fulfill his father's dream for the Precipice Medical research center, a project Andrew had inherited but never managed to bring to fruition. That should have been his most significant source of happiness about the offer, yet he felt strangely conflicted about it. But he shouldn't get ahead of himself. He wasn't about to get his hopes up. But he could at least investigate it.

Andrew scanned the letter for the third time and read the proposal, entering the contact info into his phone. Then, grabbing a new file folder, he handwrote a title and slipped it into the front drawer on the right side of his desk. He made plans to call that afternoon, then pulled out the portfolio on the Precipice project and perused it. He'd done this a hundred times, running the numbers, factoring the labor, material cost, and the promotion and marketing campaign. It always added up to a winner. He'd just never found someone who would believe in it like he did and step up with the cash. Maybe now he'd found his angel.

Andrew spent the rest of the morning attending to various tasks. He went through the rest of his mail and made a few calls. He paid his bills for the month, agonizing over his shrinking bank numbers. If this deal really happened, it was coming none too soon. Even though he was busy with other things, he couldn't seem to take his mind off the Teknon 2 offer. It was exciting but also made him anxious. He stopped, got up, and walked around. He headed down the hall to the reception area and spoke to Evelyn. She routed phone calls for the dozen or so businesses that operated out of the co-op. He strolled into the conference room. No one was using it now, so he was able to do a few laps and walk off some of his unease.

Andrew headed back to his office, buzzing with the feeling of possibility. The beauty of the day drew him to the window. He breathed in deep, feeling his spirits soar. And then just as quickly, his gut plummeted, and every happy thought disappeared. The Black Range Rover was back, just up the street. It was just turning the corner. Once again, the license plate was just enough obscured that he couldn't read it. Today of all days, it had to show up and bring all his anxieties crashing back in.

No. He wasn't going to let it ruin this one good thing. No. Andrew turned away, put it firmly out of his mind, and went in search of some lunch.

He decided on Jeff's Café just off the 101. When he walked in, he was greeted by the hostess. She smiled and showed him to his seat. He waved at a few locals he knew. He ordered his usual, a ginger soft taco and one of the local draft beers. While he waited for his order, he called Jimmy's office. He wanted to tell him about the Range Rover that had appeared at his office again. Jimmy wasn't in, but the girl said he'd call him back. He had called Andrew earlier in the week and said that the license plate he had given him had pulled up a car registered to a tech corporation, but the details had been intricate to confirm. Jimmy said he'd try to get a name.

The excitement over the new offer didn't dissipate even with the taco and beer. So, Andrew finished it off and headed back to the office. Evelyn said there was a call for him while he was out. He took the note from her long fingers.

The message, in Evelyn's neat handwriting, said it was from one of his creditors. He was only a month behind on that bill, and he couldn't believe they were pressing him for payment. If this thing with Teknon 2 Partners panned out, that would all be in the past. There he went again, raising his hopes. Did he really want to rely on what might be some random fishing expedition by some big corporation? It might just be one of a host of offers they were making to groups in the area.

CHAPTER SEVEN

RANCHO SANTA FE

JULY · 2000

T he California sun beat down, unforgiving and glorious all at once, casting shimmer across the surface of Donovan's lavish swimming pool. Landon reclined on a plush lounge chair, savoring the weight of luxury surrounding him, here in the exclusive enclave that had once been the Atchison, Topeka & Santa Fe Railway's failed eucalyptus plantation.

In the early 1900s, the railroad had purchased thousands of acres to cultivate more than one million Australian eucalyptus seedlings for railroad ties, but severe drought and freezing temperatures killed most of the trees, forcing them to abandon the project. The railroad then formed the Santa Fe Land Improvement Company to develop a planned community of country estates, renaming it "Rancho Santa Fe" in 1922. The towering eucalyptus groves that now provided shade for mansions like Donovan's were the living remnants of that grand miscalculation, transformed from industrial failure into symbols of old California elegance.

It wasn't long before the community attracted celebrities like Bing Crosby, Howard Hughes, and Douglas Fairbanks, with Crosby hosting his famous "Clambake" golf tournament at the local country club from 1937 to 1947 before moving it to Pebble Beach. How far Donovan and Landon had come since their grad school days of tight budgets, celebratory beers after swims at the Y, and occasional dinners out. Those days felt like another lifetime now.

Donovan lounged beside him, both men basking in privileged repose while keeping casual watch over the children splashing in the azure water nearby. The kids' laughter punctuated the afternoon air, a soundtrack of innocence against the backdrop of opulence. the maid, approached with Caipirinhas on a silver tray, the condensation beading on the glasses like tiny diamonds. After the first sip coated his tongue with sweet lime and cachaça heat, Landon knew a second would soon follow. The maid kept watchful eyes on Payton, Eva, and Jared, allowing the adults their deserved reprieve.

This California Shangri-La sprawled across eight magnificent acres, encompassing a twelve-thousand-square-foot home, riding stables, tennis court, and fitness center. Though Landon and Britney had been Donovan's guests several times before, each visit left them enchanted anew by the staggering display of wealth. Landon's tastes differed somewhat from the Lasseters, but the raw power of his boss's unlimited purchasing capability planted seeds of ambition in his mind. He believed he was on track to achieve similar success someday.

Britney, ever the urban woman, had insisted on a downtown high-rise penthouse for them, four thousand square feet with every imaginable amenity. It was impressive, but it paled in comparison to this spread. Landon remembered when Donovan first purchased the estate four years ago. The housewarming tour had lasted a full hour, necessary to appreciate the vastness of the grounds. They'd struggled to find words adequate to express their awe, or to acknowledge how fortunate Donovan was to acquire it for under fourteen million. Now, Donovan rarely mentioned the property, keeping conversations firmly anchored to work and upcoming projects. Landon still felt overawed by the estate but kept those impressions to himself, like secrets too vulnerable to share.

The day had been full, the women had gone riding earlier, while Landon and Donovan rose with the sun for a full round of golf at the club. Landon found it fascinating that despite the exorbitant membership fees Donovan paid, he rarely took advantage of the golfing privileges. But that was just one symptom of the larger issue: Donovan seemed so consumed with making money that he scarcely found time to enjoy the luxuries it afforded him. He'd told Landon there would be plenty of time for enjoyment later in life. For now, the thrill of the deal provided the ultimate rush.

Landon took a long pull on his drink, the ice cubes clinking softly against the glass as he swallowed. "So, we've moved into the temporary space in Franklin Tower."

"Good. How does the place look?" Donovan's voice carried the casual authority of a man accustomed to having his questions answered promptly.

"Not bad. Almost like we've been there for years. The other tenants on that floor have been quizzical. But we had them over for an open house and gave them the scenario you suggested."

"Excellent. What have you heard from the developer?" Donovan's questions came rapid-fire, betraying his intense interest despite the leisurely setting.

"He responded to my letter, and we've got a meeting set up for after the holiday."

Landon hesitated, swirling the melting ice in his glass. "Donovan, before we go any further, can we talk about this name change?"

Donovan turned to him, eyebrow raised.

"Hyden Quinn," Landon said. "I've been Landon Steele since birth, and now, just before we go online with the new Teknon project, you make me switch identities? I mean, it's not just a quirky alias. It feels… covert."

Donovan's eyes narrowed slightly. "You think I'm setting you up?"

"No," Landon said quickly. "But I do think you're hiding something. Maybe from competitors, maybe from someone else—I don't know. I trust you, but this cloak-and-dagger stuff is messing with my head."

Donovan leaned back, letting out a slow breath. "Look. I didn't pick the alias to throw you off. I picked it because we need distance. There may be eyes on it. Eyes that don't want it to succeed. Going under the radar with a fresh name buys us space."

Landon looked down at the water glinting in the pool. "So this is a play against your rivals?"

"Among others," Donovan said. "Let's just say there are parties I'd rather not alert until this thing is too far along to stop. You trust me?"

Landon sighed. "Yeah. Yeah, I do. It's just… weird."

"I get that. But sometimes weird is the only way forward."

The air between them settled, tense but trusting. And now it was their current deal, the Precipice project, that dominated the conversation.

Landon still couldn't fully grasp why Donovan had taken it on, or why his involvement needed to remain cloaked in secrecy. The more he tried to untangle the logic, the more elusive it became. like the shimmer on the water's surface, there and gone the moment he reached for it.

"Okay, you need to continue to focus on this project. I want it to move forward without a hitch." The words came out smooth, but with an undercurrent of steel.

Landon took another sip and studied Donovan over the rim of his glass. Though seemingly focused on the children splashing in the pool, something lurked in Donovan's eyes, something simmering just beneath the surface. That same intensity Landon had witnessed the day this assignment was handed to him. An energy quietly smoldering inside the man, carefully contained but unmistakably present. It was something Landon instinctively knew not to touch, something better left unacknowledged. Yet curiosity and a sense of self-preservation compelled him to probe further.

"So, I know you're eager to get this thing launched, but it's so different than our other developments. And this Foster guy... I don't think we've ever partnered with such a small operator. Why all the effort?"

Donovan set his drink on the table with deliberate care, turning toward Landon. A flicker of irritation crossed his face, quickly masked but audible in his measured response. "Like I said the day I gave you this assignment, you've got to trust me on this one... Just know that every now and then I like to do these sorts of projects. The last five years we've been focused on huge endeavors, so from time to time it's nice to have something small like this one. Something unique. Remember when we did it with the Johnson site out in Springfield?"

"Okay. But why all the secrecy? I mean, all the others have been done under Lasseter Enterprises. Now you've created a totally different entity plus an alias?" Landon pushed, sensing the importance of what remained unsaid.

"You forget that when we did the Bradshaw building out east, we created another corp."

"Yes, but your name was all over that one."

"I know it seems odd, but I'm going with my gut on this. I think there are opportunities in the marketplace that we haven't explored before. Guys like Foster have options on some great properties. I'd like to investigate the possibility of taking on some new partners without our competition knowing what we're up to. That's why I'm going under the radar on this one."

"Okay, I guess that makes sense," Landon conceded, not entirely convinced.

Donovan's smile returned, the irritation evaporating from his features. "Glad to hear that."

"This won't be the first time I've seen you go with your gut on something, and it turns out to be a winner."

"Let's hope it works again."

Just then Payton's voice called out from the pool, cutting through their conversation. "Hey, Dad, can you toss us some balls?"

Donovan rose with surprising eagerness, striding toward the water's edge. He grabbed a football resting near the pool and called to his son, who was poised to dive from the opposite side. "Okay, Payton, catch this on your next dive?"

"Sure, Dad. Go ahead."

Donovan tossed the ball in a perfect arc. Payton leapt to meet it mid-jump, but his wet hands betrayed him, and the ball slipped from his grasp as he plunged into the crystalline water empty-handed.

He surfaced with a splash, spitting water and grinning. "Sorry, Dad. Let's try it again." Before Donovan could respond, Payton swam back to the other side in quick, determined strokes. In one fluid motion, he hoisted himself out of the pool, ready for another attempt. "Throw it, Dad."

"Okay, now."

Payton missed again but remained undaunted, visibly thrilled by both the game and his father's attention. The boy raced back to his position on the pool's far side, ready for another round. "Let me try it again?"

The harsh ring of Donovan's cell phone shattered the moment. He paused, reaching for the device, then turned back to toss the football to Landon. "Uncle Landon's going to take over for me. I've got to take this call."

Landon caught the toss, grateful that their families were close enough to share these terms of endearment. He liked being an "uncle." He moved closer to the water's edge, watching as Donovan retreated toward the house. Looking across the pool at Payton, he could see the boy was ready for his toss, but the earlier enthusiasm had dimmed. Disappointment shadowed the child's eyes as he watched his father walk away.

"Ready?" Landon called.

The boy mustered a smile that didn't quite reach his eyes. "Yeah."

Landon tossed the ball in a gentle arc. This time, Payton's hands held firm, and he surfaced triumphantly with the football still clutched in his small hands. "Way to go, Payton!" Landon shouted across the water. "Shall we give it another try?"

"Yes!" The boy swam back to his spot with renewed energy, and they continued their game. But despite Payton's apparent enjoyment, the disappointment over his father's departure lingered in his expression. After tossing the ball, Landon glanced toward the house just in time to see Donovan disappear inside. He noticed, with a twinge of unease, that Donovan wasn't speaking into his phone.

Payton surfaced with the ball again, tossing it back to Landon before swimming to the far side. His coordination was impressive for his age. They continued playing for several more minutes until Payton swam to Landon's edge of the pool and clung to the rim, clearly trying to mask his earlier disappointment. "I'm going to go play Marco Polo with Jared."

"Okay." Landon watched him swim toward the other children, knowing it was only a matter of time until the moment was forgotten, and Payton lost himself in new adventures.

Dinner that evening proved to be the culinary delight Landon had anticipated, enhanced by wonderful moments of laughter and joking between their families. Later, he joined Donovan for drinks in the study, where his boss predictably returned to the subject of the Precipice project. "So, you've prepared a letter of intent for Foster?"

"Yes, after our initial conversation, I drafted it up."

"Good, and I'd like to …" The study door burst open, interrupting Donovan mid-sentence as Payton ran into the room.

"Daddy, Mom said we've got to go to bed. Can you tuck me in?" The boy's voice held equal measures of hope and expectation.

"Sure. I'll be up in a few minutes," Donovan promised, his tone casual.

"Okay." Payton approached his father, giving him a quick hug before turning to Landon. "Good night, Uncle Landon. Thanks for playing catch with me."

"It was fun. Good night." Landon returned the boy's hug, watching as he dashed from the room, a small blur of energy against the study's rich wood paneling.

"All right, where were we?" Donovan asked, immediately refocusing on business matters.

Soon they were both immersed in the details of the project. Before Landon realized it, an hour had passed. They shared another round of scotch before heading to bed, both looking forward to their morning golf game.

Just before sleep claimed him, Landon's thoughts drifted back to Payton. The boy's hopeful face, his quiet "Can you tuck me in?," so easily brushed aside. Donovan hadn't meant to forget. He rarely did. But tonight, he had. Business had swallowed the moment whole. Landon stared up at the ceiling, unease pooling in his chest. All the success, all the scotch, all the acreage, none of it could fill the space left by a promise unkept.

CHAPTER EIGHT

LA JOLLA

JULY · 2000

Getting off on a new project put Andrew in high gear. He made his way up La Jolla Village Drive, heading toward the offices of Teknon 2 Partners, the afternoon sun casting sharp shadows across his windshield. His conversation with Quinn had given him new hope. It looked like Quinn's group was serious about working with him.

The first thing Andrew had done after getting off the phone with Quinn was to send over the site map, architectural drawings, and projected costs for the Precipice project. After reviewing them, Quinn called back and set up a meeting for today. He had seemed very positive, even with the possible roadblocks. When Andrew brought up some of the regulatory hurdles they might face, Quinn assured him he'd put some of his top people on it. It seemed they had friends in high places.

Andrew had already reconnected with contractors like Bill Atkins, with whom he'd worked in the past. Atkins had been reluctant at first, but when he heard the full proposal, he was ready to move forward with just one caveat: if this deal fell through, he wouldn't work with Andrew again. He remembered the last time they had worked on a project together and how the New York hedge fund they were collaborating with had strung them out, ultimately killing the deal. Andrew wouldn't let that happen again. Not this time.

Bill's firm took on projects of all sizes, from smaller developments, such as Andrew's previous work, to major commercial complexes. But even though he was a seasoned general contractor, he'd been honest about this project's scope, The Precipice was bigger than his firm could handle alone. He'd worked with Meridian Pacific Construction Group on previous research facilities and could bring them in as an associate contractor. They specialized in advanced laboratory construction, with expertise in vibration-isolated labs and modular clean room systems that could be reconfigured as research needs evolved. Their proprietary air handling designs exceeded ISO standards for particle control, exactly what The Precipice would need.

He pulled into the basement parking garage of Franklin Tower. It was one of the high-rises off La Jolla Village Drive, its glass exterior reflecting the cloudless sky like polished sapphire. He squeezed his car between a Porsche and a vintage Chevy Malibu. Quinn had said his offices were on the twelfth floor, so Andrew didn't stop to check the directory when he reached the entrance hall, but he couldn't help but admire the large seawater aquariums in the vast lobby. They were filled with colorful and exotic fish, their scales catching the light as they darted between coral formations.

That's got to cost a chunk of change to maintain, he thought to himself as he touched the button to call the elevator. The whole building didn't shout money at him, it didn't need to speak; it didn't stoop to that, instead, it just looked down its nose at visitors in a hip sort of way. Andrew caught his reflection in the glass of the fish tank and smiled back at himself. This was going to be a great meeting.

He was hopeful. It seemed as though his destiny might finally be changing. The thing he'd dreamed about for years was finally coming true. But still, somewhere at the fringe of his thoughts, there were whispers of worry. Maybe it was just another dead end, another pot with no gold at the foot of a false rainbow. He wondered how Quinn would respond once he met him face to face. Maybe he'd change his mind and choose not to go forward. Andrew was hoping with everything in him that it wasn't just another empty dream.

He was joined in the elevator by another man, who wore a big smile. The stranger reached for the buttons near the door. "What floor?"

"Twelve," Andrew replied, adjusting his tie with nervous fingers.

"That's our floor. Coming to see us?" The man's expensive cologne filled the small space.

"I'm not sure. I'm meeting with Teknon 2 Partners."

"Oh, yes, our law offices are across from them. I'm Dan Chambers of Chambers, Glenn, and Smithson."

"Good to meet you."

"Good to meet you too," said Chambers, pulling out his PalmPilot and tapping through his schedule, already disengaging from the conversation.

They rode up in a whoosh of movement, accompanied by smooth jazz coming from the speaker above Andrew's head. The doors opened to a glittering reception area featuring expensive tile, stainless steel, and polished wood, which hosted representatives from three firms. Chambers motioned for Andrew to go ahead of him. "Thanks," Andrew said.

Chambers responded in kind with, "Have a good day," then disappeared through frosted glass doors to the left.

To Andrew's right was Dreschal Management; to the left was Chambers, Glenn, and Smithson. Straight ahead, announced in embossed frosted letters on the massive glass doors, was Teknon 2 Partners. Andrew opened one of the doors and was greeted by a svelte thirty-something woman wearing one of those body-fitting, monochromatic dresses that female anchors on cable news often wear.

"Can I help you"? she purred at him with a well-controlled sophistication, accented with a hint of sensuality. She was quite a package.

"I've got a two o'clock meeting with Mr. Quinn."

"Mr. Foster?"

He confirmed with a nod, trying to project an air of confidence that he didn't entirely feel.

"Ah, yes, Mr. Quinn is expecting you." A row of perfect teeth complemented her smile. "I'll let him know you're here. Please take a seat." She motioned for him to sit on one of the dark upholstered chairs nearby and pressed a button on her phone console. "Mr. Foster is here for your two o'clock," she hummed into the headset. She looked his way with another well-crafted smile and announced, "He'll be right with you."

Andrew took one of the San Diego magazines from the glass end table but had barely lifted the cover when the door opened to his right and Quinn stepped into the reception area. Andrew recognized him easily from his photo on the website.

"Thanks for coming over to meet with me so soon," Quinn said, leading Andrew along a well-lit hallway and into his office. "Have a seat." Andrew settled into one of two large leather-bound chairs, a glass coffee table between them.

He made a quick scan of the room as Quinn moved to take his seat across from him. To his right was a wall of glass that offered a stunning view to the west. The UCSD dormitories rose in the distance against the backdrop of the blue Pacific. Past that, a bank of fog was held at bay by the high-pressure front that had finally arrived to give them days of sunshine.

July was usually sunny along the coast, unlike the previous month's weather, which longtime San Diegans affectionately referred to as June gloom. To his left was Quinn's desk. It was one of those glass models, situated near the window, which provided a perfect view.

"Nice view," Andrew offered. He'd seen it before in meetings here in La Jolla's Golden Triangle and other places around the county. These office suites were like high-tech palaces where the financial elites ruled their domains, all the while enjoying breathtaking vistas.

"Thanks," said Quinn. "Yes, it's great. Surprisingly, one can get used to it, so it's always nice when someone reminds me how lucky I am to work here."

"Lucky indeed," Andrew echoed, shifting in his seat.

"So, tell me a little about yourself, your operation."

"Well, I came to San Diego thirty years ago, and after graduating from SDSU, I got a job in the design department at a local architectural firm downtown. As much as I liked designing, I realized quickly that I wanted to expand my scope, to get out of the office and into something more hands-on. I then transitioned into construction, which turned out to be a much better fit. From there, I made the jump into development."

"Sounds like a wise decision," Quinn said with sincere agreement reflecting through his bright-blue eyes. "We've all heard the adage about finding a job you love, and you'll never work a day in your life."

"Yes, it's a job with a lot of potential," Andrew offered in response to his comment, putting on his best smile. He couldn't honestly agree with the latter part of the proverb because, as much as he loved development when he first got into it, it had been difficult for the last ten years. But he was too old to try anything else, so he'd just been slugging it out. "Well,

I've had some great years and some lean ones. I'm sure you know what I'm talking about."

Quinn nodded, but judging by the wealth around him, he really had no idea what Andrew had faced. He looked like he'd had nothing but a gilded path since childhood and the brains to capitalize on it. He seemed young for the position of power he held, but it was clear he was at ease with it. He exuded a certain sense of accomplishment, it was evident in his relaxed yet alert manner, the cut of his hair, and his attire. He was dressed in the business-trendy style common among many successful young men.

"Anyway, I've been able to build some things I'm proud of. I'm sure you must have looked over the portfolio I emailed you yesterday."

"Yes, I looked it over. You've done well for a small firm."

That was interesting—not at all what Andrew had expected to hear. Quinn must not have done as thorough a check as Andrew thought because he wasn't proud of the last few years. Of course, the prospectus he'd sent over to Quinn had all his wins prominently displayed.

"That's part of the reason I contacted you. You see, I have a silent partner who enjoys giving back. His operation was small once as well, and he knows how hard it can be sometimes to reach the next level. So, he finds guys like you and gives them a hand up. But to be honest, I think he feels like you'll work harder than some of the bigger guys."

"Well, that's nice to hear, but it seems odd for a huge outfit like yours to be so benevolent. I don't think you got here by being nice to the small guys."

Quinn laughed, the sound bright and polished like everything else about him. "True, we're in this to make money. However, we've learned that when we share the wealth, so to speak, it comes back to us in more ways than just monetary. It's kind of a principle that's part of our philosophy."

Andrew was a little troubled that he was seen as a charity case in some ways, but he was eager to get down to business, so he sloughed it off and moved on. "So, where do we go from here?"

"Well, as I said on the phone, my team has done a thorough investigation of your Precipice project, and we also agree with your projections on the costs. We feel like this will be a win-win for both companies. So, we'll go ahead and set up an LLC that we'd like to use on this project. You'll be the managing member, but I'll function as the CEO. You'll run the day-to-day operations, bring in your crews, and work with the local officials. How does that sound?"

"Sounds great," Andrew said, his shoulders releasing tension he hadn't realized he was carrying. "As far as profit sharing, it will be a forty-sixty split."

"Sure, that's typical when you're putting up the funds."

"There will be checks and balances, of course."

"Of course, I'm used to that," Andrew nodded, trying not to show too much eagerness.

"Our comptroller will have to sign off on the major stuff," Quinn continued. "We'll stage out the funding at appropriate times. I'll put you in touch with our legal and management team later this week to work out the details. Once everything's signed and underway, you can make your first draw. We're suggesting thirty grand as an up-front incentive. How does that sound?"

How does that sound? Andrew thought. *Is he crazy?* Quinn didn't really know how desperate Andrew was at that moment. Andrew found it hard to believe that Quinn was offering him so much up front. But he kept his calm and paused for a moment, pretending to weigh it all out as if he had a lot of options. Things seemed to be moving fast, but he guessed these guys had counted the cost and had all their bean counters look things over in detail. Quinn looked at him, waiting for an answer, his eyes bright and the slightest smile on his lips.

The thought crossed Andrew's mind that real developers usually faced weeks of grueling due diligence, financial audits, and partnership negotiations before seeing a penny—yet here was Quinn offering thirty thousand upfront, as if it were nothing. But after two years of closed doors and polite rejections while his father's health declined, Andrew wasn't about to question the first investor who actually believed in the Precipice vision.

Inside, Andrew was amazed that this deal was actually happening. Not wanting to seem too eager, he paused before responding.

"So, are you in?" Quinn said, his grin widening.

Andrew returned his smile. "Yes, I'm in."

Quinn's smile grew even wider. "Shall we shake on it for starters?"

"Sure," Andrew agreed, reaching out to take Quinn's extended hand.

"Great. I'll have you meet our legal gal, Tasha, before you go. She'll need to get some details from you so she can have the contracts drawn up. If everything goes well, we should be off and running right away."

"Good. I want to get started as soon as we can." There Andrew went, exposing his eagerness, and in the next moment doing his best to hide his embarrassment.

Once again, Quinn didn't seem to notice; he continued, "I'll check in with you at least once a week. I'm also looking forward to visiting the site and seeing things firsthand. In fact, I'll bring some of my team, and we can take you to lunch after that. I'd like them to get to know you, too. How's next Monday sound?"

"Sounds great."

"All right. Of course, if you need to reach me, you have my number." Quinn stood up.

Andrew followed his lead and rose. "Got it." He fidgeted a little with his hands, as they were a little sweaty from his nerves and excitement. He decided to put them in his pockets.

Quinn picked up his phone and punched in an extension. "Tasha, would you please come to my office?" He paused to listen and then set the receiver down. As they waited for Tasha to arrive, he invited Andrew to join him at the window for a view. They stared out at the ocean again. The fog had advanced along the coast and might put a damper on the evening.

"Yes, Mr. Quinn?" came a lilting voice from behind them. Andrew turned to see a medium-height, slim woman standing in the doorway. She was in a business suit and nearly as attractive as the receptionist.

"Thanks for coming over. This is Mr. Foster. He's going to be our lead on the Precipice project."

"Ah, yes," said Tasha. She reached out a slender, manicured hand. "Great to meet you, Mr. Foster. I've gone over your project, and I'm looking forward to working with you on it. It looks lovely."

"Very well," said Quinn as he reached out to shake Andrew's hand goodbye. Andrew was glad he'd put his hands in his pockets earlier—it had been a good call, with all the handshaking. "I'll let Tasha take care of you from here, and I'll have our receptionist call and confirm our meeting on Monday. I have to make a quick trip to Phoenix tomorrow, but I'll be back by the weekend. If you need me, just call."

"Great. I look forward to showing you the site."

"Goodbye, then."

"Goodbye," Andrew said. Then Tasha led him down the hall. They passed four or five nicely appointed offices until they reached her equally impressive one.

It didn't take Tasha long to gather the information and compile the details she needed. She promised to have the final contract drawn up for their signatures in a few days. Andrew was out the door and, on his way, back to his office in less than thirty minutes.

He decided to drive home along the PCH. He just wanted to savor this sudden good turn of events. He ran the figures over and over in his mind. Even with Teknon 2 taking the bigger percentage, he should walk away with a nice payday. It would get him that fresh start he needed. With a win like this under his belt, he should be back in the game in a big way.

The sun was gradually moving toward the west. The sunset would soon be lost behind a wall of gray. Andrew decided to capture the moment. He stopped along the highway just south of Del Mar and turned off the engine. The ocean stretched out below him, the gulls glided on the updrafts, and surfers cut across some great waves. He rolled the windows down and let the breeze waft through the car. It was just a great spot to think, to let his thoughts drift like the gulls on an inner, quiet wind.

He wasn't sure how to take in all that had happened in the last few days. Was fate offering him one final run at success? Part of him said that he deserved it—that all his hard work and persistence were finally paying off. But something else was in there at the back of his mind, threatening his joy. *You're getting what you deserve, Foster*, the voice would tell him. *It's payback.*

Andrew did his best to fight off such thoughts. But despite his efforts, long-abandoned memories surged into his mind like the rising tide, and he just couldn't find peace. Frustrated, he started the engine and drove away as the sun dipped into the gloom.

Since he was in Del Mar, he was reminded of an antidote for his depression. He stopped by 15th Street, a local pub, and decided to celebrate with a few old friends. It had been a great day, he told himself. He needed to cheer up and be grateful for the offer Teknon 2 Partners had made him.

When he finally got home, it was late, and all the stress and excitement of the day caught up with him. Even with the effect of all the alcohol he'd consumed toasting his good fortune, it still took him an hour to get to sleep. When he finally drifted off, it was with thoughts of hope buzzing warmly in his brain.

Hours later, though, he bolted awake from a dead sleep. Long-forgotten faces and tormenting words swarmed in his mind like a hive of angry bees. People he hadn't seen in years swept by him like a revolving kaleidoscope at some eccentric creep show. They paraded by, taunting him, intimidating him. He gathered one of his blankets across his shoulders and paced around the condo, hoping to shake off what he was feeling.

He walked to the window and stared out into the night. Only a distant streetlight gave any illumination to the darkness. There was no moon, no stars, just the fog drifting slowly past, dimming and brightening the light like the tide of a dream. His blood ran cold. The black Range Rover was back. Only now, the dome light inside was on, and there was a face, or was there? In the hazy glow, the features seemed to shift and blur, morphing from one half-remembered visage to another. Someone from Big Sur? A phantom from those desperate days after? His guilt-addled mind couldn't fix it. The face swam in and out of focus like a fever dream. He blinked once, and the features rearranged themselves. He closed his eyes and counted to ten, wishing it away.

When he opened them again, the SUV was gone. All that remained were the identical familiar vehicles parked up and down the lane, his neighbors' cars, resting like usual under the distant halo of the streetlamp.

He squinted through the glass. It hadn't even been a Range Rover, he realized—just a similar model, something his imagination had twisted into a threat. That single overhead light now seemed like a remote sentinel, its pale eye unblinking, watching him, exposing the raw truth buried deep in his chest: fear, lingering and unresolved.

But instead of giving in to it, he willed it away. He refused to let some apparition or booze-soaked vision worry him. He resolved that, despite his anxieties, a new day was ahead for him. With that determination, he headed back to bed knowing that tomorrow would be a good one.

Chapter Nine

BIG SUR

July · 1970

The stone house pulsed with evening chaos, its thick walls trapping the mingled aromas of woodsmoke, rosemary, and simmering herbs. July's coastal breeze slipped through open windows, carrying the tang of salt from the invisible ocean. In the main room, the massive stone hearth crackled with a cooking fire that threw dancing shadows across rough-hewn walls like ancient cave paintings come alive.

Lust coursed through Andrew as he navigated the bustling kitchen, weaving past Maya, who was grinding spices, and Tom, who was cleaning vegetables in a basin on the floor. The air hung thick with the scent of cumin and sandalwood incense.

Amber stood at the hearth, silhouette framed by flames as she stirred vegetables in the black iron pot. Heat had turned her cotton peasant dress transparent with sweat, clinging to curves that made his mouth go dry. Auburn hair escaped her braid, curling against her neck like question marks.

He slipped behind her, breathing in her natural musk mixed with woodsmoke, and pressed his lips to her damp neck. She laughed and twisted away, firelight painting her skin gold.

"Andrew, you're going to make me spoil dinner."

"I'd rather have you for dinner anyway."

She turned, her tie-dyed dress plunging low, hem riding high on sun-browned thighs. The pendant at her throat caught the light, their split heart of silver and turquoise, two stones that had once been one. A promise in jewelry form.

"Dessert comes after dinner," she teased, eyes glinting with danger.

"Am, you're a seven-course meal."

"Just don't go sampling the buffet." She meant some of the commune girls who spread their charms as freely as they shared joints.

The earlier incident with Blaire still haunted him. The way he had responded to her subtle provocations, those lingering looks, the reckless flirtations, left a bitter aftertaste. He hadn't crossed any physical boundary, but something inside him had faltered. There had been a moment, a shift, when desire, or maybe a deeper ache for affirmation, interrupted his clarity and clouded his devotion to Amber. Now, as he stood beside her, trying to be present, he attempted to shake off those lingering thoughts of Blaire. But something clung to him like mist in his lungs. It wasn't just guilt; it was the unsettling sense that Blaire had stirred something raw in him, something he thought had died in the desert. He hated how that moment had dulled his care for Amber, even briefly. They had left school together chasing truth, not illusions. He owed her better.

Yet despite the internal war, Andrew had remained faithful. In this era of free love and fractured promises, he had seen too many couples crumble under the guise of liberation. What he shared with Amber was different, deeper than the physical, rooted in something sacred, something he dared to call spiritual. Yes, he was in love. Deeply. Amber stood barely five-three, with a cherubic face, sparkling green eyes, and a figure that stirred both desire and protectiveness in him. Someone had nicknamed her "Sunshine" when she was just eight, and it still fit—not just because of her warmth, but the way she lit up the darkest parts of him. They'd met at SF State, bonding over poetry, Dylan, and dreams of escaping society's mold. So they'd bailed, heading to Big Sur to find something real among this vagabond tribe.

And now, here in the quiet aftermath of his own doubt, Andrew knew he'd have to face the shadow still lodged in him, before it grew into something that could cost him everything.

Soon, the great room filled with their ragtag family; hippies, bikers, seekers, all feeding bodies after feeding souls. Ash and Blaire sat close, beautiful in that careless way that made others stare. Eric Bishop ended dinner with his usual sermon about brotherhood, words floating on cannabis smoke.

The room settled into drowsy contentment. Candles flickered. Conversation drifted.

Then the temperature dropped ten degrees.

Pesha and Aishe didn't enter; they materialized. The gypsy couple had arrived a week ago in their fantastical caravan, a Reading Wagon painted in swirls and mystical symbols, mounted on a rust-eaten pickup like something from a fever dream. Ever since, they'd been testing boundaries, circling Eric's authority like predators.

Without invitation, Pesha's companion struck his guitar. Not gentle folk, but something that crawled up your spine, flamenco rhythms dark as old blood.

Pesha stood statue-still, beauty terrible in firelight. Silver glinted at his throat. His eyes were black holes swallowing light.

But Aishe commanded the room like a queen of some lost tribe.

She moved as if music was inside her, trying to claw its way out. Raven hair whipped like a storm-tossed sea. The commune formed a circle without meaning to, moths to flame.

Then she began shedding civilization like a snake sheds its skin.

First scarves floated away like dying butterflies. Then fabric pooled at her feet like spilled wine. Each layer removed was another wall torn down, another boundary crossed. She danced around Pesha, circling him like smoke around fire, becoming less solid with each turn.

The guitar shrieked higher. Aishe shed the last pretense of the ordinary world.

She stood before them completely naked, transformed by firelight into something beyond their understanding. The flames painted her in shadows and gold, turning flesh into myth. She'd become a force of nature that belonged to older times, to stories whispered around ancient fires.

Men leaned forward, hypnotized. Women turned to stone.

Amber's nails bit into Andrew's arm hard enough to draw blood. Janice, Eric's woman, looked ready to commit murder. The sisterhood was breaking, fault lines spreading across their perfect community.

Aishe melted into Pesha's shadow, and the guitar died with a sound like a neck snapping.

Silence.

Then Janice hissed something in Eric's ear that made him flinch.

Eric approached Pesha, trying for calm. "Hey, man, that crossed a line. You can't just...."

"Can't?" Pesha's accent made the word a curse. "In this place of freedom?"

They escalated to shouting in seconds.

"You've challenged me since you arrived," Eric towered over him.

"I challenge your small vision." Pesha smiled like a knife. "Your little kingdom is built on rules."

"Get out. Pack your wagon and go."

"Your authority?" Pesha laughed. "You're a boy playing at being king."

"I'll show you who's playing." Eric's fists clenched.

Pesha sauntered out, Aishe following, still completely naked but wrapped in defiance like armor, a war banner unfurled against the night.

Relief flooded the room with nervous laughter. But Andrew saw Ash's hand on his knife, saw something in his eyes that made his blood run cold.

The air went electric. The fire cowered.

Pesha returned with an ax that caught light like a smile.

"Let's discuss manhood properly," he purred, death in his voice.

The commune pressed against the walls. Someone whimpered. Fear-sweat overwhelmed incense.

Eric ripped off his shirt, his massive chest heaving. "Come on then."

Pesha danced with the ax, barefoot and beautiful and completely insane. The blade whispered promises as it sliced through the air.

"Big muscles, tiny courage," Pesha taunted.

Then Ash moved.

Fast as thought, silent as shadow. His knife flashed down and opened Pesha's wrist like a flower blooming red. The scream that followed wasn't human. The ax rang against stone.

"Nobody threatens my family." Ash's voice came from a cold and empty place. He slammed Pesha down, knife kissing his throat.

"Move and I open you up."

Blood pooled on ancient stones. The smell, mixed with wood smoke, became something that would haunt this place forever.

"Ash, enough," Eric's voice cracked like a boy's.

"Not until he learns."

"Let me handle it." Eric's hand found Ash's shoulder. "Please."

The knife vanished. Ash rose, still vibrating with murder.

"Lesson learned, I think."

Janice appeared with towels, the nurse's hands shaking. The spell broke slowly, and people remembered how to breathe.

"Let's go," Amber whispered, pulling Andrew toward escape.

At the door, Andrew looked back. Ash stood in the center of their ruined paradise, still ready to kill. Their eyes met, and Andrew saw the truth, they'd been playing at peace while absolute darkness waited in the wings.

They stumbled to their tent on the hill, shared a joint with shaking hands, wrote in Amber's diary side by side, a ritual that grounded them and then they fell into nightmares disguised as sleep.

Morning came like a hangover. Pesha's caravan still squatted by the oak tree.

"Let's hit the high meadow," Andrew suggested. "Get away from this."

"Ah, yes." Amber's laugh had sharp edges. "Before round two starts."

They fled up the mountain trail, following the stream through trees wearing fog like shrouds. At the meadow, they found Ash and Blaire already there, naked on sun-warmed rocks, as if last night's violence was just another trip.

"Heavy scene," Blaire said as they approached.

"Eric better run them off," Amber said.

"Or I will." Ash's tone made clear he'd enjoy it.

They swam until the water washed away the blood-memory, then sprawled on the rocks like lizards. After sharing lunch, sandwiches, jerky from Ash's kill, sliced apples, Ash produced orange tabs.

"Want to fly?"

They placed acid on tongues like communion wafers. The world began breathing. Colors bled outside their lines. Reality became negotiable.

The LSD transformed the grove into a living cathedral. Each leaf pulsed with heartbeat, each blade of grass hummed ancient secrets. Time stretched and contracted like breath itself.

Andrew wandered to an oak whose bark moved like the skin of a serpent. Amber communed with clouds. Ash built civilizations in the grass.

Then Blaire floated to him or maybe he floated to her. The universe bent around her, reality warping to accommodate her passage. She knelt, hands on his thighs, moving higher. Her touch sent electric messages straight to his spine.

Her eyes were oceans with dangerous tides. "I want you," she breathed, and the words rewrote his DNA.

Desire hit like a sledgehammer. Amber's face flashed a warning, accusation, but his body screamed louder than conscience. The LSD made everything permeable, no boundaries, morals, the notion of self, lost in the bliss.

No. You can't. You won't.

Then Blaire was gone, spinning away like smoke, leaving him gasping and trembling and confused.

Later, when they formed their coming-down circle, her hand found his. She squeezed, tickling his palm with promises, and then released. Again. And again. Morse code that said, *'I'm waiting.' Choose.*

The sun fled west. Reality reasserted boring rules.

"Time to go," Andrew managed.

They descended toward their wounded paradise, Amber's hand in his, Blaire's touch still burning his palm like a brand.

"Home for sunset," Amber said.

"And dessert," he agreed, but the word felt hollow now, ordinary compared to the electric promise still burning his palm. He pushed the thought away, conscience wrestling his desire back into its cage.

CHAPTER TEN

CARLSBAD COAST

AUGUST · 2000

The late summer sun cast long shadows across the undeveloped site as Andrew surveyed what would soon become his crowning achievement - Precipice, a state-of-the-art medical research facility. So far, everything had moved forward without a hitch. Teknon 2 had been a joy to work with. The weight of possibility hung in the air like the salt from the nearby ocean.

Standing on the bluff, Andrew could see it all in his mind's eye—glass and stone structures rising organically from the coastal landscape, their curved lines echoing the waves below. Where there was once only wild grass and native shrubs awaiting the Coastal Commission's approval, there would soon be cutting-edge laboratories with floor-to-ceiling windows, flooding workspaces with natural light. The residential villas would cascade down the hillside, each one a private sanctuary with ocean views for the world's top researchers. He imagined the five-star restaurant's terrace at sunset, scientists and guests dining as dolphins played in the distance. Walking paths would wind through native gardens, connecting the lab complexes to the recreation center, the amphitheater, and the meditation spaces. Everything is designed to nurture both breakthrough discoveries and the human spirit—an ecosystem of innovation wrapped in sustainable architecture that seems to grow from the earth itself rather than impose upon it. All of it is waiting for the final signatures from the Coastal Commission, city, and state officials to transform the vision into reality.

Quinn had visited the site the first week and taken Andrew to lunch with some of his team afterward. All of them had been encouraging and expressed their support for the project. Since then, Quinn had met Andrew at the site several times and had never kept him waiting. He continued to greenlight each phase. A week after their first meeting, Andrew had signed the development agreement and made his first draw, as Quinn had suggested. Thirty grand never looked so good. Quinn had wanted him to have some serious incentive. Well, he'd given him that. Andrew had been putting in the hours, twenty-four-seven. To say he was driven would be an understatement. He wasn't going to let this thing fail.

There had been a couple of concerns that troubled him. The first was that when he signed on, he also agreed to carry his part of any liability that might come from it. He had insurance, but it would still be a headache if this thing fell through. Broken agreements with contractors and failure to carry through with the city would be a nightmare. The second was that they held all the power. The way the agreement was drawn up, they could pull out at any time. Andrew couldn't imagine any reason why they would, though; this whole idea had been theirs from the start.

But he was haunted by one possible scenario. He recalled how a dear friend had joined one of the big banks a few years ago. Then they mysteriously yanked the LOC, and the builder was forced to go bankrupt even though he had some great projects in process. It turned out later that the bank was protecting itself from a recession that hit shortly thereafter. Hopefully, that wouldn't happen, but whatever the case, Andrew was in this thing with all his heart. It was a dream come true.

Despite these concerns, he saw plenty of positive signs. He'd had regular meetings with Quinn at his Franklin Tower offices since they kicked things off, and each one had been encouraging. A few times, he needed to run some unexpected detail by him, and Quinn had always been available by phone.

Whenever Andrew visited the Teknon 2 offices, he was always impressed by the warmth he felt there. It wasn't just the sincere greeting he received each time. It was the whole atmosphere they'd created. The place said welcome in every aspect, from the recessed lighting in the ceiling and floor of the reception area, to the way the light spilled out into the arrival area just outside the elevator doors. The frosted glass with the Teknon 2 logo etched into the doorways scattered a glowing array onto the tile just outside the door, subtly inviting "Come in." They'd designed the entire motif to make their guests truly feel at home.

Now Andrew sat in Quinn's office, sipping coffee and nibbling on some delicious scones the receptionist had brought them. That was another thing, a personal touch that put him instantly at ease. They were going over some final adjustments to the development plans, and Quinn was being really affirming. This had not always been the case with some of Andrew's past partners. They'd fight him on every point, second-guessing his ideas, more out of a sense of maintaining control than really wanting the best for the project. But Quinn seemed content with the progress they were making and hadn't been the least bit contentious.

The afternoon light filtering through the floor-to-ceiling windows cast a golden glow across the blueprints spread between them. Andrew explained his latest brainstorm to boost their profit margin. "Looks like the Coastal Commission and the city are going to accept the additional lab modules we've requested as long as we commit to another quarter acre of open space."

"I'm glad we had that extra area to exchange," Quinn said, his voice smooth as polished stone.

"Well, there wasn't a lot that we could do with it anyway, and to get four more state-of-the-art research labs out of the deal is golden. Additionally, I've reconfigured the top floor of the main building, allowing us to add a five-star restaurant with panoramic ocean views. It'll serve both the researchers and paying guests, creating another revenue stream."

Quinn set his coffee down and pointed to another detail on the plans. His manicured finger traced the outline of the buildings. "And these residential villas for the senior researchers?"

"Yes, each one has ocean views, which means we can attract the absolute top talent in biomedical research. They're not just labs, they're lifestyle destinations." Andrew could almost feel the sea breeze that would one day stream through those windows.

"Good work." Quinn's praise hung in the air between them.

"Thank you." Andrew was sincerely grateful that Quinn was being so supportive. For a guy so educated and savvy, he hadn't been the least bit patronizing. Andrew took another sip of coffee before moving on to his next point. "I've come up with another idea as well. If we consolidate the utility infrastructure on the north side, we can save about two million in construction costs and create space for an amphitheater—perfect for conferences and symposiums."

"Where is that located?"

Andrew flipped a few pages into the plans and showed him the schematic for that portion. The paper crinkled under his fingertips. "Here, between the main lab complex and the recreation facilities."

"And the city's cool with this, too?"

"Yes, I spoke to the planner yesterday. They love that we're creating a campus that integrates with the community rather than walling it off."

"Excellent." Quinn got up and walked to the window, taking his cup with him. The sunlight caught the rim of the ceramic mug, creating a slight halo. "So, with these changes, we're still on target to launch?"

"Absolutely."

Andrew looked over at Quinn to affirm what he just said. Quinn's smile remained steady, but there was something about the way he held his coffee cup, too still, too careful, that made Andrew pause. "Yes, the dream is just about to become a reality," Quinn said, enunciating each word with peculiar precision. A shadow seemed to cross his features, there and gone so quickly, Andrew wondered if he'd imagined it.

"Yes, the dream is just about to become a reality," Quinn said.

"Yes, that's my hope." Andrew took another quick bite of his scone and joined him at the window. Out over the horizon, the fog had cleared, and sunlight sparkled on the distant water. "It's been great working with you, Quinn," he said, smiling. He was a little embarrassed that he'd let his gratitude show so openly, but to be honest, Quinn's endorsement had left him feeling confident and happy. It all seemed too good to be true. But that was the great thing, it was true.

"It's mutual. I'm satisfied that you're doing all you can to make this project a success, and what you've just shared with me confirms that once again." Quinn's words were warm, but something in his tone sent a chill down Andrew's spine.

"I hope to come up with a few more money-saving ideas before we break ground."

"Good. So, what's next on the agenda?"

"Well, I'm meeting with Jeff Clark of Clark Strategies Group and a team from his firm tonight. It's an informal meet-and-greet at his home. He wants to introduce his group to the project. We've had some initial talks, and he's reviewed the plans, but after tonight, I'd like to secure his full commitment, so they'll have sufficient lead time to match our schedule. Jeff's firm has the connections to bring in the top public relations types, the kind who can put Precipice on the map and make sure the entire biomedical research world knows what we're building here."

Quinn took a sip from his cup and turned to him. He looked a little concerned for the first time today. The late afternoon sun cast half his face in shadow. "Well, don't make them any promises until you've got final approval from all the officials."

"That might not be for another month."

"Then it's better to wait." Quinn's voice hardened slightly.

"I think I can get them to move on this even before that. I've known Clark for years, and we've collaborated effectively on another project. He trusts me."

"All right. If you're sure." Doubt lingered in Quinn's words like fog.

"I am."

Quinn walked back to the sitting area, set his coffee down, and looked back at Andrew with a warm smile. "Great, then go for it. Like I said earlier, the dream's just about to become a reality!"

There it was again, that phrase. Every time Andrew met with him, he was always impressed by Quinn's gracious manner and appearance. Many of these young executives had developed the ability to carry themselves with a certain poise and confidence. They not only exude an easygoing demeanor, but their casual business clothes matched their manner perfectly. It was all so different from the suit-and-tie look of a generation ago. It was interesting to see how styles evolved from one era to another. But what impressed Andrew even more was the way Quinn engaged him in conversation. It was as if he was working extra hard to put him at ease.

Sometimes all this left Andrew wondering, though. Why was Quinn so affirming? Was he like this with all his partners? Then, of course, he started to wonder about other things. How had this whole thing landed in his lap at this time when he really needed a breakthrough? Was it just a coincidence, or was he somehow destined for it?

The setting sun cast long shadows across Quinn's office, painting everything in shades of amber and gold. Whatever the case, it couldn't have come at a better time. This project was not only going to generate a substantial amount of money for Teknon 2, but it was also going to set Andrew up for the foreseeable future. The flip side of that reassurance made him anxious, though. Still, he convinced himself all was well. He would need that sort of internal assurance going into his meeting with Jeff Clark and his team tonight to discuss marketing strategies for Precipice. This medical research facility would soon change everything.

As Andrew gathered his things to leave, he couldn't shake the feeling that something about Quinn's smile didn't quite reach his eyes. But despite this, he had to tell his dad the good news.

Andrew dialed Joseph's number. "Dad, I've finally found the funding for Precipice. Teknon 2 Partners—they're ready to back the whole project."

There was a long pause on the other end, then his father's voice, cautious despite the hope threading through it. "That's wonderful, son. But you've checked them out thoroughly? There are a lot of phonies out there, people who promise big and deliver nothing."

Andrew laughed, riding high on certainty. "Dad, these guys are the real deal. Professional offices, with a full staff, they've been nothing but straightforward with me. Quinn knows the business inside and out."

His father sighed, that sigh of someone who'd seen too much to trust easily. "I hope you're right, Andrew. Just... be careful. Double-check everything." "I have, Dad. I have. Your designs are finally going to see daylight." The joy in his father's voice then, restrained but real, had made Andrew feel ten feet tall.

"Ok, keep me posted."

"Will do, Dad, love you."

CHAPTER ELEVEN

DEL MAR

AUGUST ᐧ 2000

The Pacific could transform from ally to enemy in the space of a heartbeat, but tonight it was putting on a luminous light show. It was the first day of the month, and the coast seemed to know it, like the calendar itself had summoned this extra shimmer. Amber hues painted the underbellies of clouds as the sun descended, casting a warm glow across the deck of Jeff Clark's palatial home. The view was especially stunning from this elevation, where the ocean stretched toward the horizon like a sequined blanket unfurled by an unseen hand. This was San Diego at its most seductive—that magical hour when the light turned everything to gold, when the temperature hit that perfect seventy-two degrees that made people sell their homes back east and never look back.

Andrew Foster stood near the railing, nursing a glass of Pinot Noir, observing the gathering. Jeff had arranged this evening to introduce his team from Clark Strategies Group to the Precipice opportunity. His firm had built a strong reputation in San Diego, but Jeff knew that a project of this magnitude would benefit from additional firepower. That's why he was bringing in Helix Strategies as a partner, their sleek waterfront office downtown housed the West Coast's go-to public relations firm for science and innovation. Jeff had told Andrew that while Clark Strategies had the local connections and biotech experience, partnering with Helix would give them access to global media networks and specialized science communications expertise that Precipice deserved.

Andrew had to admit this smart and attractive crowd was exactly the kind of talent he needed. There were a handful of eager communications specialists mingling around the outdoor bar, along with a couple of seasoned account directors who had caught his eye. Of course, he had to remind himself of what he'd said to Jade on the beach that day. He didn't ever want another Carolyn failure. If something did happen, he'd approach it differently right from the start.

The aroma of tri-tip sizzling on the grill wafted across the deck, mingling with the salt air—it was that incredible tri-tip from Seaside Market that everyone was raving about, the stuff they were calling "Cardiff Crack" because once you tried it, you couldn't stop coming back for more. Jeff had picked up a few pounds of the Burgundy Pepper marinated beef that morning, and from the way it smelled, Andrew could already tell why people were lining up at the market every weekend to get their hands on it.

Andrew noticed some IPAs nestled in ice, while Malbecs and Pinots were in abundance too, along with what appeared to be the best salsa and chips he'd tasted since his last meal at Las Olas. The sound of laughter punctuated conversations that floated across the space like music.

After his meeting with Quinn earlier that day, Andrew approached this gathering with fresh confidence. But he had to admit there were times when he was still visited by the specters of past failures. In fact, when he told Kevin Long at Altamont Builders about his new project, Kevin had been happy for him, but Andrew could see skepticism in his eyes. He'd run into him at 15th Street last week in Del Mar and shared with him about his partnership with Teknon 2. Kevin had listened politely, but Andrew could tell he was doubtful. He'd seen Andrew excited about projects before, only to have them fall through. His subtle incredulity had left Andrew troubled. He knew Kevin could be right. In his business there were always risks, and with them came all sorts of worries. He didn't know if he'd survive if this thing fell through.

Tonight, though, Andrew was just grateful for the opportunity to get a break from his hectic work schedule and enjoy some of the beauty that this beach community offered, both natural and human.

The sun finally slipped into the sea, and nature's light show on the western skyline was grabbing everyone's attention. The sky began its nightly transformation, from molten gold to coral, then to that impossible shade of blue that photographers called the magic hour. Two of Jeff's senior account directors, both attractive women, had moved to the edge of the deck and were drinking in the view. Andrew was taking it in too, and it wasn't just the sunset. The golden light made everything seem possible, softened edges, turned ordinary moments into something cinematic. Again, he reminded himself that the physical stuff was great, but he was looking for something deeper. Others first, he told himself.

As he approached them, they instinctively turned and greeted him.

"Mister Foster, right?" said the one on his left. "I recognize you from your picture in the project brief Jeff shared with us." The other chimed in with, "We've reviewed the Precipice development materials, and we're really excited about the storytelling possibilities."

Their enthusiasm seemed genuine and sophisticated, not the sort of thing Andrew had seen in some younger professionals who were all flash and no substance. He was still amazed that forty-something women could look thirty. Maybe in southern California forty was the new thirty. Some might say these women were past their prime, but Andrew knew that frequent trips to the spa and a session with Dr. Snyder's youth clinic could do wonders. It wasn't just looks, though; maturity was a plus in the public relations business. No doubt the years had taught these women a lot about navigating complex narratives and managing high-stakes campaigns.

"Please call me Andrew," he said, the sea breeze ruffling his hair.

"Okay," said the taller one. "I'm Joyce, Senior Vice President of Strategic Communications, and this is Nicole, our Director of Science and Innovation Accounts."

Nicole extended a hand. It was tan but free of sunspots that often plagued women who spent too much time in the California sun. Her handshake was firm, confident, but she held it a beat longer than strictly professional. When she smiled, it reached her eyes, dark brown with flecks of gold that caught the fading light. There was something else there too, a directness mingled with intelligence, just below the surface of her smile.

He gave them both his best smile and hoped that his crinkles weren't too obvious. Although, they said what a man really needed to be attractive was a fat bank account, especially one that was much heftier than his midriff. Andrew was happy to say his waist was slim, too bad he had to say the same about his financial statement. But not for long. Not with Precipice around the corner, he reminded himself. The thought stroked his confidence and made him think that he might still be appealing even at fifty. But he reminded himself that the best part of him should be his character, who he was at his core.

"So how long have you ladies worked for the Clark Strategies Group?" he asked, his voice carrying over the sound of waves crashing against the shore below.

"I joined the team three years ago," Nicole said with a smile. Her warmth and perfect teeth were instantly charming. "Joyce brought me over from our previous firm. We've been colleagues for ages," she explained.

"Yes, we've been supporting each other's careers since we graduated in the same class at Sac State," said Joyce. "We both started in the Bay Area when the tech boom took off there, but I decided I'd like to try the biotech scene down here and joined Jeff's firm first. Once I saw the potential for science communications in San Diego, I convinced Nicole to make the move too."

Nicole was quick to respond. "We've been building something special here. The firm has given us incredible opportunities to work with cutting-edge research. That's why we're so excited about Precipice. From what we've seen in the preliminary materials, it should generate significant media interest."

Andrew felt refreshed by their professional confidence. "Well, thank you. That's encouraging to hear. I think we're positioned perfectly for the kind of narrative that will resonate with both the scientific community and the general public. With the biotech sector heating up and so many breakthrough discoveries happening, Precipice should capture attention quickly."

After just a few minutes with these women, Andrew could see them crafting compelling stories around the facility. Their sophistication, industry knowledge, and communication skills would be perfect for reaching the influential audiences that Precipice needed to attract. The research spaces would be expensive, but these professionals wouldn't have any trouble articulating the prestige and innovation that would make working at Precipice one of the most coveted positions in West Coast medical research.

"I can see you understand the vision already," Nicole said, her eyes meeting his. The breeze picked up, carrying the scent of night-blooming jasmine from the gardens below, and she tucked a strand of hair behind her ear, a simple gesture that somehow held his attention.

"It's a compelling story," she continued. "We reviewed the architectural plans and research focus areas you provided. The narrative practically writes itself; visionary science meets world-class design on one of the most beautiful coastlines in America."

Andrew noticed that the two of them had nearly finished their wine, so he volunteered to refill their glasses. He came back with theirs replenished, balancing a local IPA for himself. They continued to chat amiably, swapping pleasantries and getting to know each other. They were soon sharing everything from their love of the outdoors to their professional backgrounds in science communications. Perhaps it was the wine and the picturesque view that made them all feel so open to share.

His ears perked up when Nicole started talking about her personal life. "Well, other than building my career in science PR and some great international travel, I've had a good run. Though I'll admit the personal side hasn't always been as successful as the professional. Let's just say my ex-husband and I had very different ideas about loyalty."

Andrew was a bit taken aback by her candor, especially since it was his first time meeting either of them. But Joyce laughed softly and waved a hand, as if to explain. "We were just talking about this before you walked up. I got a call out of the blue this morning, from an old flame who wants to get back together. It got us down the rabbit hole of past loves and near misses."

Nicole glanced at her and smirked. "And questionable taste in men."

There was a warmth between them, a rhythm that came from shared history or at least kindred experience. Whatever initial formality the evening might have held had evaporated. Maybe it was the wine, or the twilight hour, or simply the kind of honesty that rises when people feel unexpectedly understood. And Andrew, with his quiet presence and open face, didn't seem like the type to interrupt that, if anything, his listening made space for it to deepen.

Joyce was quick to chime in. "That's putting it diplomatically. At least you learned early. I almost married someone who... well, let's just say he showed his true colors before we made it to the altar."

"Sounds like you both dodged some bullets," Andrew said, a smile playing at the corner of his lips.

They all had a good laugh, and then Nicole added, "We've definitely learned to trust our instincts. No more ignoring red flags. It serves us well in PR too, you have to read people quickly when you're managing crisis communications."

"Or when you're vetting potential relationships," Joyce added with a knowing look.

That brought another round of laughs. Andrew liked their openness, enough honesty to be real without dumping their entire histories on him. He couldn't help but wonder if he had prospects. So, he ventured this query, "Well, I hope those experiences haven't closed any doors permanently?"

"Not at all," said Joyce. "We're just more selective these days. I'm enjoying my independence too much to settle."

"I'm definitely open to the right situation," Nicole added, meeting his eyes briefly. "I still believe in partnership, just with someone who shares the same values. Working with brilliant innovators like yourself reminds me there are still people worth getting to know better."

Andrew was taken back by their candor with someone they just met. Maybe there was some truth to the old saying: In vino veritas. Or perhaps it was their way of letting him know they weren't attached to anyone right now.

Just then Jeff announced the food was ready. "Come on, friends, the tri-tip is sliced, and there's some great kale salad to go with it. The chow line forms right behind Madi," he said, pointing to his twenty-eight-year-old trophy wife. And from the look of her figure, it was obvious she wasn't often first in line for dinner.

"I'm famished," said Joyce. "I skipped lunch to work on the Genomics Institute campaign." She turned to lead the way to the line. Nicole stayed close to Andrew as they let others move into place ahead of them.

"So, Andrew, Jeff told us you've been here in San Diego for over thirty years," said Nicole with a warm familiarity that drew him in. "I can see why. The weather, the lifestyle, and the innovation ecosystem are hard to match. Is that what keeps you here?"

"You know, I've talked to people who've lived here but travel a lot, and they say nothing can match it for climate and beauty. As fun as their vacations are, they can't wait to get back here. In all your travels for Clark Strategies, you must have seen some wonderful places. Which one has been your favorite?"

Nicole took a plate and moved down the line ahead of him, briefly turning back to respond. "It's hard to say. There are so many amazing places, but I guess I enjoyed my time in Africa the best. I went with a documentary crew covering a medical mission, part of a humanitarian campaign we were developing. The work there was amazing, and the land is so diverse, so different than here. But most of all, it's the people. They're open and warm."

Andrew took a plate and followed her, savoring the aroma of the feast spread out before them. "I've heard that before. I'd love to go there someday. The people sound like my type. I think I'd fit right in."

"Yes, I think you would," she said with just a hint of a smile.

"Well, maybe next time Clark Strategies has a project there, I'll join your team," he said with a wink.

"We'd love to have you, Andrew," she said, smiling bigger this time.

They got to the end of the line and started to look for a place to sit. Joyce was with a group at a table inside, deep in conversation about media strategy.

"Looks like Joyce is deep in campaign mode," Nicole observed with a laugh. "Want to find somewhere quieter where we can actually hear each other?"

"Great idea," he said, relieved she'd suggested it. "There's a spot over there that's not taken," she said, pointing to two seats by the edge of the deck.

He followed her to the spot, noticing how the blue hour had begun to settle over the coast, that ethereal time when the sky matched the ocean in impossible shades of indigo. String lights had come on around the deck, creating pools of warm light that made everything feel intimate, like they were in their own private corner of the world. Even though it was clear that Nicole was not afraid to be frank, Andrew sensed there was also a sweetness about her. Her face reflected it in her sincere smile.

After a few bites, they both paused and picked up the thread of conversation. Each of them had returned from the buffet line with fresh drinks, Nicole cradling her third glass of wine, and Andrew now sipping a cold IPA. Maybe it was the earlier honesty between the women, or maybe the drinks had lowered the usual guardrails, but there was an unexpected ease in the air. First meetings rarely felt this unfiltered. The warm evening, the slow drift of conversation, it all lent itself to something more open, more human.

"So, I don't see a ring on your finger," Nicole said, tilting her head slightly. "What's your story? We spilled a bit of ours to you."

She laughed as she said it, but her eyes held a spark of real curiosity.

Andrew smiled, taking a sip. "That's a loaded question. I've had a few disappointments too. Nothing has ever really seemed to click."

He paused, hearing himself—and realized he was dodging. If anything was going to change, it had to start with telling the truth. "Actually... if I'm being honest, I've been a big part of why things haven't worked out. Even if I met someone, I felt I could live with for the rest of my life, I'd have to be willing to change."

"Being willing to change is good. Pain changed me... pain I went through with my former spouse."

"I've had a few hurts too, some deep ones even though I've never been married." Andrew was surprised at how open he was suddenly being with this woman. Perhaps it was the alcohol, or maybe Nicole was bringing out something genuine in him.

"Being hurt like that once was enough, but I can't let that keep me from hoping one day it will all click."

They lapsed into silence for a while, enjoying their meal. Andrew took the time to think about how to respond.

"And what would that look like?" he asked. "I mean, what kind of person are you looking for?"

"That's hard to say. It's kind of like your question about travel. There are a lot of great guys in the world, but I'm looking for a special one. Remember what I said about the people in Africa?"

"Warm and open?"

"Yes, it would have to be someone like that."

"Sounds like a good plan."

"Yes, I guess you could call it that. A good plan."

Nicole finished her plate and set it aside. "Speaking of plans, what are yours?"

"Well, for starters, I don't plan to ever move away from San Diego. That's why I'm working so hard right now. I mean, I love the idea of travel, but I've got to get through this current project. Then after that, I plan to build my dream house and take some time to enjoy all this place has to offer."

"That's not what I meant," she said with feigned anger, reaching out and touching his arm briefly, a playful smirk on her face. Her fingers were warm against his skin, and the touch sent an unexpected current through him. "I was talking about relationships."

"I know you were," he said, smiling back, aware of how close they were sitting, how the soft evening air seemed to wrap around them like silk. "I guess I'd have to say I'm like you, I'm looking for someone warm and open." That wasn't just a line he was feeding Nicole. At this point in his life, it had to be real.

Just then, Jeff announced that they all needed to gather inside. Andrew picked up Nicole's plate and pointed the way to where the group was gathering. Nicole went ahead, and he dropped off their plates near the serving table. Once inside, Jeff stood at the center of his vaulted living room, a glass of whiskey in hand, the strategic lighting making his silver temples gleam.

Jeff closed out the evening with a short speech about the Precipice project and the partnership opportunities. As he spoke, Andrew noticed a slight tightness around Jeff's eyes, a subtle tension in his smile that didn't quite match his enthusiastic words. Jeff took a few minutes to praise Andrew for his vision in bringing this development to where it was now, but beneath the polished veneer, Andrew detected the faintest note of caution in his voice, the sound of a man who had witnessed promise dissolve into disappointment before.

"In all my years of working in this San Diego market," Jeff said, raising his glass, "I've only found a few developers like Andrew who truly understand that vision matters more than scale. We met back at SDSU, and I watched him grind through projects when everyone else was out partying. Sure, he's mostly done smaller residential and commercial developments, but that work ethic, that's what counts."

He paused, his eyes briefly meeting Andrew's with a flash of something, confidence mixed with anticipation, before continuing. "When he came to me with Precipice, I'll be honest, it's bigger than anything he's tackled before. But I did my homework on Teknon 2, and with their backing plus what we can bring to the table, along with our new partnership with Helix for global reach, this isn't just about building labs. This is about putting San Diego biotech on the world stage. The three of us together? We're going to make Precipice a name that resonates from here to Geneva to Singapore."

Jeff's smile widened. "I've got a great feeling about this project, and I can say for all of us here tonight, we're looking forward to seeing how far we can take this vision."

There was a courteous round of applause, during which Jeff took a longer sip of his drink than necessary. Then he added, with practiced enthusiasm that didn't quite mask his underlying uncertainty, "Be sure to look at the project materials in the foyer again on your way out. This is going to be a landmark development." The unspoken "I hope" hung in the air between them, discernible only to Andrew, who had learned to read the subtext of doubt in even his staunchest supporters.

Within half an hour, most of the guests had left for the evening, stopping in the house to look over the floor plans, research facility specifications, and PR strategy outlines that Clark Strategies had prepared. Nicole lingered near the materials, studying them with genuine interest.

"Shall we go back outside? It's still warm," Andrew suggested.

"Yes, that would be nice," she replied.

The moon was near the horizon, enormous and amber, painting a silver path across the water that seemed to lead directly to them. The air had that perfect San Diego quality, warm enough to be comfortable, cool enough to make you want to move closer to someone. Andrew took it as a sign and invited her to join him near the railing.

They stood there for several minutes not saying much except for comments about how beautiful the night was. The distant sound of waves provided a rhythmic soundtrack to their silence. Nicole stood close enough that he could smell her perfume, something light and citrusy that mixed with the ocean air. When she shifted slightly, their shoulders almost touched, and neither of them moved away.

Soon Andrew could tell it was time to allow their hosts to close. "It's been great getting to know you," he said with a warmth he hadn't felt for a woman in a while.

"Absolutely, I hope this won't be the last time we talk."

He took that as an invitation that it was okay to follow up. "Let me give you my cell number," he offered.

"That would be great. I'll give you mine too."

Andrew took out his phone and punched in her number, then he texted her his contact info. "I guess we better go. Jeff has been gracious to host this evening, but it looks like he's ready to close for the night. Can I walk you to your car?"

She smiled. "I'd love that."

They said good night to the Clarks. From the way they were hanging on to each other, Andrew guessed they were glad their guests were moving on. They stopped at Nicole's Lexus, and he wondered how he should end this. There was a moment of uncertainty, both hesitating.

"Thank you for a lovely evening," Nicole said, turning to face him. The moonlight caught in her hair, and she stepped slightly closer, but maintained just enough distance to keep things professional. He could see her considering something, a decision playing out in the slight tilt of her head.

Andrew took her hand and squeezed it gently. "I really enjoyed talking with you. I'd like to see you again, if you're interested."

"I'd like that too," she said softly. Then, surprising them both, she leaned in and kissed him lightly on the cheek. Her lips lingered just a moment longer than casual, and he caught that citrus scent again. "For luck with Precipice," she said with a smile that suggested it might be for more than that.

He opened her door, and she slipped in, touching the button on the window control. It glided down, and she reached out to him. Taking his hand one more time through the open window, she said, "Call me. I mean it."

"I will," he promised. "Drive safe."

She smiled a final goodbye, started the car, and then smoothly glided out into the street and was gone.

Andrew stood in the moonlight, watching the red taillights of her car disappear around a curve. He wondered if Nicole might be the one to break his pattern of failed relationships, even as he questioned whether Precipice would finally break his pattern of unrealized dreams. In the cool night air, both possibilities seemed tantalizingly within reach, yet somehow just beyond his grasp.

Chapter Twelve

DEL MAR

AUGUST · 2000

The wine glass trembled in Nicole's hand, just slightly, as he asked the question that would change everything between them.

"Why are you even entertaining the idea of getting serious with me?"

It had been just over three weeks since they met, now their fourth date and things were moving faster than either of them had expected. Whatever this was, it had a gravity neither seemed quite prepared for, but both kept orbiting closer.

Andrew watched the tremor. A tiny vibration in the crystal, catching the candlelight. Most people wouldn't have noticed, but he'd learned to read the small signals, the way her index finger tapped once against the stem, how she tucked that strand of hair behind her ear when she was nervous. The gesture released a hint of her perfume, jasmine and something else, something that made him think of sun-warmed skin.

Outside Jake's windows, the Pacific crashed against the shore with unusual force. High tide. The salt-laden breeze slipped through the restaurant's open-air section, carrying with it the primal scent of seaweed and brine. The summer sunset had been perfect an hour ago, at eight o'clock the sky still held color, painting the water in shades of copper and gold, the light transforming Nicole's skin to honey. But now, past nine, dusk was finally settling in, intimate and enveloping

"That's easy," Nicole said, steadying her hand. "I see your heart."

The words hung between them. Andrew shifted in his chair, the worn leather creaking.

"But there's another side of you I want to know more about."

"There is?"

She hesitated. Her earrings, small silver drops, caught the light as she tilted her head. The candle between them flickered in the ocean breeze, throwing dancing shadows across the weathered wood of their table. "I'm a bit hesitant to bring it up."

The restaurant hummed with summer evening energy. Families lingered over dessert, couples shared appetizers at the bar, and the cheerful chaos of a busy beachside eatery wrapped around them. Andrew had chosen Jake's deliberately, no tablecloths, no pretense, just weathered wood and good food. The kind of place where flip-flops were welcome and the Pacific provided the soundtrack. The air tasted of salt and possibility, tinged with the smoke from small gas grills on the beach where people cooked their catches of the day.

"Don't be. What is it?"

Nicole's gaze was direct now. "After all you've told me about your successes, you haven't been all that open about your failures."

The word hit him like cold spray from the ocean. Failures. Precipice loomed in his mind, his company poised to leap into territory he'd never navigated before. Not failing but reaching higher than he'd ever dared. The meetings with Jeff Clark, the ambitious plans that made his previous ventures look like practice runs.

"Jeff told me about them."

Heat rushed to his face. His hand clenched on the table.

Nicole reached across, her fingers cool against his fist. "I asked him. And I'm grateful he was honest." Her touch was firm, grounding. "He believes in you, or he wouldn't even consider working with you."

Andrew forced his hand to relax. Through the window, he could see the foam of breaking waves, white lines in the darkness. A seagull cried somewhere in the night, its call lonely and wild. The restaurant's warmth wrapped around them like a cocoon, the mingled scents of grilled fish and garlic butter making the moment feel both real and dreamlike.

Three weeks. That's all it had been since Jeff's party, since he'd stood with Nicole in the driveway under the rustling palms, leaning toward a kiss that never quite happened. Three weeks of conversations that stretched until dawn, of careful touches and careful words.

"This relationship is too wonderful to rush anything," she'd said that second night, candles flickering between them in her living room. *"If I ever give myself to someone again, I've got to trust them completely."*

He'd seen it then, a flash of something raw in her eyes. The betrayal she'd mentioned. Her husband and her best friend. The kind of wound that changed the shape of a person.

"Why would you want to hear the bad stuff?" Andrew asked now, genuinely puzzled.

"Because it's part of what makes you, you. That's where I can shine." She leaned forward, the candlelight throwing shadows across her face, turning her eyes to liquid amber. "One of my best gifts is being a support. But to do that, you've got to let me in."

The waiter approached, then retreated, reading the intensity of their conversation. Outside, a group of teenagers ran past on the beach, their laughter sharp and sudden before fading into the distance. The smell of grilling burgers and hot dogs drifted in from the small gas cookers dotting the beach, families roasting marshmallows, making s'mores, squeezing the last moments from the summer day. They couldn't have fires on Del Mar beach, but the portable grills served just as well. It mixed with Nicole's perfume and the wine on her breath when she spoke, creating an intoxication that had nothing to do with alcohol.

Andrew studied her face. The determined set of her jaw, the vulnerability in her eyes. She was offering something he'd never had before, someone who wanted to see him fail, just so she could help him stand back up.

"Okay," he said quietly. "I promise to do my best to let you in, even with the bad stuff."

But even as he said it, something twisted in his chest. A memory, distant but persistent. Another promise, made to another woman, broken like glass on stone.

"Can I ask you something?" Andrew's voice was careful now.

Nicole nodded.

"That whole thing with your husband, will you be able to fully trust again?"

Her fingers found the rim of her water glass, tracing circles in the condensation. "I have to believe I will. But..." She looked out at the ocean, then back at him. "Right now, I'm hoping that maybe I've found the kind of man who would never betray me."

Betray.

The word lodged in his throat like a fishbone.

"Absolutely, you have," he heard himself saying. "I would never betray you. That would be the worst thing I could imagine."

Somewhere in the back of his mind, a quiet laugh echoed. He pushed it away, focused on Nicole's face, on the hope he saw there.

She reached up, touched his cheek. Her palm was warm. "Yes, I'm sure you mean it."

The drive home followed the coastal highway, headlights cutting through the marine fog that had rolled in with the tide. Just past the racetrack, the road veered inland at Via De La Valle, threading beneath the 5 and into the quiet streets of Solana Beach. Nicole sat close, her warmth radiating through his shirt where her shoulder pressed against his arm. Her perfume, that maddening blend of jasmine and mystery, mixed with the salt air streaming through the cracked window. The fog transformed the familiar route into something otherworldly, softening the edges of reality, like they were drifting together into some shared dream.

They didn't speak much, the important words had all been said. But her hand found his on the gear shift, fingers intertwining as naturally as breathing. The radio played something soft and forgettable, barely audible over the rhythmic swoosh of waves breaking against the cliffs below.

At her door, under the porch light that attracted moths in dizzy circles, they stood close enough that he could feel the warmth of her breath. The night jasmine in her garden bloomed heavy and sweet, mixing with the ocean air to create a perfume that would forever remind him of this moment.

They kissed. Soft, brief, her lips tasting faintly of wine and promises. When she pulled back, her eyes held depths that matched the ocean's, beautiful and terrifying in their vastness.

"Goodnight, Andrew."

"See you soon."

Simple words. Ordinary. But as he walked back to his car, Andrew felt the weight of everything unsaid pressing against his ribs.

Andrew could have taken the 5 north to get to his apartment in Encinitas, it would've been faster, direct, uneventful. But he needed time to think. So instead, he turned west at Via De La Valle and rejoined the coast highway, choosing the longer way home. The fog had thickened, and the familiar road took on a quiet, contemplative mood that matched the churn inside him.

Alone on the highway, the word returned.

Betrayed.

It brought with it images he'd buried deep. Amber's face, years ago, when she'd found out. The way her mouth had opened but no sound came out.

He'd been different then, he told himself. Younger. Careless with hearts, including his own.

The road stretched ahead in dim arcs of light, the fog swallowing everything beyond the reach of the high beams. The ocean, just out of sight, breathed steadily in the dark. He cracked the window and let the salt air in, hoping it might clear more than just the windshield.

He thought of Nicole's trust, offered so carefully. Of his promise never to betray her. Of how easily promises could break, like waves against stone.

Alone on the highway, the word returned.

Betrayed.

He'd said it so easily. *"I would never betray you."* As if the words could erase what he'd done before. As if Nicole's trust could somehow absolve him. But the past had weight, and it pressed against his chest now, demanding acknowledgment. Amber's face materialized in his mind—not as he chose to remember her, laughing in the sunshine, but as she'd looked that last morning.

CHAPTER THIRTEEN

BIG SUR

JULY · 1970

It had been seven days since Andrew's trip in the meadow, the memory fading like mist rising from the ocean. Things at the stone house had settled into a lazy rhythm of contentment. The strange couple with their gypsy caravan had moved on, leaving only footprints in the dust and whispered stories around the communal fire. Eric was full of good words and seemed more confident than ever in his idyllic dream of brotherly love and good vibes. For the most part, the group was happy to let him spout his platitudes. There was plenty to eat, plus lots of dope to share. The days blended in a haze of smoke and sunshine.

The July air was thick with the scent of wild sage and eucalyptus when a new guy arrived at the compound around noon. He was tall, dark-haired, broad-shouldered, and several of the women were clearly intrigued, their gazes following him as he moved about the camp. But what was more interesting was the teepee he'd brought with him in the back of his pickup, a structure that would become the stage for what happened next.

The teepee had several lodgepole pines that created its frame, with white canvas laid over it, forming a space at the top for smoke to ascend through. The canvas cover, if not completely true to the pattern the Lakota

Sioux used, looked otherworldly at night because it glowed from within, transformed by the fire into a luminous beacon against the dark hillside.

As the sun began its descent towards the Pacific, a group gathered around the hearth at the center of the teepee. The floor was covered with a series of rugs and burlap, offering an inviting place to lounge. The air inside was still, heavy with anticipation. Before long, joints were being passed around, and several began a jam session. The notes from the guitar floated up with the smoke, disappearing through the opening at the top of the teepee.

Amber sat at Andrew's side, trying her best to enjoy the moment, but she was visibly uncomfortable. She hadn't been her usual bubbly self all day. Her face, normally flushed with excitement, was pale and drawn. She thought she had a flu bug or perhaps food poisoning. She had vomited when she woke up and stayed in the tent most of the morning. A few others at the camp had suffered the same sort of malady and had been missing from the communal gatherings.

Blaire, who was sitting near the tent entrance with her knees pulled up to her chest, mentioned to the group that Ash had gone to the city to take care of "business" and wouldn't be back for a week. They missed his flute playing, and without it, the jam session soon faded as the pot and heavy atmosphere put most of them in a chilled-out state.

Andrew glanced over at Amber; she looked weary, her hair hanging limp around her face. "How are you doing, babe?" he asked, his voice low.

"The nausea's gone, but I'm really tired," she squeaked out, resting her head on his shoulder. "Whatever I've got has really drained me. If it's all right with you, I'm going to go back to our tent and try to get some rest."

"Sure. I'm sorry you're not doing well. I'm sure it'll pass. You know how flu bugs are. I don't think it was food poisoning. No one else got sick, and we ate the same food." Andrew placed his hand on her forehead, checking for fever.

"You're probably right. Must be the same thing Sara has," Amber replied, her eyes half-closed.

"Do you want me to walk you up to our place?" Andrew asked, giving her a hand up off the floor. Her fingers felt cool and fragile in his. "I can go back with you now if you want."

"Thanks," she whispered, her voice barely audible over the murmur of conversations around them.

"Looks like we're going to call it a night. Am's not feeling well," Andrew said to a few friends nearby as he helped her to the tent opening.

As Amber ducked to exit the teepee ahead of him, Andrew glanced at Blaire sitting nearby. Her eyes fastened on him, dark and knowing. Her face reflected that same alluring look she had given him a few days ago—a look that had lodged itself in his mind like a splinter, impossible to ignore. He smiled at her and then stooped to follow Amber. But he paused just before going through the opening and gave Blaire a quizzical look. She returned it with pouting lips and a wink that seemed to say, *Come back when you've taken care of her.*

Outside, the night air was brisk compared to the warmth of the teepee. The sky was brilliant with stars, a vast canopy of light stretching from horizon to horizon. The cry of a coyote echoed in the distance, a lonely sound that sent a shiver up Andrew's spine. They made their way up to their tent using a flashlight to guide them. The beam cut through the darkness, illuminating patches of dried grass and the occasional wildflower, closed tight for the night.

Near the stone house, two trails came together, one led to the spring, and the other from the clearing where the teepee had been pitched. Just beyond the house, another trail split away, leading them up the side of the hill to their camp. The path was narrow, forcing Andrew to walk behind Amber, guiding her with a hand on her lower back.

He helped Amber get settled, and she turned over in her sleeping bag to get some rest. Andrew sat on his gear and considered his options. He wasn't ready to go to sleep, and he was intrigued by what had just happened with Blaire. It set in motion a surge of desire, a warmth blooming low in his belly. Since their encounter in the high meadow, her face had haunted him. As hard as he'd tried to shake it, it seemed to cling to him like a shadow.

He was torn. He loved Amber, loved the way her laughter filled a room, loved the gentle way she touched his face when they kissed. But there was this other part of him, this animal sense, that had been aroused, and it gripped him with a ferocity that both frightened and exhilarated him. He'd resisted its force for days, but now something told him to respond. Maybe, he thought, he could just go and confront Blaire and let her know that she needed to quit coming on to him, that he and Amber were serious, that she needed to keep her distance.

The tent was quiet except for Amber's slow, even breathing. Outside, an owl called, three distinct hoots that seemed to be asking a question.

Andrew placed a gentle hand on Amber's shoulder. She moved, trying to get comfortable. "Sorry, Andrew. I'm a bit of a comedown, I know. But I just need to rest." Her voice was thick with fatigue.

"It's okay, I'm not really tired. Do you mind if I go back and join the group?" His heart beat a little faster as he said the words.

"Sure, you go ahead. I'll see you in the morning." She rolled back toward him and gave him a little peck on his lips. Even when sick, she smelled like wildflowers.

He returned her kiss. "Rest easy, sweetie." The endearment felt like a betrayal even as it left his lips.

Emerging from their tent, Andrew heard the coyote again, closer this time. The moon was just cresting the hill behind their dwelling. It was only a quarter full, so he still needed the flashlight. Making his way down the trail toward the others, he ran the options through his mind again. It would be so easy just to give in to his urges and respond to Blaire's advances. But if he did that, how would he live with himself? He knew it would devastate Amber.

But she doesn't have to know, a voice whispered in his head. *Maybe just this once, tonight. Amber will be sleeping; she'll never know.*

He came to the spot where the two trails split: one to the spring and one back to the teepee and the stone house. He could go to the spring and fill his canteen with some fresh water for Amber; she'd love it in the morning. Then there was the more inviting thought, continue on his way to the teepee.

Andrew stood motionless in the darkness, torn between his choices, the flashlight beam creating strange shadows on the ground. He waited, unable to move for a few moments, teetering between his two options. The coyote howled again, and something stirred inside him. It was a raw, visceral craving compelling him to quench his curiosity.

He took the path away from the spring.

The light from the teepee grew stronger as he approached, the canvas walls glowing amber from within. Andrew could hear muted laughter and the soft notes of a guitar. His pulse quickened with each step.

As he ducked through the entrance of the teepee, he could see the fire had died down considerably. The air was heavy with the smell of pot, a sweet, earthy scent that clung to everything inside. Dave Hester was gently strumming on his worn Spanish guitar, the notes drifting lazily around the enclosed space. Most of the others were settled on their backs, high and drifting, a few locked in amorous embraces that seemed more languid than passionate.

Andrew found Blaire sitting to his right, her face transformed by the shifting firelight. She passed him a joint; he took it and settled down beside her, close enough to feel the warmth radiating from her body. He took a deep hit, as if it would give him the courage to say what he needed to say. The smoke burned his lungs, bringing a moment of clarity amidst the fog of desire.

He expelled the smoke and then whispered to her, "Why do you keep coming on to me? I thought you and Ash were an item?" His voice sounded strange to his own ears, tight and controlled.

She flashed him those wanton eyes, dark and knowing. "We are, but he's gone now, and I'm really turned on." She leaned closer, her breath warm against his ear. "Pot does that to me, so does acid."

"Why me? There are lots of other guys here." He gestured vaguely toward the others in the teepee, though his attention never left her face.

"Yeah, but I've tried a few of them and, well, to be honest, they're duds." Blaire ran a hand through her hair, the movement calculated to draw his eye. "I've seen the way Amber is with you. You clearly know how to satisfy a woman." Her lips curved into a predatory smile.

As much as he hated to admit it, her appeal to his male ego was working. Andrew told himself that he shouldn't be taken in by such a ploy. "That's cool. I must say that you know how to turn a guy on. But I've got to think about Amber." Even as he said the words, he knew they lacked conviction.

He took another hit on the joint and then passed it back to her. She took a deep drag, the ember brightening momentarily, illuminating the hollow of her throat. She sent it on its way around the gathering. She expelled the smoke slowly and sensually into his face and then murmured to him, "Come on, Andrew. She doesn't have to know." The words hung between them, heavy with possibility.

"Yeah, but I would." His resistance was weakening with each passing moment, like ice melting under a hot sun.

"You're such a prude," Blaire said with a laugh that was both mocking and inviting. "Haven't you heard of this little thing called free love?"

"I know, but that's for people not into a committed relationship." Andrew shifted uncomfortably, aware of how close they were sitting.

"I disagree," Blaire said, her fingers tracing idle patterns on the rug between them. "I've made it with guys who were shacked up with one chick and really love them. It's called an open relationship." Her voice dropped to a conspiratorial whisper. "Besides, Amber's probably gone out on you. You just don't know it. I've seen the way some of the other guys around here come on to her, and she always smiles back."

The suggestion sent a jolt of jealousy through Andrew, though he tried to dismiss it. "She's just playful. She's like... sunshine twinkling through tree branches. But I'm pretty sure that's all it is, just being playful."

"Are you sure, Andrew?" Blaire's question was like a needle, probing for weakness.

"Yes, I'm sure." His argument was not winning him over. But he couldn't say the same for her raw sensuality. As the effect of the pot increased, he sensed himself giving in to her piercing eyes and inviting words. The teepee seemed to contract around them, making the rest of the world fade away.

"Take it easy, Andrew. Here, lay back on my blanket." She gently touched his arm and pulled him down beside her. The contact sent a spark of electricity through him. She rolled over toward him and began to stroke the side of his thigh. "Come on, Andrew. Just once. Make a girl happy. Amber will never know."

Desire surged at his core, and his body flushed with passion. It took everything within him to push her hand away. "Are you kidding?" he whispered, his voice hoarse. "Half the people in here will tell her. I've got to go back to her. Sorry, Blaire," he said as he got up and ducked outside.

The night air hit him as he emerged from the teepee, and the chill temporarily broke the spell he was under a few moments ago. Stars wheeled overhead, indifferent to the human drama playing out beneath them. Andrew took a deep breath, trying to clear his head.

But only a moment later, he heard movement and turned to see that Blaire was following him, with her blanket draped over one shoulder. The moonlight caught in her hair, turning it to silver. "You can't get away that easily," she said, her voice carrying in the still night air.

"What is it with you?" Andrew asked, not moving away as she approached.

"I can teach you some things you've probably never dreamed of. I can show you things you've never seen." She caught up to him and slipped her hand into his. The light from the moon spilled over her face, her eyes bright and beckoning. The confusion he thought was gone returned with an even greater force, a tide rising inside him.

She pulled at his hand and led him back down the trail, away from the camp and toward the stream. Soon they were under a stand of trees, their feet walking over a matting of ferns and leaves. The night sounds surrounded them—the distant murmur of the stream, the rustle of nocturnal creatures in the undergrowth, the sighing of the wind through the trees.

"No one can see us now. Amber will never know." Blaire's words were a whisper in the darkness.

The moment was charged with tension, the night suddenly warm despite the coastal breeze. Blaire dropped the blanket to the ground, the fabric making a soft sound as it settled on the forest floor. She stepped closer to him, her hand reaching for his face.

Andrew stood frozen for a heartbeat, suspended between temptation and loyalty. The scent of her perfume, mixed with the forest air, surrounded him. In that moment, he faced a choice that would define him: the faithful man he could become, or the betrayer he was about to be. He couldn't see himself thirty years later, sitting across from Nicole in a Del Mar restaurant, swearing he'd never hurt her. Couldn't know how this moment would poison every future promise.

He chose wrong. He kissed her.

Time passed under the canopy of stars, the forest around them silent except for the distant stream. Andrew sat on the blanket, his head in his hands, feeling a coldness seep into him that had nothing to do with the night air. What had seemed so compelling just moments before now felt hollow. He stared up at the sliver of moon visible through the branches and wondered how he would face Amber in the morning.

Blaire sat beside him, seeming pleased with herself. "See? That wasn't so hard, was it?" There was triumph in her voice, as if she'd won some game he hadn't known they were playing.

"I should get back," Andrew said, standing abruptly. The guilt was already eating at him, a reminder of the real world waiting for him up the trail.

"You're not going to get all guilt-ridden on me now, are you?" Blaire watched him pace. The moonlight cast her features in stark relief, making her look both beautiful and somehow calculating.

"I need to check on Amber." He didn't look at her as he spoke.

"She'll be fine. She's sleeping. Stay a little longer." Her voice was coaxing, but there was something hard beneath the softness.

"I can't." Andrew stood awkwardly beside the blanket. "This was..."

"Amazing?" Blaire supplied, smiling up at him. "Unforgettable? Everything you hoped?"

"A mistake," Andrew finished, the word hanging between them like an accusation.

Blaire's smile faded. "You didn't seem to think it was a mistake a few minutes ago."

Andrew had no answer for that. He turned and began walking back toward the camp, each step taking him closer to Amber and the lie he would now have to live with. Behind him, he heard Blaire laugh softly, the sound following him up the trail like a ghost.

By the time he reached their tent, his mind had constructed an elaborate fiction about filling the canteen at the spring, about sitting by the water listening to the night sounds, about anything but what he had actually done. Amber was still asleep, her breathing deep and regular. He slipped into his sleeping bag, careful not to wake her.

But sleep eluded him. Every time he closed his eyes, he saw Blaire's face, felt her hands on his skin. And beneath that, like a bruise that ached when pressed, was the knowledge that he had betrayed Amber. The word echoed in his mind: *betrayed, betrayed, betrayed.*

It was a word that would follow him through the decades, a shadow that would never quite leave him, no matter how far he ran or how much he changed. Though Amber would eventually fade from his life, that singular act of betrayal would become a pattern he couldn't seem to break. The guilt would resurface with each new relationship, with each promise made and broken.

Thirty years later, in a seaside restaurant in Del Mar, he had sat across from Nicole, promising he would never betray her trust. He had meant it with every fiber of his being, just as he had once loved Amber with all his heart. But the seeds planted that night in Big Sur had grown deep roots within him, roots that continued to shape his choices in ways he couldn't fully understand or control.

Because some betrayals aren't just acts, they're revelations of character. And Andrew Foster, even as he built Precipice and reached for success, even as he tried to become someone new, remained haunted by the man he had first discovered himself to be under the stars of Big Sur.

CHAPTER FOURTEEN

CARLSBAD COAST

OCTOBER · 2000

The stillness of early morning clung to the Carlsbad coastline as Andrew stood on the bluff where Precipice would rise. October thirty-first, and the marine layer hung thick over the site, refusing to lift, as if the coast itself was holding its breath. Usually, October meant clear skies in San Diego, the marine layer taking its leave until May, but here it was, dense and stubborn, like nature was trying to hide something. He checked his phone again, the city inspector was due any minute for the environmental impact assessment, another crucial step before breaking ground. The fog seemed to muffle everything, even the waves below sounded different, muted and strange.

Four months since Quinn's letter had arrived with Teknon 2's offer. Four months of planning sessions, endless meetings with county supervisors, city council presentations, and the delicate dance with the Coastal Commission. Each approval felt like climbing another rung on a ladder that stretched beyond sight into the fog.

The Pacific churned below, gray-green and restless, waves grinding against the sandstone cliffs with methodical persistence. Salt mist drifted up from the breakers, coating everything with a fine sheen of moisture that made the wild grass glisten like steel wire. The fog pressed close, erasing the horizon, turning the world into a narrow corridor of visibility.

This inspection was just one more hurdle, but each one carried weight. The environmental impact report had to be perfect. One red flag about drainage or endangered species habitat, and months of work could unravel. Fortunately, Andrew's years of preparation were finally bearing fruit. Long before he had an investor, he'd spent countless hours navigating the maze of agencies—working through permits, zoning regulations, environmental reviews, and meetings with the Coastal Commission, city planners, and state and county officials. He'd done it all on the hope that, when the right partner came along, he'd be ready.

Now that partner had arrived. Teknon 2. Their influence behind the scenes was something he didn't fully understand, but it was real, and powerful. Approvals that once took months were now moving in days. Bureaucratic roadblocks disappeared with a quiet word from the right person.

Andrew walked the perimeter of what would be the future building pad, his footsteps leaving dark prints in the dew-soaked earth.

The October gloom pressed down, that particular North County coastal weight that made every breath taste of salt and uncertainty. Not the theatrical darkness of Halloween, but something more patient, more grinding. Like the approval process itself.

A text from Nicole lit up his screen, filled with affectionate words. He responded in kind. They were truly connecting on a level he hadn't experienced with anyone in years. Andrew had never been great at texting, always preferring voice-to-voice or face-to-face communication. But bonding with Nicole had given him a new appreciation for how intimate this process could be.

She texted again that she was hurrying to get dressed and on her way to a meeting with a client. He replied to tell her about his meeting with the City representative on the job site later that morning. They promised to meet after work for drinks and dinner. Their relationship was about to enter its fourth month, deepening with each passing day. What had begun with cautious conversations and tentative curiosity had grown into something steady, quietly significant, like the tide creeping higher with each return. She seemed to trust him completely now, and he felt confident they had a future together. He was eager to get through the day's work so he could spend time with her that evening.

Andrew had called Quinn yesterday afternoon, and the man had answered on the second ring. Andrew had offered to pick him up at the office and drive over to their meeting. He was still amazed that he'd been able to secure it. But with Teknon 2's help, they had locked in the option he had on the land.

To kill time before the meeting, Andrew walked around the site, trying to put Nicole's ideas into practice. He congratulated himself for his perseverance. Just a few more hours and this thing would be a reality. The purr of an engine caught his attention as Ben Pringle from the city planning department drove his pickup onto the site. Andrew walked over to greet him.

"Sorry I'm late. Traffic was awful," Ben said, climbing out of his truck.

"Oh, I hadn't noticed the time," Andrew replied, suddenly realizing that meant Quinn was late too. Quinn was never late. "No worries, Ben. My finance guy is running behind too."

"Well, while we're waiting, let's take one more look at those plans," Ben suggested.

Andrew went to his car and popped the trunk. He took the plans to the front of the car and rolled them out on the hood. Ben had seen them a dozen times at his office, but he just wanted one final conference out here at the site before promising to go back, put his stamp on the copies in his office, and sign off. Andrew was certain Ben just wanted another excuse to get out of his office. He'd known the man for years, clear back to when Ben spent most of his time out on sites like this. But since his promotion, he spent much of his time riding a desk and not enough out in the sea air.

Ben looked over the renderings and surveyed the site. As he rolled up the papers and handed them back to Andrew, he said, "It's going to be a great place, Andrew. Kudos for all your efforts."

Andrew glanced up toward the road and then back to Ben, trying to ignore the growing pit in his stomach. "I don't know what happened with my guy from Teknon 2. He's always been on time before."

He reminded himself that Quinn wasn't required to be here. Quinn had simply said he wanted to join them to affirm their deal and take in this moment when the dream would be at the threshold of becoming a reality. There was something in that phrase he always repeated: "The dream's going to become a reality." It was almost like some mantra he'd been instructed to repeat. He never sounded completely convinced. In fact, one time Andrew had caught a glimpse of something strange in his eyes, just there for a moment before the Quinn he'd known for months returned.

They waited another ten minutes, but still no Quinn. Finally, Ben broke an uncomfortable silence. "Listen, Andrew, I've got another meeting. If you want me to sign off on those plans today, I should be getting along."

"Sure, no problem. Thanks for coming out. I'll stop by later this afternoon and pick them up. Around four—is that a good time?"

"Yeah, I should have everything ready for you by then."

Ben drove off, kicking up dust that swirled around Andrew in a ghostly cloud. Where was Quinn?

Andrew texted him, but it pinged back as undeliverable. Must be a problem in the network. He waited, walking around the site, trying to keep his growing anxiety at bay. Five minutes later, he texted again. Same result, undeliverable. How odd. His pulse quickened. He knew Quinn didn't have to be here, but then why had he said he would be?

Andrew dialed Quinn's number. A strange buzzing sound filled his ear before a recorded voice announced the number was no longer in service.

He tried Quinn's office landline as a last resort. It rang three times before a recording informed him it was no longer in service. What? An unmistakable feeling that something was wrong washed over him. Nicole's words were starting to fade; they provided cold comfort now. He kept punching in the number on his speed dial, but the message remained the same. After another lap around the site, Andrew finally decided there was only one way to find out what was really going on. He would go to Quinn's office. Maybe Quinn had lost his phone and had to temporarily shut off his service. Yeah, Andrew told himself, that must be it. But that didn't explain why the office line would be down. With dread building in his chest, he jumped in his car and headed for Franklin Towers.

When he pulled into the parking garage, Quinn's Mercedes was nowhere to be seen. Maybe he had parked on an upper level. Andrew hurried through the foyer and punched 12 on the console. The elevator rushed him to Quinn's floor. His pulse finally slowed. He just knew that once he saw the man face to face, this whole mix-up would be resolved.

The doors opened, but instead of the usual comforting and familiar landing, Andrew was greeted by an unexpected sight. He'd been up here at least half a dozen times since his first meeting with Quinn, and this was not right. Nothing here was as it should be. The lights of Teknon 2 Partners, which always cast their glow on the polished tile floor of the entryway, were completely dark. The doors to the office, usually marked with the sleek Teknon 2 logo, were blank, void of any words.

Andrew blinked hard, trying to clear his blurring vision. He walked up to the doors and pressed his face against the cool glass. It didn't help. Peering inside the reception area, all he could make out in the dark was an empty waiting room. There was no hint of the former furnishings that had so impressed him, no reception desk, no smiling receptionist, just dust and a few crumpled papers swept into the corner.

"This can't be happening," he whispered, his breath fogging the glass.

He pounded on the doors, but the only response was a hollow echo bouncing back at him. "Quinn, are you there?" he shouted through the glass. Nothing. Maybe it was just a nightmare, and if he shouted loud enough, he'd wake up. Somewhere in his mind, reason called for him to stop, but he couldn't. Pure terror fueled him. He just kept pounding and shouting, determined to make Quinn hear and come out and face him. The glass vibrated under his attack. All the while, his mind was slipping deeper and deeper into a shadowy, murky hole.

He continued pounding, sweat dripping down from his forehead and into his vision. He closed his eyes to shut out the burning moisture. Then it was there, a face coming to him out of the gloom. There was light in the eyes. Hope. An answer. But then he saw the glowing cigarette and the glowing eyes. It was Ash Murik, and he was laughing at him. Andrew pounded his fists harder than ever until something finally broke. He'd broken through. Warmth flooded over him, wonderful warmth. It flowed over his hands and arms.

He opened his eyes, but it was all wrong. His arms were stained red, not the red of a glorious sunset but the red of the warning light in his mind. It was sticky and wet. In a rush back to reality, he realized he'd broken the glass. The shards had cut into him, and it was his blood that was warm and red and flowing over him.

Suddenly he heard sounds and felt arms take hold of him. People were streaming out of the other two offices on this floor. He instantly became totally aware of his surroundings. The staff of the legal offices had spilled into the landing. One of them was speaking to him, pulling him out of the swirl of his confusion.

"What are you doing, friend?" came a voice through the fog. Andrew recognized him. It was Dan Chambers of Chambers, Glenn, and Smithson.

"Where's Teknon 2 Partners?" Andrew mumbled, his voice distant even to his own ears. "Where's Hayden Quinn? Where's his staff?"

Chambers looked at him, his face incredulous. "Why, they closed things up. Said that they were moving to Sorrento Valley."

"But I was just up here Monday... everything looked normal. They said nothing about moving." Andrew's words came out slurred, his mind struggling to process this information.

"They moved on Tuesday. We all thought it was odd the way they moved out so quickly."

Another voice chimed in from the growing crowd. "Except for their staff, you were the only person any of us ever saw in their offices."

It all hit Andrew like a physical blow. The tormenting voices he had confronted last night were all real. Their predictions were coming true right before his eyes. They had pegged him for the loser he was. It was all too much. Every positive thought Nicole had planted in his mind withered and died, replaced by a wasteland of hopelessness. It all swirled around him, the darkness closing over him like a shroud. He was swallowed like some tiny insect spinning on a churning tide until he sank into unconsciousness.

CHAPTER FIFTEEN

ENCINITAS

OCTOBER · 2000

Nothing feels quite like the rush when pain suddenly vanishes. Andrew remembered it from years ago during his first and only experience with a kidney stone. One minute there was excruciating pain. The next came a tingling explosion in the brain that somehow expelled the agony as quickly as light exorcised darkness from a room. That's what Andrew felt the moment Jimmy Ramirez walked into his room at Scripps Memorial ER. He immediately started feeling better. Jimmy arrived full of smiles and comforting words, and suddenly things weren't so dark. There was hope. At least one person in the universe cared about him.

But beneath the morphine haze, questions swirled. The fluorescent lights above hummed with an insect persistence that made his teeth ache. His right hand throbbed beneath fresh bandages, evidence that he had indeed pounded on that office door until his knuckles split. Quinn's office. Except the suite had been empty, furniture gone, not even indentations in the carpet where desks should have been.

The ER's particular chaos pressed in through the curtain walls, someone retching two bays over, the squeak of gurneys, a child's persistent wail. Late afternoon light filtered through high windows, casting everything in that institutional gray that made time feel suspended.

The IV drip kept time like a liquid metronome. Real. Not real. The papers in his car, the contracts, the four months of meetings, those had to be real. But the medication made everything feel underwater, dreamlike, as if he might wake up and find himself back in his apartment, no Precipice, no breakthrough, no betrayal.

His split knuckles argued otherwise.

"What happened to you, hermano? "Man, you look rough. Like someone dragged you through the hedge backwards," Jimmy lovingly taunted.

Andrew tried to sit up straighter in the hospital bed. "Quinn and his company, Teknon 2... they disappeared. Just vanished. Like they never existed."

"What?" Jimmy's eyes went wide in disbelief.

"It's a long story. I've been trying to make sense of it myself. The law firm called an ambulance, and I landed here. It must have been the sight of my own blood. The nurse cleaned me up and got me in a hospital gown, but I guess I still stink."

Jimmy smirked before growing serious again. "Why are you all busted up?"

Andrew held up his bandaged hand. "They found me in a fist fight with a glass door. I was trying to pound my way into a locked office. Cut myself pretty bad."

"Well, you need to pick your opponents better," Jimmy said with a taunting laugh. "I told you years ago that you're the kind of guy that brings a felt tip pen to a knife fight."

"You know what they say about the pen being mightier than the sword," Andrew threw back in his face, laughing along with his friend despite the pain throbbing in his hand.

"Yeah, well, the guy who said that was never in a gang fight in Logan Heights."

This was classic Jimmy, making light of Andrew's situation. This would go down as another of the many times they'd helped each other out. Andrew was just thankful he was here. "I really appreciate you getting over here so quickly. How'd that happen anyway?"

"I was running down some leads in Del Mar when I got your text. Lucky for you, I'm normally not up this far north."

Andrew held up his bandaged right hand again. "I had to use my left hand to punch in your number. Guess I'll be learning a new technique." His phone vibrated on the bed beside him. "Speaking of my phone, it's vibrating right now." He glanced down to see it was Nicole. "Just give me a minute, Jimmy. It's Nicole."

"Sure."

Andrew answered with a tentative, "Hi, Nicole."

She asked about the meeting with Quinn and the city planner. The concern in her voice carried through the phone, making Andrew's chest tighten.

"I'm sorry to say things didn't go well," he said. She sounded increasingly worried and pressed for details. "Listen, Jimmy's here with me. I'll call you right back. I'll explain it all then."

She told him she loved him and was worried.

"I promise to call as soon as he leaves. Bye, babe." He set the phone down and looked up at Jimmy, who was obviously anxious to know about everything that had occurred.

"So, what exactly happened?" Jimmy leaned forward in the plastic hospital chair; his eyes narrowed with concern.

Andrew took the next twenty minutes explaining the whole scenario about the development plans, the meetings with the officials, the tormenting nightmares, and then the final revelation at Teknon 2's empty offices. With each detail, the heaviness in his chest grew, the reality of what had happened settling in more firmly.

When he finished, Jimmy looked not only perplexed but angry. "What's going on? What sort of crazy people would do this to someone?"

"The more I think about it, the more it doesn't seem to make any sense." Andrew stared at the ceiling, trying to find patterns in the speckled tiles. "At first, I thought they'd gone dark on me because they ran out of funds and were trying to avoid a lawsuit. But that sort of thing wouldn't really work in this situation."

He shifted uncomfortably in the bed. "Deals fall through all the time, and one party's left holding the bag with no viable alternatives. People just lawyer up and stonewall you. That's what happened to me on the Stradford deal. I just had to count my losses and lick my wounds. Gemini Federal went bankrupt, and I couldn't do a thing."

The bandages on his hand had started to show spots of blood seeping through. "Besides, I don't have the kind of deep pockets where I could afford to pursue them. Then there's that huge first draw of thirty grand. Why did they give it to me? It was almost like bait on a hook. Once I got that, I was sold. I really needed the money. The fact that they looked legit gave me the incentive to roll the dice and go for it." All these thoughts rambled through Andrew's mind, each one darker than the last.

"It's got to be something more, something intentional, something they planned. It's like they set me up. But why would they do that? Who am I to them?" he said, conflicted and confused.

Jimmy squinted, pursing his lips. His investigative mind was in high gear. "There's something evil behind this whole thing. Something sinister. It must be connected to the black SUV. This is the sort of sting people do to those they hate. I've known you a long time, man, and in all those years you've never had an enemy."

"I know, but there is someone out there who has it in for me. What am I going to do?" Andrew's voice cracked slightly, betraying the fear that had been building since the moment he'd seen the empty offices.

"Well, hermano, I'm not going to leave you hanging. I will come up with answers." Jimmy's voice carried a certainty that Andrew desperately needed.

"You're a real friend. Thanks." Andrew closed his eyes, grimacing. "I really need to close my eyes; my hand is really aching right now. I need something to knock out this pain."

Jimmy jumped up and pulled back the curtain to their cubicle. "I'll go find the nurse."

"Thanks, man." Andrew sank back into the bed, trying to find relief from the pounding in his hand. It was intense, and the ache rushed up his arm and into his brain. Once more his world was a swirl of perplexity, enhanced now by the throbbing in his wound.

But there were other wounds. They were more than physical. They were emotional and psychological. Something deep in his gut was throbbing. The voices had returned full force now, and nothing he did could drown them out. He was a failure. And worse, he was a fool. It wasn't just the embarrassment over how he'd handled the situation at Franklin

Tower. Sure, those legal folks must think he was a real nut case, but it was so much more than that.

How was he going to face his colleagues? Jeff Clark and his marketing team had put hours into this project. They were going to be really angry. How was he going to explain this to them? Ben Pringle and all the other officials were going to think he was a fool. Bill Akins would never work with him again. He was a great guy, and Andrew couldn't even imagine how to break the news to him.

But most of all, Nicole was the one he worried about. How would she react to this? Something told him he was going to lose her. She wouldn't want to hitch her wagon to a loser like him. He wouldn't have anything left.

It was all too much. Everything he'd hoped for was crashing down around him.

"The nurse is on the way with something to help," said Jimmy. Andrew opened his eyes to see him standing beside the bed like an angel of mercy.

"Thanks, bro. You're a godsend."

"Glad I can help." Jimmy's smile held a warmth that momentarily pushed back the darkness crowding Andrew's thoughts.

The nurse swept in and injected something into his IV. And there it was, that scintillating explosion in his brain that sent all his misery fleeing, and with it, all his worries. He drifted in and out of awareness for a few minutes until he heard Jimmy's voice softly comforting him.

"Listen, Andrew, you're going to be okay. These folks here are going to take good care of you. They want to keep you here for observation for a few more hours. I'll be back to drive you home."

"That would be great," Andrew murmured through his temporary euphoria.

Jimmy gave him a knowing smile. "Sometimes drugs are a real lifesaver."

"You've got that right," Andrew mumbled, smiling back at him as he waved goodbye and slipped out. Andrew was slipping out as well, gliding into the warmth of the drug's comfort and its chemical assurance. All will be well, it told him, and for the moment he believed it.

But then he remembered that he owed Nicole a call. Through a wave of narcotic contentment, he did his best to hit the autodial on his phone to call her.

Moments later she picked up. "Hey... you won't believe..." he said, his words running together.

"So, what happened at your meeting with the city today?" she asked, still sounding concerned.

The room seemed to spin slightly as the medication took hold. Andrew struggled to focus on her voice. "What happened?" she repeated, a deeper note of concern rising in her voice. "You sound strange, Andrew. Is everything okay?"

"No, it's a long story. Listen, I'm at Scripps Memorial in Encinitas." His tongue felt thick in his mouth, the words coming out slurred.

"What? You're kidding." The alarm in her voice cut through the haze.

"No, I'm not."

"What happened to you?"

"It's a long story. I got cut on some glass." Andrew looked down at his bandaged hand, which now seemed very far away.

"Well, I'm coming right over."

"I'm in emergency. They've treated me, but I think they're going to keep me for a while for observation."

"I'll be right there." The urgency in her voice was the last thing Andrew registered clearly.

"That would be nice," he murmured, already feeling the meds pulling him slowly down into a slumber, where at least temporarily, the voices of doubt and fear couldn't reach him.

Chapter Sixteen

BIG SUR

July ·1970

An act of passion can change everything in a moment. Andrew was still dealing with the consequences. His insides felt like broken glass grinding together with each breath. It was the second day since his first tryst with Blaire, and Amber had another bad morning. He could hear her outside their tent throwing up, each retch an accusation his body remembered in the place where shame lived.

The sound twisted in his gut like a rusted blade. His skin still carried Blaire's scent, that earthy musk laced with some exotic herb he couldn't name, no matter how many times he'd scrubbed himself. It clung to him like a second skin he couldn't shed.

"I hate this flu," Amber called out weakly, her voice shredded. "Someone from the city must have brought it up here. I'm going down to the well to get some water."

Andrew felt massively guilty, but beneath it pulsed something worse, the memory of Blaire's body against his, the way she'd moved like liquid fire, the sounds she'd made that still echoed in his skull. Even now, with Amber sick and trusting, his treacherous flesh responded to the memory.

He was two people trapped in one body: the man who loved Amber and the animal who'd taken Ash's girl while his best friend was gone to the city.

"I can go and get some water for you. Why don't you stay and rest?" Even as the words left his mouth, they tasted like ashes and lies. The voice inside didn't question, it screamed: You're still thinking about having her again, aren't you? Even now. Even with Amber puking her guts out.

His hands shook as he reached for his canteen. Not from guilt. From want. From the knowledge that Blaire was somewhere in the camp, hungry for him in the same way he hungered for her, both of them caught in this thing that had ignited between them like a grass fire. And God help him, that knowledge made him want her more.

"No, I'll get the water myself. I need to get up and move. Thanks for the offer."

"Okay."

"Keep the bed warm for me." Her voice was sweet. She was doing her best to stay cheerful even as she dealt with the lingering sickness. Andrew sensed her vulnerability and her need, her need for him. How could he have been unfaithful to her? How could he let his lust take him from her? Not just once, but twice.

That thought brought him up short, and he almost stayed with Amber to comfort her through her sickness. He did linger for a while, feeling all noble but then simply gave in as images of Blaire's supple body filled his head. How was it possible that a woman could have that kind of power?

After their first time, Blaire and Andrew had met again. It was the night after their first encounter. Amber's weakness had returned, and she went to bed early. Andrew slipped out after she fell asleep and met Blaire beneath the trees. He was clearly sinking into something he had very little control over. He knew if Amber ever found out, it would hurt her deeply, but he'd done the deed, and now he was riven with self-reproach. But despite it, he was still overwhelmed with a yearning to return to Blaire as soon as he could.

By the time Amber came back from her trip to the well near the house, Andrew was drowning in his dark thoughts. She'd cleaned herself up but was still feeling drained.

"I don't understand why I'm so weak," she whimpered. "This is the worst flu I've ever had. I think I have a fever now."

"I'm so sorry, Am," Andrew offered with as much sympathy as he could muster. He opened their joined sleeping bags to her. "Come inside the covers." He drew her close and sought to comfort her. She was so tender, so vulnerable. His conscience shouted at him. How could you have been so wicked, so selfish? He hugged her tight, hoping to appease the cry inside his soul with this show of affection.

Part of him wanted to tell her the horrible thing he'd done, but something at his core gripped him. Images of Blaire filled his thoughts, erotic and sensual. The taste of her mouth and the smell of her body seemed to linger with him. It was as if a beast had emerged from his core and longed for its meal of lust. Now he was its captive, and nothing, not even the fragile body of his lover, could defer its craving. He had to have Blaire again and soon.

They had made plans to explore the upper meadow and find a trysting place there. She had warned him that Ash would be returning soon, and then their little fling would have to be put on hold. As guilty as it made him feel, Andrew looked for an excuse to leave Amber again and meet up with Blaire.

"You probably need to rest and drink lots of fluids. I've got some aspirin in my pack." He pulled it out from a bundle of gear near their heads. "Let me get you an apple, and then you can take a couple of these with the veggie juice I bought from the store." He extracted two pills from his kit and handed them to her. "I'll leave you alone so you can rest. The aspirin should reduce the fever and let you sleep. I'll check up on you regularly."

"Thanks, babe," she mumbled, her eyes heavy, her breath short.

Andrew opened a can of vegetable juice and placed it beside her. "My canteen's here if you need more fluid," he said, setting it nearby.

"I'm going down to the house to get some breakfast. If you want, I can bring you some."

"No, I'm not the least bit hungry. Just let me rest." That was exactly what he wanted to hear. Now he was free.

"Okay, be sure to take a few bites of the apple before you take the aspirin. You don't want to make your stomach more upset."

"Thanks." Her voice was weak but tender. The sound cut him to his core, but the force of his lust pushed it aside.

When Andrew got outside the tent, he looked down the hill. He could see Blaire sitting on a rock, her eyes closed, her face drinking in the morning sunlight. Others were milling about, one strummed a guitar, another lit a joint. A few were munching on chapattis dipped in honey. He waited for a few moments, hoping Blaire would open her eyes and look up at him. Finally, she did, and a huge smile broke across her face. He waved at her, and she grabbed her pack and made her way up the hill toward him.

He met her where the path crested their little hill. He quietly led her away from his tent and out of sight of those below in the camp. "Listen, Amber's resting and probably will be out of it all day. So, I'm free." He slipped his arms around her and pulled her close. "Things are working out great."

She responded to his embrace, pressing her body against his. "Yeah, Ash left at just the right time. I only wish he'd stay away longer. But we've got today, so let's make the most of it."

They took the path through the redwoods, hand in hand. They stopped to remove their shoes at the stream, waded across, and then continued their climb. She began to pour out her heart to him, sharing what she'd only hinted at in their previous rendezvous. She hadn't been happy with Ash for months. Oh, she still enjoyed sex with him, especially when she was stoned. But there'd been something missing, and she said she'd come alive again since they'd been hooking up.

Andrew assured her the same sort of thing was going on in him. Of course, he didn't share with her all the shame and guilt he was feeling about abandoning Amber. It wasn't just Amber, it was Ash. He was a friend, and Andrew was betraying him too. Ash was creepy, and maybe he deserved it, but what Andrew was doing seemed kind of creepy too. But he was so overcome with the pleasure of this woman's allure that he found it easy to suppress that feeling in exchange for the gratification she brought him.

A half an hour later, they reached the meadow. They spread out a blanket in the sun, and soon found themselves in each other's arms. Time seemed to stop as they gave in to the moment, the world around them fading away.

Later, they sat side-by-side on the blanket, disheveled and catching their breath, sharing the corn biscuits and some honey Blaire had brought in her pack. Andrew's shirt was carelessly tossed aside, and Blaire's hair was loose from its braid. He offered her a biscuit drizzled with the sweet syrup and stole a kiss, tasting the honey on her lips. He'd forgotten completely about Amber. All he could think about was Blaire and what had just happened between them. Her touch, her whispered words, the way she looked at him now, he was lost, truly lost.

Later, completely exhausted, they pulled their makeshift bed under the trees and napped. When Andrew awoke, he had a massive urge to pee, so he made his way into the nearby brush. Afterward, he started back toward Blaire when something out of place in the foliage caught his eye.

At first, he thought it might be a snake, but he was quickly reassured when he looked closer. It was a piece of thick brown rope sticking out of the ground in an odd way. So, he reached down to investigate. There were a few broken fern branches spread over some loose soil. Brushing them aside, he saw the rope was attached to something heavy. He knelt and pulled. It wouldn't budge, but with more force, it quickly emerged and brought with it a backpack.

Why would anyone bury a backpack here? His curiosity was completely aroused now. He unloosed the buckles on the bag and flipped the flap open, scattering dirt and small pebbles aside. He saw several bundles of what appeared to be money wrapped in plastic. He opened one, and twenty-, fifty-, and hundred-dollar bills spilled out. His hands trembled as he reached deeper into the bag, finding more bundles. He did a quick cursory estimation of what he'd found. There had to be at least fifty thousand dollars here.

His heart hammered against his ribs. "Blaire, come here! You won't believe what I've found."

Moments later she was beside him, her naked body still glistening with sweat from their lovemaking. "What in the world?" she gasped, wrapping the blanket around herself. "You've got to be kidding me."

"Look at this." Andrew's voice cracked with excitement and fear. He held up a bundle, the bills crisp and real in the dappled sunlight.

Blaire stepped back instinctively, as if the money might bite. "Put it back, Andrew. This is bad news."

"But think about it…"

"No, you think about it." Her voice had gone cold. "That's drug money. Has to be. Nobody buries legitimate cash in the woods."

Andrew stared at the bills in his hand. Benjamin Franklin stared back, multiplied by hundreds. "Fifty thousand dollars, Blaire. At least."

"I don't care if it's a million. It's not ours." She pulled the blanket tighter around herself, suddenly looking vulnerable despite her defiance.

"But what if—" Andrew stopped himself, his mind racing. The weight of the bundle in his hand felt like possibility itself. "What if this is a sign?"

"A sign?" Blaire laughed, but there was no humor in it. "A sign of what? That we should get ourselves killed?"

"No, listen." Andrew set the bundle down carefully and took her hands. They were shaking, or maybe his were. "We were just talking about getting away from here. About starting fresh. And then this appears? Right here where we…"

"Where were we screwing around behind our partners' backs?" Blaire pulled her hands away. "Some sign."

The words stung, but Andrew pressed on. "You said you wanted out. That Ash was controlling, that you were unhappy. This could be our chance."

"Our chance to what? Steal from drug dealers?" But something in her voice had shifted. The absolute refusal was softening into something else, consideration, maybe. Or fear of a different kind.

Andrew saw the opening. "Whoever left this here… they're criminals, Blaire. They didn't earn this money honestly. Why should we leave it for them?"

"Because they'll come looking for it, that's why." She was pacing now, the blanket dragging through the pine needles. "These aren't people who just shrug off fifty grand."

"But they don't know we took it. How could they? We're just two more hippies in a camp full of them." Andrew stood up, energy coursing through him. "We could be in Mendocino by tomorrow night. Or Oregon. Or anywhere."

Blaire stopped pacing. "You're serious about this."

"Dead serious." He met her eyes. "You said Ash scares you. That he's into dark stuff, that he might hurt you if you try to leave. Well, this money means we don't have to stick around and find out. We can disappear tonight."

"And Amber?"

The question hung between them like smoke. Andrew's stomach clenched. "I'll... I'll figure that out."

"Figure it out?" Blaire's voice was sharp. "She loves you, Andrew. She's sick right now, and you're still all she talks about."

She stopped herself.

"She's what?"

"Nothing. Just—forget it." Blaire looked back at the pack, then at Andrew. "You really think we could get away with it?"

"I know we could." But even as he said it, doubt crept in. The woods suddenly seemed full of watching eyes. A branch cracked somewhere in the distance, and they both jumped.

"Crap," Blaire whispered. "I'm already paranoid and we haven't even taken it yet."

"That's just nerves. It'll pass." Andrew knelt back down by the pack, running his fingers over the bundles. "Think about it, Blaire. We haven't even made plans yet, but now we could go anywhere. Paris, Bali, Buenos Aires, wherever our hearts lead us. No more limits, no more schedules. We could explore the world while we figure out... us. In comfort. In style. Everything's different now."

"With stolen drug money."

"With money that appeared right when we needed it most." He looked up at her, trying to pour every ounce of conviction into his words. "Doesn't that mean something?"

Blaire was quiet for a long moment. When she spoke, her voice was smaller. "What if Ash finds out?"

"How would he? We'll be long gone."

"He has ways of knowing things." She shuddered despite the warm afternoon air. "Sometimes I think he can read my mind."

"That's just him getting in your head. Making you afraid so you'll never leave." Andrew stood and pulled her close. She resisted at first, then melted against him. "I won't let him hurt you. I promise."

"You can't promise that." But she wasn't pulling away. If anything, she was holding him tighter. "You don't know what he's capable of."

"I know what we're capable of. Together." He pulled back to look at her face. "This morning, when we were... when we were together... didn't you feel it? Like we were meant to find each other?"

Blaire's eyes glistened. "Don't do that. Don't make this about us when it's about stealing fifty thousand dollars."

"It is about us. Everything is." Andrew heard himself speaking and wondered at the conviction in his voice. Three days ago he'd been in love with Amber. Now... "This money is just the universe's way of saying yes. Yes to us. Yes to getting away from here. Yes to starting over."

A tear slipped down Blaire's cheek. "You really believe that?"

"I do." And in that moment, he did. The guilt about Amber, the fear of getting caught, even the basic knowledge that this was wrong, all of it faded beneath the intoxicating possibility of escape.

Blaire looked at the pack for a long time. Then, so quietly Andrew almost missed it: "How would we even carry it?"

His heart leaped. "I'll put it all in my pack. Leave most of my clothes behind, donate them to the commune." He gave a bitter laugh. "They'll need them more than I will."

"All of it in yours?" Blaire looked uncertain. "That's a lot of weight."

"Better than splitting it up. Safer. If anyone checks your pack, you're clean." Andrew was already thinking ahead to the motorcycle ride, the bag secured behind him as they fled.

"This is insane." But she was already kneeling beside him, watching as he pulled out more bundles. "We're really doing this?"

"Only if you're sure." Andrew paused, a bundle in each hand. "I won't do it without you. We're in this together or not at all."

Blaire reached out slowly, as if the money might burn her, and took one of the bundles. She hefted it, feeling the weight. "It's real."

"Very real."

"And if someone comes looking for it?"

"Then we'll be somewhere they'll never think to look. It's a big country, Blaire. We can go where Ash wouldn't even dream of looking."

Andrew's mind was racing with possibilities. "New names, new lives, new everything."

Blaire turned the bundle over in her hands. "I must be crazy."

"Crazy in love?" Andrew tried for levity, but it came out more desperate than he intended.

She laughed, a broken sound. "Something like that." She looked him in the eye. "Promise me something."

"Anything."

"If this goes bad, when this goes bad, we don't turn on each other. No matter what."

"Never." Andrew sealed it with a kiss, tasting fear and excitement on her lips.

They worked quickly after that, Andrew stuffing all the bundles back into the same pack he'd found them in, wrapping them in a spare sweatshirt someone had left behind. He'd come back later with his own gear, but for now, it was safer to leave it where no one would notice. Every snap of a twig made them freeze. Every bird call sounded like a signal. By the time they finished, they were both slick with nervous sweat.

"I can't believe we just did that," Blaire whispered.

"We haven't done anything yet. Just reorganized my pack." Andrew tried to sound casual, but his hands shook as he covered the empty hole where the money had been. "No one has to know until we're ready to leave."

"And when will that be?"

"Soon. A day or two. Just let me..." He thought of Amber, sick in their tent, trusting him. "Just let me handle things."

Blaire nodded, but her face had gone pale. "I need to get back. Separately. If anyone sees us together with this pack."

"Right. Smart." Andrew watched her stand. She just turned and started walking, like she couldn't get away fast enough.

"Blaire?" She paused, glancing back over her shoulder.

"We're doing the right thing."

She smiled faintly, but it didn't reach her eyes. "Keep telling yourself that. Maybe one of us will believe it."

Then she was gone, disappearing into the trees.

Andrew stood alone beside the pack, the weight of what they'd found pressing down on him. The forest, so familiar an hour ago, now felt uneasy, full of listening shadows and shifting light. He looked around, checked for movement, then grabbed the bundle and moved quickly.

About twenty yards off the trail, he found a shallow depression beneath the tangled roots of a pine tree. He widened it with his hands, lined it with dry leaves, and slid the pack inside, tucking it deep in the shadowed space. He covered it with a crisscross of branches, then kicked dirt and needles over the top until it looked like nothing at all.

When he stood, his hands were filthy, his heart pounding harder than he wanted to admit. He didn't want to carry it. Not yet. Not like this.

Not until he knew what they were really going to do.

As he made his way back toward camp, his mind churned with plans and justifications. They'd need to leave separately to avoid suspicion. He'd need a story for Amber. So many details, so many ways it could go wrong.

But underneath the fear, something else pulsed, a wild, intoxicating sense of possibility. Fifty thousand dollars. A new life with Blaire. Freedom from everything that held him here.

The thought of the money seemed to burn against his brain, a reminder of the line he'd just crossed. There was no going back now. Whatever happened next, he and Blaire were bound together by this secret, this theft, this desperate grab at a different future.

He could only hope it was worth the price they'd both eventually pay.

When Andrew arrived back at his tent, he could hear Amber snoring quietly. He was grateful to know she'd been resting but more grateful that she hadn't missed him. It would be no fun making up a story about why he'd been gone so long. When he slipped into the tent, she stirred, murmuring softly. "How long have I been asleep?"

"It must have been at least four hours."

"I guess I needed it. I think my fever's gone."

"Then I'm sure you're hungry."

"Famished."

Andrew saw a quick way to release the guilt hovering at the edge of his thoughts. "Let me go down to the camp and bring you something to eat."

"That would be great. You're really sweet, Andrew."

Those words pierced him. He felt like a rat. How could he do this to her? How could he break her heart? But he knew. Deep inside, something that had been hiding had suddenly found a way out, and he wanted to let it out. Besides, he told himself that she'd find someone else just as he had, and if his heart could have been turned from her so easily, then it must not have been with her in the first place.

When he arrived at the stone house, he found that some of the women had cooked a delicious pot of stew, and there were several chapattis left over from breakfast. He gathered them up and poured a hearty amount of the stew into one of the carrying containers nearby. He thanked the cooks and headed back to their tent.

Once again, Amber was sweet and grateful for his concern and care. So, he settled in to nurse her back to health. It was something he knew he must do before he confronted her with his change of heart.

The intervening nights brought tormenting dreams. In one, he found himself in a dark place, holding stacks of cash in his hands. Amber and Blaire both approached him, smiling and alluring. Suddenly the money caught fire, and the flames began to melt his flesh. Searing red-and-green liquid dripped from his body, flowing out from him until it reached the women. When the fire touched them, they each erupted like blazing pillars that soon turned to ash and were slowly carried away in a churning wind.

In another nightmare, the money had been glued to him like a second skin. He could feel the adhesive penetrating his body until the cash and his soul seemed to be one. Then Ash, his face and body like that of a demon, crept toward him. He reached out and took hold of a single bill, slowly pulling it from Andrew's body. His flesh tore away with the money, along with a piece of his heart. Ash repeated this, tearing away each fragment of cash until all that remained of Andrew's body was a carcass of bone and muscle, completely empty of spirit.

These two dreams came each night. He woke in a cold sweat, wondering what they meant. But with a few hits on a joint, he always managed to drift back to sleep, waking the next morning to wonder what it all meant.

By the time Ash returned two days later, Andrew had managed to slip away from Amber once more to meet with Blaire. His absence almost got him discovered. He had to make up some excuse about intervening between Ash and Blaire to stop some fight they were having. It was a flimsy pretext, but thankfully she was unaware that Ash was still gone, so she believed him.

Her health had improved, and they'd had some intimate moments she initiated. He'd done his best to show her that his affections hadn't changed, but it had been difficult, and he found himself haunted by his conscience.

Early in the morning, when he was having breakfast, Andrew saw Blaire and Ash head off up the trail toward the high meadow. It left him wondering if she'd tell him about their tryst and her new affection for Andrew. But more than that, he wondered if they'd discover the empty hole where fifty thousand dollars used to be buried. The thought made his breakfast turn to concrete in his stomach.

The money was hidden now, all fifty thousand dollars, waiting for the moment they'd flee. His clothes would stay behind, a donation to the commune, he'd joke, though the irony tasted bitter. But with each passing hour, the weight of it seemed to grow heavier, the stolen bills burning like accusations through the canvas. Andrew knew that very soon, everything would come crashing down. The only question was whether he and Blaire would be far enough away when it did.

CHAPTER SEVENTEEN

ENCINITAS

NOVEMBER · 2000

ndrew's mind had become so focused on one thing that he found it impossible to sleep. His thoughts were tethered like a captured feral animal circling a stake, unable to break free from the recurring loop. Each time he tried to pull away, the hold on his soul pinned him with a guilty conscience, leaving no escape. He told himself he somehow deserved what had happened, as if some crafty karma had finally come due, as if Ash had unleashed astral hounds that had tracked him down and were now circling in for the kill.

A nightmare jolted him awake, but then his medication momentarily lifted him only to slowly drag him down again into a trance. When he finally awakened fully, he was drenched in sweat. The sound of windblown mist beat a hellish rhythm against the window above his head.

He had explained his dilemma to Nicole when she visited him at the hospital. She had been as mystified as he was about the Teknon 2 situation, but she'd worked overtime to lift his spirits.

"Listen, Andrew," she had said, her voice steady and determined. "Whoever did this to you is evil. You can't let this thing go without finding out who's behind it and holding them accountable."

Despite her encouragement, Andrew had been in a stupor with very little incentive.

"I'm really discouraged," he had told her, his voice barely above a whisper. "I can't explain it, but I almost feel like I had this coming to me. Whoever did this obviously planned it out way ahead of time, and I'm sure they've covered their tracks well."

She had looked back at him, shocked and somewhat incredulous. "Don't talk like that. I know you're down, but listen, maybe Jimmy can help you find out who these guys are?"

"He's already on it," Andrew had replied with as much hope as he could muster.

Jimmy had offered to come back after his visit earlier, but when Nicole arrived and offered to take him, Andrew had texted Jimmy to let him know he was covered. *Nicole's got it. Thanks again for everything,* he'd written.

"I know this thing has set you back, but I believe you're the kind of man that won't give up," she'd said as they stepped into the cool corridor. "Get some rest, and I'm sure you'll have a better perspective in a day or two. Remember, I believe in you."

With that, she had given him a kiss, soft, unhurried, and they'd headed to the parking lot in silence. No more pep talks. No dramatic gestures. Just a quiet steadiness between them, as if she knew what he needed more than he did.

The medication numbed the pain but also wreaked havoc with his waking thoughts. At 3 a.m., according to the clock on the stand beside his bed, the light of its green display was the one constant amid the spinning questions, changing faster than the seconds that ticked by on the nearby timepiece. What happened to the Teknon 2 Partners? Who was this Hayden Quinn? Was that even his real name? Why would he leave Andrew hanging? Was it all some enormous trick? How did he not see it coming? Was he merely dreaming?

In fact, he had been dreaming, off and on all night. He finally fell asleep around five, grateful for a moment's relief. But then in a delirium, Quinn approached him, hand outstretched, holding a glowing piece of paper in his palm—their contract. Quinn smiled, and Andrew felt comforted. He took the document, seeing the fine print, the details of their agreement. Everything seemed right, and his heart surged with hope. He drew the paper close, and pride rose inside him, warm and heartening.

Then the document grew warmer until it became uncomfortably hot in his hand. Suddenly it was burning him. He looked down to find his hands filled with flames. He dropped the paper, and it spiraled toward the floor, leaving a trail of tiny dark laughing faces, like some demonic helix twisting inside its smoky wake. The former agreement at his feet was mere ashes now, gradually being whisked away by some unearthly wind.

There were voices in the wind. They mocked him with harsh whispers.

You fool, they chanted. *Do you remember now what you did? All those you hurt? Did you think there'd be no payback? Did you think you could steal and never have to face the consequences? You've reaped what you've sown, all those moments when you pissed away the money and abandoned those who loved you. There's only one way out. Just crawl away into some hole and vanish. You'll soon be forgotten like all your schemes and dreams.*

He tried his best to shut out such voices, but they challenged him to disappear like he did so many years ago. But now he seemed to have only one route out: death. Their voices rose again, swirling around him like some shrieking vortex until he was sucked to the bottom and held there by a vengeful steel hand. Its grip was relentless, smothering him, choking the life from him. Depressed beyond words, he waited to slowly expire.

But for some strange reason, he didn't. Things gradually changed, and he managed to find hope. Here at this depth of desolation, he found resolve and a glimmer of courage. Nicole's words of encouragement came back to him.

"Believe in yourself, Andrew. You can do it. We're a team, and I'm here for you. You're going to hear encouraging things, don't listen to those negative voices in your head. Listen to the happy voices instead, they're like the melody of birds."

Her words inspired him. He told himself the most cowardly thing to do at this time would be to run. If he was ever to lift his head again, he must find out why this had happened to him. He must find those who had betrayed him.

Fever-like sensations drove Andrew from the bed. He walked to the kitchen and opened the fridge, leaning against the shelves to feel the coolness wash over him, gradually chasing away his temperature. He pulled a can of sparkling water from the side pocket and closed the door. The snap of the can opening cut through the silence of the apartment. He lifted the drink to his lips, letting the cool liquid pour down his throat. Gradually he became alert, and for the first time, he sensed some sort of direction.

"Whatever it takes," he promised himself, his voice barely audible in the empty kitchen, "I'm going to hunt down those who've done this to me and confront them."

With each gulp of the chilled fluid, a plan slowly formed in his mind, crystallizing like ice in his veins.

Two days later, Andrew was having lunch with Jimmy at a sushi place in Pacific Beach. Andrew was eating sashimi, but Jimmy was sticking with his California rolls and going heavy on the wasabi. He was paying again, so Andrew could enjoy this meal without worrying about his finances for a moment. They both were quaffing Asahi between bites. Jimmy was still concerned with Andrew's appearance, and Andrew had to agree, he looked as bad as he felt. But at least one thing had changed: there was a fire in his eyes now, and Jimmy could sense it.

"There's got to be a way to find out who shafted me," Andrew said, his voice low but intense.

Jimmy set his chopsticks down and folded his hands, resting his chin on them and staring at Andrew. The fluorescent lights of the restaurant cast shadows across his concerned face.

"I told you, man. Everything I've tried so far has come up empty," Jimmy said with a sigh. "The contact info I got from the property management group that runs the Franklin only led me to some offshore shell. It's all been a dead end. It was the same way with the license plate. I can't get past the bureaucratic roadblocks. Whoever has that vehicle has some great connections. It's the same way with the website. It's like they just slithered down some cyber snake hole. I even used my best tech guy, and he's confounded."

"Well, there's one place you haven't looked yet," Andrew said, leaning forward.

"Where's that?"

"Franklin Towers." The name hung in the air between them like a challenge.

"It's a dead end," Jimmy said, shaking his head. "I went up there and looked through those front office windows. The place is empty. I even asked the guys at the law firm next door, and they don't have a clue."

"I know, but I want to get inside. I want to get into those offices and search." Andrew's voice dropped even lower, almost conspiratorial. "I'm sure whoever did this took great precaution to cover their tracks, but there's got to be some clue there, something they've overlooked. Can you get us in there?"

Jimmy started to reply but then stopped to think, taking another mouthful. Finally, a smile curled ever so slightly at the corners of his mouth. "My cousin Leticia works for a property management firm that's contracted out to some of the offices in the Golden Triangle. She may know someone who can get us in there."

"She'd do that for us?" Hope flickered in Andrew's voice.

"Absolutely, we're family."

"Man, that's what I was hoping for. Just one break!" For the first time in days, Andrew felt something close to excitement.

Jimmy took a gulp of his beer. "Give me a few days, and I'll get back to you."

"Great! Thanks, man. You'll never know how much your friendship means to me right now." The gratitude in Andrew's voice was palpable.

"I've got your back. But please take care of yourself. You look like crap." Jimmy's bluntness was tempered by genuine concern.

"I will. I must. I've got a date with Nicole tonight, so I'm going to put on my best face both mentally and physically."

"Good. How's she taking your bad news?"

"She's been great. Lots of encouragement from her corner, it's been keeping me motivated."

Jimmy finished off his beer and smiled at Andrew. "She seems like a keeper and with the both of us, you've got a strong corner. You'll find a way out of this."

"Yes, I'm finally starting to believe that," Andrew said, and for the first time in days, he meant it.

Hours later, Andrew was at Nicole's house. She'd made some great pasta and salad, complemented with a bottle of Cabernet. They were eating on her deck, and there was a slight breeze coming up the nearby canyon. The sun was hanging near the edge of the encroaching cloudbank, threatening to end their hope of a nice sunset. Still, Andrew was optimistic that when the evening was over, at least things wouldn't be setting on their relationship.

Nicole looked great as always, her hair and makeup nicely in place with the lightest of touches. The fading daylight caught the highlights in her hair, giving her an almost ethereal glow. More importantly, her focus was not just on the food but also on their conversation, moving it forward as graciously as possible.

"So, you think you've found a way of running down the jerks that did this to you?" she asked, her fork poised midair.

She could tell he was finding it difficult to talk about it, but her warmth was encouraging.

"Yes, I think so. I was with Jimmy today, and he thinks he can get me into the Tower offices."

"You think there's something there? When we were there, it looked like they'd cleaned it out completely." Skepticism tinged her voice, but not disbelief.

"Jimmy has checked with the property management group, and he also ran down all the possible cyber leads he could and still came up with nothing."

"Well, I guess it's the only real link you've got. I mean actual physical one." She took a sip of wine, her eyes never leaving his face.

Andrew took a bite of the pasta and chewed slowly, thinking before he spoke. The flavors reminded him of better times, of normalcy.

"I've always been a fan of the Sherlock Holmes stories," he said finally. "He would find answers where no one else could and in the strangest ways. That's how I feel about this. There's got to be some clue they've left behind. If it's there, I'll find it."

"I hope you're right," she said after a mouthful of salad. "Yes, you'll need some of that Sherlock stuff. The whole thing seems so random, like it's out of some bizarre mystery novel."

"It's weird beyond belief," Andrew agreed, his fork scraping against the plate as he gathered another bite. "But I'm determined now to get an answer. I'm going after this thing with a vengeance. I don't care how long it takes, I'm going to find out who did this to me and why."

Nicole smiled, set her fork down, and took a sip of her wine. When she looked up from her plate again, her countenance had changed. She was centering in on him now, deep concern in her eyes.

"What about your company? I mean, now that this deal has fallen through, what are you going to do? If you're not careful, you could get sidetracked."

Andrew knew this would be coming. What woman wouldn't want her guy to be working hard and winning? He knew that's what she'd done, pulled herself out of a bad marriage and made a career for herself, a good one. He was sure she expected him to do the same.

"This thing could finish me professionally," he admitted, his voice quiet against the background noise of waves in the distance. "But it's like a spear in my heart. I've got to pull it out. It's simply a priority now."

"I know," she said, reaching across the table to touch his hand. "It's just I don't want it to ruin you in the process."

Andrew had stopped eating as well. The pasta grew cold on his plate as he struggled to find the right words.

"Let me explain," he began, his voice heavy with things unsaid. "There are some ghosts in my life. Things I've never told anyone about. Not even Jimmy, my best friend. It's those ghosts that I'm chasing."

"We've all got ghosts or skeletons in our closets," Nicole said, her expression softening. "But we move on. You don't let them hold you back. I've told you about mine, and I assumed you'd told me about all of yours. It sounds like you haven't," she added with a disappointed sigh.

"No, I didn't tell you," Andrew admitted, the weight of his secrets pressing down on him like a physical force. "I haven't shared everything."

The confession hung in the air between them, as the last remnants of daylight faded from the sky and darkness settled over the ocean.

CHAPTER EIGHTEEN

BIG SUR

JULY · 1970

Even the best high couldn't drive away Andrew's anxieties. It was afternoon now, and several of their little tribe were gathered at the great table in the stone house. He was on edge, wondering what was going on with Blaire. Eric was in the middle of one of his spontaneous lectures on brotherhood, his words flowing through the haze of marijuana smoke that hung in the air like an ethereal fog. The mellow effect of the pot made his talk somewhat hypnotic, his voice rising and falling in a rhythm that matched the distant sound of waves crashing against the cliffs below.

Eric added a special note to his spiel by saying that he was some sort of ordained New Age minister and he'd love to do weddings here at the stone house if any of the couples were so inclined. A meaningful silence fell over the room at the suggestion, conversations suspended as couples exchanged glances.

Amber was beside Andrew, much improved. It seemed that a few tokes on some weed really helped. He passed the joint to her, and she took a deep hit, the cherry glowing bright red. They smiled at each other and then gazed dreamily back at Eric, whose face was animated as he spoke, afternoon sunlight streaming through the windows casting him in golden light.

Blaire appeared abruptly in the doorway, her silhouette framed by the bright afternoon light behind her. She scanned the room, and once she saw Andrew, she motioned for him to come to her. Her movements were urgent, her eyes wide with something that looked like fear.

Andrew turned to Amber, quickly making up an excuse. "It looks like Blaire and Ash are still at each other. Maybe I should see if I can help? What do you think?"

Amber's eyes lingered on Blaire for a moment, then drifted back to Andrew. Something flickered across her face, a shadow of doubt, perhaps, before the weed smoothed it away. "Sure," she said, her voice slow and thick with the buzz. "Just be careful. You don't want to get in the middle of some sort of weird confrontation." She paused, her gaze sharpening slightly despite the high. "Especially with Blaire."

"Don't worry, I'll watch myself." He threw her a little reassuring kiss and headed for the door, feeling her eyes follow him across the room.

Blaire led him outside to a couple of chairs under a nearby oak. The ancient tree's sprawling branches created a canopy of dappled sunlight and shadow above them. They were tucked just beyond a gentle rise, out of sight from the stone house, secluded enough that no one could see them from the porch or windows.

Looking back to ensure that no one had followed, Andrew took her hands as they sat together. The warmth of her skin against his sent an electric current running up his arms. He looked into her eyes, hoping for a luscious response but found only fear, her pupils dilated with anxiety.

"What is it, Blaire? You haven't told Ash about us?" His stomach clenched at the thought.

"No, but earlier today he wanted to go up to the meadow and have some fun."

Her words sent a surge of jealousy through Andrew. He saw them in his mind, Ash doing to her what he wanted to do to her right now. Her face and body were so close to him, her eyes so inviting. But he suppressed his envy and desire as quickly as he could and encouraged her to continue.

"Once we were through," she said, her voice barely above a whisper, "he went into the woods where we found the cash the other day. He rummaged around in there for a long time, shouting and cursing. Then he came out really mad. He didn't say why he was angry, but I knew. He was looking for the money."

She leaned in closer, her breath warm against Andrew's ear.

"Andrew... it's his. It's Ash's money. We stole Ash's money."

She pulled back just enough to look him in the eye.

"I didn't say a thing to him, but I'm really scared he's going to figure it out. He has this uncanny way of knowing things, I told you, he's kind of psychic. And if he finds out, we'll..."

Her voice trailed off, but the fear in her eyes said everything.

Andrew interrupted her, wanting to calm her fears. "Listen, I don't believe in this psychic stuff. It's all just some mumble jumble." He squeezed her hand reassuringly and looked encouragingly into her troubled eyes. "Look, there are at least forty people up here on the side of this mountain. Any one of them could have taken the money as far as he's concerned."

"He's never told you anything about the money, right?"

"Right."

"Okay, then there's no reason he should suspect you. As far as me, well, I'm just another one of his friends and have no idea about his business dealings. So, do you get it? There's nothing to worry about." His tone was confident, but a knot of unease tightened in his stomach.

"Okay, but he's really angry, and when he gets this way... he takes it out on me." Her voice faltered, a shadow crossing her face that made Andrew's pulse quicken.

"That's even more reason we need to blow this place right away. Where is Ash now?" Andrew glanced around nervously, half expecting to see Ash materialize from the woods.

"He's still up there in the meadow looking around. He told me to come back here, and he'd join me later."

"Don't worry, I've hidden the cash really well. He'll never find it." Andrew paused, trying to think about their next move, the weight of their decision pressing down on him. "Okay, here's the plan: later tonight after he's back, you try to calm him down. Get him high and take him to bed. I'll tell Amber about my decision to leave with you."

He reached up and touched her cheek, stroking it reassuringly, feeling the softness of her skin beneath his fingertips. "It's going to work, don't worry. Once Amber's asleep, early, before dawn, I'll head back to the meadow and get the stash. I'll bring it back along the creek trail to where my bike is parked and head down to the highway before anyone wakes up. As far as Ash, once he's asleep, slip out quietly and join me near the highway. We'll be on our way before he finds out you're gone. How does that sound?"

Blaire's expression was a mixture of hope and doubt. "It's going to be tough. He's been this way before, and it's taken all my feminine charms to get him under control."

"From what I've experienced, those 'charms' should do the trick." Andrew smiled, but it didn't reach his eyes. "I must say, though, I'm just a little jealous that he can still have you."

"Well, that won't be for much longer." Her lips curved into a smile that sent a thrill of anticipation through him.

They rejoined the group and spent the rest of the afternoon hanging out. The hours stretched and compressed in that way they do when altered by substances and anxiety about what was to come. Around dinnertime, Ash came into the house clearly agitated, his energy disrupting the mellow vibe of the communal space. He refused the offer of a hit on the pot but joined them for a dinner of pasta and chicken that some of the girls had rustled up. Before long, he took Blaire with him, and they retreated to their tent, his hand gripping her wrist a little too tightly.

Andrew realized he was going to have to come clean with Amber, so he took her hand and motioned toward the door. "Let's call it a night, Am. Besides, I need to talk to you about something really important."

As they made their way up the hill to their camp, they looked west toward the horizon. The sun was sinking into the fog near the coast, a red-orange orb disappearing into a blanket of gray that hugged the shoreline. Andrew could tell Amber was captured by the moment, her face illuminated by the last golden rays.

"Let's just sit out here for a while and watch the sunset," she said, her voice dreamy and content.

"Okay," Andrew acquiesced, knowing he needed her to be in the best possible mood for what was ahead.

They sat there long after the sun had gone down, each in their own quiet space. When they finally decided to go inside, it was dark, and a chill had come over them. In the distance, there was a now-familiar cry. It was a coyote, keening away in one long mournful call, the sound hanging in the air like a warning.

Later, when they were settled in and were snuggling together, Andrew started to break the ice. But before he could, she looked into his eyes. She gently touched his face and then affectionately ran her finger along his jaw.

"I've got a question for you, Andrew," she said softly. "It's about our future together, and I want you to know how I feel."

Andrew anticipated what he thought she was about to say. When they were listening to Eric's little announcement about doing weddings here on the mountain, she had looked really inspired. He didn't want her to start going down that road because of what was coming, so he interrupted her as gently as he could.

"Listen, I really need to come clean with you about where I'm at."

Her body immediately stiffened beside him, and she drew away a little. It was almost as if she knew what was coming. Andrew took a deep breath, steeling himself for what had to be done.

"I've been thinking about our relationship for a while now. You seem happy with it, but I've got to be honest, I'm not."

Her mouth turned down, her brows knitted, and she bit her lip. The soft lamplight cast shadows across her face, deepening the hurt in her eyes.

"What do you mean you're not happy? This is the first I've been aware of it. I know I've been out of it for a few days, and I'm grateful for the way you've cared for me, but you say you're not happy? What gives?"

Suddenly, her eyes widened, and her mouth went slack as understanding dawned on her. "I know what it is... it's Blaire. You've been hooking up with Blaire, haven't you?"

Tears spilled down her cheeks, glistening in the dim light of their tent, and a mournful cry rose in her throat. She choked it back and burst out with a bitter tone, "Something told me you were making it with her. I knew it. You were gone so long that first day I was sick. I woke up and called for you, and you didn't answer. I even got out of the tent and wandered around a little. I looked down the hill and didn't see you there. I just wondered where you'd gone. You acted so nice later, but all the time you'd been hooking up with her."

She turned over in their bed and was crying deeply now. Huge sobs shook her body. Andrew gently placed his hand on her shoulder, but she shook it off violently.

"I'm sorry," he said, his voice hollow even to his own ears. "You've just got to understand. I just felt like our relationship wasn't going anywhere, and I needed something new."

That was a lie. Their relationship had been great. If he were being honest with himself, he would admit that it wasn't about their relationship. No, he'd been completely sucked into this thing with Blaire, and it had swept over him like an amazing new drug. He had found the ultimate sensual, fleshly high, and he wanted it even if it meant an end to what he and Amber had going.

She suddenly turned around toward him, her face tormented and full of questions. The lamplight caught the tear tracks on her cheeks, making them shine like silver ribbons.

"I thought we'd had a future. That's why we quit school and headed out on this adventure. I gave you my heart and soul." She started to cry again but forced herself to stop. "I know that sounds cliché and corny, but I mean it. Why would you just betray me like this?"

Andrew reached out to her again and tried to touch her shoulder. She drew back as if his touch would burn her.

"Why?" The single word hung in the air between them, laden with pain.

"I don't fully understand why either, Am. All I can tell you is that what's been happening to me is overwhelming and it's real. I know it's painful for you, but it's better that I'm honest now and not drag this thing out."

"Fine. You want honest? If you want the truth, I think it's all about some sex thing. I've seen the way she comes on to guys. I've seen her body..." Her voice broke on the words. "But just give it some time. It will get old after a while."

"It's more than that," Andrew insisted. "There's a connection there that I haven't had with anyone... ever!"

Her lips drew tightly together again and then pursed out. Her eyes snapped closed, almost like she was trying to shut out the pain the way one would shut all light from entering. "I just can't believe that you would do this to me."

"I'm sorry. But you'll live through this and find someone who will take my place. You're a beautiful girl full of sunshine."

"Yeah, well, the sunshine's gone out now."

She reached up to the pendant around her neck and pulled hard on it. The leather cord snapped, and it came free in her hand. She thrust it at him, the silver gleaming dully in the lamplight. "Here, you take this. It obviously didn't mean a thing to you."

Andrew pushed her hand away. "It did mean something. It will always mean something. Please keep it." His voice was thick with emotion he didn't fully understand.

"It means nothing now," she cried as she threw it toward the tent entrance near their feet.

Then in a second act of rejection, she unzipped their two sleeping bags from each other and then curled up in her own, the sound of the zipper like a final punctuation on their relationship. "You'll never touch me again," she cursed in anger.

With that, she turned away from him again, moving as far as she could from him, pressing herself up against the edge of the tent on her side. Sobs came from deep in her core, her body shaking with each new quake of sorrow.

Andrew tried to remain still, but he was shaken as well. His own conscience was burning, refusing to excuse his selfishness. No, he told himself. No, this isn't selfish. This is... His mind scrambled for the right words, the right framework to make this crushing guilt disappear. There had to be a way to see this differently. There had to be. And then, like a life raft in stormy seas, the words came: "To thine own self be true." Shakespeare. Yes. This wasn't betrayal, it was honesty. It was courage. It was...But then there was a part of him that said, Andrew, you're a fool, and all this stuff about following your heart is no excuse for a serious act of total betrayal. But that part of him was no longer in control. Something deeper, almost primordial, had taken over, and he was going with it. It was shutting out any empathy. How could he do this to someone he was sure he had loved so much? What kind of person was he? Whoever that person was, he was taking over.

Then he told himself, he was on a journey of discovery. Wasn't that what this whole generation was about? Turning their backs on the old, worn-out ways and looking for new paths. As hard as this was, it would turn out for the good for both of them. Amber would eventually heal and then find someone who would care for her in a way he had failed to. As far as Blaire and him, well, there was danger there as well. It might not work out, and he might be left alone. But it was a risk he was willing to face and a price he was willing to pay for the pleasure he saw before him.

So, he stayed tranquil and listened for nearly an hour until Amber's crying finally stopped. Mercifully, she had fallen asleep, her breathing now even and deep.

Finally, Andrew found sleep as well, but the tormenting dreams of previous nights returned, only this time there was a new one joining them. Blaire moved toward him like a gazelle, her motion fluid and luxurious, appearing out of darkness. Her body was full and inviting. He reached out to embrace her, his heart alive with pleasure, his flesh fully aroused, but as soon as he touched her, his hands passed through her as if through an apparition. She dissolved like a ghost into the darkness. The dream repeated itself, melding and morphing into the others that had returned.

He was stirred from his fitful sleep; dawn was still four hours away. There was plenty of time for him to get to the meadow and back again before the camp awoke. He slowly unzipped his sleeping bag and slipped out of the tent as quietly as possible, taking his things with him. The crisp night air hit his face, a stark contrast to the stuffy warmth of the tent.

Andrew turned on his flashlight and explored his surroundings. Something was caught in its beam beneath his feet. He looked closer, and there at the entrance, he saw the pendant Amber had tossed away. If she didn't want it, then he guessed he should keep it as a memento of the good times they had together. He picked it up and stuffed it in his bag. He took a wrinkled piece of paper and a pen from his pack and scratched out a few words of goodbye. He folded it twice and then ducked back into the tent to tuck it into her bag.

Back outside, the air was filled with the chill of the predawn. He breathed it in deeply, his senses waking. In the waning moonlight, he could see the fog rising from the ocean far below, like steam from a cauldron. Despite the drama of the night before and the tormenting dreams, he felt alive and full of hope. The future looked good for him. He had plenty of cash, and soon he would have a beautiful woman at his side. He couldn't wait to set off with her on a new adventure, leaving behind the mess he had created and the heart he had broken.

The promise of dawn was still hours away as Andrew melted into the darkness, his footsteps fading into the mist like a ghost disappearing into the night.

Chapter Nineteen

DEL MAR

November · 2000

There's nothing quite like laying yourself bare to someone you care about, revealing the darkest corners of your past. You wonder if your hidden secrets might end up on the next daytime talk show or in some lurid account on those tabloids that shout at you in the checkout line at the local market. That's how Andrew was feeling this morning. It had been two days since he'd made his confession to Nicole, and the pain of it still clung to him like the morning fog that refused to lift.

He sat at an outside table at Stratford Court Café in Del Mar, finishing his breakfast. The morning air was thick with marine layer; everything wrapped in gray cotton. The sun struggled somewhere above, casting the world in that peculiar California half-light that made everything feel suspended between night and day. Del Mar's elegant shops were still mostly closed, their windows dark. A few early joggers passed on their way to the beach, their footsteps muffled in the mist. Andrew checked his watch. Jimmy should be arriving soon. He was taking the morning off to help Andrew dig into the mystery, and Andrew was immensely grateful. But even his obsession with finding answers couldn't quiet the echo of Nicole's words from two days ago.

Nicole had texted him out of the blue, could they meet at Pannikin in Encinitas? She'd suggested the old Santa Fe Depot location, with its high ceilings and constant flow of people. Andrew understood the choice immediately. Neutral ground. Public enough that things would stay civil, busy enough that she could leave whenever she wanted. The kind of place where difficult conversations dissolved into the hiss of the espresso machine and the chatter of other people's lives.

She had handled his confession about Amber and the betrayal with a grace he hadn't deserved. Her words drifted back to him now with the salt breeze.

"I can understand why you didn't want to share those things with anyone," she had said, her voice steady but carrying an undercurrent of hurt. "You were a very selfish person in the past, and I would have hated you if I'd known what you were doing to Amber at the time. But I can see that you've changed. You're not that guy anymore. I'm glad you finally opened up to me." She had paused, her hazel eyes searching his face across the small café table. "If I'm honest, though, I'm just wondering why you couldn't have told me earlier."

"You know what they say, guys got the short end of the stick when God handed out transparency," Andrew had replied, trying for levity that fell flat between them.

Nicole had leaned forward, pressing her point. The soft lighting couldn't soften the steel in her voice. "I'm not sure I agree with you on that issue. In fact, to be honest, I think a lot of guys are cowards when it comes to being vulnerable. They're afraid if they open up, they'll become less manly."

Andrew had raised his palm in weak defense. "I'm with you there. It's a struggle for a lot of us, so can you understand why I was having a hard time?"

She was having none of it. "Not really. I want to be sympathetic, but I'm beyond that wimpy way of approaching life. Real intimacy requires risk, Andrew. Trust requires transparency. I'm not into the lifestyle where everyone keeps his and her own private little world." Her voice had cracked slightly. "I've always been upfront with you, and I'd hoped you would have been that way with me. Do you remember the night I poured out all my hurts to you? I didn't hold back."

Andrew had wanted to look away, but her honesty demanded his presence. The silence that followed felt like drowning in slow motion.

"It's just strange to me that it's taken this whole disaster to get you to open up," she'd continued, each word precise as a scalpel. "I wonder if it hadn't happened, if you'd ever gotten to this place of transparency. What else are you holding back? What other shadows am I supposed to just accept?"

Andrew had searched for words to reassure her, but his mouth had gone dry as sand.

"I'm just wondering if it will last. I hope it's not an anomaly. Because relationships built on partial truths are houses built on sand, Andrew. One good wave and they're gone."

He'd finally managed, "I guess time will tell," and immediately saw how wrong those words were in the flinch that crossed her face.

Nicole had sat back, her silence more damning than any accusation. When she finally spoke, her words fell like stones.

"Andrew, I think I need to give our relationship some time off."

His heart had plummeted. "Time off?"

"Just a few weeks to let me reflect, but more importantly to let you sort out where you're headed. As critical as this whole openness thing is to me, I want to make sure that the man in my life knows where he's going, and I'm not sure you know that right now."

This was what he got for finally being completely open, the good, the bad, and the ugly? He had been dumbstruck by the whole thing. That was where their conversation had ended. There was a tender but short kiss goodnight. Since then, he'd texted her a few times, but her replies had been cursory. He'd decided it was best to give her the space she asked for.

It really hurt, to say the least, and Andrew knew he deserved what he was getting, but those things he'd hidden from her were simply too painful to talk about until now. He'd done everything he could to forget them, but they refused to go away. They were like relentless specters chasing him even in his moments of rest. So, he'd run and shut the door on them.

And all this coming right on the heels of the Teknon 2 Partners deception. At least this crisis had kept his mind occupied, distracting him from the worries about his relationship with Nicole. He saw it as a bit of mercy and a possible antidote to his pain. He was going to let his search for answers drive him now and sidetrack his torments.

The marine layer was finally beginning to lift. Andrew's phone buzzed. He glanced at the screen, Jimmy.

He answered, pressing the phone to his ear as the low hum of the café surrounded him.

"Hey, just letting you know, I'm heading over to the towers now," Jimmy said. "You still good to meet me there?"

Andrew glanced at his half-eaten breakfast. "Yeah. I'll head over now."

He finished his coffee, pushed aside the cold remains of his eggs, and paid the bill, leaving a generous tip despite barely touching his food. He stepped outside as the day began to awaken.

He jumped in his car and made his way to Franklin Tower. They each found a spot in the parking garage and took the elevator to the twelfth floor. Time to find some answers, even if he couldn't find them in his own life.

"So, Leticia got you a key?" Andrew confirmed again. It had turned out she owed Jimmy a favor, and he had cashed it in. After being extra sweet to her boss, she had been able to get it through one of his connections along with a letter of permission.

"Yes, and now I'm the one with the deficit," Jimmy said with a wry smile. "But she's blood, she won't ride me about it."

"I'm the one with the deficit, Jimmy," Andrew said, his voice heavy with gratitude. "I just hope I can pay you back someday."

"I know you'd do the same for me. Besides, this thing is becoming sort of personal. It's got my investigative juices flowing." Jimmy's eyes had a gleam of excitement that Andrew hadn't seen in a while.

Andrew pointed to the backpack slung over Jimmy's shoulder. "What's in the bag?"

"Oh, just a few tools of the trade," Jimmy replied with a mysterious smile.

The elevator opened, and they walked into the vestibule. It was Sunday, and the other offices on this floor were closed. That was why Jimmy had suggested they wait until today. They didn't want to attract any unwanted attention.

They approached the doors. Andrew was amazed to see the shattered glass had already been replaced. The janitor had done a good job cleaning and polishing the tile; there were only a few tiny flecks of red he'd failed to expunge. The sight of it almost pulled Andrew into a flashback, but Jimmy inserted the key in the lock, and the rattle of the door snapped him out of it.

"I'm not sure if we'll find anything here, but it doesn't hurt to take a look," Jimmy said, his voice dropping to a near whisper as if they were entering sacred ground.

"There's got to be something, some hint they've left behind or failed to erase," Andrew replied, desperation coloring his words.

"Here's the light," said Jimmy, flipping the switches near the door. A few fluorescents flickered on in the former reception area, and a row of recessed LEDs in the hall leading to the offices lit up. The place had been swept clean and the floors polished.

"Let's start in Quinn's office. Do you remember which one it was?"

"Yes, just up the hall here. It's the one with the nicest view."

"Wow, you're right about the view," said Jimmy as he followed Andrew into the room and walked over to the ceiling-high windows. The marine layer was retreating, and just the slightest blue of the sea was poking through the dissipating mist out near the distant horizon. Andrew hoped this was a good sign, that the fog of deception and confusion around this whole thing would clear, and they could find some link to these jerks who had played him for a fool.

"Yeah, it's pretty impressive. The ambiance here really sucked me in," Andrew admitted, looking around the empty space that once seemed so promising. "Their whole operation looked top shelf."

"But this thing must have cost them a ton of money. Who'd spend that kind of dough just to shaft you? It's just so crazy." Jimmy's brow furrowed as he tried to make sense of it all.

Andrew wanted to tell him about his secret theory about why it may have happened. But digging the whole thing up again after having just lived through it all with Nicole was too much now.

"Apparently I do have a serious enemy," was all he said, his voice tight.

"Well, that's why we're here. We're going to find out." Jimmy unzipped his bag and took out a pair of nitrile gloves and slipped them on. Andrew followed him as he toured the room, examining the walls, the floor, and doors. He checked the door handles. "It looks like these have been wiped clean, the same with the walls." He reached back in his bag and pulled out a scope-like device.

"It's called RUVIS, that's short for Reflective Ultra-Violet Imaging System," he explained. "It allows me to see if there are any latent prints. I don't want to start random dusting if there's nothing here."

"Wow, pretty cool-looking device," Andrew said, impressed by Jimmy's thoroughness.

"Yeah, it's amazing what they're developing these days for crime scene investigation."

Jimmy moved around the office, looking into the eyepiece and slowly scanned the windows. The sunlight was beginning to stream in more fully now, giving him better conditions for his work. "Not a trace anywhere else except right here on the glass. Come take a look."

Andrew stepped up beside him and looked. Nothing.

"No, you need to move to the side a little and let the exterior light highlight the image," Jimmy instructed. Andrew remembered all the times he'd cleaned a window and then when the sun hit it later, he saw all the streaks he'd left. He moved to the side and looked again.

"Oh, yes, I see it now. Looks like three fingertips." The ghostly impressions were faint but unmistakable.

"Yes, definitely three prints. But it's weird, they look out of place. It's almost as if someone put them there after the surface had been wiped clean. Notice the streaks left from cleaning. The prints are on top of them, not beneath them."

Andrew could clearly see the streaks now, and sure enough, the prints were on top. "Are you able to lift them?"

"Should be easy enough. First, I'm going to photograph them." Jimmy took a camera from his bag and stepped to the side to catch the right angle of the light. The camera's flash briefly illuminated the room. He snapped a few photos and then returned the camera to his bag and took a small black case from it. "It's a simple fingerprint kit. Nothing special. You can get them online now for less than fifty bucks." He started to dust the prints with a small brush that he gently swirled over the surface. Then he reversed the motion. A black powder residue adhered to the glass surface.

"I thought it was white powder that was used on prints?" Andrew said, remembering some scene he'd seen in a CSI episode.

"Yes, that works on a lot of surfaces, but when you have light coming from outside flooding through the glass, the black dust makes the prints stand out better," Jimmy replied confidently.

Gradually, the image began to stand out. Then Jimmy took a bulb-shaped object from his kit and blew away the excess powder. After that, he removed three strips of tape from his kit and applied them to the prints. Then slowly, he lifted each piece of tape from the glass one at a time, pressing them into a card. "They're called transfer cards. I'll have these scanned later and see if I can get a match. I got some friends on the force who can run these for me."

"You made that look simple enough," Andrew said, impressed by Jimmy's professionalism.

"Well, it helps that I was trained in all this back when I worked in law enforcement."

"Now what?" Andrew asked, eager to continue.

"We keep looking, cover every inch."

Over the next half hour, they went through almost every room, searching each corner, even getting down on their hands and knees to look. Nothing. Not one single print on doors, walls, or windows. Finally, in the last room, on the back of the door, Andrew found a yellow Post-It note, which had apparently been overlooked.

"Jimmy, come here," he called, his heart quickening at the discovery.

"Is there anything on it?" asked Jimmy, hurrying over.

"Yeah, someone scribbled, 'Briana, don't forget to stop at Costco on the way home, Bill.'"

"Let me see it."

Andrew handed it to him, and Jimmy took out a plastic baggie and slipped it inside. "I'll check for prints later."

They spent another twenty minutes giving each room another once-over before heading back to their cars. In the basement, they stopped to confer. The underground parking garage was dimly lit and smelled of concrete and car exhaust.

"Listen, I think we've got a couple of possible leads here," Jimmy said, his voice echoing slightly in the cavernous space. "The prints on the glass are kind of an enigma. But let's see what comes up."

"Thanks, Jimmy. It's something, some hope," Andrew said, feeling the weight on his shoulders lighten just a bit.

"Well, don't get overly optimistic yet," Jimmy cautioned, but his eyes held a glimmer of determination.

"I'm not, but at least there's a path forward now."

"Give me a couple of days, and I'll let you know what comes up. I'm also going to keep my tech guys going on that phony website. Even though it's offline, you know what they say, nothing ever goes away once it's out there in cyberspace."

"Can I buy you lunch, Jimmy?" Andrew asked, wanting to extend their time together.

"Thanks, but my granddaughters are in town, and we've got plans for the rest of the day. I'd better take a rain check." Jimmy clapped Andrew on the shoulder, a gesture of solidarity.

"Okay. Thanks again. I really appreciate all you are doing."

"You're welcome, and we'll talk as soon as I get the lab reports back."

"Adios amigo."

"Hasta pronto," Jimmy said with a smile, knowing Andrew probably hadn't heard that one in Spanish lately.

Andrew headed to 15th Street to celebrate the progress they'd made but also to help him forget about Nicole for the rest of the day. He had a few drinks and hung with some friends. Their laughter and conversation provided a temporary balm for his troubles. He made it through the rest of the day without too much pain.

Finally, as the sun began to set, casting long shadows across the landscape, Andrew took a long walk on the beach. The rhythmic sound of the waves breaking against the shore seemed to settle his nerves before heading home to what he hoped would be a restful sleep. But even as the sand gave way beneath his feet, he couldn't shake the feeling that he was walking a path that would lead him back to a past he'd tried so hard to escape.

CHAPTER TWENTY

LA JOLLA

NOVEMBER · 2000

The aroma of perfectly prepared sushi wafted through the air, mingling with the scent of the ocean breeze that drifted in through the open windows. Landon took a deep breath, savoring it as he and Donovan waited for their food. They sat across from one another, immersed in the refined simplicity of the restaurant, sipping on some Stone IPA's, the amber liquid catching the light from the windows.

Landon loved to come here not just because of the taste and texture of the food, but because of its appearance. It suggested the Japanese aesthetic; Miyabi, a presentation reflecting elegance and refinement. That was something close to his heart. As long as he'd worked in development, he recognized that something of true quality and excellence would reflect a certain but subtle elegance and refinement. Not just on the surface, but also at its core. The quality then emerged externally. To put it simply, it was the ideal of integrity, something he believed in and tried to hold to.

Then there had been that suspicious call, traced to an agency that had contacted a state prison, inquiring about a specific inmate. Not a consultant or a contractor. A convict. As if Donovan were trying to track someone down from a world Landon had never associated with him. A world of violence, not business. Was he planning to bring someone in? A fixer? A hit man? The thought chilled him. It was so far outside what he believed Donovan capable of.

Landon never would've known about the call if his secretary hadn't mentioned it, something she'd picked up from Donovan's assistant during a casual coffee break. A throwaway comment, half-whispered, that had lodged in his brain like a splinter.

All of it was adding up, and it deeply concerned him.

He was struggling with this very matter right now. It surrounded what he'd done, what Donovan had had him do and it had turned sour within him. He'd racked his brain, but he couldn't find any good reason why Donovan had made him pull the plug on Foster like that. It felt premature. Cold. And now it was eating away at him.

He felt as if he'd compromised his own integrity. And as much as he admired and trusted Donovan, he couldn't let this go. Not without answers. Not when the shadows around Donovan were starting to look real.

"So, Don, I need to get some things off my chest," Landon said as casually as possible. He didn't want to add any additional stress to what he knew would be a difficult conversation. Perhaps if he approached it in a matter-of-fact manner, it would soften the impact and allow him to get to his point without being shut down.

Donovan looked up from his beer, his eyes narrowing slightly. "Sure, what is it?"

"Well, first of all, how am I going to deal with the city on what we've done to Foster?"

"I had legal handle it," Donovan replied, his voice level and calm. "We have some connections with the head of the department. They will make sure it gets buried and that there's no connection with us."

"That's a relief," Landon said, though the feeling of unease remained lodged in his chest like a stone.

"Then there's the issue with the contractors Foster lined up. What if they try to come after us?"

"Like I had legal explain to you when we started, they set up the contracts with Foster in such a way that he's on the line once we pull out."

"I know, but what if they decide to come after us anyway?" Landon pressed, leaning forward slightly.

"They'll never find us. Our tech guys have covered our tracks," Donovan said with confidence that bordered on arrogance. "But if they do find us, we'll tie them up with legal stuff for years."

"I hope you're right."

"Our lawyers know what they're doing."

"There's one other issue," Landon said, his voice dropping a notch.

"What is it?"

"It's what's happened to Foster. I…"

Donovan interrupted him. He was already on edge, his posture stiffening. "Before you get started, I need you to know I understand your frustration. I know it's been difficult. That's why I needed you to trust me."

"I've got…"

He interrupted again. "I know you've been struggling with it, and that's why I didn't let you know my plans until right before we shut it down. I had to be sure you didn't have time for second thoughts."

"So, you'd been considering this for some time?" Landon asked, a chill running down his spine despite the warmth of the restaurant.

"Yes." Donovan paused and took a sip of his beer. His eyes, normally steel blue, had turned almost gray and hardened like river stones.

"And you held that from me?"

He took another sip of his drink and looked down at the table, avoiding Landon's gaze.

Landon looked down now. He took a sip of his beer, trying to understand. Somewhere inside, the liquid met his stomach, and he started to lose his appetite. He took another drink and looked up, his eyes as determined as Donovan's were earlier but angry. "So, the whole Teknon thing was a scam, a setup? Why? What in the world were you thinking?"

"I've had my reasons. It's a long story and I..." Donovan began, his voice trailing off.

Just then their food arrived, and they both drew back to allow the waiter room. The dishes were placed in front of them. Landon's was an Ebi and Ahi roll. Donovan had a Lobster California roll and Lakanilau roll. Landon took out his chopsticks, grabbed a dollop of wasabi, and stirred it into a small bowl he'd filled with soy sauce.

"What possible reasons could there be for defrauding Foster?" Landon asked, stirring the solution. It was as muddy and black as his thoughts. "Do you realize what we've done to him? Someone told me he ended up in the hospital."

"I know. I'd heard that as well, terrible," Donovan said, though his tone suggested minimal concern.

He prepared his sauce, dipped his sushi in it, and put it to his mouth. He closed his eyes as he chewed, savoring the taste but perhaps hiding from Landon's gaze.

Landon couldn't start on his meal yet. He was too upset. "So, if this was the plan the whole time, why didn't you run it in person?"

"You know in the last few years I've let you run some of our special projects," Donovan said, his eyes now open and fixed on Landon.

"What in the world are we gaining from this? How did this help me grow?" Landon demanded, his voice rising slightly.

Donovan took another bite. He chewed slowly, his eyes clear and unyielding. There was a fire there now, almost as if the heat of the wasabi had ignited them. "Let me tell you about this guy. In fact, all the guys on the list I gave you. They're thieves."

"Thieves?" Landon echoed, confusion evident in his voice.

"That's right. Thieves. They steal." The words hung heavy in the air between them.

"What did they steal? Whom did they steal from?" Landon pressed, leaning forward.

"It's a long story, and I don't know if you'd believe it if I told you."

The waiter came and asked if everything was okay. He'd obviously noticed that Landon hadn't touched his food. Landon assured him everything was fine. But it wasn't. His earlier turmoil had only been increased by the growing revelation of Donovan's scheme.

"Are you kidding? I've trusted you completely. You owe me an explanation," Landon said once the waiter had left.

Donovan took another sip of his beer and continued, "I regret that I didn't tell you earlier. I've been conflicted by that. But I feel strongly about what I'm doing, and I don't want anything or anyone to get in the way."

"Doing? You mean to tell me that you're going to do this again? Is that what the list is about? Is this a vendetta? And you're using me to enact it?" Landon pushed his plate away in irritation, the ceramic making a sharp sound against the table.

"Lanny, just calm down for a moment and listen," Donovan said, his voice dropping to a near whisper.

Landon crossed his arms and leaned back, his chair legs scraping the floor, a perfect echo of his feelings. "Okay, I'm listening."

Donovan finished his beer in one long pull. But the chilled liquid did nothing to cool the fire in his eyes. "I've told you how my family came from back east and settled in LA in the late sixties. Even though both my parents came from money, they ran off together against their families' wishes. Therefore, they were left out of any inheritance."

"Yes, I remember," Landon said, trying to keep the impatience from his voice.

"Well, my dad went to work as a grunt on a construction site, and Mom worked at a Bob's Big Boy until she had me and my brother, Ryan. But after a couple of years, my dad had worked his way up to foreman and eventually put together his own construction company."

"Yes, you told me that too and how your dad made a fortune in the housing boom," Landon said, not hiding his annoyance with hearing the recap.

"Yes, we had a great home in Brentwood and a great lifestyle. And at the height of his success, he died of a heart attack, and my mom got cancer and died within a year after him."

"Of course, it's a tragic story. It's sad. You've told me this at least a half a dozen times. And I know you think it was the stress of your dad's death that brought on the cancer."

Donovan paused like he was searching for the right words or maybe the courage to say them. He couldn't seem to look Landon in the eye as he finally confessed, "But what I didn't tell you is what brought on my dad's heart attack." He placed both his hands flat on the table between them. He took a deep breath and slowly breathed out, leaning back and letting his hands slip off the table into his lap.

"No, you didn't tell me that," Landon said, his anger ebbing as he noticed Donovan's struggle. His thoughts of Andrew Foster faded, and he couldn't seem to stay mad at his friend. He took a long drink of his beer. He felt its chill calming him.

"So, Dad's business is booming. But there's a lot of competition in that market. The rivalry is cutthroat," Donovan continued, his voice gaining strength. "There were a group of young hotshots that wanted to control the market, and they were willing to do anything to achieve their goal. Someone went to my dad's bankers behind his back and got his line of credit cut off. He was right in the middle of his biggest development. It was his dream project. If he'd brought that one in, he would have been set for life, and so would the rest of us—my mom and us kids. But then his credit went to hell, and he was faced with losing everything he'd worked so hard for." Donovan's hands were back on the table, and he leaned in toward Landon.

"Did he lose everything?"

"Not at first. He found a partner that helped him with financing. This new guy also found out who had knifed my dad in the back."

"They were three rival developers, some who are on that list I gave you."

"Foster?" Landon asked, his pulse quickening.

"Yes, Foster was one of them. They stole from my dad. Stole his livelihood, stole his life." Donovan looked off to his right, out toward the parking lot. His eyes followed an older man walking away from them, toward his car. It was almost like he was searching for something he'd lost, a father he never got to know, a mentor he never had to guide him. He squinted and clenched his teeth ever so slightly.

Landon took a moment before he spoke. He could see the hurt in Donovan's eyes clearly now and understood better some of what his friend must have gone through when this whole thing was coming down on his family. "So, what happened with the new partner?"

Donovan's focus came back to Landon. "He was a real strange guy. He had tons of money and was willing to bankroll the project through to completion. Dad always suspected it was dirty money. You know, drug money or something like that. But he was desperate."

"So, he took the money?"

"Yes, but once he did, really weird stuff started happening. Mysterious fires broke out on the construction sites. Theft of materials went through the roof. My dad was burning through the loan and ran out of money. The construction insurance company dropped him, and before he knew it, he was out of funds again. He couldn't complete the project. Both he and his partner suspected the three rival developers, but they couldn't prove it. That's when the pressure got too much for my dad, and he had the heart attack. Killed him instantly." Donovan was looking down again, his gaze intent on his hands, his thumbs rubbing against one another.

Again, Landon was slow to respond, realizing this must be difficult for Donovan to relive, but he pressed on in hopes that this whole process was therapeutic or at least helping their friendship deepen. "What happened to your dad's partner?"

"He sued the developers."

"How did that work out?"

"It went nowhere."

"Why?"

"They lawyered up, and then after they won, they cashed in and left town."

"Just like that?" Landon asked, finding it hard to believe.

"Yes."

"Was that the end of it?"

"Well, it was for my mom," Donovan paused again and stared out toward the parking lot, his gaze distant. "Right after that, she found out she had cancer. She heard one more time from my dad's former partner. He said he would track down the thieves no matter how long it took. That he had a score to settle with one of them and that he would find them all eventually. He heard some rumor that they'd headed down here to San Diego."

He looked down at his plate, his food half-eaten. He pushed his dish away. He lowered his head into his hands and took a deep breath. He was obviously drained by what he told Landon, reliving the pain as he shared the story.

Landon was completely transfixed now and thirsty for some strange reason. He called for their waiter and ordered another round of beers. They arrived a few moments later, and he drank almost half of his in one long pull. Donovan ignored his.

Landon had run the gamut of emotions in the last few minutes. He was really perplexed why Donovan would do what he did to Foster, but he was gradually beginning to see his point of view. He continued, almost tiptoeing into his next statement. "It must have been really hard for your mom."

Donovan looked up at him with tears spattered under his eyes. He wiped them away. "Those last few months for my mom were terrible. Not only was she in excruciating pain, but she'd also lost everything. We were on welfare those last months of her life."

"I thought you had a house in Brentwood. What happened to that?"

Dad had taken out loans against it and even leveraged his life insurance policy. He put everything on the line. When Mom found out we were left with nothing, well, she was devastated. She had such dreams for our family, such dreams for us boys. They all been stolen, and my dad had been murdered. That's how she saw it, those men had killed my dad as sure as if they'd pulled out a gun and shot him. That's how I felt too. When I saw the way my mom suffered and realized that those guys had killed her dream, I took it personally. They killed my dream as well. And I vowed if I ever found them, I'd make them suffer."

Another beer arrived as if on cue, Donovan took a sip and then continued. "That's what this is all about. I hired a PI firm last year, and they found all of them. I can't tell you how great it felt to know that I could get back at Foster and the others. But I wasn't ready to tell you yet. It was just too painful, too raw. So, I just made a plan and went with it."

The waiter came over and asked about their food. They told him it was okay, but he could see that most of it was uneaten. Donovan asked him to bring the bill.

"So, I understand now. It's about revenge. It's about some sort of justice for what they did to your family," Landon said, the pieces finally falling into place.

"Exactly," Donovan said, looking directly in Landon's eyes.

Landon sipped the rest of his beer slowly to buy time to think and consider the whole matter. He could sense his own empathy for Donovan gradually brewing into a quiet rage. The waiter arrived with the bill, and

Landon stared at the beer bottle, watching the moisture drip slowly down onto the surface of the table and then pool around its bottom.

"But why did you do it the way you did? I mean, it seems like a strange way to go about revenge."

"I know. But I had thought about it for a long time, and I wanted them to feel the full impact of what they did to my family and me. I wanted them to dream like my dad did, like my mom did and then have their dreams die just before they came to fruition. It seemed to have a certain ring of poetic justice to it, don't you think?" There was a fierce satisfaction in Donovan's eyes now.

"I kind of get it," Landon admitted. "Foster's been dreaming for four months now, and then just like that, he loses it all."

"That was the goal."

"Well, I think you've attained it." Landon was still somewhat conflicted about the way they'd gone about this whole matter, but if he was honest, something deep inside him was happy to know Foster was paying for his sins. Just then his cell phone buzzed. It was a message from his assistant. He ignored it.

"So, what will you do about the other two?" he asked, curious now about the extent of Donovan's revenge plot.

"We'll hold off for now. I want to see what Foster does first."

"So that you'll know what happens to him."

"Yes, I've got someone keeping an eye on things for me," Donovan said with a cryptic smile.

Landon nodded, still sifting through everything he'd just heard, trying to piece it all together. He'd read stories about people who carried these sorts of hurts and buried them for years. He remembered in college how one of his psych professors had explained that to them. But this was the first time he'd seen it firsthand. Looking back, he could suddenly see that what he'd always assumed to be Donovan's air of mystery was this untold story, this essential part of his story he hadn't told Landon. Now that he knew it, he was seeing a whole new perspective on things.

He'd always seemed to side with those who'd been betrayed and hurt by injustice. Now he felt he was part of a real-life situation where he could see it lived out. A close friend had betrayed him years ago. It was nothing as horrific as what Donovan faced. Still, he'd struggled with the pain for months. But he'd finally just given up rather than carry the burden of it; he'd just forgiven him. He'd realized if he hadn't, he would never have been free of the torment. He guessed Donovan wasn't about to do that anytime soon. Perhaps someday he would. Maybe at the right moment, Landon could share with him how he'd gotten through his pain.

Landon looked at Donovan, realizing suddenly how much his confession was affecting him. If he thought he was loyal to the man before, it was nothing to what he felt now. He was going to do whatever he could to help Donovan put these demons to rest.

Donovan paid the bill and folded his napkin. "Shall we go?"

"Yes," Landon said. He tossed his napkin on the table and followed Donovan's lead across the restaurant.

They walked out the front door into the parking lot. The traffic was typical for this part of town in the afternoon. The lots were full of people, and the bustle of cars coming from the street nearby had a distinctive sound to it. The sun was high in the sky, and there was a slight breeze that kept the temperature at its usual mid-seventies for this time of year. The atmosphere was invigorating and echoed the freshness Landon sensed in the relationship with his longtime friend. Now that the air had been cleared, he was looking forward to a better week ahead.

As they parted ways in the parking lot, Landon couldn't help but wonder what would happen next in their revenge plot. The knowledge of what they'd done to Foster weighed on him differently now. It wasn't guilt he felt anymore, but a strange sense of complicity in something larger than himself—a story of betrayal and vengeance that had begun long before he'd entered the picture and would continue to unfold in ways he couldn't yet imagine.

CHAPTER TWENTY-ONE

SOLANA BEACH

NOVEMBER · 2000

The ringing of a phone always evoked unwelcome memories for Andrew. Perhaps the worst was when Amber called years ago, entirely out of the blue. He had no idea how she'd even found his number. He'd braced himself for anger, for bitterness, and tried to apologize before she could speak.

But instead, she said softly, "I forgive you."

Those three words hit harder than anything she could've screamed. She didn't excuse him or pretend it hadn't mattered, she just forgave him. And that, somehow, made the weight of what he'd done even heavier. Her grace carved deeper than her anger ever could have.

He'd sat in silence after she hung up, the dial tone humming like a verdict.

Then there were calls from bankers rejecting his funding requests after months of effort, or angry contractors lashing out when projects fell through, blaming his poor management skills.

These thoughts ran through Andrew's half-awake mind as his phone rang on the nightstand. He'd been gripped by another tormenting dream, one of many haunting him for weeks. In it, he stood in an ancient courtyard, barefoot on cobblestones, dressed in rags. Guards escorted him from a prison cell toward the gallows. Familiar faces circled the execution site, people he'd disappointed or betrayed over the years, their accusations spewing from bitter faces. An antique gong struck by a hooded executioner matched his footsteps, mocking him. Gradually, the gong's ring shifted pitch, becoming his modern cell phone.

Andrew emerged from his dream and reached for his phone, hoping to still the tones that had dogged his walk toward doom. He grabbed it just in time to see that it had gone to voicemail. Seeing Jimmy's name, he didn't wait for the message; he hit redial and called him back.

"Sorry, Jimmy," he said, his morning voice cracking. "I guess I just overslept." It had been something he'd been doing for the past few days, burying himself in slumber, not really looking forward to the possibility of another day of depressing news.

Thankfully, Jimmy's voice carried a ring of hope. "Well, it's good news today, Andrew," he chirped. "I've run down some of those leads I've been chasing, and I think we're close to an answer."

"That's great," Andrew squeaked out, pushing himself up on his elbows, the sheets tangled around his legs.

"Yes, so get your bones out of bed and meet me at the restaurant for breakfast in thirty minutes. I'll fill you in then."

Andrew struggled out of bed and went to the sink, splashing water on his face. Looking in the mirror, he was seriously disappointed with its effect on his countenance. He was staring back at the gritty stubble along his jawline and the wrinkles near his eyes that seemed to shriek out his age. As he shaved, he sorted through the last few days. He still hadn't heard from Nicole. To be honest, he didn't really expect to. But he was still holding out hope that his confession would garner a bit of sympathy and he'd get some sort of signal from her. He continued to fight the urge to call her. He needed to respect her space for her to process as well.

At least he had Jade and his time with Chandler on the beach. They'd been therapeutic. He knew he was supposed to be there for the boy, but to be honest, he was the one being helped. They were meeting on Saturdays now that school was back in session, and he was looking forward to some much-needed therapy, making sandcastles, and answering Chandler's questions. He cared for that boy so much; he'd do anything to help him. Then there was Jade. She'd been so good to him, and helping her with Chandler had turned out to be an unexpected blessing. He'd always be grateful for the grace she brought into his life that day, years ago, in Joshua Tree. She had sat and listened to his heartache, offering the words he needed to hear. It was amazing what a great friend she'd been to him over the years. He'd heard people tell him that they'd been estranged from their siblings. That was sad to him. Jade and he had always been there for each other; she more for him, but he knew if she ever needed him, he'd be there.

He jumped into the shower, and the steamy stream of water quickly chased away all his agonizing ruminations. Half an hour later, he was sipping coffee and reading a menu at L'Auberge with Jimmy, looking out at the ocean as a ridge of fog slipped westward. Below them, beside the pool, people were lounging in the hazy sunlight filtering through the last bit of morning mist. It wasn't hot enough for most of them to take the plunge. A few were still wrapped in the lovely white robes the hotel provided. Others were lathering on sunblock. It was one of those days that made this coastal town a welcome destination for the rich. Andrew wished he had the money to enjoy some of what this great place offered, but such hopes were now distant dreams. His internal pity party was interrupted when their waiter arrived.

"What will it be, guys?" the waiter asked, pen poised over his notepad.

Andrew looked at Jimmy sheepishly. He hadn't picked this spot to meet. In years past, he'd enjoyed splurging here, but not now. His bank account was empty, and he wasn't about to put any more on his Amex card.

"I've got this," Jimmy said and then pointed to the menu. "I'll have the Eggs Benedict and wheat toast."

"Same for me," Andrew said. The waiter smiled and took their menus before walking away.

Jimmy sipped his coffee and set his cup down on the white tablecloth. "So, you've been sleeping in? That isn't like you, buddy."

"I know. Things are caving in on me. I'm hardly sleeping, and when I do, well, I'd rather not wake up." Andrew stared into his coffee cup, the dark liquid reflecting his mood.

"I hope you're not drinking too much." Jimmy's concern was evident in his voice.

"No, just a few beers in the evening. No dinner. That seems enough to get me into a stupor. Then I wake up around midnight and can't sleep for a few hours. Finally, I drift off around three. It's just been a nightmare. So, your call was a welcome respite."

"Well, I don't want you to get your hopes up. But I think I've got something solid." Jimmy's eyes gleamed with the thrill of the chase.

"Great. Let's hear it." Andrew leaned forward, desperate for anything that would shed light on his situation.

"First, I checked with the leasing agency that handles the suites in Franklin Tower. They gave me the runaround, claiming they can't divulge their clients' information. So, I had Frank Marshal, one of my friends at the PD, give them a call, and after a little intimidation, they coughed up the name."

"What was it?" Andrew asked, his heart quickening.

"They're called Kryvo Development. They're up in the Bay Area and part of a larger conglomerate with outlets around the country. It's really a labyrinth of networks and shell companies. There's nothing illegal, but there's a clear intent of keeping anyone from finding out who's at the top. I've got a friend who specializes in these types of searches, and he's running down all the possible links. It may take him a few days, but he's always come up with a source for me."

Andrew was deeply touched that Jimmy had expended so much time on his problem. He was reminded once again how indebted he was to his friend, and he responded with as much sincerity as he could express. "That's great news, Jimmy. I know I've said it before, but I really appreciate what you're doing for me. I hope you know how much this means to me."

"You're like family," Jimmy said, his voice gruff with emotion.

"I know, but I don't have any way of repaying you."

Jimmy took another sip of his coffee, set the cup down, and leaned toward Andrew. "I've never expected any sort of reciprocity on this matter. If there's one thing I've learned in all my years, it's that you help your close friends. I've only got a handful of people who have been in my life as long as you. I treasure each of those relationships."

"Well, I know that I can never repay you for this, but I'll go the extra mile if you ever need my help."

"I know you would, bro, and that's the best payment a guy could ever get."

Andrew looked out toward the ocean. "Thanks," he said sincerely.

Jimmy smiled back and followed his glance. The last wisps of fog had melted away from the horizon, and the sunlight sparkled on the water of the pool below them. It was creating tiny gems of light that danced their way, almost as if to confirm the one thing that was crystal clear in Andrew's dark world right now: good friends who go the distance with you.

Jimmy bent back, stretching and then leaning forward. He rested his elbows on the table, bringing the focus back to the matter at hand. "The next bit of good news is that I've located someone who may have been on the staff at Teknon 2."

"You've actually found someone?" Andrew's voice rose with excitement.

"Yes. I figured that if they set up a false company, they might have hired some temps. So, I had my secretary check with every agency in the area. She got a hit on the fourth call. It seems that they sent a gal over to Franklin Tower four months ago. They wouldn't give any details on the company that hired her, but they did slip up and give us her name."

"And what was it?" Andrew held his breath, waiting for the answer.

Jimmy took a couple of heartbeats to reply, relishing the anticipation of his following statement. "Briana," he whispered, his mouth pleasantly savoring the word as if it were an appetizer.

"That's the name on the sticky note we found," Andrew said, nearly spitting out the sip of coffee he'd just taken.

"Right," Jimmy confirmed, a satisfied smile spreading across his face.

"So, what are we going to do?"

"Well, that's the 'sticky' part," Jimmy said, amused at his play on words. "We've got to be careful approaching this gal, but my secretary, Juanita, came up with a great idea. Seems she's been needing some more help around the office and might be looking for a temp worker."

"Perfect." Andrew could feel a surge of hope rising in his chest for the first time in weeks.

"She's having Victor, one of my associate PIs, make the call later today."

"Well, things are looking up indeed," Andrew said, allowing himself a moment of cautious optimism.

Just then, their food arrived, and they thanked their waiter and started on their eggs. After a few bites, Jimmy continued. "The final bit of good news is that I've got the report back from the lab on those prints. They belong to some drug dealer."

"How did you find him?" Andrew asked, his fork pausing halfway to his mouth.

"I located a DA up in Monterey County; Ash has a rap sheet a mile long. At first, he was reluctant to share any information, but it turned out we had a mutual friend from the force, and he opened up after discovering that. I'd explained to him that we'd found this guy's prints on a window here in San Diego. He said the guy's got a million aliases. His real name is Shane Samuelson. He said he'd email a full report on the guy later in the week. It turns out this Samuelson guy was a big-time drug dealer with links to one of the syndicates out of Laguna Beach."

Andrew reached for his coffee with both hands, hoping to suppress the sudden trembling that had come into his body. He knew that name, and the mention of Laguna, well, that was a different matter altogether. But for now, he couldn't go there. So, he shut out those fears and turned back to the conversation. "So how do the fingerprints from some con end up on the window of a high-rise in La Jolla?"

Jimmy crossed his arms and leaned back in his chair. "That's an enigma to me as well. The DA said this Samuelson is still in prison. He also said, this Samuelson guy is involved with some hippie syndicate, The Sons Of Malku, with a leader they call the Omraxis. Really heavy into the occult.

The officer's teams are working on some leads, and he promised to get back to me if he finds anything."

"This is really freaky, Jimmy," Andrew said, setting his cup down on the table. Some of the coffee spilled, staining the white tablecloth. He moved his saucer to cover it.

"I know. That got me thinking about those prints. They were in such an obvious place. The whole office had been swept clean, and they missed those? Totally freaky. But for now, that seems to be all the information we've got on this guy. I should know more once that email arrives."

Andrew was grateful for Jimmy's efforts, but he wondered where these new revelations would lead. He tried his best to put a good face on his response, but inside, he was shaken. "This is great news," he said, trying his best to hide the hesitation in his voice.

"Well, I'm not sure where this is all heading, but at least we've got some leads." Jimmy stabbed at his last piece of egg.

"Let me know if I can do anything."

"Nothing right now, but when I find out where this whole thing leads, you're going to have to decide how we're going to confront this situation. But don't do anything rash," Jimmy warned, tilting across the table with a look of worry in his eyes.

"I won't, but I am going to demand answers," Andrew said, a hardness creeping into his voice.

"Okay, but I'm going to be there too."

"I wouldn't think of doing it without you."

"Good, I'm looking forward to seeing you get some satisfaction on this matter."

"Thanks again." Andrew changed the subject and asked about Jimmy's wife and kids. Jimmy shared the joys of fatherhood between bites, and Andrew soon found himself wishing he'd made the same choices Jimmy did to get married and have a family.

Twenty minutes later, they'd finished their meal, and Jimmy had paid the bill. Standing outside the front entrance, Andrew told him goodbye with a hug as Jimmy waited for the valet to bring his car. Andrew's was parked down the hill, a block away, and on the street. He told Jimmy he was going to walk for a while and reflect on everything Jimmy had told him.

Andrew strolled back through the lobby and then down the hallway leading south. Once outside, he turned right and headed down the hill toward the park. The beach was on its right, a short distance from the L'Auberge, and he was soon caught up in the feel of sea breeze and sand beneath his feet. As he walked along, he found himself staring west, gazing out at the apparent horizon, empty of the previous fog, but wondering about the murkiness that was now filling his mind. But slowly as he walked along, he found his thoughts clearing.

Then, almost as marvelously as the warming sun melting away the bank of fog, everything became clear.

The name Shane Samuelson had triggered something in the recesses of his memory. Now, as the Pacific stretched endlessly before him, the pieces were starting to fit together in a way that made his blood run cold. He stopped walking, his feet sinking deeper into the sand as the waves continued their relentless rhythm against the shore. The morning sun was warm on his face, but Andrew felt a chill run through him as realization dawned. He knew who was behind this.

CHAPTER TWENTY-TWO

MOUNT SHASTA

JUNE · 1969

The mountain watched them.

Andrew felt it even through the lingering haze of the morning's joint, a presence that pressed against his skin like the chill from his last dive into the glacier-blue lake. Mount Shasta loomed in the distance, its snow-covered peak piercing clouds that writhed around it like smoke from some ancient fire. Beautiful. Terrible. Full of secrets that had drawn their small band of seekers to this pristine wilderness.

Ash leaned against the stone outcrop; eyes fixed on the canopy above like he was waiting for it to whisper something back. "The Amstel brothers weren't just tripping," he said. "They knew things."

Phillip raised an eyebrow. "You mean the houseboat guys?"

"Yeah. Out past gate six. They guided some of the bands in the Bay Area, LSD, chanting, transcendence. Real scene-makers. Then one day they disappeared. Moved up here, somewhere near Mount Shasta."

Andrew glanced at him. "They're still around?"

Ash nodded. "Yeah. Their place has turned into a kind of retreat. Some of the musicians still go up there, quietly. It's not on the maps. But they say the mountain pulses with power. That it sits on a convergence point, energy lines, ancient ley channels, whatever you want to call it."

There was something off in his tone. Not just awe, something thinner, glassy.

Andrew noticed a faint tremor in Ash's fingers. His pupils were too wide for daylight. His skin had a waxy pallor, as if he hadn't been eating or sleeping enough.

"They introduced me to the Sons of Malku," Ash went on. "Not just burnouts. These people are serious. They discuss contact forces that predate any religion. They believe they're conduits."

Phillip gave a short laugh, but it didn't carry. "Sounds like a cult."

Ash didn't blink. "Their leader's called the Omraxis. He's not just spiritual, he's scientific. He claims to have merged Eastern mysticism with quantum physics and genetics. They put me through this whole program, showed how ancient pagan worship connects to modern chromosomal theory. Like the old rites were trying to unlock something buried in the human code."

His voice didn't rise or fall. Just steady. Too steady.

Andrew watched him closely now. Ash hadn't blinked once. His breath came shallow, too regular, like someone holding still in a role they weren't entirely controlling anymore.

And then the memory returned.

Two weeks ago. The Kettle Café.

Ash had leaned across the table, hands unmoving around a cold espresso.

His voice had been flat, matter-of-fact:

"They trained me to summon forces at will."

Phillip had laughed. Andrew had smiled, uncomfortable, thinking Ash was just off on another fringe tangent.

They weren't laughing now.

The girls, Kimberly, Michelle, and Blaire, sunned themselves on nearby rocks, their tan bodies still glistening from the lake. Blaire was Ash's, and everyone knew to keep their eyes elsewhere. Even the mountain seemed to bend away from her radiance.

From the campsite, smoke twisted in the wind, bringing the smell of Philip's cooking. He always had eggs and bacon when he was high. Always.

"Getting on my nerves," Ash muttered, just loud enough for Andrew to hear.

Andrew thought of the drive up, Philip's careful pace in the VW van, Ash's constant needling. And that night as they passed Corning, something had flashed between them. Andrew could have sworn he'd seen Ash's eyes fill with red light before Philip cried out about being stung. Just a trick of the dashboard lights. Had to be.

But here, under the mountain's shadow, Andrew wasn't so sure.

That evening, they jammed around the fire, guitars and flute weaving through old blues standards. The pot had brought them together, unified in the music until Philip refused to yield his lead.

Twelve bars passed. Then another twelve. Philip kept playing, possessed by some inner force. The girls swayed, entranced. "You're really cooking, Phil," Blaire purred, her body moving like smoke.

Andrew saw it building in Ash's eyes, that same red glow from the van. Brighter now. Angrier. The air between them seemed to thicken, and Andrew found himself leaning back, sensing what was coming.

The ember struck Philip's hand like a tiny meteor.

"Yeow!" Philip dropped his guitar, a black mark scorched into its neck.

"Must have been a spark from the fire," Ash said, his voice silk over steel. "Pine logs can spit sometimes."

The girls fussed over Philip, Blaire hiking up her skirt to apply cool lake water to his burns. Ash watched, his jaw tight, until he pulled out the leather pouch from around his neck.

"Best peyote you'll ever have," he announced. "An Indian shaman blessed it specifically for this place. Under this mountain."

They all took the buttons. The sickness came first, Kimberly stumbling to the lake to retch, Philip vomiting directly into the fire. The smell made Andrew's stomach turn, but he held it down.

Then the visions began.

Stars exploded in kaleidoscope patterns. The fire shrank to a pinpoint, then swelled until it filled the world. Ash transformed into something bear-like with an eagle's face, regal and terrible. The girls became felines with scales and fur that shifted in the firelight.

All except Philip, who writhed on his mat like a wounded snake.

"My fingers are on fire," he hissed. "The pain's spreading everywhere."

"Let it take you," Ash commanded. "Don't fight it."

But Philip couldn't stop fighting. His cries pierced the night until Ash rose, and the red energy radiated from his entire being.

"I won't let you ruin this for everyone," Ash said.

"Your sorcerer's tricks don't scare me," Philip spat back.

Andrew watched, frozen, as the energy leaped from Ash and enveloped Philip. Like a puppet on invisible strings, Philip lurched toward the fire. He fell into the flames, rolling, screaming, before some unseen force expelled him into the darkness.

A splash. Whimpers. Then silence.

"He'll be fine," Ash said, his authority absolute. "I'll take him a blanket later."

By dawn, Philip lay by the lake wrapped in wool, breath misting in the cold air. He returned subdued, almost robotic, his minor burns treated with Blaire's herbs. The magic of the night had evaporated like morning dew, leaving only a strange, sober heaviness.

They packed in silence and headed south.

At a stop near Dunsmuir, Andrew finally asked: "Those things the Amstel brothers taught you—did you use them on Philip?"

Ash studied him. "What you saw was real. As real as rockets to the moon, just from a different realm. They even gave me a new name for my new life."

"What's your real name then?"

Ash pulled out a crumpled business card from his days selling cars in Menlo Park. "Take it. A memento."

Back in the van, wedged between Michelle and Kimberly, Andrew examined the card:

Menlo Park—Foreign Car Sales - Shane Samuelson, salesman

He stared at the name, feeling a chill that had nothing to do with mountain air. Somehow, he knew this card would matter. He just didn't know how much.

The mountain receded behind them, but Andrew felt its presence still, watching, waiting, keeping its secrets.

CHAPTER TWENTY-THREE

SAN DIEGO

NOVEMBER · 2000

The phone had rung at seven-thirty that morning. Jimmy's voice carried something Andrew hadn't heard in weeks, hope.

"Andrew, I think we're getting somewhere," Jimmy had said, his tone warm and reassuring, like a lifeline tossed to a drowning man. "Meet me at the coffee shop in the UTC Mall. Noon."

"Thank God." Andrew had felt his shoulders drop, tension he hadn't even realized he'd been carrying suddenly releasing. "Tell me what you've found."

"Not yet." Jimmy's voice held that sage-like calm, the patient wisdom of someone who knew when to wait. "You need to hear the whole story first. No jumping to conclusions. No making plans until you have all the pieces. Trust me on this, Andrew."

Now, one hour later, Andrew merged onto the 5 South, the Pacific a flickering silver ribbon to his right. The morning commute moved in waves, and the coastal air streaming through his half-open window carried the faint scent of eucalyptus and sea salt.

A digital sign flashed overhead, warning of slowing ahead near the Del Mar Heights exit. Andrew glanced in the rearview mirror, catching his own tired reflection, creased brow, thinning patience. Somewhere between the fading morning fog and the rising tension in his chest, he wondered how many more betrayals he could survive.

He passed the UTC without really seeing it, Jimmy's words replaying in his head like a refrain. Whatever he'd uncovered about Teknon's disappearance, it was significant. The Teknon team had disappeared overnight, phones disconnected, emails bouncing back, even their building lease terminated without a trace. It was as if they'd never existed, and Andrew was the only one who believed they were real. Maybe, just maybe, Andrew wouldn't have to carry this disaster alone much longer.

But first, he had to survive the morning.

Jeff Clark at nine. The Coastal Commission at ten-thirty. Three city council members are slotted throughout the week. Each meeting felt like stepping into a minefield of his own making, every handshake another act of professional penance, another apology for the impossible.

The morning fog hung heavy over San Diego Bay as Andrew navigated through downtown toward the waterfront, Clark Communications occupied prime real estate in one of the sleek high-rises overlooking the harbor. Over the years, Jeff had built his PR firm into a powerhouse, and Andrew had been happy to throw smaller development projects his way when he could. It had been a good working relationship, Jeff got steady business, Andrew got solid PR support.

Which made today even worse. This time, Jeff had really gone out of his way for Andrew.

He'd called ahead to make sure Nicole was out on assignment. Their relationship remained suspended in limbo, another casualty of the Teknon disaster. The last thing he needed was to navigate those emotional waters while trying to face Jeff.

Jeff's corner office commanded a view that would have been spectacular on a clear day, the harbor spread out below, Coronado Island in the distance, Navy ships dotting the gray water. Today, the fog reduced visibility to mere suggestions of shapes. The view matched Jeff's expression as his assistant showed Andrew in.

"Sit," Jeff said, not getting up from behind his mahogany desk. The usual warmth was gone, replaced by something Andrew had never seen directed at him before, cold fury barely held in check.

"Jeff, I…"

"Do you have any idea what position you've put me in?" Jeff's voice was controlled, but Andrew could hear the anger underneath. "I vouched for you. I brought in Helix Strategies specifically for this project. Do you know what it took to get them interested? They specialize in biotech, medical research, and pharmaceutical launches. They don't do real estate. But I convinced them that Precipice was different, that Teknon's environmental technology made this a game-changer worth their time."

Andrew's stomach churned. He knew all this, but hearing it laid out made it worse.

"I hosted meetings in this office," Jeff continued, his hands flat on the desk. "I put my reputation on the line. I told them that Andrew Foster doesn't make mistakes; if he says a project is solid, you can bank on it. And now? Now I've got Helix threatening to pull their entire account. Not just Precipice, everything. Three pharmaceutical launches that my firm desperately needs."

"Jeff, I'm sorry. If I could …"

"You can't." Jeff cut him off. "That's the problem. Teknon is gone, and I'm the idiot who championed a phantom project to one of the most prestigious PR firms in medical research. They think I'm either incompetent or was in on some kind of scam."

Andrew felt each word like a physical blow. Over the years, he'd brought Jeff probably a half a dozen smaller projects, strip malls, office complexes, residential developments. Steady work that had helped Jeff build his firm. And Jeff had returned the favor by putting his credibility behind Precipice.

"I've spent hours on the phone in damage control mode," Jeff said, leaning back in his chair. "Helix finally agreed not to pull their other accounts, but only after I personally guaranteed to cover any losses they incurred from the Precipice planning phase. Do you have any idea what that's costing me?"

Andrew knew better than to ask for a number. It would only make things worse.

"The irony is," Jeff's laugh was bitter, "I actually believed in the project. Your presentation on their state-of-the-art medical research center was brilliant. Even the Helix team was impressed, and they've seen every kind of innovation pitch in the medical field. But it was all smoke and mirrors, wasn't it?"

"I believed it too," Andrew said quietly. "Every word."

Jeff studied him for a long moment. "I know you did. That's the only reason you're sitting here instead of talking to my lawyers." He rubbed his temples. "Look, we go back too far for me to burn you completely. But this is it, Andrew. Whatever friendship we had, whatever professional relationship we've built over the years, it's done. I can't afford to trust you again."

Andrew nodded. He'd expected nothing less.

"And one more thing," Jeff added as Andrew stood to leave. "Nicole doesn't know how bad this got with Helix. I prefer to keep it that way. She respects you, or at least she did. No need to poison that well any more than necessary."

The dismissal was apparent. Andrew left the office feeling the weight of another bridge burning behind him. Jeff had risked his firm's most crucial new client relationship on Andrew's word, and now he was paying the price.

The meeting with Bill Atkins yesterday had followed a similar script. The contractor had shown up at Andrew's office, his face dark with barely controlled anger. Bill had reminded him of every work-up, every estimate, every hour his team had spent preparing for a project that would never break ground.

"You're lucky I've got that casino project keeping my crews busy," Bill had said, his calloused hands gripping the arms of the chair. "Otherwise, I'd be coming after you for breach of contract. As it is..." He'd stood up, towering over Andrew's desk. "We've known each other, what, fifteen years? That's the only reason you're not talking to my lawyer right now. But we're done, Andrew. Don't call me again."

Two good men. Two burned bridges. And Andrew had a week full of similar meetings ahead, the Coastal Commission, which'd fast-tracked permits based on Teknon-backed promises of environmental innovation; the city planning department, which'd revised zoning regulations; the county supervisors, who'd championed the project as a model for sustainable development. Each one would want answers Andrew didn't have, explanations for how a company could simply evaporate, leaving him as the sole bearer of responsibility.

But he'd soon be sitting across from Jimmy in that mall coffee shop. Whatever his friend had discovered, it had been enough to change the tone of his voice, to inject hope where there had been only resignation.

Andrew checked his watch as he walked to his car. The Coastal Commission meeting would be brutal, but it was just one more stone in the avalanche of consequences from Teknon's betrayal. He had to keep moving, keep apologizing, keep taking responsibility for the phantom company that had played them all.

Jimmy's call this morning had been the first good news in days. Whatever he'd found, it had better be substantial. Andrew wasn't sure how many more of these meetings he could survive with his sanity intact.

He just had to make it to eleven.

Five minutes after leaving Jeff's office, Andrew was in his car, driving to the Coastal Commission's offices in Mission Valley. It was well past rush hour, and the traffic was lighter than its usual crawl. It gave him time to review what had just gone down and prepare a little bit for what was to come.

The meeting with the Coastal Commission was as tricky as it was short. He arrived at their Mission Valley offices in decent time, but he was out the door in twenty minutes. They'd listened to his explanations about the delays, his assurances about the environmental impact studies, but their attention was clearly elsewhere. The controversy surrounding the Children's Pool Beach in La Jolla had exploded in the headlines, the endless battle between seal advocates and beach access supporters consuming all their bandwidth.

"We'll get back to you, Mr. Foster," the commissioner had said, already shuffling papers for the next meeting. "The harbor seal situation has to take priority right now. You understand."

Andrew understood all right. He realized his project was being pushed further down their priority list as baby seals garnered more attention than biomedical research facilities.

When he arrived at the UTC Mall, he managed to find a spot on the lower deck of the parking lot and then made his way through a throng of shoppers to the coffee shop. True to his usual punctual self, Jimmy had arrived a few minutes before Andrew. He was smiling, which was a great sign.

"Hello, bro," Andrew greeted him, the tension in his shoulders already easing at the sight of his friend. "Don't get up. Can I buy you a latte?"

"You know me better than that, hermano," Jimmy punctuated with a laugh. "A small dark roast with a little cream."

"Okay. I'll be right back."

The coffee shop was bustling with midday customers, a mix of shoppers taking a break and business people having informal meetings. The aroma of freshly ground beans and baked goods enveloped Andrew as he waited in line. Five minutes later, he returned with their drinks.

When they finally got settled at one of the nearby tables, Andrew wasted no time starting in with questions. "So, what did you find?" he asked, leaning forward eagerly.

Jimmy took a sip of his coffee before answering, savoring both the moment and the brew. "It's pretty amazing the way these guys set up this whole scenario. It must have taken them a lot of effort. My IT man finally sorted through all the false leads and concluded that a for-hire group put together this Teknon 2 Partners website out of Eastern Europe. They've been able to cover their tracks well, but the source finally led back to a company called Lasseter Enterprises with headquarters here in La Jolla's Golden Triangle, not that far from the Franklin. They're located in the

Brenton Tower." He spoke quietly, his eyes scanning the room occasionally to ensure no one was listening.

"That's great," Andrew said, his voice low but intense. "Now what about this Hayden Quinn guy?"

"That's the other interesting development. Remember the sticky note with the name Briana on it?"

"Of course."

"Well, my assistant, Juanita, did hire her and quickly got into her confidence."

"How did she get her to talk?" Andrew asked, impressed by the efficacy of Jimmy's team.

"She had my IT guy go to Lasseter Enterprises' web page. She had him print out a few pictures of some of the lead players over there. She started leaving copies on her desk, and Briana walked by and recognized one of them. She asked what a picture of her former boss was doing on Juanita's desk. She made up some story about him being part of my peers' group and that we were going to honor him. Juanita's got a curious sense of humor. She has the funniest way of covering some things up."

"So, who is he? I mean what's his name?" Andrew pressed, his coffee cooling and forgotten in front of him.

"His name's Landon Strand. But he's just the VP at Lasseter. I'm sure he didn't put this whole thing together on his own. It's got to be his boss."

"How would you know that?" Andrew's brow furrowed in confusion.

"Hang on, it gets better." Jimmy leaned in closer, his voice dropping to just above a whisper. "Turns out Briana ran into one of her old coworkers at Teknon 2. Her name's Abbey. They exchanged contact info and agreed to go out for drinks. So, Juanita invited herself along to their little reunion.

After a few drinks, this Abbey girl starts to talk. Says she's back at her boss's old office in the Brenton. The moving thing had her perplexed. First, they leave their offices in the Brenton and move into the Franklin. Four months later, her supervisor instructs her to report to her old desk in the Brenton instead of the Franklin. She thought it was weird but didn't ask any questions. She says the pay is great, and she likes her job and wants to keep it."

"Did she tell her anything else?" Andrew took a small sip of his coffee, his eyes never leaving Jimmy's face.

"Yes, Abbey also said that she spent most of her time working on stuff for Lasseter and that she only handled one new client at the Franklin. That struck Abbey as odd."

"How so?"

"Well, odd that they would move several of their staff and offices to the Franklin for just that one new client. This goes all the way to the top." Jimmy's eyes gleamed with the thrill of the chase.

"Who was the new client?" Andrew already knew but needed to hear it.

Jimmy grinned. "Foster and The Precipice project."

"Bingo!" Andrew gave Jimmy a high-five, drawing curious glances from nearby tables. "That's it. You've found the connection! I can't believe you did it. Thanks so much."

"Well, it really wasn't me. It was my staff. If you want to thank someone, then send Juanita some flowers and buy my IT guy a set of tickets to the next Star Trek movie."

"Gladly," Andrew said, his face animated with excitement for the first time in days.

"So, it looks like we've found the source. What do you want to do now?" Jimmy asked, his expression turning serious.

Before Andrew replied, he had a question. "One more thing. Any more about this Samuelson guy?"

"Nothing yet. I spoke with his PO, and he still hasn't heard from him."

"Well, guess what?" Andrew said, his voice dropping even lower. "Remember back when we were in school, and I was giving you a little of my history?"

"Yes, that was ages ago."

"Well, I think I told you about this Ash guy that I hung out with during my druggie days. He had a lot of names."

"Oh yeah, I remember. You said he was a real spooky guy." Jimmy's eyes widened in recognition.

"Well, the name you gave me the other day, Shane Samuelson." Andrew paused, letting the name hang in the air between them.

"Yes."

"That was Ash's real name."

"What!" Jimmy's exclamation caused a woman at the following table to look over. He lowered his voice. "Okay, so why are his fingerprints showing up here?"

"I don't know, but it's not a coincidence." Andrew ran a hand through his hair, a nervous gesture he'd started to develop. "I never forgot that name."

"Why would he be linked up with this Lasseter outfit? Maybe he's a silent partner? Maybe they're related?"

"Remember, when you asked me when this whole thing started with the SUV about enemies. It was so long ago. I never thought Ash and I would ever cross paths again, but now my past may be catching up with me." The realization sent a chill down Andrew's spine despite the coffee shop's warmth.

"The whole thing just keeps getting weirder by the minute." Jimmy shook his head, bewildered by these new connections.

"But now at least I've got some answers."

"So, where do we go from here?" Jimmy asked, already shifting into action mode.

"I need to confront this Strand guy and find out why they did this." Andrew's voice hardened with determination.

"When?" asked Jimmy.

"As soon as possible."

"Okay, just call me when you're ready. You're not going alone." Jimmy's tone made it clear this wasn't up for debate.

"Thanks for being available. I'm going to need some moral support." Andrew felt a surge of gratitude for his friend's unwavering loyalty.

"I'll be bringing more than that," Jimmy said, patting his side beneath his coat. "I'll be packing some heat. I have a feeling you'll need some protection."

"I never thought that my past and present would collide like this." Andrew stared out the coffee shop window at the bustling mall, feeling oddly detached from the everyday life unfolding around them. "Looking back to four months ago, life wasn't great, but I never felt like my life was in danger. I never thought the dreams that haunted me would actually show up in real life."

"One last thing," Jimmy said, finishing his coffee. "I did some research on the Brenton. You need clearance to get past their security. But don't worry. There's a firm in the building that I've done business with in the past, and they've already added me to the visitors list. Once we're in the elevator, we'll just bypass his floor and go right to Lasseter."

Andrew nodded, his mind already rehearsing the confrontation ahead. The pieces were finally falling into place, but the picture they revealed was far more menacing than he had imagined. The ghosts of his past weren't just haunting his dreams anymore, they had materialized in his waking life, and they had come with a vengeance.

Outside the coffee shop, the sun was shining brightly now, all traces of morning fog burned away. But for Andrew, a different kind of fog was only beginning to lift, revealing a landscape far more treacherous than he had anticipated.

CHAPTER TWENTY-FOUR

ENCINITAS

NOVEMBER · 2000

A hush fell over the beach as the sun met the horizon, and if the timing was just right, the green flash could be seen, for just a moment, the last remaining nub of the sun suddenly turned the color of emerald and then vanished as the last bit of light slipped beneath the horizon. It affected those who saw it differently, some gasping in awe while others shrugged and said, "That's cool," but for Andrew, it seemed to offer a sort of promise, like the old tale about the bucket of gold at the end of the rainbow or the good luck that comes from finding a four-leaf clover. To him, that emerald flash had always heralded the end of a great day with the promise of a better one to come. Though he wasn't Irish, it was interesting that all his metaphors of luck came from those folktales that had originated on that tiny green Gaelic island across the ocean.

Sitting on one of the weathered benches overlooking Swami's beach, Andrew recalled all that had transpired over the last four months, amazed at the twists and turns, high points and low points his life had been through in a third of a year, and now all those memories flowed by, one after another, like the row of breakers crashing on the beach below, each wave bringing with it a different impression as it spilled across his consciousness.

There was the elation that came with the check from Teknon 2 Partners and the way it raised a flood of hope in him. He saw the joy that was on Nicole's face during their last date together before everything came crashing in on him.

Following that came a current of painful thoughts as he recalled the confusion he sensed when he stood on the Precipice development site and wondered why Quinn hadn't shown up. Next, there was the shock of the empty office in Franklin Tower and the utter confusion that washed over him when he realized he'd been deceived.

But overall, this evening, there was a sense of closure pushing its way toward him, as sure and as steady as an incoming tide. This matter would be resolved by tomorrow; he was sure of it. Jimmy had been lucky so far with what he'd found. They got the break they needed. Andrew was trusting his good fortune would hold. The sun passed into the sea as he got up to leave. A ruby haze had covered the horizon, so there would be no green flash tonight.

Five hours and two beers later, Andrew was trying to go back to sleep after being awakened from another set of nocturnal torments. In each one, he was flat on a surfboard, something he hadn't done in years, stroking with all his might, doing his best to catch a wave. Each time, he missed it just as it crested, and he dipped back into the after-wake. But something kept driving him to try to ride the next one. Over and over, he attempted the same vain effort, only to slip down the back of every wake.

With each effort, the sea grew darker and more menacing. Black-skinned predators appeared, their fins slashing through the water. They seemed to grow in number with every endeavor until he was surrounded by a frenzy of sharks homing in on him. That's when he awoke, drenched in sweat, the smell of stale beer and perspiration assaulting his senses. He pulled himself out of bed and made his way to the bathroom. A set of cold-water splashes shocked him out of his lingering delirium, a self-prescribed therapy that was becoming all too routine.

Andrew stared at the ceiling, restless. The resolve he found at Swami's Beach still held, he would confront Quinn and anyone else behind the deception. He'd already texted Jimmy to meet him at ten at Brenton Tower in La Jolla. Jimmy had pulled strings to get them in but hadn't said a word to Strand. Still, that was hours away. What mattered now was getting some rest so he'd be sharp for what lay ahead.

Sleep finally came, but it was short-lived. He awoke from a nightmare, heart pounding. In the dream, he stood in the middle of his street. It was dark, the streetlight blinking through the swaying limbs of a tree. One by one, black SUVs tore toward him, each swerving at the last moment, until the final one. It emerged from a smoky cloud of burning rubber, its ghostly driver holding the vehicle in place like a beast waiting to strike. Then its brakes screamed, and it barreled at him with no sign of turning. Just before it hit, he jolted awake, drenched in sweat and certain he wouldn't sleep again.

To settle himself, Andrew paced the apartment, poured a glass of chilled water, and stood by the window. The street rose the hill, lined with quiet, parked cars. Then he saw it: the shape that had haunted him so many nights. At the crest, partially obscured by fog, sat a black SUV, still, watchful, familiar. His pulse quickened. It looked just like the Range Rover from his visions, crouched in silence.

He had to be sure. Throwing on jeans and a jacket, he stepped out into the cold marine air and climbed the incline. As he neared the vehicle, its outline sharpened. Same shape, same size, same gloss-black paint, but a different brand. Not a Range Rover after all. His breath escaped in a long, unsteady exhale. Just another SUV. His mind had been playing tricks again.

Back inside, he showered, shaved, and dressed with purpose. Whatever else the day might bring, he would meet it head-on. First, breakfast at Hide Away Café in Solana Beach. Then, the confrontation that might finally shed light on all of this.

As he stepped out into the street and headed for his car, the early morning breeze seeped through his lightweight, casual tan blazer and brought on a shiver. He was wearing his semi-dress shoes, with dark socks and his best blue jeans. He jumped into his car and headed toward the top of the hill. As he passed each vehicle on his left, their shadowy exteriors, ghost-like in the fog, troubled him. Turn back, there's only terror and more pain ahead, they seemed to declare, prophesying his demise. But he ignored them and stepped on the accelerator, determined to face his fate and whatever lay at the top of the hill.

Just as he reached the crest of the street, he saw it clearly. Parked along the curb with its wheels turned in was the same black Chevy Suburban he had investigated the night before. It confirmed what he'd already discovered, it wasn't a threat. Just an old vehicle, ordinary and still. A phantom born of his own spiraling dread. Still, the relief wasn't immediate. The voices, the accusations, they were lies, he reminded himself. Smoke screens from hell meant to rattle his resolve and keep him from his appointment with the swine at Lasseter Enterprises. But they wouldn't hold. They'd crumble beneath the weight of his demand for justice, just like the fear that had clung to that Suburban. In the east, the sky seemed to nod in agreement, its deepening orange glow hinting that dawn was near.

Twenty minutes later, Andrew parked on the street and made his way to L'Auberge in Del Mar. The morning sun shimmered off the ocean as he joined Jimmy at a quiet corner table on the terrace, away from the hum of other diners. They had agreed to meet over breakfast to go over their approach and then ride over together in Jimmy's car.

"You made it, hermano," Jimmy said with a grin as Andrew approached the table. "How are the nerves? You look a little green around the gills."

"It's been a bad night," Andrew admitted as he sat down. "But, yeah, I'm ready."

Jimmy leaned in, concern softening his tone. "What happened?"

Andrew gave a tired smile. "Some old demons stopped by. It was rough, but I beat them back."

"You'll have to tell me about it sometime."

Andrew shook his head. "Not worth rehashing. I'm done giving it space."

Jimmy nodded. "So, you're ready then?"

"I can't wait to get this over with," Andrew said, jaw tight with resolve.

One hour later, after a hearty and much-needed breakfast and a drive up the coast, Jimmy pulled into the parking garage beneath the Brenton Tower. They took the elevator to the main lobby, immediately struck by the building's imposing grandeur. A massive bronze and glass sculpture spiraled upward in the center of the soaring atrium, something between a hawk and a phantom, twisting toward the skylights above. Walls of glass and acid-washed steel loomed like sentinels, echoing wealth and power.

At the far end of the lobby, a row of elevators stood behind a sleek security desk operated by a hulking guard in a pristine uniform. Jimmy looked at them and back at Andrew with a knowing glance and a nod. No words were needed this time.

They walked over to the reception desk and spoke to the guard. "We're here for a ten o'clock appointment with Gallagher's Associates," announced

Jimmy with confidence. He'd done several PI jobs for Gallagher's over the years.

"Yes, Mr. Ramirez and Foster," said the guard, scanning the computer screen mounted on a flat area behind the polished wall of the reception counter.

"That's us," affirmed Jimmy.

"Take the elevator to the tenth floor."

"Thanks," they both said and walked to the row of elevators. A directory was embossed in gold letters on the granite walls near the keypad. There was a list of offices. On floors eleven and twelve, at the top of the list, was Lasseter Enterprises. It was the only firm there. Twelve was the top floor. The directory said, reception, floor eleven. They stepped in and pushed the button for that floor. With a firm swoosh, the door closed, and they were whisked silently to their destination. Stepping out of the elevator, Andrew was once more fighting the feeling of intimidation.

The reception area was expansive with a two-story ceiling. Several modern chandeliers set at different levels in the ceiling hung over their heads, each glowing with a constellation of tiny lights. Directly ahead of them was a curved reception desk, faced with highly polished wood, enhanced by indirect lighting that emanated from a white trim that carried on around the entire station. It seemed to invite and yet overawe them at the same time.

An equally elegant and intimidating middle-aged woman sat behind the bureau, striking and confident as if she were in command of a starship. On each side of them, opaque glass with colorful hues of supple greens and grays was set in matching arrays reaching from floor to ceiling. A curved stairway with polished metal handrails and white marble steps ascended behind the reception area and led to another floor above it.

"May I help you?" asked the lady behind the desk, in a tone and accent that matched her refinement.

"Yes, we'd like to see Mr. Strand."

She glanced over at her screen and then back at them. "Do you have an appointment?" she said, the conceit in her voice hinting that she knew they didn't.

"No, but it's vital that we speak with him."

"I'm sorry," said the woman, with just a trace of condescension. "Mr. Strand is very busy, and his appointment calendar is full for the day. Perhaps you'd like to leave a message, and I can have him get back to you later."

"I'm sorry, but I'm afraid that won't work," Andrew said with as much authority as he could muster, but adding an equal amount of grace. He could feel a growing sense of irritation rising in his chest. He should have asked for an appointment, but at the same time, he knew he'd never get near this office once Strand knew what they were up to. This was the only way he could see that they'd get through to him. Now that he was here, he wasn't about to let this woman stand in his way. He was even more irritated now that he had a few seconds to review in his mind the whole injustice he'd been through. The more this lady tried to stop him, the angrier he became.

"Well," responded the woman, clearing her throat to add a firmness to her response. "Like I said, Mr. Strand is not available right now, but I'd be happy to take your name and number so he can get back to you when he's available."

"I'm sorry, but that's not going to work," said Jimmy, injecting himself into the conversation with a sense of authority that came from years of working in law enforcement. "I'm with a private investigative firm, and we have some serious issues to discuss with Mr. Strand. I think it would be best for you to inform him of our presence, or you may regret it later."

Jimmy's abrupt announcement obviously flustered the woman, but she kept her composure, and Andrew could clearly see why she had her job. "If that's the case, let me call our security team, and they can speak to you about this matter. I've dealt with your type before, and I don't recall ever having someone come in unannounced like this. This approach is completely unacceptable."

Jimmy wasn't about to be put off by this woman, and he leaned ever so slightly in her direction. "Ma'am, I don't think you understand. We came in here unannounced precisely because of the type of runaround I've gotten from people like your boss. Now would you kindly notify Mr. Strand that we'd like to see him?"

"I will not," asserted the receptionist, clearly unimpressed with Jimmy's Jedi mind trick approach. "I'm calling security right now." She grabbed her handset and brought it up to her ear, simultaneously punching in a few keys on the phone's pad.

"Security, we've got an issue here. Would you send someone up right away?" The lady firmly planted the headset back on the base and announced with a new boldness. "I suggest you leave now. If not, security will be here any moment and escort you out."

As Andrew watched this lady stand up to them, he was impressed with her confidence, but his own frustration was nearly at the limit. She was clearly within her rights to ask them to leave. They'd been rude and pushed their way into the room. But she had no idea what Strand had done to him. He wasn't about to back down at this point. So, he asserted himself and leaned toward her with all the firmness he could muster. "Listen, lady, I'm sorry you're not happy with our approach, and I'm sure you don't have a clue why we're here, but I can tell you right now I'm going to see Strand today or there's going to be hell to pay."

Andrew knew that they only had a few more minutes before security arrived, and then it would all be over. He knew Jimmy was packing, but he wasn't about to see matters get out of hand. Realizing he only had one option, he moved away from the desk and quickly headed for the stairs behind her.

She moved to stop him, but he was already halfway up by the time she put her foot on the bottom step. He was at the top of the stairway in the next second. Now that he was on the second floor, he moved down the hallway, glancing at the names embossed on each door. He passed one that said, Sheryl Banks, Acquisitions, the next, Philip Yates, COO. Then, near the end of the hallway, he saw the name, Landon Strand, Executive Vice President. He grabbed the handle and pushed his way into the office. There with phone in hand, obviously being warned by a call from the receptionist, stood Landon Strand, whom Andrew had known as Hayden Quinn for the last four months, with a look of shock and slight humiliation on his face.

"What are you doing here?" he declared, not quite sure what to make of the situation.

"I'm here because I'm looking for answers." Andrew's voice was steady but charged with emotion.

"Who let you in here?" demanded Strand.

"You're going to tell me why you set me up and then walked away and left me hanging?" Andrew took a step toward him, his hands clenched at his sides.

"Listen, Foster, this is not the time or place to handle this matter," Strand said as he moved out from behind his desk. "Here, let me walk you down to reception and we can discuss this in the conference room on that level," he demanded, as he pushed past Andrew and out into the hall.

"I'm not going anywhere until I get answers," Andrew shouted, refusing to move any further.

"Ms. Blanchly," Strand called down the stairway. "I need security up here right now."

"They're on their way," barked the receptionist, her voice carrying up the stairwell.

Things were clearly not developing the way Andrew had hoped. But now that he was here, he was going to make the most of the final moments he had to confront Strand. His anger was boiling over, and he wasn't about to go peacefully. He grabbed Strand by the arm, spinning him around till he was facing him and yelled, "Did you think you could just get me to walk away without making you face what you did to me?"

Suddenly, a door to his right opened, and another man stepped into the hallway. He was angry and perplexed, shouting at Landon, "What in the hell is going on here?"

"It's Foster. I don't know how he found us," Strand replied, his voice tight with tension.

The man looked at Andrew, and a flash of recognition crossed his face. Andrew looked at the name on the half-open door behind him. It read Donovan Lasseter, President. At that moment, Andrew realized that this must be the guy behind his nightmare. Instantly, he felt a flood of anger rising in him, and he moved toward Lasseter. "So, you're the one in charge here. Did you put Strand up to this?"

"How did he get in here?" bellowed Lasseter as he backed away and into his office.

Andrew followed him, hoping to get up in his face, but Strand moved between them. "Sorry, Don, I tried to get rid of him."

Lasseter moved behind his desk, clearly trying to put as much space as he could between them. Andrew pushed Strand aside and forced his way to the front of Lasseter's desk, pouring out his hatred. "Like I told Strand here, you're not going to usher me out of here without a fight. I've got to know why in the hell you set me up."

Just then, security arrived in the hallway with Jimmy right behind them. He obviously wanted to jump in, but given his background in law enforcement, he was holding off for now. But he signaled to Andrew. "You good?"

"Yes, I'm just getting to the bottom of things."

"Well, don't do anything rash."

"I'll try."

The security guy, the man who was at the desk in the lobby, stepped into the room. There was another equally huge man with him. He spoke to the man Andrew knew as Quinn. "What's going on, Mr. Strand? Do you want me to remove this guy?"

"Don?" said Strand, looking at his boss and then back at the security team.

"Have them stand down and wait outside." Looking at his security team, Lasseter said calmly, "I can handle this. Just close the door behind you. But you stay in here," he added, looking at Strand.

"Okay, but we'll be right outside if you need us." The security team backed out of the room, taking Jimmy with them, and closed the door behind them.

"So, you're the jerk behind this whole thing?" Andrew declared, spitting out his anger with deep conviction. "Who do you think you are to set me up the way you did and then ruin my life as if I'm some speck that means nothing?"

Andrew held his position at the front of the desk, shouting again in his anger, "Who do you think you are?"

Lasseter lowered his hand and opened the top drawer of his desk. Then slowly, he pulled from it an object Andrew hadn't seen in years. He looked up from it into an angry set of eyes.

"I'll tell you who I am," Lasseter said, his voice dropping to a menacing whisper. "I'm your son."

In his palm lay a pendant, half of a piece of Native American jewelry, its turquoise and silver pattern jagged where it had been broken. Andrew's breath caught. Amber had worn it every day until that final night when she'd ripped it from her neck and threw it at him in bitter hurt.

The words hung in the air between them, as suffocating as smoke. Andrew felt the room tilt slightly, his mind struggling to process the revelation. Everything, the deception, the sabotage, the nightmares, suddenly took on a new and terrible meaning.

CHAPTER TWENTY-FIVE

BIG SUR

JULY · 1970

Andrew moved carefully along the moonlit trail, flashlight beam bobbing ahead of him. The light made him feel exposed, like a target. He'd spent so much time keeping secrets, hiding in the shadows of his own deceptions. But now that he'd told Amber the truth, he felt like he was carrying a beacon that might attract attention from dark places he'd rather leave undisturbed.

From the moment he started down the path toward his rendezvous with Blaire, he'd sensed that he was too abrupt with Amber. They'd shared so many wonderful times together, and with each of them, their souls had knitted together a little more. Sure, a good clean break seemed like the least painful way to end things, but he couldn't deny that he still had deep feelings for her. As silly as it might seem, he suddenly felt grateful for all she'd been to him, and he needed to leave her with some token of thanks before he was gone from her life.

Besides, he wanted her to keep the memento that they created from the Indian relic. He certainly didn't want it. There was always the possibility that Blaire might ask him about it. At the same time, he didn't want to throw Amber's half away; somehow that seemed foolish. It was valuable, even though it was only one half of the former ornament.

Andrew stopped and used his flashlight to search for it in his bag. Finding it, he held it in the beam and watched as the light danced over the silver surface and the precious inset stone, bringing out the warmth of the turquoise. Of course, there was always the possibility that she'd toss it aside or in some other way destroy it in an act of vengeance. But that would be her choice and not his. Whatever happened, he was going to keep his half. Clutching the pendant in his hand, he turned back up the path on one final errand.

Arriving back at the tent, he could see a light glow cast on the ground as it shone through the gap where the entrance was. Amber was still awake, so he softly announced his presence not to startle her.

"It's me, Amber," he said in a whisper, the words barely disturbing the night air. "I've come back to bring you something."

He knelt and pulled the entrance flaps aside. She'd turned on the small battery-powered lantern and was writing in her journal. She looked up at him; her eyes were red, and her cheeks spattered with dried salt from her tears. The sight of her pain sent a pang through him, but he pushed it aside.

Andrew held out the pendant to her. "Amber, I just felt the way I left was too abrupt. I'm sure you're so mad at me that you never want to see me again. I know you tossed this away in anger, but I really want you to have it."

He was expecting her to repeat her earlier rejection of the pendant, but there was a strange look on her face, so he just continued. "And more importantly, I just wanted to say that I will always be grateful to you for the wonderful things you brought into my life. We had some great times together and created some wonderful memories I'll never forget." The words sounded hollow even to his own ears, but he meant them, in his way.

"Well, Andrew, you need to know that we've created something else," she said, her voice steady despite the tears beginning to fill her eyes again.

"Oh, yes, those poems and drawings we wrote together in your journal." He smiled, trying to keep the moment light.

"No, not those."

"Are you referring to that song we composed together? Don't worry, I'll always give you credit for the lyrics." He shifted uncomfortably, sensing something deeper in her tone.

"You really don't get it, do you?" Amber's voice took on an edge. "All these days I've been sick, there's a reason. It wasn't the flu."

"What was it?" Andrew asked, a nagging worry beginning to form.

"I'm pregnant, Andrew."

The words hit him like a physical blow. He rocked back slightly on his heels, steadying himself against the tent's entrance. "Pregnant. You've got to be kidding me."

"It's true. I've missed my period for the last two months. I didn't tell you because I wanted to be sure first. While you were off on your little fling, it finally hit me why I might be so sick. So, when I dragged myself out of bed and went to wash up the other day, I spoke with Janice. She's done some nursing, and I told her it might be the flu, but I could be pregnant. She agreed when I told her I missed. She has that little first aid kit, and sure enough, it included a pregnancy test. Once I took the test, I knew without a doubt. It's for real, I'm going to have a baby."

The flashlight beam trembled in Andrew's hand, casting jittery shadows across the tent walls. "How could this possibly be?"

"Are you really asking that?" Amber's face was a mixture of disbelief and irritation.

"I thought you were on the pill?" Andrew's voice rose slightly, panic edging in.

"I was, but you know those things aren't foolproof. My doctor told me there's about a five percent failure rate."

"Failure? How could that possibly have happened?" He was scrambling now, looking for an escape route from this new reality.

"I might have missed taking it one day. Sometimes when I'm stoned, I forget things. I was told something as simple as that could cause this." Amber's voice was matter-of-fact, but there was a brittleness to it.

"Well, that's clearly one of the things you don't want to forget," Andrew snapped at her, his voice rising, pushed by his growing anxiety. He was suddenly wondering what his options were now. Was she going to hold this over him? Use it as some sort of ball and chain to keep him with her? But then he wondered why she didn't tell him this earlier. Before he walked off and left her.

"Why are you telling me this now? Why not earlier when I told you about Blaire?" The question hung between them like an accusation.

"I was about to tell you just before you announced your decision to run off with Blaire. After that, I was too stunned. I was so overwhelmed by the pain I couldn't think straight. Besides, I thought you'd say I was making it up as a ploy to hold you. But now that you're back and we may not see each other again, I just thought you ought to know. I'm through with you, Andrew, so don't worry that I'll use this to manipulate you."

Relieved by that statement, Andrew slipped his pack off and settled into a sitting position, resting his bag beside him on the ground. He was concerned for her and tried to offer some sort of condolence. "You have options. You don't have to have this child. There are plenty of clinics in the city that will help you eliminate this dilemma." He tried to keep his voice gentle, but the words came out clinical and detached.

"I know," she said, her brows nearly meeting, her mouth twisted, a mirror of the anger in her heart. "Listen, it's no longer your worry, and I don't want or need your advice."

"Of course, you don't, but I would think you'd want to put both of us at rest by doing away with the problem." As soon as the words left his mouth, he knew they were the wrong ones, but he couldn't stop himself.

"Like I said, it's not your problem any longer. I'm not sure what I'll do. I heard the state supreme court just made it legal now in California. It will be a lot easier, especially since I'm going to be alone. But I'm not sure I want to rush off to the city and have a procedure." Her hand unconsciously drifted to her stomach; a gesture Andrew couldn't help but notice.

"At least you won't have to have some back-alley job. You know how dangerous those are." He was trying to sound concerned, but it came out as dismissive.

Even though Amber had let him off the hook on this matter, Andrew still felt responsible. But he was also really frustrated and growing angrier at her apparent failure to remember to take her birth control. He knew that having sex with someone meant it was both their responsibility to be careful and use the proper methods, but he wasn't the one that needed to take the pills. Why wasn't she more careful? He could sense that he wasn't handling this very well, and the next minute his irritation got the best of him. "What were you thinking, Am? I just don't understand how you could be so irresponsible."

Now she was back in full-blown stress mode. He could see that his outburst was not helping matters much. Her face flushed, the lantern light catching the gleam in her eyes.

"Responsible. Is that what you were being? Going off with Blaire behind my back?" Her voice rose, trembling with emotion. "Well, you don't have to worry. I'm going to do the right thing. I must be responsible for what happens from now on. It will be my choice, and I'll decide what to do."

"Yes, it's your choice. I don't want to have this thing hanging over me the rest of my life, wondering if you did what is necessary." Andrew leaned forward, his expression intense. "Listen, if you've ever cared for me at all, then do me a favor and have an abortion. I know you're not interested in listening to me right now, but it's going to be hard to raise a child without a dad, and the truth is I'm simply not going to be there."

Some part of him recoiled—at the thought of a child, his child, entering the world alone. But he buried it. Fast.

"Like I said, it's not your problem," she said, a fresh wave of anger clearly rising inside her. "And I definitely don't want any remembrance of you either, so don't worry, I'll take care of it."

"Good." The word hung in the air between them, cold and final.

"Good," she echoed. "You'd better be on your way. You don't want to keep your new girlfriend waiting. If you're gone too long, she may get bored and find some other guy to start hooking up with."

After the intensity of what they'd just said and the news of the pregnancy, Andrew wasn't sure what Amber would do with his offer of the pendant, so he just set it on the bottom of her sleeping bag and started to move away. "I do wish you the best, Amber." The words felt empty, a social nicety that couldn't begin to cover the chasm that had opened between them.

Amber didn't say a word as he slipped on his pack and moved out of the tent.

"Good-bye," he said with as much gravitas as he could bring to his voice.

She didn't say a word, but her sobs spoke volumes, following him as he stepped out into the night. Each step he took away from the tent seemed to echo with the weight of what he was leaving behind. The night was cool now, the stars sharp overhead, but Andrew barely noticed. His mind was racing ahead, to Blaire, to the money, to the life he thought he wanted.

An hour and a half later, he'd unearthed the money and was at the bottom of the hill on the west side of the highway, waiting for Blaire. The cash was stuffed into his backpack, his future seemingly secured. The night pressed in, and he realized he had buried more than the cash. He had buried something of himself, too. The road stretched silent and black before him, empty but full of tension. Every sound, a shifting breeze, a distant engine, sent a jolt through his nerves. Was it Blaire? Or someone else entirely, coming to settle a score he hadn't yet accounted for?

The highway stretched empty before him, a ribbon of black in the moonlight. And Andrew waited, his decision made, the consequences left behind in a tent on the mountainside.

CHAPTER TWENTY-SIX

BIG SUR

JULY · 1970

The motorcycle tires bit into the asphalt, every piston firing in unison as they fled their pursuer. Moments before, they'd eluded him, but now he'd seen them again. Andrew cranked full throttle on his bike as they flew down the road toward the next turnout. Ash was in pursuit, but because he had gone beyond them when they'd hidden earlier, he'd had to reverse on the narrow highway, and that had given them needed time. If they could keep at their current pace, Andrew believed they could outdistance him.

The night was a tempest of shadows and fog, the beam of Andrew's headlight barely cutting through the thick marine layer that had rolled in from the Pacific. Behind him, Blaire clung to his waist, her body pressed tightly against his back. In the rearview mirror, the distant glow of headlights appeared intermittently through the mist, a predator stalking its prey.

For the next several minutes, Andrew weaved in and out of the turns they'd maneuvered through earlier, only this time they were heading north. Sometimes they came dangerously close to hurtling off the road and down one of the cliffs to their deaths. The drop-offs were invisible in the darkness, but Andrew could sense them, yawning chasms just beyond the guardrails, waiting to swallow them whole. But each time, he was able to rein in his bike at the last moment and sail safely on toward the next curve, the motorcycle tires screeching in protest.

Blaire's arms tightened around his waist with each precarious turn, her breath warm against the back of his neck. She didn't scream or ask him to slow down. Instead, she moved with him, leaning into the curves as if they were one being, joined in their desperate flight.

Finally, as they passed their starting point, it was evident that Ash was too far behind to close the gap. The distance between predator and prey had widened, giving them a crucial advantage. By the time they hit the first straightaway, the fog had thinned, and Andrew found another side road that led up a hill into the brush where they could hide. He cut the engine, and they sat in silence, listening to the ticking of the cooling metal, their breathing gradually slowing.

Andrew looked back from their perch at the empty road, but soon he saw Ash's truck racing up from the south, its headlights cutting twin swaths through the lingering wisps of fog. They watched as he passed on the road below and continued heading north, the sound of his engine fading into the distance. They waited ten minutes after he was out of sight, confident that he'd continue in the same direction. Then they dropped down from their hideout and back onto the highway. Andrew headed south again at full force, the open road before them now a path to freedom.

They didn't stop until they were safely onto Highway 46 an hour later. The sun had just peeked over the horizon as they pulled into a service station to fuel up, bathing the world in a soft golden light that seemed to promise a new beginning. The morning air was crisp and clean, carrying the scent of eucalyptus and distant salt spray.

Blaire jumped off the back of the bike and looked down the highway from where they'd come and then back toward Andrew. Her face was flushed with excitement and alive with a sense of awe at his racing prowess. Her hair, wild from the wind, framed her face like a dark halo, and her eyes sparkled with the thrill of their escape.

"It looks like we've lost him," she declared. She patted the seat of the bike, her hands still trembling slightly from the adrenaline. "You're amazing. You really know how to handle this thing."

Andrew climbed off the bike, reached out, and pulled her to him, his heart still pumping with adrenaline. The leather of his jacket creaked as he embraced her, their bodies fitting together like puzzle pieces. "You're amazing," he said, his voice husky with emotion.

She smiled back at him, her eyes dancing with delight. "I can't wait to see where this adventure takes us." The morning light caught the gold flecks in her eyes, making them seem to glow from within.

"I can't either," Andrew said, the smile on his face almost as bright as Blaire's. The weight of the money in his bag felt like a promise, a ticket to wherever they wanted to go.

They fueled the bike, took a restroom break, grabbed cups of coffee, and headed into the bright sunlight of a new day. The coffee was hot and bitter, a perfect counterpoint to the sweet taste of freedom. The service station attendant barely gave them a second glance, just another young couple on the road, seeking whatever lay beyond the horizon.

For just a few moments, the drama of last night rolled through Andrew's mind, setting off little bursts of guilt somewhere inside. He briefly recalled Amber's tears and her surprise announcement that a new life was stirring in her womb. The image of her face, shocked and hurt, flashed before him, but only for an instant. Hopefully, she would put that intrusion off for another time and find another lover to build a family with someday.

As for him, well, those thoughts were soon lost in a swirl of other thrills: the celebration of the chase through the early morning fog, the grip of Blaire's arms around him, the adventure that waited before them both. All these thrills consumed him, the chase through the mist, Blaire's arms around him, the open. He let those pleasures wash over him, crowding out anything that might resemble regret.

As they merged back onto the highway, the motorcycle purring beneath them, Andrew couldn't help but feel a surge of something like triumph. They had escaped, from Ash, from responsibility, from consequences. The road stretched before them, a ribbon of possibility unrolling toward a future that seemed limitless and golden in the morning light.

But even as they accelerated down the open road, a small voice whispered in the back of Andrew's mind, barely audible over the roar of the engine. It wondered how long they could run, how far they could go before the past caught up with them. Andrew pushed the thought away, focusing instead on the warmth of Blaire's body against his back and the freedom of the open road.

The morning sun climbed higher, burning away the last wisps of coastal fog, illuminating their path forward and erasing any trace of the darkness they'd left behind. They rode on, the past shrinking in the rearview, unseen but not undone.

CHAPTER TWENTY-SEVEN

LA JOLLA

NOVEMBER · 2000

S tanding in Donovan's office, Landon was watching an unfolding scene he could never have imagined. Donovan's declaration that he was Foster's son had left him speechless. What was going on? Why had his boss, his friend, done this to him? It was all too much to take in. All this time he'd had Landon believing a total lie. He'd been on Donovan's side, completely understanding his anger, quietly rooting for him, but now he felt betrayed. He wanted to shout out his frustration, but the jolt of what he'd just learned left him feeling as if all the air had been sucked from his lungs. All he could do was stare at his boss in a state of shock.

The morning sunlight slanted through the floor-to-ceiling windows, casting long shadows across the plush carpet of Donovan's corner office. Outside, the Pacific stretched blue and endless, a stark contrast to the turbulent emotions churning inside the room. Landon watched in stunned silence as Donovan tossed an object, which appeared to be some pendant, onto his desk and then ordered them to sit down. The pendant caught the light, its turquoise stone gleaming like a small, accusing eye.

"You see, Mr. Foster, that should be my name, Foster," Donovan said, his voice tight with barely contained emotion. "But my mother chose to have us take an uncle's last name rather than her maiden name. Someone I could respect."

Landon looked over at Foster. Most of his earlier anger had strangely dissipated, replaced by a stunned confusion that seemed to have numbed him. His face had gone pale; his eyes fixed on the pendant as if it were a poisonous snake. He was barely able to get out a few words. "What are you talking about?"

"My mother is Amber Reed. Surely you haven't forgotten her?" Donovan's voice was razor-sharp, each word honed to cut.

"Of course not," Foster stammered. Landon could see he was still in shock, his mind struggling to process the revelation. "It was years ago; we both moved on."

"Correct, but perhaps you remember what transpired the last time the two of you were together." Donovan's fingers drummed once, twice on the polished surface of his desk, the only outward sign of his inner turmoil.

Landon's gaze went back and forth between Donovan and Foster. He was overwhelmed by the revelation that was pouring out of his friend. The scene unfolding was staggering. His mind seemed frozen in a state of amazement as he absorbed the fact of who might be sitting in the chair across from Donovan.

Foster's face was a picture of confusion. He was clearly unable to grapple with what he was hearing. Landon could see his brows knitting as his eyes stared at the object on the desk. Finally, he found the presence of mind to respond. "We said our good-byes and then went our separate ways," he said, his voice thin and uncertain. "I did what I thought was best for both of us at that point."

Donovan gritted his teeth, doing his best to hold back his rage. But still, his words came out with a guttural tone. "Really? By breaking the covenant that you and my mother made. Maybe that was best for you, but was it for us?"

"How could you possibly know what happened between the two of us all those years ago?" Foster shifted in his seat, the leather creaking beneath him like a distant warning.

Donovan picked up the pendant and held it out toward Foster to make a point. The chain dangled from his fingers, swinging slightly like a hypnotist's watch. "Because my mother told me all about what happened between you two. This pendant was something you'd made for her as a sign of your love. She told me how you fashioned it from some ancient Native American jewelry. But then you broke your promise and betrayed her by running off with some other woman."

Foster's face turned slightly pale, and his gaze distant, as if he was remembering things in his past, things he didn't want to deal with. The weight of those memories seemed to press him deeper into his chair. "That's true, but it kind of went with the territory back then. People had sex all the time with whoever came along. It was the era of free love. But I paid for it. I was betrayed, too. You just had to learn to deal with it."

"My mom wasn't the only one who was hurt. She told me about Ash, how you took off with Blaire right under his nose. Maybe I'm not the only ghost from your past. Perhaps there are others out there, looking for revenge." Donovan's words hung in the air like storm clouds, dark with threat.

"That's it!" blurted Foster, suddenly sitting up straighter, a realization dawning. "Ash is behind this whole thing. We found his fingerprints on the window in the Franklin."

"That's because I wanted you to find them in case you tried to track us." A small, cruel smile curved Donovan's lip. "I was hoping it would put you off our trail. I also wanted to put some fear in you. I wanted you to think your karma was catching up with you."

"What do you mean? Are you telling me it was part of this whole crazy scheme?" Foster's voice rose with incredulity.

"Yes, it was. I hunted Ash down. Found out he was in prison. I had a friend in the DA get a hold of a copy of his prints and had them planted there in case you came looking for me. Mom told me all about the way you feared him. I was hoping it would add to your torment; I hear he should be out of prison soon. Maybe you really should be concerned." There was a satisfaction in Donovan's voice that made Landon's skin crawl.

"Why would you want to torment me?" Foster asked, his voice barely above a whisper.

"You still don't understand all the pain you caused my mom. You broke her heart, and that's exactly the reason you need to pay for it." Donovan's voice hardened, brooking no argument.

"Listen, I cared for Amber. I really did." Foster leaned forward, his hands spread in a gesture of pleading.

"If you cared so much, then why did you leave?" Donovan's question cracked like a whip.

Foster was clearly taken aback by the force of Donovan's disclosures but struggled to defend himself. "It was a different time. People were experimenting, having open relationships, and I'd found someone who fulfilled me on a new level." Even as he spoke the words, they sounded hollow to Landon's ears, a feeble justification for abandonment.

Landon couldn't help wondering what must be going through Foster's mind. His face was a twisted scrim of turmoil as if a storm of confusion was fomenting just beneath the surface. It was as if two raging emotions were fighting one another in his heart. Here he was, realizing for the first time that he had a son, someone he should want to embrace, sitting before him. But at the same time, he was confronted with the fact that it was his own offspring that had put this whole scenario together to torment him.

"It was selfish," Donovan said, dropping the pendant back on the table with a slight metallic sound that seemed to echo in the tense silence.

Foster looked into Donovan's eyes. Donovan's face was flint, unyielding. "But you left something else with her, too, didn't you?"

"What?" Foster's voice was barely audible.

"But I agreed to let her choose what to do with the pregnancy." His words hung in the air, hollow and inadequate.

"True, but not without laying a huge guilt trip on her and then leaving her with the option of raising me by herself or doing away with me." Bitterness dripped from every syllable Donovan spoke.

"But we weren't ready to have a child. At least I wasn't. It just wouldn't have been fair." Foster's voice had taken on a pleading quality.

Landon could see the intensity in Donovan's face as he listened to Foster's excuses. His eyes narrowed as a blistering focus took over his countenance. "Fair to whom, Mr. Foster? Fair to you or fair to my mom and to me?" Each word was delivered like a physical blow.

The intensity of Donovan's argument clearly subdued Foster. His hands were in his lap, and he looked down at them for a moment as if searching for a reply. Then, raising them and folding them together on his chest, he responded in what must be as transparent and honest an answer as he could find. "But you've got to understand how I felt then. I thought if I'd stayed with your mom, it would have sidetracked my life, it would have killed my future and my dreams."

Donovan rose halfway out of his chair and leaned across the desk, raging out a bitterness Landon had rarely seen in him. "That's exactly the point I want to make to you now. It's exactly why I set this whole thing in motion. I wanted you to understand what it is like to have your dreams shattered. But you didn't just try to have my dreams shattered, you wanted me to die. And that's the whole point of what I did to you with Precipice. I let you conceive a dream in your heart, and then I killed it. I needed you to dream. That was the only way I could make you feel what you tried to take from me."

"What possible connection do the two things have to one another?" Foster asked, his face a mask of confusion.

"My mom waited another two months into her pregnancy before she made her final decision not to have an abortion. So, for four months, I grew inside her womb, becoming the life I was destined to be. During those four months in the womb, my heart, brain, limbs, and bones formed and became the man I am today. Instead of the tiny little speck you thought I was and wanted to get rid of. That's why I gave you the dream of The Precipice project for four months. For four months, you worked to grow your dream, and then, like you wanted to do to me, I killed it." Donovan's voice had risen to a shout, the veins in his neck standing out like cords.

"I'm sorry." Foster's words fell into the silence that followed, small and inadequate.

"Sorry? Sorry that you betrayed her, sorry you broke her heart? You're not sorry, it's because you're a despicable man, and it's about time you learn that." Donovan was standing now, pointing across the desk and shouting at Foster. His rage was out of control. Landon was just shocked at the way his friend was acting. Did he even know this man anymore? He'd deceived Landon as well, but what he'd just heard made a strange sort of sense. The faintest hint of understanding was starting to form in his mind.

Landon looked at Foster, wondering how he'd respond to this attack. For a few moments, he seemed cowed by the bitterness and intensity of

Donovan's rage, but he gradually appeared to collect himself. He slowly stood to his feet and looked at Donovan and then declared, "So you're my son then?" His voice was thick with emotion, the words seeming to catch in his throat.

"Yes, but only by birth. I want nothing to do with you after today." Donovan's words were like ice.

Donovan's statement hit Foster at his core. Landon could see the rejection in his face. "I am sorry. I was..." Foster began, extending a hand across the desk.

"Stop, I'm done," Donovan said as he turned his back, the gesture as final as a door slamming shut.

"Donovan," Foster said with brokenness in his voice. Donovan spun around so quickly that Landon thought he was going to lunge at Foster. He stepped in front of him and the desk, his body a barrier between the two men.

"Don't ever repeat my name and get the hell out of my office," Donovan yelled, his face contorted with rage.

At that, the doors burst open, and the security team moved in on Foster, followed by the friend he'd brought with him. The sudden intrusion broke the tension in the room like a thunderclap.

The security guys came up to Foster and moved him toward the door. His friend stepped in between them, but Foster waved him off. "Don't mess with them, Jimmy. I'm leaving." There was a defeat in his posture that hadn't been there before, as if something vital had been crushed inside him.

"Follow them out and make sure they don't ever come back," Donovan ordered, his voice strained with the effort of control.

Landon walked with the four of them to the top of the steps. As they descended, Foster's friend sought to console him. "You okay, Andrew?"

"Let's just get out of here." Foster's voice was hollow, shellshocked.

"What happened?"

"You won't believe it." With that, Foster and his friend quickly paced down to the foyer and over to the elevator with the security guys close behind. They disappeared inside the elevator, the doors sliding shut with a soft hiss.

Landon walked back up the hall and into Donovan's office. He was sitting at his desk, his head in his hands. Landon approached slowly, realizing that his failure to quietly get rid of Foster when he burst into his office earlier had set off the whole confrontation. "Listen, I'm really sorry for not getting rid of Foster without bringing you into it." He realized he was taking the blame when it was really Donovan who needed to take the blame for setting this thing in motion. But after what he'd just heard, he realized how conflicted Donovan must be right now. He'd just met his father face to face for the first time and tossed him out like some worthless bum. But Landon was still mad and wanted him to understand that he was hurt too. Donovan had built the company fast; driven by a fire most couldn't understand. Now Landon saw where that fire had come from. Could he even trust Donovan again after this? He might continue working for him because he respected his management skills and loved the company he'd built, but he wasn't sure he could ever have confidence in what Donovan told him.

"Listen, Don, I can see that Foster has left a huge wound in your heart, but is that any reason to drag me into this whole thing? You deceived me, too." By now, Landon realized he was nearly shouting, so he lowered his tone and spoke the truth to his friend. "I feel used and don't know if I can trust you anymore."

Donovan was shocked by Landon's outburst and recoiled for a moment but then responded in a hoarse voice. "I understand," he said, looking up at Landon, his face pale, tears at the edge of his eyes. He looked totally drained, as if the confrontation had sapped all his strength. "I never expected Foster would find us. I never wanted you to get caught in the middle of this whole thing."

"Why didn't you just come clean with me? I don't get it. And what was that whole story about your dad being a contractor and your mom dying from cancer?" Landon paced in front of the desk, unable to contain his agitation.

"The part about my mother is true, she did die from cancer. She never married. But I just made up the part about my dad getting the shaft to hide my real reason for what I was doing to Foster." Donovan's voice was barely audible, his admission hanging in the air between them.

"And the other guys on that list you gave me. You never really intended to partner with them, did you?"

"No, it was another fabrication. I didn't want you to find out what was really going on and try to talk me out of it." Donovan couldn't meet Landon's eyes as he spoke.

"But, to create this whole deception, it was such a huge investment of your time and money."

"It was."

"Why would you throw so much away, when there were other ways to confront what Foster did?"

Donovan looked across the desk at Landon, the look of fire and determination returning to his eyes. "That's just it, Lanny, some things cost a lot to achieve. What I did for Foster was worth every penny. I'd have paid a lot more just to know that this contemptible man would finally pay for his sins."

The anger of Landon's earlier outburst had dissipated, and he was surprised to be feeling compassion for Donovan. He was wrong, but Landon didn't want to make things worse by doing something else wrong. He didn't condone it, but he understood it. That was enough for now.

"This thing with Foster has been eating at me for years." With that, Donovan slowly let his head slip down onto the desktop. He was still for a while, and then he quietly began to sob, his shoulders shaking with each burst of grief. The sound was raw and painful, like something being torn from deep inside him.

As Landon listened to him weeping, he thought about the deep hurt that must have been inside of Donovan all these years. He still felt betrayed, but at the same time, he knew Donovan, and he would find a way to rebuild their friendship. But what must it feel like for Donovan to be betrayed by the one who helped conceive him? What must it have been like for him never to know his father? To have a massive hole in his life where a dad should have been. What must it have been like for him to hear from his mom about the pain and hurt that his father had put her through?

Landon slowly began to understand how it would cause someone to carry a deep root of bitterness within them for years. He could see how it could cause someone to want revenge and then make every effort to see the betrayer pay for it. On top of all that, what must it be like for Donovan to be haunted by the fact that the last time he was near his father, the man was leaving his mother? What must it be like for him to know that the last time he was near his father, the man wanted him dead?

Landon walked over to stand beside Donovan, gently resting his hand on his shoulder. Donovan was still now, the crying had stopped, and he was quietly drifting away somewhere in the wake of all the previous emotion. Landon considered all these things he'd just heard and searched his own heart, wondering what he would have done if he'd been in Donovan's position. His heart bled now for his dear friend. Somehow, he sensed that Donovan would never find peace if he continued to travel down this same road. Promises had been broken, dreams had been killed, but somehow, Landon told himself that maybe, just maybe, things would work out someday.

The office was quiet now, the only sound the distant hum of traffic from below. The sun had moved higher in the sky, the shadows retreating. Outside the window, a seagull soared past, free and untroubled, unaware of the weight pressing down on the men inside. Inside, two men stood in silence, surrounded by the wreckage of secrets and the weight of decisions made decades ago.

CHAPTER TWENTY-EIGHT

BIG SUR

JULY • 1970

The fog clung to Highway 1 like a burial shroud, thick and wet and suffocating. Ash yanked the pickup's wheel hard right, tires screaming against asphalt as he skidded into the turnout near McWay Falls. The engine ticked its death rattle in the sudden silence.

Gone. They were gone.

He slammed his fist against the dashboard, feeling the rage burn through him like acid. Forty miles he'd chased them up this coast, watching Andrew's taillights dance in and out of the mist like fireflies. Watching Blaire's hair whip in the wind as she pressed herself against that traitor's back, her arms wrapped around him like she used to wrap them around him.

No.

Ash kicked open the door and stumbled out into the gray nothing. The roar hit him first—that ancient, endless thunder of water meeting stone. He moved toward it, drawn by some primal need to witness violence, even if it was only nature's.

The overlook materialized through the fog. Below and to his left, McWay Creek hurled itself over the cliff in an eighty-foot freefall, a silver ribbon of fury pounding straight into the churning Pacific. No beach to soften the blow, no mercy, just water smashing into water, the way he'd wanted to smash Andrew's skull against the pavement.

But the fog had swallowed them. Somewhere north of here, maybe in Carmel or Monterey, they were laughing at him and counting his money. *The Sons' money.*

Why hadn't he seen it coming? How had Blaire fooled him, again? Was he losing his edge?" The questions tore through his mind. *How? Why?* "You think this is over? It's not." The words escaped as vapor in the cold air, barely more than a whisper, but heavy with the weight of betrayal.

Fifty thousand dollars. Not his to lose. That stash Andrew uncovered. Not some forgotten trust fund. It had come from the Sons, It was theirs. They'd fronted him the drugs, trusted him. Now he'd have to explain that he'd been outplayed. That he'd *lost*. Ash was supposed to protect, not fumble the ball like some rookie. Rage clawed at his throat.

He slammed his fist against the metal doorframe, voice hoarse with fury.

"They made a fool of me!" he shouted.

"I don't lose. I *don't* lose!"

His breath came in sharp bursts, clouding in the cold air like steam from a vent about to blow.

The Sons of Malku didn't forgive that kind of mistake. They'd made that clear when they'd initiated him, when they'd shown him what happened to brothers who betrayed the family. The canyon. The screaming. The way sound echoed off the rock when you really wanted someone to understand their mistakes.

He gripped the wooden railing until splinters bit into his palms. Below, the waterfall kept falling, kept pounding, eternal and indifferent like it had been falling when the Esselen Indians walked this coast. Like it would keep falling long after the Sons had buried him in some unmarked patch of redwood forest.

Unless.

The thought came to him sideways, the way his best ideas always did. Not from his conscious mind but from that darker place, the shadow-realm where his true power lived. The place that whispered secrets in voices that weren't quite human.

The woman. Amber. Andrew's abandoned plaything, still back at the commune, was probably crying into a pillow faintly scented with lavender and smoke. Amber, still lit from within by something Ash could never quite dim, no matter how many tricks he'd tried. Waiting for her man to come back.

His lips curved into something that wasn't quite a smile.

Janice had told him about how Amber had asked for a pregnancy test. And now the voices were telling him other things, secrets that crawled up from the depths like creatures from the tide pools.

"Perfect," he whispered.

The waterfall roared its approval, or maybe its warning. Hard to tell the difference anymore.

Ash turned from the railing and walked back to the truck, his boots grinding against the gravel. The engine turned over on the third try, coughing black smoke into the mist. He pulled back onto Highway 1, heading south now, back the way he'd come. Back to the commune. Back to Amber.

The Sons would get their money. One way or another, everyone paid their debts. And if Andrew thought he could run, if he thought distance could save him or his woman, he was deceived.

The fog swallowed that thought before it could fully form. But it didn't matter. The pickup's headlights carved twin tunnels through the gray nothing as he drove south, leaving McWay Falls to its eternal plunge. But the sound followed him, that endless crash of water against water, nature's reminder that some forces couldn't be stopped, only redirected.

Like water, he would find a way.

The speedometer crept past sixty, sixty-five, seventy. The fog rushed at him like a living thing, but Ash didn't slow down. The voices were singing now, a harmony that only he could hear, telling him about the beautiful cruelties he would visit upon them all.

By the time he reached the commune, he would be ready. The preparations would be made. The circle would be drawn.

And somewhere in the north, Andrew and Blaire would feel it, that first cold finger of dread touching their spines, that animal knowledge that running wasn't enough. It would never be enough.

Because Ash Murek always collected what was owed.

Always.

The fog closed behind him like a door. McWay Falls kept its own counsel, still falling, still judging. The sea didn't care who died next. But the shadows did.

CHAPTER TWENTY-NINE

ENCINITAS

OCTOBER · 2000

The feel of wet sand under his feet was bracing. The earthy texture made him feel like he was connecting with nature on a visceral level. Walking at the edge of the wave flow, His toes tingled with each incoming surge, the cold water scrubbing him clean. There was a sense of repeated cleansing with each surge. Andrew needed that right now, a cleansing.

It was evening at Moonlight Beach, the sun hugging the horizon. Since leaving Brenton Tower, he'd been reviewing all that had transpired. He kept seeing the angry face of the young man who claimed to be his son. His accusations and bitterness still rang inside Andrew's head. Was he really his son? Or was this just another massive deception like the Teknon debacle? But there it was in Donovan's hand—the pendant that Amber and Andrew had fashioned from that Native American jewelry. It must be real; he must really be Andrew's son.

The idea that Donovan hated him for wanting to abort him seemed bizarre. He acted as if Andrew had wanted him dead, he saw it as murder. But Andrew never saw it that way. As far as he was concerned, Donovan was nothing when Amber and he argued about the abortion. She was two months pregnant at the time, and Andrew assumed he was just a tiny obstacle getting in the way. But now he realized Donovan was much more. Now that he saw what Donovan had become, his handsome face, his apparent genius, his success, everything looked different.

If only he could go back and change things. What could Amber and he have built together? What great things could he have accomplished with his son at his side? No, that was the wrong way of looking at it. What amazing things could *they* have accomplished together? It would have been a different world, a better world. But it was too late. That future was gone. All he could do now was mourn the version of himself that might have been.

When Jimmy asked him to describe what happened, Andrew gave an evasive explanation and asked for time alone. He wasn't ready to tell Jimmy what had unfolded in Lasseter's office; it was too confusing and painful. Jimmy warned Andrew not to be alone, but Andrew assured him that was precisely what he needed. Not before a stop by the local liquor store, though, he needed something to dull the ache. So, he asked to be dropped off at the beach, assuring Jimmy he'd call someone later for a ride home.

A brief text came from Nicole: "There's always hope, Andrew. Hang in there." What did she mean? Was she ready to give their relationship another chance? He wanted to call her and pour out his pain but held off and clung to that simple phrase. But what would he even say? That he'd found a son and lost him on the same day? Don't ghosts always stay in the past?

Andrew dug his toes into the sand, trying to find something stable as this storm assaulted his heart. But he couldn't get a grip on anything permanent. One bitter memory seemed to be replaced by another, like the breakers spilling onto shore. He slipped on his hoodie and took a long gulp from the whiskey bottle he'd bought. He knew it wasn't the answer, but it was the only comfort he could think of.

The sun was almost gone. The final nub of sunlight hovered above the ocean, then flared into emerald before the deep swallowed it up. There had been so many golden moments in his life, with a momentary flash of green near the end, only to be swallowed by something dark and unfathomable.

Out in the waves, a lone surfer caught his last ride of the day. Andrew watched him expertly maneuver along the crest until he unexpectedly caught an edge and tumbled into the foam. Like the surfer, Andrew saw himself cutting through the years, gracefully maneuvering to the crest of each new adventure only to be caught suddenly by a shock that sent him tumbling into bitter brine.

All these thoughts ganged up on him in a riptide threatening to pull him down. What made each one worse was the haunting voice of the man claiming to be his son, with his bitter accusations that Andrew had called for his death. It was too much. Seeking relief, he fell back as sobs rolled out from his soul. Tears spilled down his face and into the sand.

As night fully descended, the beach grew quieter. The bottle in his hand was lighter now; its contents diminished with each sip. A chill wind picked up, but the cold seemed to be coming from within. The waves continued their endless rhythm, offering and then taking, giving moments of joy only to reclaim them in sorrow.

He stared out at the moonlit water, the silver path it cast toward the horizon seeming to offer an invitation. To what? Andrew wasn't sure. He only knew that the pain of confronting his son, a son he never knew he had, a son he had once wished away, was almost more than he could bear.

Mercifully, stupor and sleep came shortly, and he rested without dreaming. The bottle slipped from his fingers, the remaining whiskey spilling into the sand like the opportunities he'd let slip away.

CHAPTER THIRTY

JOSHUA TREE

SEPTEMBER · 1970

The way the desert looks at twilight creates two conflicting possibilities in the mind. In one, its stunning beauty is enhanced by the stillness in the air here south of the Mojave. In this light, the barren landscape has a cleanness that brings a mantle of peace. The second option that slowly makes its way into consciousness is the increasing orange glow that gradually spills over the eastern skyline. It reminds Andrew that the bright orb just below the horizon would soon become a blazing, white-hot ball, burning its way into his head with unrelenting heat. Such is the joy and torment of this place, where he and Blaire had finally landed.

Andrew was awake now, standing in front of their humble dwelling, enjoying the lingering coolness of early morning and recalling the events that had led them here. Nearly two months had passed since they first left Big Sur, weeks filled with drifting, avoiding Ash, and chasing something undefined. First, they traveled north on Highway 101 to Mendocino for a two-week stay at a commune. But the threat of being found caused them to head east and then south. They retreated down the 101 and across the bay, stopping with friends in Berkeley for a few days. From there, they trekked through the Central Valley, made a brief detour to Yosemite, and eventually cut southeast through Bakersfield to a small ranch on the edge of Joshua

Tree National Park. The trip alone had taken close to three weeks. Now they'd been in the desert for more than a month.

Their relationship was as hot as ever, and it seemed at times they couldn't get enough of the sensual pleasure they found in each other. Andrew was clearly addicted to this woman. She was like dope to him. The only problem was that she knew it and now had a certain power over him. He tried his best not to let her know it, but it was evident he was seriously failing. He had moments when he wasn't sure she was as committed to him as he was to her, and that worried him a bit. But for now, he was hopelessly ensnared and actively pushing aside any thought that would tell him this sort of thing couldn't possibly last.

When they left the commune in Mendocino, they managed to hook up with a band of hippies heading out on a road trip. The group was traveling in a couple of vans, so from time to time, Andrew would let one of them ride his bike, and he'd spell them at the wheel of their vehicle. It gave them time to get to know their traveling companions, and they soon found themselves fitting in with these wandering pilgrims. They were on a quest for the perfect place to set up the teepee they'd recently sewn together.

Andrew suggested Joshua Tree because his sister Jade was there. Months ago, when she came through Big Sur, she told him about the little colony of artists and eccentrics that had made their way to this lonely place. They claimed it was some cosmic intersection between the celestial dimensions and Mother Earth.

Once their wandering caravan finally arrived at this ranch near the national park, most of them decided to stay for a while. The place was a broken-down farm with a main house and a scattering of shacks, some converted chicken coops, a few rusted-out campers parked under struggling trees. This spot was so barren that Ash would never guess they'd come here.

Jade was happy to see Andrew and gave their group a tour soon after they arrived. Oh, there was the typical group of artists and hippies, happily sharing their dope and food, but interspersed within the group were some peculiar individuals. Andrew thought the crew at the stone house in Big Sur was odd, but some of these folks were real ozone warriors.

Justin Gator, one of the farm's self-appointed gurus, was really into aliens. He claimed to be one of their contacts and persuaded them to hold vigils on several nights under the stars. It was beautiful waiting, but nothing showed up. If you asked Andrew, his ideas were all a bunch of hokum, but he went along to make Blaire happy. She seemed to see something in the guy and was getting increasingly bored with the place, so any intrigue was a welcome change.

Then there was Vlad, a short, thin dude with haunting eyes and sharp cheekbones. He held séances in his converted henhouse, which he'd decorated with hammered tin cans, weathered wood, animal bones, and colored glass from soda bottles. The twisted, inky symbols he'd painted on the front appeared to be zodiac signs, creating an inviting place away from the heat of the day.

Blaire and Andrew sat with him the first week they arrived. He offered to tell them their future, and some of his insights proved accurate. At first, it was intriguing as he went into a trance, his skull-like countenance glowing with mystique. But then the atmosphere turned edgy. His face started to morph before their eyes, and his voice deepened. At that point, Andrew was over it. He grabbed Blaire's hand and pulled her out of the place.

Later that day, Andrew ran into Vlad, and he seemed friendly enough on the surface, but his eyes flickered with a strange intensity that Andrew took for anger. Blaire remained fascinated and wanted them to go back for another session, but Andrew wasn't about to. It was too much like the sort of thing Ash was into, trances, chanting, and then demonic stuff that turns deadly.

This morning they'd been treated to scrambled eggs with tomato puree and day-old bread with butter and jam. They were sitting around the table, faces shining with satisfaction as they ate. Their appetites had been enhanced by several joints that circulated before the meal began. Today, they were joined by one of Jade's friends who had recently arrived at the farm. Her name was Carolyn. She had recently arrived at the ranch—barely out of her teens, but she'd left home at sixteen and drifted ever since. You could see it in her eyes: she was young, but not innocent. There was a fire in her questions, and a sadness that made her feel older than she was.

She didn't say much during the meal, but Andrew noticed the way her eyes kept drifting toward the open desert beyond the property line. She asked Jade a few questions about the big Yucca tree out past the fence, something about its shape and how it looked in the moonlight. "It feels like it's calling," she had murmured, almost to herself. Andrew had chalked it up to another dreamy hippie fantasy. Still, something in her expression suggested she might wander out there if the mood struck her.

Carolyn was lithe and striking with dark eyes and long kinky hair. Her nose curved down ever so slightly at its tip; her bright teeth, one slightly twisted inward, gave her a bewitching and mysterious look. She immediately smote Andrew, but he did his best not to let Blaire notice. Apparently, he didn't have to worry about that now. She was sitting beside him in deep conversation with Vlad and didn't catch on. They had fought earlier, and Andrew was sure she was still angry. He was, too. So, for now, this new girl was a welcome diversion that reminded him that Blaire was not the only woman who could intrigue him. But the next minute, he was struck with a sense of possessiveness, startling in its intensity. He looked over at the two beside him and realized that he was jealous. Why was Blaire so fascinated with Vlad?

Andrew leaned close to her, touched her arm gently, and whispered, "Hey, babe. I'm sorry that I went off on you earlier."

She hardly seemed to notice but did turn back to him and whispered a reply before continuing her conversation with Vlad. "Thanks, Andrew, I was wondering if you'd cop to your attitude."

He leaned in even closer, "Well, it's just that I'm worried about what happened in that last session with Vlad. It was really strange."

At this, she excused herself from her chat with Vlad and looked at Andrew. He could see that he'd become a nuisance now because she was agitated. She got up and motioned him to come over to the corner. "I don't get it, Andrew," she said, her voice low but tense. "There was something deeply spiritual going on with Vlad in that session. What made you bring it to such an abrupt end?"

"We've talked about this already. I just don't understand why you don't get it. Didn't you see the way his face was changing? It was scary, almost kind of demonic."

"I think it's all because you're still worried about Ash." She paused, reached out her hand, and gently placed it on his arm. Her mood had changed. She softened, slipping into that maternal tone she used when she wanted to calm him down. "I know you're anxious that Ash might be tailing us, babe. I've heard you say his name when you've been asleep. But don't worry. He's not going to find us, so don't let it stress you out. Chill a bit. Maybe you need to take one of those ludes Gator's been passing around. The tea he gave me to make for you was supposed to help you chill out. He said it would calm your nerves, settle your mind—but it just knocks you out and drags you into those weird dreams. Honestly, I thought it would keep you from stressing over everything, especially Ash. I didn't expect the nightmares to get worse."

Andrew recalled those dreams. Pot sometimes had a crazy effect on him when he'd had too much. He seemed to go deep into his subconscious and get trapped there. Ash was there, just at the edge of his thoughts, threatening him. A few times in this dreamlike state, a dark specter rose out of a hideous black pit and spread its vapor over him like a living sticky gel. He found that he was suddenly unable to breathe and tried to wake up, but escape evaded him, and he was forced to struggle until he fell into a deeper place of torment. He forced himself awake and reached for Blaire in his dreams. But she wasn't there. The spot beside him was empty, and he was alone. When he woke later, she told him she'd been with him the whole time, stroking his head and whispering comforting words to him.

"Yes, the dreams have been a torment. I'm glad you've been there for me. I really hope I can shake them."

"I hope so, too."

"Right now, that's not the issue. It's this dude Vlad, he's not helping. There's something cracked about the guy. Besides, he's hitting on you."

Her eyebrows raised, and a slight smirk formed at the corner of her mouth. "You're jealous. That's kind of weird coming from a guy who stole me from my former lover." She turned and faced him fully, placing her other hand on his arm as well. "Don't worry about Vlad. You know I have this mystical side to me, and that sort of stuff really gives me a contact high. And those faces? Well, he was explaining it to me. He was telling me that I will have many gurus in my life as I continue to evolve, and those faces are the faces of the ones I'll meet in the future."

Now, Andrew was the one with raised eyebrows and a smirk. This was one of the issues that had been growing between them. He wasn't as sensitive to all this spiritual stuff like she was, and he'd let her know it. "I know I'm not tuned into all this 'transcendence' stuff you find so fascinating. Are you still hanging onto some of the things you saw with Ash?"

Her face flared a bit at this, and then she settled back into her mothering mode. "Ash was really out there. Yes, I was scared when he practiced the dark stuff, but there's also a good side to these things, and Vlad seems to be onto that. He's not conjuring anything evil, he's channeling higher guides, not demons." She stroked his arm and then tickled the inside of his wrist with her fingertips. So, don't worry." She stroked his arm and then tickled the inside of his wrist with her fingertips. "You're the one who turns me on. This other interest is just my quest for higher consciousness. That's all."

Andrew relaxed a little at her explanation and tried his best to corral his possessiveness. "Okay, I'll take your word for it. But don't expect me to have another session with the guy."

"I won't, but I hope you're not going to forbid me to have one."

Now his antennae went up, but he'd just told her he wouldn't worry, so he said, "Sure, no problem."

"Great, because Vlad just told me that tonight's a perfect time for another session. He wants to do it under the full moon. Something about cosmic forces aligning when the moon is at that stage."

Oh great, Andrew thought, but he didn't say it. He could see it all now in his mind's eye. She'd be out there in the desert somewhere, looking into Vlad's hypnotic eyes under the moonlight. Now that's "spiritual." Come on, give me a break. But he held his tongue. "Well, if it's what you want, go for it."

"Great, I knew you'd understand."

Understanding was the last thing Andrew could do, but he realized he had few choices left. If he wanted to hold onto this relationship, he was going to have to bend a lot.

"How about a little action before I have the session with Vlad?" Blaire suggested, her voice dropping to a seductive whisper.

Andrew was immediately aroused and under her spell. "That would be nice."

She turned and went over to Vlad, "So I'll meet you at ten like you suggested. Out near the big Joshua tree, right?"

"Right," he replied, his eyes emitting a distant, evocative gaze.

Late that night, Andrew found himself still awake. Blaire had gone to meet with Vlad and left him to sleep. The passions of the previous hours had left him exhausted, and he sought slumber but didn't find it. He was left wondering as he lay in their sleeping gear. If she left Ash for me, what would prevent her from doing the same with someone else when I'm unaware of it? After all, that's what we did to him and Amber. Perhaps she's genuinely into this guy and just feeding me a line?

The moon was full, high in the night sky now, and the desert was bathed in a silver sheen. As he gazed out at the surrounding desert, he turned his attention to the giant Yucca tree where Blaire and Vlad's rendezvous was supposed to be, but he saw nothing but shadows. That was strange, she had pointed out where the giant yucca stood and assured him that if he got worried, he could always come over and check on her. But from where he stood, there appeared to be no one there.

He tried his best to shake off his fears, but it wasn't happening. He was too attached, too bound to Blaire to allow anyone else to have his way with her. He knew he stole her away from Ash. But he justified it. Ash was a monster, and Blaire was clearly looking for a way out. And as far as Amber was concerned, Andrew gave little thought to their relationship when he ran off with Blaire. It was sad, maybe even mean, but he had to be true to himself.

Andrew walked out toward the opening in the fence that led into the desert. He squinted into the twilight, looking in the direction of the large Yucca tree, hoping to see something recognizable. But there was nothing, just shadows and forms that wreaked havoc with his imagination. So, he pressed on through the gate into the dark.

Finally, he reached the spot where Blaire was to meet Vlad, and there was nothing there. All he could see in the moonlight were two indentations in the sandy soil and some strange markings between them. Maybe they're nearby, he told himself. So, he called to them, his voice barely above a whisper.

"Blaire, are you there?" his words seemed to disappear into the night with no effect. He waited another minute and then raised his voice a notch and called out again. "Blaire, where are you?"

"It's Carolyn," the voice behind him suddenly announced itself. The unknown sound pulled at the skin around his ears, stretching them to open wider as the shock of its abrupt declaration sent shivers through him. He whipped around, not sure what to expect. There was Carolyn, her striking face and dark locks caught in the moonlight, stark and unsettling. Immediately, all his anxieties melted away and, in their place, came reassuring warmth.

"Where did you come from?" he asked, his heart still racing.

"From the house." She pointed back toward the farm. "I couldn't sleep. It's so hot in there. Gator told me at dinner that this Yucca tree is magical, and I thought, Why not take a stroll out here and see for myself?"

"Are you looking for Blaire?"

"Yes, I can't find her."

"Oh, I see. Well, I hope you find her. You're Jade's brother, right?" She reached out a hand to greet him.

Andrew shook her hand. "Yes, Andrew. I saw you at dinner. You're a friend of hers."

He wanted to keep the conversation going. It was helping him get his mind off his fears about Blaire. "So where are you from?"

"San Diego. That's where I met Jade."

"Cool. I'm from up north. We've been here a few weeks. I've heard San Diego's a beautiful place. What brings you all the way out here to the desert?"

"First, Jade, and then a bunch of our friends back home told me about this place. The ranch, the desert, the Yucca trees. People said they give off these mystical vibrations. I also love the beauty of the desert, especially on a night like this. I'm an artist like Jade. That's why we've become such good friends."

"Well, this place certainly has a special beauty to it."

"It certainly does. Also, it looks like there's quite a unique group here at the ranch."

Andrew smiled inwardly, thinking about Vlad and Gator and a few others he'd met. "Yes, quite a unique group."

"So, what brings you here, Andrew?"

"Well, that's a long story. But in brief, we've just been exploring. It's been kind of like one of those road trips. You know, like what Kerouac did in On the Road. We came in with the little tribe of teepee builders. I guess you saw the tent when you arrived."

"It is hard to miss." Her smile was luminous in the moonlight.

"We came from Mendocino down the five and then to here."

"You've come a long way farther than I did."

"This place has a reputation that's even reached up north."

It felt weird standing here in the semidarkness talking to this beautiful young girl. Andrew suddenly reminded himself why he'd come out here in the first place. "Well, I guess I'd better be getting back. It looks like my effort to find Blaire has been unsuccessful. Would you like to go back with me?"

"No, you go ahead. I want to linger here a while longer and soak up the atmosphere. It's fascinating, the way the moonlight plays across the landscape."

She was an artist with an eye for unusual things. Andrew watched her as she scanned the horizon. Her face was truly angelic. There was innocence there, but also a healthy, joyous sensuality. He was drawn in by her smile and the way she seemed to embrace the beauty around her. "I'll see you later."

"Yes, I'll look forward to meeting your friend Blaire and hearing more about your journeys."

When Andrew arrived back at their shack, Blaire wasn't there. He wondered where she'd gone. How could she have left the meeting spot that Vlad had arranged with her and not come back to their place? The whole matter troubled him before, but now he was really concerned. Maybe Vlad had done something to her. What if he'd enticed her and led her off to some trysting place and had his way with her?

He headed over to the main house, but no one was in the central room. It appeared that everyone had turned in for the night. He returned to his place and lay down, forcing himself to rest and try to sleep.

Sometime just before dawn, he finally fell into slumber. In it, he saw Blaire stroking his brow and purring words of comfort. But then a strange figure moved into the doorway. He looked closer and made out the faint form of Vlad. His eyes were glowing hypnotically. They focused on Blaire, and she turned away from Andrew and rose to her feet. Spreading her arms out, she glided toward Vlad. When she reached him, she wrapped her arms around him and then her legs as he lifted her and carried her out into the night. The dream reoccurred several times until it faded into darkness.

When Andrew awoke, it was late morning, and he was still alone. He lay there still, wondering and questioning the events of the last few weeks: their session with Vlad, their arguments, Blaire's patronizing attitude, and their passionate lovemaking. He remembered the dreams and the struggles he had in the night. He remembered how Blaire told him she'd been there with him through it all. But now he distinctly remembered that she wasn't there on some of those nights. He'd been too drugged or exhausted to know for sure, but now with time to reflect, he could clearly recall that he was alone.

Andrew finally found the strength to stand and walk to the door of their shack. The sun pressed down on the landscape as he looked out toward the main house. A few people, including Samantha, were washing dishes from a late breakfast in the outdoor sink. He called out to them. "Have any of you seen Blaire?"

Samantha called back. "She's not here, but Gator told me this morning that she left with Vlad really early to go into town. He said she left a note for you in the main room. It's on the table."

Andrew was totally awake now. All his fears and concerns seemed as real as the baking sun and stark reality of this desert place. The first thing he thought of was the money. He'd been keeping it in a cabinet they found in their room. He thought he had the only key, but he was wrong. When he opened it, he found that half the money was gone. He dragged on his jeans as quickly as he could and headed to the house.

In the main room, on the table, he found an envelope with his name on it. He tore it open and read:

Andrew,

I've struggled with how to write this, but I realize now there's no perfect way to say goodbye to someone who has given me so much and yet can't go where I'm going.

You've been a passionate lover and a wild, beautiful spirit—but I need more than passion. I need transcendence. I've tried to bring you into that part of my life, my search for light and energy and deeper things, but you've been stuck—tethered to fear, to Ash, to shadows.

Vlad sees things in me you never could. Last night under the Yucca tree, something opened. I saw beyond the veil. When I looked into his eyes, I glimpsed my future—the one I thought I'd found with you. I was wrong. Those were illusions. What I feel now is real, and I can't turn from it.

I know this hurts. That's why I began giving you the tea—so you wouldn't feel everything all at once. I didn't mean it cruelly. I didn't want your anxiety and your dreams to consume you. I hoped the calm would help you ease into this parting without more damage. I was trying to protect you from yourself.

I'm leaving with Vlad. I can't say where we're going, but I need to follow this path. Maybe you'll say I betrayed you, but I was only ever following what felt true.

I took my fair share of the money. I hope you find peace. I really do.

Love,

Blaire

Andrew held the letter in his hands for a long time, just staring at the page but not reading it, the words were as out of focus as the confusing thoughts pouring through his mind. Deep at his core, he sensed this unseen hand pressing against his heart, crushing it, and at the same time thrusting needles of grief deep into its center. The pain filled his chest and then rushed to his head. He saw Blaire, her smile, her delicate features, her lithe body dancing away from him. Her laughter, which used to bring him such joy, now rang in his brain, taunting him, mocking him.

Slowly, but with all the force he could muster, Andrew crushed the letter in his hands until it was a tiny ball. Tears filled his eyes and spilled onto the table in front of him. His head followed them to its surface, and he wallowed there as time seemed to cease. Then, amid his sorrow, he heard a faint voice. It was a voice so soft and yet one full of comfort.

"Are you okay? Is there anything I can do?" Andrew looked down into his tears on the tabletop; they were like tiny jewels caught in the light streaming through the nearby window. They sparkled like beacons of hope during his torment. He heard the voice again. "Andrew, can I help?" At that moment, a tinge of courage seemed to flicker back at him in the crystalline liquid of his pain. Then there was another voice. "What happened, Andrew?" It was then that he gathered his nerve and looked up into the faces of two angels. First, he saw Jade and then beside her, Carolyn.

As he struggled to find words, the sun shifted, casting a gentle glow through the window that seemed to envelop the two women. In that moment, somewhere deep in the broken pieces of his heart, Andrew felt the first tentative stirrings of something he'd nearly forgotten existed: the possibility of healing.

Chapter Thirty-One

ENCINITAS

NOVEMBER · 2000

Waking up alone on the beach at night was alarming. Andrew's head felt heavy, and sand filled his mouth as he tried to move.

Then it all came rushing back, the confrontation at Brenton Tower: the shouting, the anger, the hollow look in Donovan's eyes. No matter how hard he tried to justify himself, nothing he said could undo the past. The pain of it settled in his chest like a cinderblock.

He staggered to his feet, brushing sand from his cheeks, and grabbed his shoes and the empty whiskey bottle.

The fog had snuck in while he slept, chilling him to the bone. Each step through the sand was difficult, as if his feet were in chains. The depression that had come over him was heavier now, smothering his heart and mind.

Through the thick fog, a figure loomed before him, dark and foreboding, with black-and-white tendrils swinging from its peak. Andrew's heart hammered against his ribs. The alcohol still clouded his judgment, but his survival instinct kicked in. He scrambled backward on the sand, hands searching for something, anything, he could use as a weapon.

"Easy there, brother." The voice was gravelly but not threatening. The figure stepped closer, and Andrew saw it was a man in a tattered overcoat, salt-and-pepper dreads swaying around his weathered face. Something about him seemed familiar, but Andrew couldn't place it through the fog of his hangover.

"You startled me," Andrew said, his voice hoarse. He remained crouched, ready to run or fight.

The stranger held up his hands, palms open. "This is sort of my space. I come here when it's empty to commune with nature." He studied Andrew's disheveled appearance with eyes that had seen too much. "You look like you've been through hell."

Andrew said nothing. Everything that had happened in the last twenty-four hours had left him on edge, unwilling to trust anyone, especially a stranger who'd just materialized out of the fog like some specter from his worst fears.

The stranger seemed to understand. "I've been living rough for three years. Tent cities, doorways, and beach caves when the weather turned mean. Lost everything when my company downsized, twenty-three years in pharmaceutical sales, gone in one afternoon." He gestured to Andrew's expensive but wrinkled clothes. "You've got that same look I had, man who built something, then watched it burn."

Despite himself, Andrew felt a flicker of recognition. "What changed?"

"My mom passed two months ago. Left me her unit in the Shamrock trailer park." The man's voice carried a weight of grief that sobered Andrew more than the ocean air. "I'd lost touch with her years ago, too proud, too angry about my own failures. Church contacted me when she died. Turns out she'd been asking about me, hoping I'd come around." His voice cracked slightly. "Never got that chance."

Andrew thought of his own situation, of all the bridges he'd burned. "I'm sorry."

"She went quietly. Probably in a better place." The stranger's eyes narrowed as he studied Andrew more carefully. "You sleeping off a stupor, or you planning to walk into those waves?"

The question hit Andrew like a physical blow. Had he been considering that? The thought frightened him more than the stranger's sudden appearance.

"Just the stupor," Andrew said, but his voice lacked conviction.

The man nodded slowly. "I've stood at that water's edge more nights than I care to count. It's a permanent solution to a temporary problem, as they say." He reached into his coat, and Andrew tensed again. But instead of a weapon, the stranger produced a small vial filled with white pills.

"Ecstasy. The good stuff. Self-medicating helps for a while." He held it out, but his expression was watchful, calculating. "Course, it's also a trap. One more thing to lose when you're already down to nothing."

For a moment, Andrew was tempted, anything to escape the pain of learning about Donovan, the son he'd once wished away and who now hated him. But then Amber's face came to him. Then Blaire's. Then Carolyn. He remembered Carolyn's gentleness, how he'd failed the women who truly loved him.

"On second thought, I'm good," Andrew said.

The man smiled for the first time, and Andrew saw intelligence behind the weathered features. "Smart choice. Pills are just another kind of quicksand." He pocketed the vial. "I'm Jonesy."

"Andrew."

Jonesy studied him again, and Andrew had the unsettling feeling he was being evaluated. "You want some real help? I got coffee at my place. Tylenol. Maybe some perspective from someone who's been where you are."

Andrew hesitated. Every instinct told him not to trust a stranger, especially one who'd just offered him drugs. But something in Jonesy's manner suggested he understood the particular kind of desperation that drove successful men to sleep on beaches.

"Why would you help me?" Andrew asked.

Andrew felt something shift inside him. The walls he'd built in the last several hours, walls of anger, self-loathing, and bitter isolation, began to crack. Maybe it was the hangover making him vulnerable, or perhaps it was the recognition that in this storm of his life, any friend, even a new one, would be a comfort. He found himself nodding.

They headed toward the trailer park, which had a "Stand by Me" vibe, toys and bikes scattered everywhere in the amber glow of streetlights. Donovan came to Andrew's thoughts. He imagined teaching him to ride a bike and catch a baseball. All his son had wanted was a father to be present.

Jonesy's trailer was surprisingly neat. They sat outside in lawn chairs, and Jonesy disappeared inside for a moment, returning with two steaming mugs. "Chamomile tea with a touch of ginger," he said, settling back into his chair. "Better than Tylenol for what ails you. Learned that from my mom, one of the few things she taught me before I was too stubborn to listen."

The tea was warm and soothing, cutting through the remnants of Andrew's hangover like a gentle tide washing over jagged rocks. For hours, they talked under the fading stars. Jonesy shared his life, backpacking through Europe in his twenties, losing his best friend in a climbing accident in the Alps, and the slow descent into homelessness after the layoffs. He spoke of couch surfing and living in shelters, of the small kindnesses that kept him human and the cruelties that nearly broke him.

"What kept you going?" Andrew asked, surprised by his own openness.

Jonesy was quiet for a long moment. "Guilt, mostly. Knowing my mom was out there somewhere, probably wondering if I was alive. Took me three years to swallow my pride enough to reach out, and by then..." He shrugged. "Sometimes the things that haunt us are the same things that save us."

Andrew found himself sharing bits of his own life, carefully editing out the worst parts. But when the conversation touched on deeper things, he pulled back. "I've got problems with something from my past," he said finally, his voice tight. "There's no hope, no possible way they can ever be made right."

"You got kids?" Jonesy asked quietly.

Andrew stared into his tea, the question hitting like a physical blow. "Yes, a son I never knew I had," he said after a long pause, his voice barely above a whisper. "But there's no hope. I can't even start to explain it."

"Then you've got something I'd give anything for, a chance to make it right." Jonesy's voice carried a finality that suggested his own chances were long gone. "Question is, what are you willing to do to earn it?"

The conversation gradually wound down as the first hints of dawn touched the horizon. Andrew felt his eyelids growing heavy, the combination of emotional exhaustion, the lingering effects of alcohol, and the soothing tea finally taking their toll.

"You can crash on my couch," Jonesy offered, seeing Andrew's fatigue. "It's not much, but it's clean and quiet."

Andrew wanted to protest, to maintain some dignity, but the truth was that going home would require too much effort, physically and emotionally. The thought of facing his empty house, of having to explain his disheveled state to anyone who might see him, felt unbearable. Right now, Jonesy's couch looked like the best choice he had. He had no energy left to pretend otherwise. Meeting Jonesy didn't feel like an accident, it felt like something else entirely, though he couldn't name what.

As sunrise approached, Andrew's eyes grew heavy. Jonesy offered his couch, and Andrew drifted into sleep slowly, as if descending into deep water. When REM overtook him, a dream arrived, vivid, surreal, and full of weight.

He found himself on the beach near where he'd met Jonesy, but now rocks were jutting from the sand like ancient sentinels. Turning, he spotted a narrow crevice in the stone. That could be a place to hide, to cover himself, to cover his shame. Instinct guided him forward, and he squeezed into the passage, but it grew tighter with every inch. Stone pressed against his shoulders, his chest, his legs, until it felt like the rock itself wanted to crush him.

Panic flared, but it wasn't the stone that frightened him, it was what he saw in the darkness. Shadows came alive, replaying the worst of his memories: the moments he had chosen self over others, pleasure over conscience, indulgence over love. Every betrayal, every justification, now stood stripped of illusion. The guilt was no longer abstract; it was personal, searing, inescapable.

Then, like a chime in the silence, the question rose: *How can I ever be free from this?*

The answer came like a surgeon's knife, swift and sharp. Not from without, but from within. He must choose. Not just vaguely regret, but forsake the path he'd walked. He must live differently. Not for self, but for the ones he claimed to love. Not for indulgence, but for redemption. It was not a punishment. It was a way forward.

And so, he chose.

With that decision, strength surged through him, not the strength of pride, but of resolve. He pushed forward, clawing toward a shaft of light that beckoned like hope itself. The struggle seemed endless, the birth pangs of a soul remade. But then he broke through. He emerged, gasping, and cried out.

An excellent brightness enveloped him. He felt his body lift from the ground, no longer crawling but rising. For a moment, he wondered if this was death. Below him lay his body, cold, still, draped across the darkened sand of Jonesy's couch.

Then came something stranger: the form he watched began to change. Before his eyes, it regressed, lines smoothing, features softening, until it was no longer a man, but an infant. Naked. New. Squirming in the surf of consciousness.

He gazed in wonder. The child was him. Vulnerable, yes, but untainted. A fresh beginning. Light surrounded the scene, golden and warm. A whisper, barely audible, reached his ears: *You are not finished. You are being made new.*

Gentle hands cradled the newborn with a tenderness he had not known since he could remember. Warmth enfolded him. Then, slowly, the dream began to fade, the light dimming.

But the peace didn't come immediately. Andrew drifted in and out of sleep, caught between the dream's promise and waking reality. Each time consciousness returned, the weight of his failures pressed down, Donovan's hatred, the years of selfish choices, the wreckage he'd left behind. The old Andrew would have reached for another bottle, would have run from the pain.

Instead, he found himself thinking of Jonesy's story, the regret of losing touch with his dying mother, the choice to help a stranger rather than walk away. The despair was still there, but something else was growing alongside it, not happiness, not even hope exactly, but something quieter. A willingness to sit with the pain instead of running from it. To face what he'd done and who he'd become.

The choice remained. And so did its promise.

When Andrew awoke, pale sunlight streamed through the trailer's small window. The couch beneath him was rough, the room unfamiliar, but something inside him had shifted. The despair hadn't vanished, but it no longer owned him.

He felt a sliver of peace. Not happiness, not even hope, at least not yet. But the possibility of it. The possibility of becoming someone new. Someone willing to stop running and begin facing the wreckage he'd left behind.

The road ahead would be long. But for now, in the quiet light of morning, he believed he could take the first step.

CHAPTER THIRTY-TWO

ENCINITAS

NOVEMBER · 2000

The vividness of his dream still clung to Andrew as he slowly awakened. He couldn't remember the last time he'd had a dream he wanted to capture, wanted to hold onto. The smell of coffee and something cooking drew him from the couch.

"Morning," Jonesy called from the small kitchen area. "Hope you don't mind scrambled eggs. It's about all I'm good at."

Andrew sat up, running his hands through his hair. "You don't have to ..."

"Already made too much." Jonesy appeared with two plates and steaming mugs. "Besides, can't send a man out into the world on an empty stomach."

They ate in comfortable silence at first, the simple meal grounding Andrew in a way he hadn't expected. The eggs were perfectly cooked, seasoned with something that tasted like hope.

"Thank you," Andrew said finally. "For last night. For this. I don't know what I would have done."

Jonesy shrugged. "Everyone needs a soft place to land sometimes."

They talked easily as they finished breakfast, about the weather, the trailer park, small things that didn't require emotional excavation. When Andrew stood to leave, he felt steadier than he had in hours.

"Thanks for the advice," he said, meaning it. "About having a chance to make things right. I'll be in touch."

"You better," Jonesy replied with a slight smile. "Don't be a stranger."

They embraced briefly, two men who'd found something unexpected in their brokenness.

Andrew stepped back, feeling oddly reluctant to leave this small sanctuary. "I should let you get on with your day."

"No rush," Jonesy said, but he understood. Some conversations had natural endings, and this was one of them.

Andrew gathered his socks and shoes, taking his time with the simple task. The trailer felt smaller now, but in a good way, intimate rather than cramped. He wondered what time it was. Looking at his watch, he saw it was eight thirty.

"I need to get cleaned up," he said, more to himself than to Jonesy. "Think I'll head to the beach showers, not wanting to impose any further."

Jonesy nodded. "Those work fine. I've had to use it back in the day."

Andrew moved toward the door, then paused with his hand on the handle. "Thanks again, Jonesy. For everything."

"Take care of yourself, Andrew. And remember what I said, some things can be made right if you're willing to do the work."

He pushed open the door and was momentarily blinded by the brightness outside. As his senses cleared, he heard the voices of kids laughing and playing. As his eyes adjusted to the morning light, he was greeted by children running around. The park was alive.

Andrew started walking towards the beach. A little girl, no more than four, smiled at him as she pushed along on her scooter. He looked at the clouds over the horizon, their edges gilded with morning light. When he reached Moonlight Beach, the ocean was alive with surfers hoping for the perfect wave. There were a few people there, some jogging in his direction, others settling in for the day with their beach chairs and ice chests. The warmth of the sun on his face reminded him of the warmth he felt in his dream.

He made his way to the water, cupped his hands, and brought the liquid to his face. After a couple of doses of seawater, he felt refreshed. He was glad to be alive. Thankful for a new day, grateful for a new friend.

It had been quite an amazing and crazy twenty-four hours. As he moved up the sand toward the public restrooms, he slowly reviewed all that had happened to him. He remembered the confrontation and revelation in Lasseter's office. He recalled the hours he spent on the beach, grappling with guilt, the encounter with Jonesy, which was unnerving at first and could have turned out very differently. Again, he felt a sense of gratitude that last night he could honestly say he made the right decision and didn't take the opportunity to escape.

Andrew was doing his best to make sense of it all when suddenly, he remembered that it was Saturday, almost nine o'clock. That was when he was scheduled for his weekly meeting with Chandler, now that he was back in school. It all made sense now why the trailer park was full of kids playing. It was the weekend.

He was in no condition to hang out with Chandler today, but he couldn't let Jade down. He had to think of something. Maybe, he'd just text her he was sick. No, he was going to have to face her and let her in on everything. He needed to meld his past and present together, finally. He needed to start looking forward to true healing and take whatever medicine was prescribed by his doctor.

By the time he reached the parking lot, her car was pulling in. He waved to her, and she headed his direction. As she pulled up alongside him, he could see the look of concern on her face. She obviously saw his condition. She guided the car into one of the parking spaces beside him and got out. She opened the back door to let Chandler out and then asked him, "What in the world has happened to you, Andrew? You're a mess."

"Listen, Jade, I can explain." Just then, Chandler ran up to Andrew's side.

"Are you okay, Andrew?" The boy's face was etched with concern, his eyes wide and questioning.

"Yes, buddy. Better now that I can see you two." Andrew tried to muster a reassuring smile, though his facial muscles felt stiff with exhaustion.

"Did you sleep here?" Jade asked, her voice tinged with a mixture of worry and disapproval.

"Jade, I have so much to tell you." Andrew ran a hand through his disheveled hair, knowing how he must look to them.

"Sleeping on the beach, that sounds fun," Chandler said, bouncing slightly on his toes.

"It was quite exciting but not really that fun", Andrew said to himself.

Jade came over to Andrew's side and reached out a hand of comfort. "Wow, you look tired." The morning sun highlighted the dark circles under his eyes and the stubble on his chin.

"I promise, I'm good, like excellent. I just need a shower." Andrew tried to sound convincing.

"Does that mean you're not going to watch me today?" Chandler said, disappointed.

"I'm afraid not, Chandler." Andrew felt a pang of guilt at the boy's crestfallen expression.

"Well then, I guess... I'll have to tell you later." Chandler turned and looked out toward the ocean; his small shoulders slumped.

Then Andrew remembered how he'd seen the boy conflicted these past weeks, wanting to reveal something to him but never quite able to get it out. "Tell me what later?" he asked.

"My secret. I was going to tell you today." Chandler looked up at him, his eyes serious and determined.

Some internal voice told Andrew that what Chandler was about to share with him was infinitely more important than his missing out on building a sandcastle.

"What did you want to tell me?"

"I asked Jade, and she said it's okay to tell you." Chandler glanced at Jade for confirmation.

Andrew looked over at his sister, and she nodded her approval. So, he turned back to the boy and knelt beside him. "Okay, go ahead."

Chandler paused just for a moment and then began. "You see, my real name isn't Chandler, it's Payton. My daddy told me that I must use this name, Chandler, when I'm out on the beach."

Andrew looked at Jade, completely taken aback. "What's he talking about?"

"It's true," Jade said, tucking a strand of hair behind her ear. "When I got hired, his dad told me I could never let anyone else know his real identity. It seemed kind of paranoid to me, but you know how these rich folks can be. They think the whole world is out to steal their child or get their money. But Payton's been bugging me to tell you the truth, so I finally agreed to let him. He says he won't tell his dad. I hope this doesn't get me fired."

Once again, Andrew had believed one thing when an entirely different situation was going on around him. He did his best to brush it aside for the moment. What was important was that this boy knew his name change wouldn't alter Andrew's feelings towards him.

Andrew gave the boy a soft smile. "So, you're Payton."

The boy nodded, still standing a little straighter than before.

"Well, now that you've been so brave, mind if I ask your last name?"

"Lasseter," the boy said.

Something inside Andrew staggered. The name struck like a chord, long buried but never forgotten.

As he looked closer into the boy's face, another face began to emerge—not in reality, but in memory, a face from thirty years ago.

There it was: the slight curl at the edge of the smile, the same rich brown eyes flecked with green. A distant echo stirred, wind in the redwoods, laughter in a sunlit meadow, voices long silenced by time. He stared for several seconds, not just looking at the boy, but through him, through years of regret, loss, and half-buried hope. The line of his nose, the shape of his chin, the subtle way he tilted his head, it was all too familiar.

He swallowed, carefully.

"And your dad," he asked quietly, "what's his name?"

The child didn't hesitate. "Donovan. Donovan Lasseter."

Andrew felt as if someone had punched him in the gut. The world seemed to spin around him, and he had to struggle to maintain his balance. He stared at the boy, trying to process what he'd just heard.

"He's a very important man. He has a huge office at the top of a building. I'm not supposed to tell anyone about me, and my daddy says I'm special. He says I must be protected from bad people."

Andrew reached out and took the boy's hands in his. He struggled not to crush them in his grasp. The sensation of those small fingers in his own nearly undid him. "Do you have any brothers or sisters, Payton?"

"No, sir. It's just me, my daddy, and mommy. But I have an uncle. His name is Ryan. He's my daddy's brother. I like my uncle better, though, 'cause he's a lot nicer to me."

Andrew couldn't believe what he was hearing. Thoughts rushed through his mind like a runaway train. Donovan was the man who had set him up. The man who had crafted that whole elaborate scheme to destroy his dream. The man who had called himself Andrew's son. And now this boy, this beautiful, innocent child he'd come to love over the past few months, was telling him that Donovan was his father. Which could only mean one thing: this child was Andrew's grandson.

He looked closer at the boy's face, searching for something in the features, something he'd somehow missed before. And then he saw it, the cleft in the chin, the way his left eyebrow arched when he was curious, even that slight dimple that appeared when he smiled. They were all markers Andrew had seen in his own mirror. And then there was that small gesture, a way of tilting his head when asking a question. It was the exact change that Amber used to give him as her eyes crinkled when she smiled. Yes, it was there, that smile, the reason they called her sunshine. Then the irony of it all hit him. He'd been rejected by a son he never knew, but here before him was the grandson he didn't think he had, and he liked him, maybe even loved him.

Andrew started to cry, overwhelmed with what he'd just discovered.

"Are you okay, Andrew?" Jade said, moving closer with concern.

"Why are you crying?" Payton asked, his small face pinched with worry.

Andrew was looking at him for the first time as his flesh and blood. It was as if he were looking at a young version of himself. He'd missed so much. If he were honest, it had always been about him, even with Payton. He was here to help Jade and to help the boy, but really, it was more than that, he liked that paternal feeling. It was filling that hole inside. The hole he'd made himself, the one that came from never being a father, never having a family. That was the real driving factor in his time with the boy. His heart began to fill with a deep sense of affection for him. He thought he was special before, but now everything had changed. Now that he knew Payton was his grandson, he didn't want to leave him. He wanted him to see the truth and know who he really was.

He knew it was risky and would undoubtedly be painful, but he had to do it. But how could he tell him? His father hated Andrew, and if he knew Andrew was here with his boy, well, he'd put an end to it right now. Looking at his innocent face, Andrew so wished there was a way to reconcile with his son. He wished there were some way for him to forgive himself. But the hurt was still there in his heart: the vast, painful revelation that he'd been deceived. Yes, he'd been deceived.

It was time to face his fears and stop running. Andrew forced himself to confront it. He stood up and faced Jade. Suddenly, the haunting voice that had troubled him repeatedly these last few months exploded in his memory, phantom words that had never actually been spoken but felt real as razors in his skull: *You're cursed, you thief. Your dreams are history. I'm coming for you. You're dead.* He shook his head, trying to dispel the imagined threats that his guilt had conjured.

"Jade, the man who hired you, who was it, Jade? Was his name Lasseter, Donovan Lasseter?"

"Yes, it was Lasseter, but ...."

Jade looked over Andrew's shoulder, and her eyes flashed with recognition. "There's his car right there," said Jade. Andrew's breath caught. He knew that vehicle, the black SUV. It had been haunting him for weeks, creeping at the edge of his vision, parked across from the café, idling down the street. His worst fears flooded back in a rush. Was this it? Had Donovan finally decided to come for him?

Was this the reckoning he couldn't outrun? A wave of panic surged through him, cold and suffocating, like drowning in ice water. His vision tunneled. His heart hammered against his ribs. The world seemed to tilt sideways, reality fracturing at the edges. Without thinking, without any conscious thought at all, he reached down and scooped up Payton, pulling him protectively against his chest. The boy's small body felt fragile, breakable, like something precious that needed shielding from a storm. Every nerve, every instinct that had lain dormant for decades suddenly roared to life: protect the boy. Get him away. Run.

This wasn't rational thought anymore; this was something primal, something that bypassed his brain entirely and went straight to his bones. He'd failed as a father once. He wouldn't fail again. Not with this child. Not when it mattered most. The boy didn't deserve to be caught in the crossfire of adult failures, adult rage, and adult mistakes that stretched back years. "Please, God," he shouted, his voice cracking with desperation. "It's too much for me. I know I deserve it, but my grandson doesn't."

Shocked by his actions and his words, Jade grabbed Chandler out of Andrew's arms and moved away from him. At that very moment, the car stopped beside them. Andrew looked to the driver's window but couldn't see in, the tinted glass hiding whoever was inside. Then, slowly, the door opened, and the man who had confronted him in the office the day before emerged toward him.

Andrew's feet scraped against asphalt as he backed away, his body moving without conscious thought, every instinct screaming danger. The man took another step forward. Andrew's vision tunneled, the morning light suddenly too bright, the ocean breeze too sharp against his skin. His hands trembled at his sides, caught between the urge to flee and the need to protect Payton.

"Andrew," Jade's voice cut through the roar of blood in his ears. "What are you doing? That's the man who hired me."

The words didn't penetrate. Andrew's gaze remained locked on the approaching figure, same angular jaw, same piercing eyes that had blazed with hatred just yesterday. The ghost of Donovan's voice echoed in his skull: *You're nothing to me. You never were.*

"Hey... It's all right," the man said, his hands rising slowly, palms open in a gesture that seemed foreign on features Andrew had only seen twisted in contempt.

"No, it's not." Andrew's voice cracked, raw with decades of accumulated wounds. "You cursed me yesterday and told me you never wanted to see me again."

The man stopped. Something shifted in his expression, not the cold satisfaction Andrew expected, but genuine confusion. Then, impossibly, his mouth curved into a smile. Not Donovan's bitter smirk, but something warmer, fuller.

"Cursed you? I never cursed you." The voice was wrong too, same timbre, but missing the sharp edges that had flayed Andrew's soul. A pause, then understanding dawned across the familiar features. "I'm not Donovan, I'm Ryan. Donovan's twin."

Andrew froze. Something wasn't right. The face, it was familiar, achingly familiar, but wrong somehow. His mind scrambled through the fog of panic. The features were there, yes, the same sharp jawline, the same deep-set eyes, the same mouth that could have been carved from his own genetic blueprint. But something was off.

Wait. Wait.

He blinked hard, forcing himself to really look. Yesterday, when he'd seen that face, it had been twisted with fury, eyes blazing with years of rage and betrayal. The man who'd confronted him had radiated violence, had looked at him like he wanted to tear him apart.

But this face was calm. Concerned, maybe. Confused. There was no fire in these eyes, no burning hatred. Just clarity. A gentle sort of strength that was utterly foreign to what he'd witnessed before.

Of course. His mind had been so clouded by fear and guilt that he'd only seen what he expected to see. He'd only met Donovan once, and in that moment, everything had been blurred by rage and shame. He should have seen it immediately, but terror had made him blind.

Now he could see the difference. This was Ryan's face, carrying all the same features that marked him as family. But there was no vengeance here. No anger. This wasn't the same man at all.

"Hi, Uncle Ryan!" Payton's delighted cry shattered the spell. The boy darted forward, small arms wrapping around the man's legs in uninhibited joy.

"Hi, Payton." Ryan's hand settled on the boy's head, ruffling his hair with easy affection. The gesture was so natural, so devoid of calculation, that Andrew felt the iron bands around his chest begin to loosen.

His knees suddenly felt weak. The adrenaline that had flooded his system moments before drained away, leaving him hollow and shaking. He reached out unquestioningly, found the hood of a nearby car to steady himself, as the truth settled over him like a blanket after a fever breaks.

Not Donovan. Ryan. A twin he'd never known existed. Another ghost from a past that kept revealing new chambers of loss and possibility.

"Wait. What?" Andrew could hardly process all that was coming at him. He looked at Jade and realized that she was just as confused as he was.

"Andrew, what the heck is going on?" Jade's eyes darted between Andrew and Ryan, trying to make sense of the situation.

In a state of wonder, Andrew looked back at the man known as Ryan. He wasn't sure how to start, but he forced himself to explain. "This man's brother... and this... man, Ryan, are my sons."

"Your sons?" Jade's voice rose in disbelief.

"Yes, it's a long story. I just found out." Andrew's hands trembled slightly as he spoke.

Jade just stood there, staring at him, her eyes clouded with shock.

"You're telling me I've been working for your son... and you never told me any of this?"

Andrew's shoulders sagged. "I didn't know. Not until right now."

She folded her arms, her voice tight. "You told me about Amber once, vaguely. But twins? That you might have kids? You never said a word."

"Because I thought it...I mean, they were gone. That Amber had..." He stopped himself, the memory crashing over him like a wave. The tent. That moment of truth when she'd told him about the pregnancy. He'd already been leaving, his lust for Blaire pulling him toward a different life entirely. Her tear-streaked face as the words tumbled out. His own panicked response, the words that had poured out of him like poison: *You have to get rid of it. We can't, I can't.* Her broken sobs, the way she'd looked at him like he'd just shattered something irreparable between them.

One baby. That's what they'd thought. One mistake to be erased.

He never saw her again after that night. Even years later, when she'd called out of nowhere to forgive him, to tell him she'd found peace, even then, she'd never mentioned them and never said a word about what had really happened.

But it hadn't been one. Somehow, that single pregnancy had been twins. Twins she'd discovered later, twins she'd chosen to keep despite his cruel demand, twins she'd raised in secret while he'd spent decades believing his words had destroyed everything.

"I didn't believe they existed until I saw Donovan. And now this. Ryan." His voice cracked. Two sons. Two lives that had grown and flourished in complete silence, while he'd carried the guilt of what he thought he'd made her do.

Jade shook her head slowly, the hurt flickering across her face. "You've kept so much from me, Andrew. You're my brother. I've trusted you."

He looked at her, guilt rising. "And I want to earn that trust back. I do."

For a moment, neither of them spoke. Then Jade exhaled, her face softening. "This is a lot. But you're here. And Payton... he matters."

She smiled at Payton and moved in his direction. "That makes you my great-nephew." She reached for his hand, and Payton took it, his small fingers curling around hers.

Ryan looked at Andrew and then at Jade. "You see, Donovan was so busy, so distracted by his work, that he asked me to find a nanny for Payton. So, I arranged this entire thing. I found Jade. It's a long story and I'll explain it all later." He paused, glancing toward the water where children were still playing. "But I want you to know—I've been here several times over the past months, watching from a distance when Jade brought Payton to meet with you."

Now, Andrew understood the appearance of the mysterious Range Rover. It had been Ryan all along. His paranoia had been misplaced; someone was watching but watching over them in a good way.

"I needed to see if there was real chemistry, real bonding happening between you two. I was hoping my plan would work." A small smile crossed Ryan's face. "And it looks like it did. The connection between you and Payton is exactly what I hoped for. But be assured, Donovan has no idea Payton's been playing at the beach with his grandfather."

Ryan reached out to assure Andrew. He rested his hand on Andrew's shoulder. "I want to confront him about it when the time is right, and I want Payton and you to come with me when I do. I want to reintroduce you to each other again, but this time as grandfather and grandson."

Andrew's heart was overwhelmed at that moment as Ryan continued. "I found a way to forgive you years ago. Mom told me what you'd done and the way you left her, but instead of getting bitter, well, as I thought through it over the years, I was able to forgive you. I just wanted to find you. I wanted to find my father and know who he was... I wanted to know him, no matter what he'd done to us. Then I discovered that Donovan had located you and what he was up to. He told me about his plan for revenge. But it just seemed wrong. We ended up in a serious argument. He still refuses to talk to me about it. I know he's filled with bitterness. But I knew there must be a better way. It's time for Donovan to start forgiving. Dad, you're not the only one who needs forgiveness."

The word "dad" sent shivers through every fiber of Andrew's body. He couldn't believe he heard it, and it was meant for him.

Ryan rested his hand on Payton's shoulder, smiled down at the boy, and then looked back at Andrew with concern. He leaned in close and whispered in Andrew's ear. "The way I've seen Donovan treating Payton, within another ten years he'll hate his dad as much as Donovan hates you today."

He leaned back, looked down at the boy, and spoke to all of them. "Maybe together we'll see Donovan find a place in his heart for his dad." Ryan smiled at Payton again. "I know his grandson has."

Payton looked up at Andrew, a huge question in his eyes. "What do you mean, Uncle Ryan? Do I have a grandfather? Dad always said he died."

Payton looked back and forth between Ryan and Andrew several times, trying to take it all in. Then, slowly, just the slightest flicker of sunshine lit up his eyes, and he asked, "Are you my grandfather, Andrew?"

"Yes... Yes, I am." Andrew stooped down and gave Payton a huge hug. The boy hugged back, his small arms wrapping tightly around Andrew's neck.

Andrew let go and tried to stand up, but he was overwhelmed. There were no words. Ryan reached down and helped him up. "Here's my address and phone number. There's a lot to talk about." Ryan handed Andrew a card.

Andrew stared at the business card in his hand, the paper trembling slightly. The morning sun caught the embossed lettering: Ryan Lasseter, GENORYX – Bio-Medical Research. His thumb traced over the name, Lasseter, not Foster, another sign of the fracture in the family tree.

He turned the card over. Ryan's handwriting was nothing like Donovan's sharp slashes, it flowed with confident ease. A home address in Del Mar. A cell number. An invitation where he'd expected only rejection.

Andrew stared at the business card, his mind reeling from everything that had just unfolded. The morning's revelations crashed over him in waves, Payton was his grandson, Ryan was his son, Donovan had a twin brother who chose forgiveness over revenge. It was too much to process standing in a beach parking lot.

"Ryan," Andrew said urgently, his voice thick with emotion, "I need to understand all of this. I need answers, about Donovan, about what happened between you two, about everything. Can we talk more? As soon as possible?"

Ryan smiled, a knowing look in his eyes. "I figured you'd need that. That's why I'm inviting you both over, tonight, if you're willing."

"Do you really think that we can reason with Donovan?" Andrew asked.

"I'm hoping so. He's got a lot of pain and anger. But I believe it's nothing; time and understanding can't heal." Ryan looked down at Payton. The boy was smiling up at Andrew. "I think the smile on your grandson's face will be a perfect place to start."

"Yes, it's a great one." Andrew felt a warmth spreading through him as he looked at Payton's beaming face.

"Sometimes a smile can do more than a ton of words." Ryan looked down at Payton one more time and then back at Andrew. "6 o'clock for drinks and then dinner," Ryan said through the open window, his tone casual as if he hadn't just rewritten Andrew's understanding of his lost family. "I'll see you both tonight." He looked at Jade and waved as he got back into the SUV.

Andrew's mouth moved before his mind caught up. "Yes, see you then."

Beside him, Jade echoed the words, her voice carrying the same note of bewilderment. They stood there like survivors of a shipwreck, watching the Range Rover pull away, the exact vehicle that moments before had seemed like a harbinger of destruction, now carrying away a promise of something Andrew had stopped believing in.

Redemption, perhaps. Or at least the possibility of a different ending than the one he'd written for himself in the dark hours of too many sleepless nights.

After Ryan left, Jade came over and hugged Andrew, her initial shock giving way to compassion.

"I really can't process all this right here," she said, looking down at Payton, who was still trying to understand what had just happened. "I need to get Payton home first, I'm still his nanny, and his father will be expecting him. Then you need to get cleaned up." She looked at Andrew's rumpled clothes and beach-matted hair. "You can't show up at Ryan's looking like you slept on the beach."

"Right," Andrew said, suddenly aware of how he must look. "I need a shower and clean clothes."

"I'll drop you at your place first," Jade said, opening the car door for Payton. "Then I'll take Payton home and come back to pick you up. We should talk more before we go to Ryan's, I still have about a thousand questions."

Six hours later, Andrew stepped out of his bedroom in clean clothes and found Jade waiting in the living room. She had returned from dropping Payton off and had taken time to freshen up for dinner at her place. Now, she sat quietly on the couch, still processing everything she'd just learned.

"Feel better?" she asked.

"Much," Andrew said, settling into the chair across from her. "Now, you said you had questions."

For the next hour, they talked, or instead, Jade questioned, and Andrew answered. She asked about Amber, about Big Sur, about the choices Andrew had made decades ago. There were definitely a few heated moments, a few wounds created, but Andrew could see his sister working through her shock and disappointment, trying to reconcile the brother she thought she knew with the man who had kept such enormous secrets.

"I did keep you in the dark about much of my past," Andrew admitted. "But wasn't that what big brothers do, protect?"

"Protect, maybe," Jade said, leaning back in her chair. "But not lie. Not for thirty years." Her voice was soft but firm. "This is going to take time, Andrew. For me to trust you again."

"I know," he said. "But I have faith that time will heal this, and our relationship will become stronger."

Jade stood up, straightening her purse. "We should go. We don't want to be late for Ryan's."

They headed out to her car in the driveway, ready to drive to Ryan's. Once they were both settled inside, Jade reached for the ignition, but Andrew's hand touched her arm gently. "Wait," he said softly.

A yellow butterfly landed on the side mirror. "Don't move for a moment," Andrew whispered, not wanting any sudden motion to scare it away.

He watched it intently, his mind racing. The dream he had at Jonesy's suddenly came flooding back, squeezing out of the rock, the out-of-body experience, seeing himself reborn as a baby. That was it. It all made sense now. It was the same as when a caterpillar emerges from its cocoon and becomes a butterfly. It becomes something totally different; it's not the same creature at all.

Today, Andrew has been given a new life as a dad, as a grandfather. He watched as the butterfly flew away and took a deep breath. "Thank you," he whispered to the empty air.

"You okay?" Jade asked softly.

Andrew nodded, then suddenly heard a vibration from his phone. He hadn't even thought about his phone since last night. There were several texts from Jimmy and one from Nicole.

He opened hers. It was two words: "Call me."

Andrew stared at the message for a long moment, his finger hovering over the screen. He took a deep breath and dialed her number; his heart filled with a hope he hadn't felt in a long time. As the phone rang, he gazed out at the clear blue sky, wondering what other miracles this day might hold.

CHAPTER THIRTY-THREE

DEL MAR

NOVEMBER • 2000

Jade's older Camry climbed the tree-lined streets of Del Mar, passing estate after estate tucked behind hedges and gates. Andrew caught glimpses of the ocean between the properties, teasing views that promised something spectacular ahead.

"That's it," Jade said, turning into a circular drive where a Range Rover sat beside a midnight-blue Mercedes S-Class. "Ryan's place."

The house rose before them, contemporary but warm, with clean lines softened by natural wood and golden stone. Not ostentatious, but quietly confident in its elegance.

"I still can't believe it," Andrew said as Jade parked. "Payton is my grandson." The words came out with the same wonder he'd felt all day, like a man repeating a miracle to make it real.

The front door opened before they reached it. Ryan stood there, Andrew's younger self, but without the damage. The revelation still made Andrew's chest tight.

"Welcome," Ryan said, then called back, "Elena, they're here."

A woman appeared, graceful, with honey-colored hair and a warmth that radiated from her hazel eyes. "Andrew, Jade," she said, stepping forward with open arms. "We're so glad to finally meet you both. Ryan's told me so much about you."

Two children materialized behind their parents. The boy, perhaps eleven, had Ryan's coloring. The girl, a year younger, made Andrew's breath catch.

Andrew smiled at them both. "Good to meet you, kids. This is Jade, my sister."

Elena took both of Andrew's hands, her expression growing more serious. "Ryan told me everything about The Precipice project," she said gently. "What they did to you was unconscionable."

"This is Marcus," Ryan said. "And Sophia."

Sophia tilted her head, studying him, and Andrew saw it, Amber. Not a ghost or an accusation, but a gentle echo of the woman who had once been everything to him. Those same luminous eyes, the delicate curve of her smile, the way she held her head when curious.

"She looks just like her," Andrew whispered to Ryan. "Like Amber when she was young."

Ryan nodded. "Mom's beauty lives on in all of us. But without the pain."

"Are you really an architect?" Sophia asked.

"I try to be," Andrew said, his voice rough with memory and wonder. "Though my father was the famous one."

Marcus stepped forward with easy confidence. "Dad says you design research centers. That's cool." Andrew smiled, but something caught in his throat. Watching Marcus, the way he stood, the spark in his eyes, he couldn't help but wonder: *Was Donovan like that once? Before the bitterness? Before the walls?* He'd missed everything. The scraped knees, the questions, the dreams. What kind of boy had he been? And what kind of man could he have become, if only Andrew had stayed?

"We thought about having Payton here," Ryan said, "but this moment needed to be about you first. About restoring what was lost. Donovan doesn't know about any of this yet, and until he does, we have to be careful."

"Come," Elena said, rescuing him from the emotion threatening to overwhelm. "Let's have wine on the terrace."

They moved through the house, understated elegance in every detail, to the French doors that opened onto a terrace. The view stole Andrew's breath. An infinity pool seemed to spill directly into the Pacific, the horizon line blurring where water met sky. The sun was beginning its descent, painting everything gold.

"This is..." Andrew stopped, searching for words.

"It's why we bought it," Ryan said, pouring wine. "Elena fell in love with the view."

"I fell in love with the potential," Elena corrected, handing Jade a glass. "The house was a disaster when we found it."

As the children splashed in the shallow end of the pool, the four adults settled into teak chairs facing the ocean. The wine was good, not showy, just good. Like everything here, Andrew thought, success worn lightly.

"Tell me about the medical research center," Ryan said. "The Precipice."

Andrew glanced at him, recognizing the genuine curiosity in his voice. "It was supposed to be revolutionary. A coastal facility that nurtured the whole person, not just their research."

"My company might be interested," Ryan said, watching his children play. "If we can get Donovan involved."

"Donovan." Even now, the name stung.

"Elena and Jacqueline, Donovan's wife, are close," Ryan said meaningfully. "My wife has a gift for helping people see past their own walls."

Elena's eyes lit up. "Talking about my superpowers again?" She smiled at Andrew. "Jacqueline says Donovan's been different lately. Questioning things. She thinks something's shifting in him. He doesn't say it, but she sees it, how he lingers in silence, asks questions he never used to. It's a crack. A beginning."

Dinner was warm and chaotic, Marcus describing his soccer game, Sophia showing Andrew her sketches, stories flowing like wine. Andrew found himself laughing at something Marcus said, then stopped, startled by the sound. When had he last laughed at a family dinner?

"More potatoes, Mr. Andrew?" Sophia asked, then looked at her father. "Dad told us you're Andrew Foster." She hesitated, glancing between Andrew and Ryan. "Maybe... maybe we could call you Grandpa? I mean, if that's okay?"

Andrew felt his throat tighten, his eyes misting slightly. "That's completely up to you, children. I'm not sure I've done anything yet to earn such a precious title, but hearing you say it... It sounds like music to my heart."

Ryan's expression was firm but gentle. "Andrew, you don't need to earn being their grandfather, you already are. And kids, calling him Grandpa isn't just okay, it's exactly right. We're all learning how to be a family together, but the love is already here."

Jade looked around the table with wonder, her voice soft with realization. "I'm still trying to wrap my head around all of this. Sophia, Marcus, you're my great niece and nephew." She smiled, tears gathering in her eyes. "And you, Elena...I never imagined... I mean, I thought maybe we'd find some answers about our family, but not this. Not all of you."

The simple domesticity of it, being included in this ritual of passing dishes and sharing stories, nearly undid him.

As the evening wound down, Elena touched Andrew's arm. "We do this more often," she said. "You're expected, both of you."

"That would be wonderful."

"Family dinner," she said simply. "All of us. And soon, hopefully, Donovan, Jacqueline, and Payton too."

At the door, Ryan pulled him into an unexpected, firm, genuine embrace. "This is just the beginning, Dad."

In the car, Jade navigated the dark streets towards Encinitas while Andrew sat quietly, processing.

"Good thing I drove," she said gently.

"I'm not drunk," Andrew said. "Just..."

"High on hope?"

He looked at his sister, she'd seen it all. The dreams when he was young, the career he'd built with such promise, and then the spectacular wreckage of every relationship he'd touched. She'd never given up on him, even when he'd given up on himself.

"Is that what this feeling is?" he asked.

"It's good to see you alive again, Andrew. Really alive."

She pulled up in front of his place and turned to face him. "All those years of watching you pour everything into your projects, dreaming, building, hoping to bring Dad's vision to fruition, thinking if you just created something perfect enough, it would fill the holes you left in people's lives." Her voice was soft, knowing. "But this, family, connection, showing up, this is the real architecture."

They embraced across the console, the gesture carrying decades of shared history, celebrations and catastrophes, dreams and demolitions.

"Nicole's call earlier," she said quietly. "The meeting she wants to have with you... that could be another miracle, couldn't it? If you two found your way back to each other?"

"Wouldn't that be something," Andrew said, his voice filled with cautious hope. "My new family wants me, and maybe Nicole still wants me too."

"I believe they all do," Jade said quietly. "And maybe that's the miracle, they're all willing to make it happen."

As he watched her taillights disappear, Andrew stood outside, looking up at stars he hadn't noticed in years. Hope, he thought. The most dangerous high of all. But this one could save him.

CHAPTER THIRTY-FOUR

SOLANA BEACH

NOVEMBER • 2000

Andrew turned off Via de la Valle and climbed into the hills east of I-5, leaving the coastal fog behind. Solana Beach's modest neighborhoods sprawled across the ridgelines, not the oceanfront glamour of Del Mar, but solid homes where real people built real lives, the November evening wrapped around him like silk, Indian summer holding on with both hands.

Nicole's street curved past ranch-style homes and mature eucalyptus trees. Two days had passed since their phone call, tentative at first, then warming as they found their rhythm again. "Come for dinner," she'd said. "Let's see where we are." He'd replayed her voice in his head over and over. Hope had crept in slowly, cautiously, but now, seeing her again, it surged like light through a cracked window.

He parked his car in front of her craftsman bungalow, its deep eaves and stone pillars solid against the amber sky. The house suited her, unpretentious but beautifully maintained, with purple sage and Mexican marigolds spilling from the garden beds.

She opened the door before he knocked. Forty-two years old, wearing a simple white blouse and jeans, her amber hair caught back in a loose knot. No pretense, no armor. Just Nicole.

"You came," she said.

"You invited me."

They stood there for a moment, testing the space between them. Too much time apart after only four months together, it should have felt awkward. Instead, it felt like breathing again.

"Dinner's almost ready. Let's go out back."

He followed her through the house, catching glimpses of the life she'd continued without him. Work files from her PR firm were stacked on the dining table. The proposal for The Precipice, which they'd worked on together, was still visible in a folder marked "PENDING."

The backyard opened to a view of the canyon, wild chaparral tumbling down to the developed valley below. No ocean view, but the space had its own beauty, string lights wrapped through the pergola, a table set for two, citronella candles flickering against the approaching dusk.

"Sit," she said. "Wine?"

"Please."

She poured a Pinot Noir, something from the Central Coast. They clinked glasses carefully, eyes meeting over the rims.

"Tell me about Ryan," she said, settling across from him. "About all of it."

Andrew took a breath, then began. The words came easier than he'd expected, Ryan's appearance at the beach, the revelation that Payton was his grandson, dinner at Ryan's house in Del Mar. Elena's warmth. Marcus and Sophia, carrying echoes of the past into the future.

"And in Sophia's face," he said, his voice catching, "I saw Amber. Not angry or accusing. Just... there. Beautiful. Like grace."

Nicole reached across the table, her fingers brushing his. "Grace. That's what you needed, isn't it?"

"What I need," Andrew corrected. "Present tense."

She squeezed his hand, then rose to check the grill. The scent of salmon and herbs drifted across the yard. Domestic. Normal. Everything he'd run from and now desperately wanted.

"Ryan thinks we can resurrect The Precipice," Andrew continued. "The three of us, him, me, and eventually Donovan."

"And you?" Nicole asked, plating the fish with practiced ease. "What do you think?"

Andrew considered as she set the food before him, salmon, roasted vegetables, a salad bright with pomegranate seeds. She'd remembered all his preferences after such a short time together.

"I think I've spent too much time in the dark," he said finally. "Bitter. Blaming Donovan. Blaming myself. Building nothing but walls." He met her eyes. "Meeting Ryan, finding Payton, seeing what's possible when you choose forgiveness over anger, it's like someone turned the lights back on."

They ate in comfortable silence as the sky deepened from Amber to purple. The November warmth held steady, that particular Southern California magic where summer refuses to surrender.

"I've missed this," Nicole said softly. "Missed you. Four months wasn't long, but it was..."

"Real," Andrew finished. "More real than relationships I'd had for years."

"I pushed you away." The admission came raw. "After Donovan's betrayal, I couldn't stand for you to see me broken."

"Andrew." She set down her fork. "I never needed you to be invincible. I needed you to be present."

"I know that now." He looked out over the canyon, lights beginning to twinkle in the houses below. "Ryan helped me see it. Family isn't about perfection. It's about showing up."

"Even when it's messy?"

"Especially then."

Nicole rose and began clearing plates. Andrew stood to help, their movements falling into remembered rhythms. In the kitchen, washing dishes side by side, he felt the ordinariness of it settle into his bones like medicine.

"Stay," she said as they finished. Not a question. Not quite a command. An offering.

They returned to the pergola with coffee, the string lights creating a pocket of warmth against the vast night. Nicole tucked her feet under her on the loveseat, leaning into his shoulder.

"What happens now?" she asked.

Andrew thought of Ryan's confidence, Elena's quiet strength, and his grandchildren's easy acceptance. The meetings are planned for next week, with the possibility of facing Donovan, with Ryan as a bridge-builder.

"Now we rebuild," he said. "The Precipice. The family. Us." He turned to look at her. "If you'll have me."

Nicole was quiet for a long moment. Somewhere in the canyon, a coyote called, wild and lonesome.

The sound transported Andrew instantly, Big Sur, thirty years ago, another canyon, another choice. The moment he'd decided to leave Amber for Blaire. A coyote had cried then, too, as if nature itself mourned his betrayal.

He shuddered, and Nicole felt it. "What is it?"

"Nothing. Just... remembering."

She studied his face in the string lights. "No more of that, Andrew. Whatever it is."

"No more," he agreed, meaning it. "Never again."

Nicole shifted to face him fully. "When you're ready to relaunch The Precipice, I can talk to Jeff Clark at the firm. He owes me, I saved his biggest account last year when things went sideways. The PR strategy we developed is still solid. But only when the time is right. When you and your sons are truly ready to build together."

Andrew's throat tightened. "You'd do that? Go back to Jeff for this?"

"The Precipice was never just another account for me, Andrew. You know that." Her voice was steady. "Jeff knows it, too. He'll make room when we're ready."

"You never gave up on it."

"I never gave up on you." Her eyes held his. "Even when you gave up on yourself."

The kiss was different from their desperate connection four months ago. Quieter. Deeper. A promise rather than passion alone.

When they broke apart, Nicole's eyes were bright. "No more running," she whispered. "No more running," Andrew agreed.

They sat together as November worked its magic, the warm air carrying the scent of sage and distant fires. Tomorrow would bring challenges, lawyers, plans, the delicate work of rebuilding trust with Donovan. But tonight, Andrew felt something he'd thought lost forever.

Hope. Not the desperate kind that denies reality, but the steady flame that says: yes, things fall apart. Yes, we fail each other. But we can also choose to begin again.

Nicole's hand found his in the rkness. Below them, the lights of Solana Beach spread like a constellation, each house a story, each story a chance for redemption.

"The future's bright," Andrew said, surprising himself with the certainty in his voice.

Nicole smiled, her face beautiful in the string lights' glow. "Yes," she said simply. "It is."

A breeze stirred the canyon, carrying the salt-sweet promise of the ocean just beyond the ridge, Indian summer's last gift before the world turned toward winter and, eventually, another spring.

Andrew pulled Nicole closer, feeling the solid weight of now, the delicate architecture of what might be. Sometimes, he thought, the best buildings are the ones that rise from ruins. Stronger for having been broken. Beautiful for having been rebuilt.

In the distance, the coyote called again. This time, Andrew heard it differently, not as judgment for past betrayals, but as wild permission to begin again. As Nicole leaned into him, Andrew was struck by the quiet miracle of being known and still welcomed. It wasn't rebirth in some mystical sense. It was reentry. A return to presence. To family.

Andrew pulled Nicole closer, feeling the solid weight of now and the fragile architecture of what might be.

Sometimes, the best structures rise from ruins, not despite the cracks, but because of them. Stronger. Truer. More beautiful for having been broken and rebuilt.

CHAPTER THIRTY-FIVE

CARLSBAD

DECEMBER · 2000

The Sterling Grove sat near the center of Carlsbad Village, a modest two-story Spanish colonial revival building of white stucco and terracotta roof tiles. From a distance, it looked more like a small luxury inn than a senior care facility. Up close, the barely perceptible medical equipment and staff in casual scrubs gave away its true purpose.

Andrew parked his sedan in the visitor's spot closest to the entrance, taking a deep breath before getting out. Today was different from his usual visits. Today, thanks to Ryan's efforts at reconciliation, he would be seeing not only his father Joseph, but also his son Donovan and his grandson Payton, all together for the first time. His stomach tightened with nervous anticipation mixed with hope.

He stepped into the lobby, with its terra cotta tile floors and arched doorways, taking in the scent of lemon polish mixed with faint antiseptic. The receptionist, a woman in her fifties with salt-and-pepper hair twisted into a neat bun, looked up and smiled.

"Mr. Foster, your father's expecting you. He's been quite excited all morning."

"I can imagine," Andrew replied. "This means a lot to him."

"You know the way," she said, buzzing him through.

Andrew had been coming to The Sterling Grove every day since Joseph's minor stroke three weeks ago. Remarkably, the hope of reconciliation and the knowledge that he had two grandsons had brought new life back into his father. The doctors were amazed at his recovery, attributing it to his renewed sense of purpose and family connection.

The extended care wing was newer than the rest of the facility, with wider doorways and handrails along the walls. Andrew paused outside Room 208, preparing himself for what lay ahead. This meeting, which Ryan had finally arranged after weeks of patient work, carried the weight of decades of mistakes and regrets. It also took the first real hope of healing.

He pushed open the door.

Joseph was propped up in bed, looking more alert than he had in months. His white hair had been combed back neatly, and someone had helped him into a button-down shirt rather than the usual hospital gown. He was studying a set of architectural drawings spread across his lap tray.

"About time," Joseph said, glancing up. "I've been reviewing these old Precipice designs all morning. They still hold up, you know."

Andrew leaned down and kissed his father's forehead. "How are you feeling today?"

"Like a man who's been given an unexpected gift," Joseph replied with genuine warmth. "The doctors say my recovery has been remarkable. Nothing like the prospect of meeting your grandsons to give an old man renewed vigor."

Andrew set a small bottle on the bedside table. "I brought you something."

Joseph's eyes lit up when he recognized the premium tequila. "Now that's more like it. Though I doubt Nurse Ratched will let me near it."

"I cleared it with Dr. Mehta," Andrew said. "One small glass before bed is medicinal, apparently."

"Bless that man." Joseph set aside the drawings. "Are you ready for this?"

"More than ready," Andrew admitted, and he meant it. The past few weeks of meeting with Ryan, visiting his bio-medical company, seeing the possibilities ahead, it had filled him with an encouragement he hadn't felt in years. "Ryan says Donovan is bringing Payton."

"Yes, my great-grandson." Joseph's voice softened. "Never thought I'd live to see that."

Andrew sat in the chair beside the bed. "Dad, I still can't believe this is happening. After everything..."

Joseph waved away his amazement. "What you told me, about Amber's forgiveness, about Ryan's grace, that's stayed with me. And seeing the change in you over the past few weeks, the hope you've found working with Ryan at his company... It's like watching you come back to life."

"Ryan's work is incredible," Andrew said, his voice carrying new enthusiasm. "The research they're doing, the potential applications, it's given me purpose again."

"That's why this meeting is so important," Joseph said. "Not just for reconciliation, but for the future. For building something together."

A soft knock interrupted their conversation. The door opened to reveal Ryan, tall and lean, with Andrew's eyes but a gentleness to his features that must have come from Amber.

"Hope this is a good time," Ryan said, moving to Joseph's bedside. "I'm early, but I needed to talk to you both before the others arrive."

"Perfect timing," Joseph replied, reaching up to clasp his grandson's hand. "How did things go with Donovan?"

Ryan's expression grew serious. "We really had it out. I mean, a real confrontation about everything, about his anger, about what it's doing to him and Payton, about the change I've seen in Dad over these past weeks."

Andrew leaned forward. "How did you make this happen? I honestly didn't think he'd ever agree to meet."

"It wasn't easy," Ryan admitted. "But I told him about the transformation I've witnessed in you, how you've thrown yourself into learning about Genoryx, how you've been designing modifications to The Precipice plans, how you light up when you talk about Payton. I told him you're not the same broken man who showed up at his office that day."

"What changed his mind?" Andrew asked.

Ryan smiled. "Jacqueline and Elena have been working their magic, too. They've been talking, and Jacqueline finally convinced Donovan that Payton deserves to know his grandfather. She pointed out that their children are growing up without that connection, and it's not fair to them."

Joseph nodded approvingly. "Smart women. Never underestimate the power of a mother's perspective."

"And," Ryan continued, "when I showed him the updated Precipice designs you've been working on, the ones adapted for Genoryx's needs, he was impressed despite himself. The businessman in him could see the potential."

Andrew felt his heart quicken. "He looked at the designs?"

"More than looked. He studied them. Asked technical questions. Started talking about funding and implementation." Ryan's voice betrayed his excitement. "Dad, I think he's ready to build something with us."

The door opened again, and the temperature in the room seemed to shift. Donovan Lasseter stood in the doorway, dressed in premium jeans and an open-collared shirt under a lightweight blazer—the uniform of a successful Southern California entrepreneur. Beside him stood a boy with blond hair and bright, curious eyes that darted around the room.

"We're not too late, are we?" Donovan asked, his voice carefully neutral but lacking the venom Andrew remembered.

Joseph broke the tension. "Not at all. Come in, come in." His gaze fixed on the boy. "And this must be Payton."

The boy stepped forward with surprising confidence. "Are you my great grandpa?"

"That's right," Joseph said, a genuine smile spreading across his weathered face.

"Dad says you design amazing things," Payton continued, moving to the bedside to examine Joseph more closely.

"I used to," Joseph replied. "I mostly dream about designing amazing things now."

Payton nodded solemnly, as if this made perfect sense to him. "Like my dad. He dreams too, but he's still building, way too much."

A flicker of something, pride mixed with recognition, crossed Donovan's face as he watched his son. He nodded to Ryan and, after a brief hesitation, to Andrew, before taking a seat near the window.

"I see you brought the Precipice drawings," Donovan noted, gesturing to the papers on Joseph's tray. "Ryan showed me some of the modifications you've been working on."

"Your grandfather's masterpiece," Joseph confirmed. "Never built but never forgotten either."

"It could be built now," Ryan said, seizing the opening. "That's what I wanted to discuss with all of you. Genoryx needs a new headquarters, and a place for a lot of others, something cutting-edge that integrates research, education, and clinical application."

"The Precipice," Andrew said softly. "It was designed for exactly that purpose."

Donovan was quiet for a moment, watching Payton examine the architectural models on Joseph's bedside table. "Ryan says you've been at Genoryx almost every day, really learning the work. Not just showing up, but digging in." He paused, eyes flicking up to Andrew. "That's not the man I thought I'd see again."

"You and Amber could have built a proper home for us," Donovan said suddenly, looking directly at Andrew. "With your talent and Joseph's reputation behind you, and Amber's spirit supporting you, maybe The Precipice could have become a reality back then. Instead of leaving us, you could have created something enduring."

The room fell silent, save for Payton's soft humming as he continued to examine the models, oblivious to the tension.

"You're right," Andrew said simply. "I threw away everything that mattered for a fleeting infatuation. There's no excuse for that."

"No, there isn't," Donovan agreed, but his voice lacked the venom it had held during their last encounter. "But Ryan tells me you're different now. That you understand what you lost."

"What I did to your mother, abandoning her when she needed me most, it's the greatest regret of my life," Andrew continued.

"Mom told us about you," Ryan said quietly. "As we got older. Not with bitterness, but with honesty. She said you were brilliant but restless. That you were searching for something you couldn't name."

"She was too kind," Andrew replied, his voice rough with emotion.

"She was," Donovan agreed unexpectedly. "Even at the end, when the cancer took hold, she never spoke ill of you. I did enough of that for both of us."

Joseph, who had been watching the exchange intently, spoke up. "What matters now is what we do with the time we have left. All of us." He looked pointedly at Donovan. "You've built an impressive business empire. But Ryan tells me your work consumes you, that you've been neglecting what matters most." His gaze shifted meaningfully to Payton.

Donovan's jaw tightened, but he didn't deny the accusation.

"I'm not saying you're like your father," Joseph continued more gently. "But patterns have a way of repeating if we're not vigilant. Ryan understands this. It's why he's pushed for this reunion. Not just for Andrew's sake, but for yours. For Payton's."

"Uncle Ryan says I should draw more buildings," Payton piped up suddenly, returning to the group with one of the models clutched carefully in his small hands. "He says I have the Foster eye for design."

"He does," Ryan confirmed with a smile. "Just like his grandfather and great-grandfather."

Donovan looked at his son with a mixture of surprise and something softer. "I didn't know you were interested in architecture, buddy."

"You've been working a lot," Payton said matter-of-factly, without accusation. "Uncle Ryan shows me cool buildings when he babysits."

The simple observation hit Donovan harder than any recrimination could have. He reached out and drew his son closer. "I'll do better," he promised quietly.

"That's why The Precipice makes sense now," Ryan said. "Not just because Genoryx needs a new headquarters, but because it gives us a chance to build something together. Father, sons, grandson. A legacy that honors our past while creating something for the future."

"Including a section dedicated to Amber," Donovan added, his voice softer than before. "She deserves to be remembered."

Andrew felt a lump forming in his throat. The weight of this moment, of the possibility of reconciliation, of honoring Amber's memory, of knowing his grandson, threatened to overwhelm him.

"I don't deserve this chance," he said finally. "But I want it. To work with both of you, to get to know Payton, to make something good come from so much pain."

Joseph reached out with his good hand, and one by one, they each moved to his bedside, Ryan first, then Andrew, and finally, after a moment's hesitation, Donovan, with Payton pressed against his side.

"The Precipice," Joseph said, satisfaction evident in his tired eyes. "A place of healing and discovery. A bridge between what was lost and what might still be found." He looked at each of them in turn. "That's what family is, when it works right. A bridge. A shelter. A place to begin again."

Andrew's phone buzzed.

Jimmy.

His breath hitched. The timing couldn't be worse, or more perfect. He slipped into the hallway, pulse still racing from everything that had just unfolded. His hands trembled slightly as he took the call.

"I saw your name, Jimmy. I'm with family but had to break away for a second."

"Final word on your friend Samuelson," Jimmy said without preamble. "The DA confirmed he's the same guy you knew as Ash Murik. Those fingerprints at Franklin Tower? Definitely planted to mess with your head."

"That confirms what I already suspected," Andrew said, glancing back at the room where his family waited. "Thanks for following through on that."

"Gets better. Samuelson's up for release next month, December. Seventeen years inside, and he'll be free. Just watch yourself, Andrew. Guys like that don't forget."

"Thanks, Jimmy. I really appreciate everything you've done. Listen, I've got to get back to my family—can't wait to tell you about everything that's happened."

"Family, huh? Sounds like things are looking up for you, hermano. We'll catch up soon."

"Definitely. Talk to you later."

Outside the window, the late afternoon sunbathed the courtyard in golden light, transforming the simple garden into something momentarily transcendent. A sparrow landed on the windowsill, cocked its head as if considering the gathering inside, then retook flight into the endless blue.

"I'll need to review the original designs more thoroughly," Donovan said, breaking the spell. "Update them for modern research requirements."

"Of course," Andrew replied. "I've been working on that. The modifications are extensive but faithful to the original vision."

"And we'll need to discuss funding," Ryan added. "I have investors interested in Genoryx's expansion, but a project this scale will require additional capital."

"I have some contacts who might be interested," Donovan said. He glanced at Joseph, an almost imperceptible softening in his expression. "Especially if an architect of your reputation is involved in the redesign."

"Can I help too?" Payton asked, looking up at the adults with eager eyes. "I could draw pictures for the walls."

"You can help me with the models," Andrew told him, smiling at his grandson. "Every great architect needs an apprentice."

"I'd like that," Payton said, his expression serious beyond his years.

A nurse appeared in the doorway, clipboard in hand. "Sorry to interrupt, but it's time for Mr. Foster's medication."

"We should go," Ryan said, rising.

"No, stay," Joseph protested, but his eyelids were already growing heavy. "We've only just begun."

"We'll come back tomorrow," Donovan said, surprising them all. "All of us."

As the nurse administered Joseph's medication, Donovan guided his son toward the door. "Say goodbye to your great-grandfather, Payton."

"Bye, Grandpa Joe!" The boy ran back to the bed and planted a quick kiss on Joseph's cheek. "I'll bring my drawings tomorrow!"

Joseph smiled, already drifting toward sleep. "I'll look forward to it, young man."

They filed into the hallway, standing somewhat awkwardly outside the door as it closed behind them.

"Dinner?" Ryan suggested. "There's a good place just down the street. Mexican."

"I love tacos!" Payton exclaimed.

Donovan checked his watch, and for a moment, Andrew thought he would refuse. Then he nodded. "Dinner sounds good. Dad?"

It took Andrew a second to realize Donovan was addressing him. "Yes," he said quickly. "I'd like that."

As they walked toward the exit, Ryan and Payton leading the way, Donovan and Andrew following a step behind, Donovan spoke softly, so only Andrew could hear.

"I'm not doing this for you. I'm doing it for Payton, for Ryan. For Mom."

"I understand," Andrew said.

"But I am doing it," Donovan continued after a pause. "And maybe... maybe that's enough for now."

Andrew nodded, not trusting himself to speak.

"Precipice," Donovan said, the tension in his shoulders easing slightly. "Mom would have liked that. She always believed in second chances."

Outside, the California sun was beginning its slow descent toward the Pacific, painting the white stucco walls of The Sterling Grove with hues of Amber and gold. As they walked toward their cars, Payton skipping ahead with Ryan, Andrew felt something shift between him and his son, not forgiveness, not yet, but possibility. A foundation upon which something new might be built, as solid and enduring as the family and future, they were finally daring to develop.

It was, Andrew thought as he watched his grandson turn to wave him forward, a beginning.

CHAPTER THIRTY-SIX

SOLEDAD, CALIFORNIA

DECEMBER • 2000

The gates of Soledad Prison opened with a mechanical groan that sounded like the earth itself protesting. The morning fog rolled across the Salinas Valley like it was trying to erase everything, the guard towers, the razor wire, the seventeen years Ash Murek had just finished burning.

He stood outside the gates in the same clothes he'd worn going in, now hanging loose on his prison-carved frame. The denim had faded to the color of old bones. His hair, once wild and free, was shot through with silver, pulled back tight. But his eyes still held that darkness, that knowledge of shadows that even Soledad couldn't beat out of him.

A van waited in the visitor's lot. Not some hippie piece of crap held together with peace signs and rust, but a custom Cadillac Escalade ESV, black as a priest's cassock, windows tinted dark enough to hide sins. The kind of ride that whispered money, the kind the Sons of Malku had only dreamed about back in '70 when he'd taken the fall.

The side door slid open, releasing a cloud of smoke that wasn't entirely tobacco. Then she stepped out.

Raven hair spilling like oil down her back. A leather jacket over a dress that clung to curves, designed to make men stupid. Red lips curved in a smile that promised everything and meant nothing.

The world tilted.

The fog clung to Highway 1 like a burial shroud, thick and wet and suffocating. Ash yanked the pickup's wheel hard right, tires screaming against asphalt as he skidded into the turnout near McWay Falls...

Gone. They were gone.

Blaire's hair whipped in the wind as she pressed herself against Andrew's back on that cursed motorcycle, her arms wrapped around him like she used to wrap them around.

"Ash." The girl's voice pulled him back. Not Blaire. This one was called Cheri, and she was reaching for him with manicured nails that could have been claws. "The Omraxis sent me especially for you. Seventeen years is a long time to go without."

Behind her, two figures emerged from the van's shadows, Felix, thin and twitchy, eyes glittering with chemical wisdom, the Sons' new cook. And Cedar, who'd replaced muscle with more muscle since Ash went inside, arms thick as bridge cables, face carved from stone.

"Brother," Cedar rumbled. "Welcome back to the world."

Ash climbed into the van, letting the leather interior swallow him. It was like stepping into a different universe, screens everywhere, a full bar, and seats that were softer than anything he sat on in years. The Sons had evolved while he rotted. Gone were the flower-power dreams and half-assed drug deals. This was something else. Something with teeth.

Cheri slid in beside him, too close, her perfume mixing with the cannabis fog. Felix passed him a joint rolled in gold paper.

"Courtesy of the Omraxis," Felix said, pupils dilated despite the morning light. "He's been waiting for you. We all have."

The van pulled away from Soledad, heading south on 101. Ash took a deep hit, feeling the smoke fill spaces that had been empty for almost two decades. Prison had taught him patience. Had taught him to listen to the voices in the dark, to practice the old arts with nothing but will and blood and time. The shamanic paths had opened wider in solitude, especially the extra four years they'd given him after that business with Rodriguez.

Poor bastard had never been the same after Ash showed him what lived in the shadows between sleeping and waking. The riot that followed had cost three lives and landed Ash in the hole for two years straight. But it had been worth it to perfect his craft, to commune with the spirits that most men couldn't even sense.

Seventeen years of bitter meditation, but not always on Andrew Foster. A hundred other betrayals, a hundred other scores to settle had occupied his mind. But seeing Cheri step out of that van—the way her hair moved, the curve of her smile—it all came rushing back. The money. The Sons' money. Fifty thousand dollars. Gone because of Blaire's seduction and Foster's greed.

"The movement's changed," Cedar said from the driver's seat. "We're not just the Sons anymore. We're part of something bigger. The Omraxis brought in the Venezuelans, ex-military, trained in things that make our old games look like kids playing in the dirt."y

"Speaking of business," Felix said, that twitchy grin spreading across his face. "The Omraxis has been tracking some prime coastal real estate. "Perfect for what he's planning. Near the heart of biotech. Prime land, great access. And get this, it's old sacred ground. Used to be a Kumeyaay power spot before the Spanish came through."

Ash's hand tightened on the joint. "Where?"

"Carlsbad coast," Cheri purred against his ear. "Beautiful piece of land. The Omraxis wants it bad."

"Here's the funny part," Felix giggled, clearly high on his own supply. "Turns out some developer's got an option on it. The whole piece collapsed in a failure with funding. And you'll never guess who it is."

The highway stretched south through California's belly, past fields and towns that looked nothing like Ash remembered. The synchronicity of it all wasn't lost on him. The shadow-realm worked like that sometimes, weaving threads together across years and miles until the pattern finally revealed itself.

"Andrew Foster," Felix said, watching Ash's face for a reaction. "Small world, right?"

The car went silent except for the hum of tires on asphalt. Even Cheri pulled back slightly, sensing the shift in atmosphere.

"Foster," Ash said slowly, tasting the name. "Now there's a name I haven't heard in a long time. Nothing since Big Sur."

He stared out at the passing landscape, jaw working silently for a moment.

"Nothing…then out of nowhere, some suit from the DA's office shows up wanting to chat about Andrew Foster. Funny timing, you know? Like someone was stirring old pots just to see what floated to the surface."

The SUV hit a bump, jarring them all slightly. Ash didn't even blink.

"The interview lasted maybe twenty minutes. Guy took notes, nodded a lot, and promised to be in touch." A bitter smile played at the corners of his mouth. "Course, that was the last I heard. No follow-up calls, no more questions. Like the whole thing just… disappeared."

He finally turned from the window, meeting Felix's gaze directly. "Small world doesn't even begin to cover it, does it?"

"Foster," Ash said slowly, tasting the name like old wine. "After all these years."

He remembered what came after Andrew and Blaire vanished, how he'd returned to the commune, offering Amber protection. Promising she wouldn't have to raise the twins alone. The family said they would care for her, and that he would.

But she saw through it.

Later, he tracked her to the hospital in Monterey. The twins had just been born. Her mother was with her, packing up to take them home. Ash followed them out and waited by the parking lot exit. When their Oldsmobile approached, he blocked the path with his rusted Ford, stepped out, and pulled a ceremonial knife from his belt.

Amber's scream cut through the air. Her mother hit the horn. The rear door held, but Ash lunged for Amber's side instead. He yanked it open and climbed halfway in, reaching past her for the infants.

She fought like a wild animal, tearing at his arms with her nails. Stitches ripped across her abdomen as she threw herself between him and the twins. Her mom circled the car, grabbing his arm, he cut her across the wrist and shoved her back.

Just then, an ambulance rolled into view. Two EMTs leapt out, a hospital security guard sprinted from the lobby, four against one. Even Ash had to retreat.

But before he fled, he looked Amber dead in the eye.

"They're his seed," he hissed. "And they will vanish from his life."

After that, Amber and the twins disappeared. Her mother moved them somewhere he couldn't find. The trail went cold—but the rage stayed hot.

"You know this guy?" Cedar asked from the driver's seat.

"Oh, we have history," Ash replied, understanding flooding through him like dark revelation. "So I get my revenge, and the Omraxis gets his land."

"See?" Cheri purred, moving close again. "The universe provides. Seventeen years you've been away, and everything's been lining up, waiting for you to come back and finish what you started."

"Foster has any idea what's coming?" he asked.

"Word is, he had a big offer on the table, but it all fell through," Felix said. "He's been struggling ever since. One good push, and he'll fold like wet paper. "But the Omraxis wants it done... special. Says you'll know how to make it poetic."

The smoke in the van was getting thicker, taking shapes that shouldn't exist. Ash could feel the spirits gathering, attracted to his return like moths to flame. Andrew Foster. After all these years, after all the blood and betrayal between then and now, it was going to come full circle.

"Tell me everything," Ash said. "Every detail about Foster's situation."

As the van rolled south toward San Diego, Felix and Cedar laid it all out, Foster's failed projects, his money troubles, his desperate grip on that coastal property. The perfect pressure points for a man who understood how to apply force in just the right ways.

Seventeen years was nothing. The shadow-realm had taught him that time was just another illusion, like mercy, like forgiveness. What mattered was the settling of accounts. And now he could serve his new master while serving his own hunger for revenge.

Andrew Foster thought he'd escaped into a new life. But some debts accumulated interest in currencies that had no intrinsic value.

The Omraxis would get his land. And Ash would get everything else.

The black Escalade tore down the highway, ghosting through the fog like a curse in motion.